Staccato Publishing
Zimmerman, MN

Originally published as an ebook called Blood Bound
February 2011

ISBN: 978-0-9892027-3-9

Printed in the USA

An Undying Oath

HK Savage

To those who serve, I have the utmost respect for all that you do and like so many others I am eternally grateful.

Prologue

Lifting a shaking hand to his brow, he wiped at the sweat threatening to drip into his eyes. His discomfort wasn't entirely due to the late summer heat. Briefly he considered how he must look; bloodshot eyes, hair wild from running his hands through it, clothing rumpled from days on the go. When had he showered last? He'd been laying endless false trails to throw them off. Days he'd been at it, working diligently to gain enough of a window to do what he needed. It wasn't optimal, but it was the only thing he could think of. She was the only one he could trust, he hoped. Unless he'd ruined that too. He hated to involve her; if he had any other option he would gladly take it. Plus, Sam was strong. She had a certain internal fortitude, he'd seen it, watched it grow with her over the years. He was counting on it now.

He was close. Finally. Forcing his pace to remain steady was painful. The muscles in his long, thin legs twitched and flexed, urging him to do as his nerves dictated and run like hell. He paused at the drug store on the corner, using the combination of sun and large plate glass windows to check all directions and see if they were following. Correction, he knew they were following. The question was: did he have enough time to send it to her before they caught up to him? Making a few swipes at his wild brown hair did nothing to tame the longish mop now standing straight up in several parts, though it did buy him a few precious seconds to frantically scan the street. Several people glanced his way. None familiar. None paid any obvious attention. What if they hired someone he wouldn't recognize? The notion brought with it a chill. Then, his overly analytical mind turned over the likelihood of that happening and was able to cast it aside as impractical. No way they would bring an outsider in on this. He'd stolen from them. No one stole from them. No one left. He did. This was personal for them. Factor in the small matter of *what* he'd stolen and he knew they wouldn't be okay with anyone else recovering it. This would need to be contained; *he* needed to be contained. They would keep this one in-house. Moving quickly down the street he ducked into the courier service he used once a year. There was no line and he was able to stalk directly up to the counter, laying one long fingered hand flat over the price chart inset on the counter and leaned against it to access the satchel on his other side.

Surprised by how far into his space the angular customer came as he hunted for his parcel in the leather satchel resting against his hip, the young man behind the counter hopped back. Covering for the less than manly movement, he nervously adjusted his nametag announcing his identity as Tyler, and took a step toward recovering his space and pride.

"This doesn't have a return address, sir." The helpful young man blinked at the plain brown wrapping on the counter. "What if we're unable to deliver it?"

"You'll be fine. You've delivered there before. It's a secured building and the driver goes to the main office. There will be someone to sign for it."

Failing in his attempt to study his curiously ragged customer on the sly, Tyler apparently decided it was more important to get a good look than to be polite. A wrinkle formed between his black brows. After a good, long look he was satisfied, or had lost interest in the speedy fast way only the younger texting generation could. Tyler shrugged and started typing. "Did you want to send it overnight or second day?"

Ch. 1

"She's dead?"

"No question about it Mr. Buckley, and as I told you before that makes this pretty cut and dried."

"But *this* baby's my whole life man. Without her I can't do nothin'. You owe me more than a couple hundred bucks."

Sam was used to being questioned in her line of work. "Look Mr. Buckley, like I've told you repeatedly, a '96 Sentra with this kind of mileage on it and its preexisting body damage give me no choice. The fair settlement amount for a 'rolling total' is what it is." She extracted her company checkbook from her black canvas shoulder bag embroidered with her employer's logo, Midwest Mutual, in white. Plain and without imagination, she wondered if the company had ever considered *that* for their corporate logo. "Midwest Mutual, you can count on us, we *never* change." Her lips twitched.

"This is *funny* to you? My life is over and you're *laughing* about it?" He took a few steps toward her, hitching at the oversized jeans drooping off his scrawny twenty-two year old rear as he tried to be intimidating.

Not much older and certainly not an imposing figure at a petite two inches over five feet, Sam had to rely upon her confidence in situations like these, and they happened more than one might think. People put up more of an argument about a rusty old car than they did a broken leg. Her mouth turned down while she was thinking and her nearly black eyes looked flat and bored as she stared unflinchingly at him with her shoulders squared and head held high. That combined with the confidence she had in herself from two years in the ring gave her an unusually strong presence. Sam wasn't challenging him, not directly. Still, she held her ground and threw the young man off balance with her suddenly flaring attitude.

Predictably, Jeff slowed in his advance, dipping his shoulders in a showy swagger attempting to save face as he raised his voice for no one in particular in the empty street and leaned a hand on the body of his beloved rust bucket as he made a few cutting observations about those "damn insurance companies."

Sensing the battle had been won, Sam lowered the checkbook to the seriously sun faded hood. It gave her no joy making people unhappy but her job was to be fair, and that was what she was.

Jeff's tone changed from argumentative to careful as she wrote out the date. "What about my pain and suffering?"

"Mr. Buckley, might I remind you that you were not actually *in* the vehicle at the time of the accident, therefore you *have* no pain and suffering." Her words were cold. Why did some people see an accident as the lottery? Did they not understand that every time somebody in the news won a huge settlement that it cost *everyone* in higher premiums? Sam wished she could explain that they were an insurance company, not an ATM.

Jeff's watery blue eyes darted under pale lashes, barely visible against his equally pale, red-dotted skin. "Yeah but now I'm out a ride and this ain't nearly enough money to get me a new one. I could sue you for pain and suffering for *that*." He hitched nervously at his pants again. Were it not for the hand firmly fixed on his waistband through his white Ludacris tee, Sam was

10

worried she would see his pasty, scrawny legs and who knew what else. Not a sight she wanted burned into her memory bank, thank you.

"*Mr.* Buckley," she held her pen aloft. "If you are intimating that you would like to pay an attorney to take your case before a judge, which will take well over a year, only to be dismissed on summary judgment, meaning you have no case, then go right ahead. You can choose to believe me or you can pay to have it explained to you by a judge."

She watched doubt take root and his face pinch up like he was going to cry. Jeff's tough guy exterior was cracking. It didn't take a genius to see that he was just a young guy who didn't have much, and he was right, five hundred dollars wasn't going to get him anything reliable. Craning her neck to look through the open window, she made a show of scanning the interior of the vehicle she knew had been unharmed in the minor collision. Sam knew she had some leeway in her settlement offer.

"Mr. Buckley, did you have some aftermarket stereo equipment in this vehicle? It looks like there is maybe a subwoofer and some decent speakers in back." She opened the passenger side door to get a better look, watching to see he didn't move toward her. People did funny things when you had a checkbook and they were broke. Pulling her head back out, she eyed him over the roof of the car. "Those are expensive speakers."

Doing the math quickly in her head, she reevaluated what she could justify on the claim. "The subwoofer is near the point of impact and I believe that's a hairline crack in the casing. The speakers have also suffered some damage I can see some tearing around the tweeters there. I'm willing to reimburse you for the system in addition to the vehicle's value." She knew it was more likely the minor cracking was due to sun exposure.

Jeff didn't try to hide the spark of hope in his blue eyes. Sam's tone softened.

"I can increase my offer for settlement to fifteen hundred dollars but that's it. Is that acceptable to you?" Though no longer hard, Sam's countenance left no opening for negotiation. She kept it clear she wasn't doing him a favor. This was a justified increase.

Wisely swallowing any further arguments, Jeff nodded. "Yeah, I guess that'd be all right."

Resuming her position on the other side of the hood, Sam finished writing out the check and release to Jeff. "Sign the form and the check is yours. The release merely confirms you have agreed to settlement of the claim for fifteen hundred dollars."

He rested his hip on the car most likely to keep his pants up while he reached for the pen, signing and pushing the piece of paper back with the pen on top. Sam watched him thinking he was probably a nice guy if he gave up the attitude. From what she had seen, Jeff showed promise under that false persona he was intent on sporting.

She slid the pen and form off in one hand, giving him the check with the other. Leaving him staring at it, Sam replaced her things in her bag and made an efficient exit.

"Hey, thanks man," he called out sincerely.

Without looking back, Sam held up a hand and slid into her SUV. Company owned, the only bit of personalization she'd been allowed was color. Her choice was a no-brainer: her favorite, lime green. A color she could never wear, she loved to accessorize with it right down to her kickboxing gloves. Settling her bag on the passenger seat, Sam let out a breath she'd been holding so long her chest hurt and sucked in another, feeling the adrenaline drain out of her and leaving her exhausted.

Raising her hand to her seatbelt, Sam frowned at the tremor she saw in her hand. These types of settlements always bothered her. A number of them that had gotten tense lately. Her territory covered a few rougher neighborhoods and job losses were high these days making some good people desperate and bad people downright dangerous. What was more surprising than Jeff's gratitude was what she had done to earn it. Her supervisor loved her for her results. Always fair yet keeping things cheap while spending the corporate dime, Sam had some of the best numbers in her department. The satisfaction from doing her job well had been enough for her, until lately. In the last few weeks Sam had begun to feel an unfamiliar emptiness tug at her insides.

Maybe it was the fact that today was her twenty-eighth birthday and she could feel thirty screaming down at her with nothing to show for it except a job she was good at but didn't love. That same company owned her car and her apartment was a rental. Sam owned nothing of real value. Nothing much about her status in life had changed since college. Except her furniture. At least she'd improved from hand me downs and actually owned a set now. Still. The closest thing she had to grownup responsibility was a boyfriend she was fond of, although now that he was pushing for more of a commitment, she was potentially losing even that. To further complicate matters, her mother and stepfather knew she was commitment phobic and as such were pushing her hard to settle for a life of comfort if not love. The whole thing was quite honestly more than a little disheartening when she sat down and let herself dwell on it.

Sam's musings were interrupted by a loud series of beeps. Punching a button on the dash, she spoke into the air.

"This is Sam."

"It's the twenty-eighth day of August. Your golden birthday," came the chipper sing-song greeting. "Happy birthday Sammy!"

Sam's mood lightened, her teeth flashing in an easy smile. "Thanks Mom. Again." She teased.

"Well, you're much more awake this time."

Twisting to double check for bicycles, which all too often came flying through the streets in this area, Sam pulled out into traffic. "That's because no one *normal* is awake at 4:27 am."

"I was." Brenda was all too pleased to enter into their annual banter. "Twenty-eight years ago *I* was awake and held you in my arms for the very first time."

Sam watched the streets go by as she wound her way back to the freeway and toward home where she could write up her reports before she could finally call it a day. A quick glance at the clock and some mental math while she listened to her mother and Sam felt a fraction of her tension dissipate. She could still make kickboxing tonight, a birthday present she'd promised herself and looked forward to having more than any other. It was her stress outlet. Some people did yoga, others played softball, and although Sam enjoyed those things when she did them here and there, she'd found nothing better than testing her mettle against a capable opponent in the ring.

"Are you coming over this weekend? We'd like to make you a birthday dinner Saturday."

"Um, I don't know Mom, I haven't talked to Paul yet. He might be planning something." She grimaced at the thought. Their time together was something she dreaded more than anticipated lately, a telling sign of impending doom for their relationship. Not surprising considering her track record.

The year she'd been with Paul had been the longest she'd been able to stay with anyone before honesty drove her to end things. At this point in her history of commitment disasters, Sam was seriously considering the possibility she was incapable of going the distance, or unwilling. It was becoming obvious she just wasn't built for it.

Brenda didn't miss a beat, only too happy to provide opportunities for her daughter to incorporate her boyfriend into the family circle. "He's more than welcome to come too, Sam. You know we like him, I don't know why you don't bring him around more often."

"I know Mom, we'll see. I have to go. Can I call you later?" She didn't want to get in to it, all too soon her mother would be in mourning for the death of another of Sam's relationships. The clock would have to start all over again on Brenda's ever-important countdown to grandbabies.

"Sure honey. Let me know soon so we have time to get things started. You know my short ribs aren't any good unless they have a solid thirty-six hours to cook."

Of course she had to throw out the tantalizing offer of Sam's favorite meal. Braised short ribs and Andouille sausage slathered on top of cheesy grits. It was gastronomic blackmail and her mother knew it. Sam could see her mother's knowing smile with her mind's eye. Brenda knew she could pretty much manipulate the situation for the best results and the gloves were coming off in the battle for Sam's domestic bliss. "I'll call you later."

"Don't take *too* long, fine dining is time sensitive. I love you birthday girl."

"You too Mom."

Her mom knew the "L" word wasn't in her vocabulary. If only Paul could be as understanding of her limitations. Sam sighed as she pushed the button to end the call and check the clock again. Merging onto the freeway, she glanced up and her foot stomped on the brake.

"Shit."

Traffic was heavy. She should have known. Every northbound route was crowded in the last weeks of summer with cabin traffic. The weather was guaranteed to be hot and school was rapidly approaching. Most of her co-workers took a week or at least a few days off to take their kids for one last hoorah this month. One more reason her supervisor loved her. No kids, no husband, no life.

"I'm a gift," she muttered dryly, quoting Mr. Silverstein's frequent compliment.

Reworking her evening plans, she figured if she didn't go home but went to the coffee shop by the gym instead she could do her reports, upload them to the

16

company's system, and still get to kickboxing by seven. Deciding that would be best, she knew what she was giving up. "Sorry Bill, you'll have to wait a little longer." She was always letting somebody down.

Sam sighed. Birthday yes, golden, sadly it was not. It was just another day.

Ch. 2

Sam walked out into the humid night air, the gym bag slung over her shoulder pressing her shirt against her shower damp skin. Absently she picked at the fabric clinging to her with one hand while the other tucked a wet clump of bangs behind her ear. The shorter hair in back angled up away from the sensitive skin of her long, thin neck, itching mildly as it dried. She saw a familiar black coupe parked beside her SUV and, with a frustrated sigh, Sam shifted her bag, disappointed in herself she couldn't muster a deeper feeling than mild affection despite both their efforts.

She infused her smile with artificial enthusiasm, watching him slide easily out of the black Honda. His return flash of teeth was more natural, lending insight into why he was the most successful salesman at his family's car dealership. Sam stopped outside the glow of the parking lot light where both their cars sat to avoid the mass of bugs now swirling around in its false moonlight. Paul closed the gap between them, his long stride easily covering the ground and bringing him close enough to wrap his arms around her. It was hard to relax into the warmth he offered knowing what she should do out of fairness and hating herself for it. When he felt her stiffen his muscles tightened. Automatically, Sam slid a hand up the back of his neck to pull him down. God help her, it was easier to kiss him than explain herself. With a low groan he pressed his lips to hers, swiping them with his tongue, asking for more. Sam opened up to allow him entrance. The passion she lacked didn't seem to bother Paul he merely poured more of his in to fill the void. *What the hell is wrong with me?*

"Sam, where have you been? I've been trying to call you all day." He pulled back, his bright blue eyes meeting her troubled light brown ones.

"I worked in St. Paul today, remember?" She cringed at the bitch in her words and worked to soften her tone. "There were a few settlements that took longer than expected and I just got out of kickboxing a few minutes ago." She gestured toward the building behind her as if he couldn't see it.

"I wanted to take you out for a birthday dinner."

"I'm sorry Paul, it's late and I'm tired. I haven't even been home yet and Bill's probably starving."

"Is there anything I could do to persuade you to come out for a quick drink?" He lifted his hands to her shoulders and grinned, some of his charisma bleeding into his offer. Car salesmen knew how to redirect after rejection. "What if I tempted you with offers of a birthday surprise?" Paul waggled his blonde brows, nearly white against his summer-tanned skin.

Sam felt the corners of her mouth twist into a smile. At his company picnic a few weeks ago, she'd been told by several fellow salesmen and one jealous receptionist, that she was the only person who had ever said no to him. For Sam, that explained why he pursued her so doggedly and continued to stay with her despite her lack of good girlfriend attributes. The kindest thing to do was to end things now and she knew she should, except the thought of admitting she was incapable of love was hard to face. Sam held out hope each time she saw Paul that something would change and she would suddenly feel that spark other people talked about. She decided right then to break up with him and let him be free to find someone who deserved and appreciated him. Tomorrow, she would do it tomorrow after work.

Backing away, she let his hands slide down and captured them in hers. "Paul that's sweet and I'd like to go out with you tonight, but I'm wiped. Can we do tomorrow instead?" She watched his glance fall to their hands.

"Sure, Sam." Paul cut his eyes back to her, the brightness of his gaze only a fraction of what it had been yet hope flickered there. "How about Baccio at 6?"

"Sounds good." She smiled back at him.

Small talk ensued. Paul asked about her day and she about his, they laughed for a few more minutes about this and that before Sam sobered up and thought of poor Bill sitting home alone, staring at his dish. She said as much to Paul.

"You know you should get him a friend."

Sighing, she stared into the bug filled light beam nearby, catching sight of a giant moth taking a breather on the roof of her car. Pulling away from Paul's, her hand slid into her pocket to hit the unlock button on her key fob. He dropped her other hand and she stepped into the light, immediately getting pelted by several small nit natty bugs dancing in the light. "I know but that just gives me one more person to worry about and that's the last thing I need." She rested a hand on her door handle.

Paul made a displeased noise and folded his arms across his chest.

Feeling like an ass for the Freudian slip, she deliberated the best way to apologize without offering something she couldn't deliver.

He ended her discomfort by stepping in and resting his hands on her shoulders. "I'll let you go." Leaning in, Paul kissed her tenderly and she kissed him back. He gave her a final squeeze and turned away from her to ease into his car, but not before she caught the injured look in his eye.

She opened her mouth to speak before he left, tried to say something kind, something that wouldn't hurt his feelings, but the door opened and closed without her making a sound. She lost her chance. Instead she raised a hand in parting, watching his taillights reach the end of the lot before he turned out onto the street.

Inside her car Sam rested her forehead against the top of her steering wheel and closed her eyes, listening to the bugs alternate between kamikaze dives at her windshield and pinging against the parking lamp's metal pole. Sitting up with shoulders slumped, she lay her hands in her lap and felt the exhaustion of the day settling in to take the place of the elation she'd found through her sparring matches. "Why can't I be normal?" she asked of a white moth perched on her windshield wiper.

Ch. 3

Sam parked on the street. She never used the underground ramp in the summer unless hail was in the forecast. It was at the back of the building and she would have to walk down a maze of hallways instead of through the secured lobby and up three flights to her top floor unit.

A small package lay beside her mailbox door with her name on it. She should have known to expect it. One just like it arrived every birthday since her tenth, the first after he left. It was always the same: plain brown paper packaging and addressed to her, never her mother. Her mother never received a thing from him, not even a note. As always, there was no return address. It was addressed to her in plain block letters, all capitals. Miss Samantha James.

With the package jammed under her arm, she let herself in and had only begun to set her bags down in the hallway of her unit when her legs were struck from behind so hard she nearly lost her balance.

"Hey Bill." She leaned over to rub the cat's big gray head. He meowed his loud reply, trotting away to disappear around the corner. The meow came again, more urgent this time. "I know, I know, I'm late."

Dutifully she danced around him stiltedly as Bill ran back and forth between her and his dish until finally she reached the kitchen and opened the cabinet to get a scoop for him. His head rubbing continued, knocking her hand with the scoop and scattering pieces of food on the floor as she tried to pour.

"Settle down, Bill.

You're in no danger of starving." Patting his head she watched him dive into his food, his purrs interrupted only by the sound of happy crunching. Bill was a big cat and carried extra weight but very little of his eighteen pound body could be considered fat. He was solid. Some of the acrobatic feats she'd seen him perform over the years had shown her how he kept himself in shape. "Cirque de Soleil would be proud to have you big man." She ran her hand down his back to sweep up his tail as she stood, returned the scoop, and shut the cabinet door securely before going on to tackle her evening chores.

It was after ten by the time she had her gym clothes in the dryer, a light dinner in her tummy, and finally settled in to flip through a health related magazine in bed. Bill lay contentedly beside her. Canting her head to one side, she watched him sleep while he purred hard enough to vibrate the blankets. "I wish I could be as content as you." Giving him a kiss goodnight, she rolled over and turned out her light.

The next morning Sam sat at her kitchen table staring at the brown package over her cup of tea. She hadn't bothered opening it last night. Why? It was the same thing every year, five thousand dollars in crisp hundred dollar bills and a little note in the same block writing as the outer wrap: *Happy Birthday Samantha.*

From the age of four, she had insisted she be called Sam and everyone except her father had honored that request. Her father never called her anything but her given name. "She's a girl," he'd said to any who asked, "Why would I call her a boy's name?" Since he'd walked out when she was nine, no one called her by her full name. She told herself she didn't miss it.

When she picked up the package to toss it in her

bag so she could deposit the money in the safe deposit box with the other nineteen years' worth of annual deposits, she felt something different. The balance of the box was off. The cash always slid because it was a little short for the box, only this time, it didn't. Intrigued, she shook it again paying closer attention. Something inside rattled.

Grabbing a scissors, Sam sliced the paper and peeled it away throwing it in the nearly full kitchen garbage bag. She slid a short, bubble gum pink fingernail under the cover of the box and sliced the tape holding it shut against the pressure of the bundle of cash inside. When the tape released, the box top popped on one side and she flipped it up to reveal the bundle inside. Unimpressed by the cash, she took it and the note out without reading it, she set them on the counter next to the microwave and stared curiously at the small silver tube.

"What's this?" She picked up the cool metal cylinder and turned it slowly around in her fingers, examining it.

The container was the size of a tube of lipstick, which is what she thought it was at first, except why her father would send makeup to her was beyond her. There was no visible means to open it and she altered her view that it looked more like a large bullet than cosmetics. The light in the kitchen was too low so she got up to turn on the brighter light over the sink. In the more direct glare of the overhead bulb Sam was able to see a tiny seam in the outer casing that went all the way around the top. It was a lid, not a cap that would screw off. The gap was too thin to put something in it and the top would not readily loosen with her tentative wiggling. The mechanically inclined bit of her mind wanted to figure it out whereas her emotional response was to throw it against something hard.

Lost in her thoughts, Sam lost track of time until she glanced up at the clock and saw she was going to be late for her first appointment if she didn't hurry and she *had* to finish her day on time if she wanted to meet Paul for dinner. Though if she ran late he knew where her spare key was hidden in the magnetic key hider on top of the metal doorframe. He could let himself in and she could meet him there. After tonight she would have to find a new place to hide a spare key, she thought. Once things were done between them she couldn't have him knowing how to get in. Already her stomach was threatening to give her trouble knowing tonight was the night for her to come clean and end things with him.

It would take a few minutes to brush her teeth so she put the water in the microwave to make another tea for the road before she went in the bathroom. The microwave dinged in perfect time and she retrieved it to pour in her aluminum thermal mug, slinging a mint tea bag over the lip. The few minutes she needed to let the tea steep Sam stood in the kitchen and her eyes were drawn again to the metal cylinder. Her eyes flicked to the note on the money and she picked it up. It was different this year, just like the contents of the package. Reading the brief message, her eyes narrowed and she spat his name in disgust.

"Steven you prick!" Crumpling the note and swiping up the cylinder up with it, she chucked them both in the garbage, the note's message becoming visible again as the paper uncrinkled itself on top of the box from last night's meal.

Dear Samantha,

I need you to keep this safe for me. For your own safety you can't tell anyone about it, not even your mother. Hide it somewhere safe and I'll come for it when I can. I am so sorry to involve you and regret that our reunion should be under such strained circumstances. I can explain everything when I see you.

Sincerely,
Dad

Wishing she could hit something, Sam did a very poor job of removing her tea bag, spilling some of the deep amber liquid on the generic white laminate countertop in the process. "Damn it." She slammed a spoonful of sugar in, not bothering to stir and put the lid on with too much force and a little jet of tea shot out the top. Cursing a blue streak that would have earned her a mouthful of soap back home, Sam grabbed the mug and money. She could stop at the bank today between appointments. The sooner she had the visible evidence of his paternal guilt out of her life the better. Briefly, Sam considered moving without forwarding her mail. Maybe he wouldn't be able to find her this time and she would never have to think about him again. That was worth five thousand dollars a year.

Hah! As much as she might be able to control nearly everything else in her life, the one thing she couldn't was her mind when it came to Dr. Steven James, the man who had left her to pick up the mess he'd left when she was just a little girl. As much as she resented him, she never moved without filling out a card with the post office. Some small part of her wanted to be found.

A last scowl at the black ink on the note in the garbage quickly running into illegibility from the wet tea bag resting on top of it, the cylinder lost somewhere in its depths, and Sam swept out of the apartment.

Ch. 4

It had been a long day and, combined with the emotional toll from her morning, Sam was seriously considering canceling on Paul. She didn't because she knew she owed him a dose of long overdue honesty. The day hadn't been *all* bad. She'd gotten a call from her closest friend Maria asking how her birthday was and her coworkers took her to lunch since she was out on appointments on her actual birthday.

The employees at the office, specifically those in her small department of six, were responsible for the majority of her social contacts. None were exceptionally deep relationships although they enjoyed each other and had happy hours at least once a month. Dinners with spouses were common as well. Paul had gone to several.

Maria was different. They met at Sam's former employer, Brookside Insurance, four years ago and shared a cubicle. Right away they developed a close friendship. Every year without fail Maria called and sang Sam her own uniquely crafted "Happy Birthday" song even if she had to leave a message, and Sam made her promise never to do it again, laughing the whole time. Every year. It was one of the things that endeared her former coworker to her, her equally agreeable and stubborn sides. It was to that combination Sam credited their entire friendship. Anyone else would have given up on Sam's thick protective outer coating long before they got to the soft inside. Most did, but not Maria.

"Come on Sam, what did you do for your birthday? You didn't just work and go to the gym, did you?" she'd asked when Sam returned her call after lunch.

It had been a coward's move and she knew it at

the time. It wasn't easy to defend. Sam swallowed to wet her mouth. "Yeah, it was my birthday and I did what I wanted to do."

"Didn't *Paul* call you?" She already knew the answer still she was going to force Sam to go through the humiliation of telling it anyway.

Squirming, Sam was glad Maria couldn't see her. "I was tired and Bill was hungry. There wasn't time for anything else after class." Saying it out loud made it sound even more pathetic. Sam felt her face heat up.

"Is he still asking you to move in with him?"

"Yes."

"Have you actually given it any *serious* consideration? Or are you trying the patented 'Sam method' and ignoring it, hoping it will magically resolve itself?" Maria didn't mess around. It was horribly inconvenient at times.

"Why keep discussing it? Nothing has changed. He wants more and I can't do it." Sam couldn't bring herself to admit she'd made her decision last night and had every intention of breaking up with him that night. "What do *you* think?"

"Well," she answered slowly, not easily giving opinions on Sam's complicated love life. "Maybe try it out for a while and see if doing it helps you, I don't know, let go a little. Trust him Sam, you know he won't leave you. He's not that sort of guy." Maria was the only one Sam would let get away with saying such a thing.

That last conversation with her friend was running through her mind as she turned onto her street a few minutes after five, thinking if she took a quick shower they could still make the reservation at six. Paul should already be inside, she'd called as soon as she knew she would be late.

"I'll pour us that drink you owe me," he'd offered jovially.

Sam felt her resolve waver when she parked her car and saw his black Accord parked up the block. Dreading the hurt she knew she was about to cause, Sam walked down the hall, keys in hand. So entirely in her own head was she, Sam was caught completely unaware as a meowing creature barreled into her legs. Reaching down, she scooped Bill up and held him tight as she craned her neck, trying in vain to see her doorway around the corner. Her skin tightened, bringing the hairs on her neck up in warning.

When she reached her unit Sam saw how Bill had gotten out. The steel door stood ajar, the light from inside visible through the crack. Bill started struggling in her grasp. Believing she was holding him too tight Sam relaxed her arms, yet he continued to wriggle.

"Stop it Bill," she scolded sharply.

Carefully, she pushed open the door and entered her apartment. The growling ball of fur in her grasp was having no part of it. Clawing at her with his sharp back claws, Bill took a few chunks out of her forearms as he finally leapt free of her, racing down the hall and out of sight. Sam didn't give chase or even turn her head to see where he went. He wouldn't go far, he never did on the rare occasion he got out. In a few minutes he would be beating at the door with his soft, declawed front paws. Her focus was on what had incited such panic in her even keel pet. Why was Bill so scared to go inside? He liked Paul. Even more unsettling was the feeling crawling down her spine. Something was very wrong.

She could feel it.

There was no sound or movement coming from
inside. When Paul was over he always had the television
turned on a game whether it was football, basketball,
soccer, whatever. He always had to have background
noise. Unlike Sam, he liked noise.

"Paul?" Sam realized she was crouching. Telling
herself she was being ridiculous, she forced herself to
stand up, pushing the door open and peering inside.
There was no answer. Maybe he was tired and had
nodded off she told herself. It did nothing for the now
painful gooseflesh covering her body. "Paul?" she called
his name again, whispering it this time. He wasn't in the
living room or kitchen. She pushed a cabinet door closed
with the back of one hand as she walked past. He had to
have been here, she never left drawers or cabinets open.
Glancing around, she noticed a piece of mail hanging
over the edge of her sorter. What had he been doing in
here, snooping? With considerably more effort, she
forced her feet toward the bedroom, stepping over one of
Bill's toys lying in the middle of the floor.

"Paul?" His name died on her lips as she walked
past the open bathroom door and froze. Without knowing
what she was doing, Sam drifted inside and stopped just
inside the doorway. Her hand flew to her mouth too late
to stop the scream.

The hammering of her heart in her ears drowned
out her ability to hear herself as she sank down to her
knees and pulled her phone from her pocket. Sam didn't
hear anyone answer when she dialed 911. She pushed the
buttons, waited a few seconds, and spoke. Her voice felt
rough, jagged as she recited the necessary information
for help to come.

"This is Samantha James. I live at Pheasant Ridge

apartments in West Bloomington, unit 309. My boyfriend is here. He's dead." She dropped the phone and heard nothing of the woman's requests for more information.

Time passed, it had to, though nothing registered until someone's hands grabbed her under her arms and hauled her, stumbling to her feet.

A man's voice spoke softly to her. "Here Miss, come on out. This isn't something you need to see."

But it was too late, she knew it. The image of Paul's once tan body gone dusky blue, dangling from the showerhead, his face splotchy with dark purple marks under his bloodshot eyes and glassy stare were frozen in her mind forever. The likelihood of that image ever leaving her was doubtful. She knew the guilt never would.

Ch. 5

"No, it doesn't make sense. Paul wouldn't kill himself."

Sam was sitting at one end of her olive green, brushed canvas sofa with her favorite cream chenille throw over her shoulders while a seasoned patrol officer sat at the other end. His nametag said Officer Davies. The younger partner, Officer Nelson, handed her a glass of water as he returned from the kitchen. She flashed him a tight smile as a thank you. The youthful blue eyes that met hers registered no emotion when he nodded back.

Officer Davies rested a large, dark fleshed hand on the cushion between them, bridging the distance without intruding. "I know it's hard but sometimes we miss the signs and we're taken by surprise when these things happen." He patted the cushion once, comforting, like he would her leg fifteen years ago when they were allowed to do that sort of thing without fearing a lawsuit.

Shaking her head, Sam threw off his explanation as ludicrous. "Miss the signs? There were no signs to miss. You can ask anyone he works with or his friends. Paul is," she caught herself with a guilty pang, "*was* cheerful, he was social, he was outgoing. Paul was the poster child for who *isn't* going to commit suicide." She pointed a shaking finger at the bathroom where the coroner had taken down her boyfriend's body and carted it away in a sterile black bag on a gurney with one squeaky wheel only a few minutes ago.

The officers exchanged a look. Davies tried again. "Sometimes, when we love someone, we aren't able to think that they might be so unhappy that they would do something like this."

Sam's gut wrenched at his mention of love. She *hadn't* been blinded by love, yet to admit that now made her seem callous. Sam reverted to her practical self, initial shock aside as she sought refuge from the agony ripping through her insides. She knew she was right and this wasn't suicide. "Listen to me," she spoke concisely to emphasize her point, "Paul *wasn't* unhappy. He *wouldn't* kill himself. Besides, it doesn't add up." Their unconvinced faces pushed her to share the evidence confirming her instincts were right. "If Paul wanted to kill himself wouldn't he want privacy? Why would he leave the door open and let the cat out? My neighbors know Bill and would bring him back once they saw him." Speaking of which, why hadn't one brought him by yet? He had to be hiding somewhere with all this commotion. Hopefully he would come back when everyone left.

Young Nelson took over. "He must have left the door open by accident and the cat got out. He had bigger things on his mind I'm guessing. "

Furious with both of them for not listening to what, to her, were obvious facts, Sam pressed on. "Why would he do it *here*? Wouldn't he have to plan it out? I only asked him a few hours ago to meet me here. That's not much time to do," she waved a hand at the bathroom, not daring to look at it, "that."

Officer Davies retracted his hand from where it lay on the cushion, resting it on his dark blue pants. The paternal concern leaked from his features revealing the harsh cop face below. "Maybe his message was for you. You'd been together for a while, he'd probably showered here before and knew the head was high enough and there was no tub to step on if he changed his mind. All he had to do was bring a rope, which I might remind you, he did. That looks a lot like a plan." He let that sink in for a moment but he wasn't done. "Were you two having any big disagreements? Something he might have been upset with? Something he might have been sad over?" The way he was eyeing her made Sam feel like he could hear her thoughts. He sat back, seeing he found a nerve, and waited.

Ducking her head, Sam hid her eyes behind the wave of dark hair that swept forward off her forehead. "He wanted me to move in and I didn't want to." Her voice broke. He'd died here not knowing tonight was probably going to be the last time they would be together. It turned out it was after all; she sniffed back tears. Now was not the time, she told herself. She squared her shoulders and straightened her back. "That's not enough to kill himself over. Paul was stronger than that, you didn't know him."

"Let me ask you this, Miss James," Davies returned his hand to the cushion. He must be a touchy person, she thought in passing. "What do *you* think happened here?"

"Paul didn't snoop but a few of my drawers and cupboards were open. Someone went through my stuff and Paul wouldn't do that. I think someone was robbing me and he walked in and surprised them." Sam kept her voice calm. To make them listen she had to sound reasonable, in control. It was a challenge but she fell back on her professional persona.

"Was there anything missing?"

"No, nothing obvious but I haven't really looked very close." *I've been a little preoccupied with my dead boyfriend's body hanging in my shower,* she didn't add.

"Would there be anything of any special value someone might be looking for? Any jewelry, do you keep large amounts of cash?" Officer Nelson asked.

All of a sudden it hit her, her father's package. That would explain the randomness of the search. Someone *had* been going through her things but carefully. They hadn't wanted to be caught but she had an eye for detail and knew her house. Relieved she'd been right about Paul took her breath. To hide it, she put her hand over her eyes.

Sam couldn't tell the police about the package, not without revealing the years of cash she hadn't reported to the IRS, not knowing where he was and not knowing if her father was in danger now. Whatever it was he'd sent her, it was something worth killing for. Enough to draw him back into her life after nearly two decades. Her frustrated response was brief. "No." She frowned.

Officers Davies and Nelson exchanged another look, this one a "we're done here" look. Officer Davies rose and Officer Nelson shadowed him to the edge of the room.

"We're sorry for your loss, Miss James. You can call if you think of anything else." He laid his card on the corner of the television before he reached the hall leading to the door.

"Thank you, Officers. For everything."

Ch. 6

After the door was closed and locked behind them, Sam shot off the couch and ran to the kitchen to dig both hands deep in the garbage. No one had touched it. Who would? No one would think to dig in dirty garbage for something valuable. Her tea bag was still lying on top of the now entirely illegible note. Had they seen that? Had it been readable enough to let them know she'd received something from her father? Searching past the remnants of the last week's meals and other discards, Sam fought back the urge to retch. She was assaulted by a vile mixture of textures including several piles of smush that sank under her fingers. At last, her search was rewarded when she reached the middle of the bag and her fingers touched the smooth metal she sought. Grabbing it, she lifted it out and examined it with renewed interest. Dirty but intact, the clean parts of the cylinder glinted silver in the light.

"What did you send me, Dad?" So distracted was she, she forgot to disparage their relationship by calling him by his first name as she'd done since her teen years. After she gave up believing he would come home to them and bitterness had taken the place of hope. "And what kind of people are willing to kill for it?"

The smell of her arms as well as the itching of egg shells drying to her forearms drove Sam to the kitchen sink where she sat the cylinder down on its edge and washed her arms up to the elbows twice. When she was clean, she turned her attentions to the dirty object dripping some sort of smelly trash juice on her counter. Examining it closely, she decided it was water tight enough to survive at least a thorough wipe down with a damp cloth. Scrubbed free of its filth, Sam gave it a test sniff. Just the faint scent of metal, no mucky odors.

"It'll do for now." She nodded to herself.

The green digital numbers on the microwave clock read seven forty. Sam dried her hands on a dishtowel then picked her cell up off the coffee table where someone must have put it after her 911 call earlier. Grateful she didn't have to go near the bathroom to find it, she checked her call log. Two missed calls, only one voicemail. Her tired body collapsed on the couch, her phone dropped on her stomach without a button pushed.

Her impulse to call her mother evaporated with thoughts of that call and what she'd seen in the bathroom. She wasn't so sure she could talk to anyone. What would she say? *I was too chicken shit to tell a good guy he wasn't for me and now he's dead?* The guilt plaguing her was oppressive. *And deserved,* she couldn't help thinking. If she'd had the nerve to tell Paul how she felt months ago, hell if she'd done it yesterday, he would still be alive, probably laughing with someone else right now. Part of her despaired she would never hear his laughter again. It was her fault he was dead.

Curling up on the couch, she fell into a fitful sleep filled with men chasing her with ropes tied into nooses yelling, "Where is it?" And her father's voice saying, "Trust me, Sam." When the sun rose and shone directly in her eyes she made a cup of tea and opened the door to look both ways for her cat. He was nowhere to be found. She was scared to wander the halls looking for him and retracted her head back into her apartment, locking the deadbolt against any unseen threats. After her third cup of tea it was after seven and she could no longer put off calling her mother.

"What do you mean Paul's gone?" Brenda sputtered, her voice getting all high and choked.

Sam's throat closed up. Saying it out loud made it more real and, in her fear and shame, she wanted her mother's comfort. Not that she deserved it. She sniffed once before the tears finally came. "Paul's dead Mom," she repeated in a hoarse whisper. "I came home and he was hanging in my bathroom." Her voice broke on the last word and tears turned into rivers.

"Oh my God honey. Are you okay?" Her voice was muffled as she slid her hand over the receiver but Sam heard her talking to her husband and mention going to Sam's. "Honey, are you home? I'm coming now." Keys rattled over the phone line.

All she could manage was a choked, "Okay," before the phone went dead and she let hers drop back on her lap. Sam lost track of time again. What seemed seconds later, she heard a knock at the door. When she opened it, her mother was there with a bonus.

"Bill!" She took him, gratefully rubbing her face against his fuzzy cheek. Sam avoided letting her thoughts turn to *why* Bill had run off. Regardless, she had a flash of glassy, bloodshot eyes once so full of fun and life and fought down the urge to be sick. The cat struggled to be free and Sam let him go, watching him dart into her bedroom surely to hide in his safe spot under the bed. She couldn't blame him a bit. In fact, if she could fit she might have joined him.

"Sammy, honey." Was all her mother had to say for Sam to lose what remained of her self-composure and crumble completely into an emotional puddle. Brenda directed her to the couch and Sam collapsed into her mother's side.

"Mom, they killed him." She lay her head on her mother's chest and sobbed as if she was eight years old again and Jimmy Keating had cut her hair on the bus.

"He's dead and it's all my fault."

Sam tonelessly related the story in its entirety. As it came out Brenda learned of the mystery cylinder in this year's birthday package and understood how Sam could believe Paul's death was not a suicide. Despite looking like she had just swallowed a baby goat, Brenda managed the report of her ex-husband resurfacing and putting her daughter in life threatening danger reasonably well.

"Honey it's not your fault. How could you know these people would find you and do it so quickly? Have you told anyone else?" She asked, stroking Sam's smooth hair.

Sam's head rocked side to side against Brenda's body where it rested heavily. "No," she mumbled.

Brenda's hand stroked her cheek and head until finally, exhausted, she rested. Sam's open eyes stared unseeing at the pattern in the arm of her couch until she lost consciousness.

It wasn't much later when, hoping to catch the call before it disturbed her daughter, Brenda snatched Sam's vibrating cell from the rectangular dark wood coffee table and answered in a hush. "Hello?"

"Sam?" The woman's mature voice was rough, she'd been crying. Brenda could easily surmise the identity of the caller even if the number didn't show up as Paul's home phone.

Heartsick with sorrow for the woman, Brenda's reply was naturally infused with sympathy. "Mrs. Fuhrman? This is Sam's mother, Brenda. I'm so sorry."

"Is it true? Did he really...?" she hesitated to say

the words. "Did he really hang himself?"

Brenda's heart went out to the woman. No parent wanted to outlive her child; it was unnatural. But even more awful was the thought that he would die by his own hand. That would have destroyed Brenda were she in Mrs. Fuhrman's shoes. However, the decisions she made from here out had to be in her own child's best interests and the fewer people who knew about this the better. So it was out of love for her daughter that Brenda put the final arrow through another mother's heart.

"Yes, Mrs. Fuhrman. I'm sorry for your loss, Paul was a good man."

Paul's mother said no more. It was unnecessary to be standing in front of the woman to know that she was utterly devastated. She did not cry, crying was not enough to express the desolation that was consuming her.

"Is there anyone there with you?" Brenda had no clue if she was still married to Paul's father.

"Jim is coming home from a business trip he was on in Iowa as we speak. He should be here in a few hours." Her words were distant and hollow. It was good she wouldn't be alone long.

"I am truly sorry, Mrs. Fuhrman." Brenda said again, knowing it wasn't enough. Nothing would ever be enough again for his parents.

"Thank you." The woman's breeding and manners provided her a base to operate from when her sensibilities failed her. "Please let Sam know that we will have a service for Paul. It will just be family but I'm sure he would want her there. I can call when we have the details settled."

"Thank you, I'll let her know."

"They're going to have a service?" Sam asked after her mother laid the phone down on the arm of the couch. Sam's confidence was shaken completely. Unable to trust her own decision-making abilities, she looked to her mother for guidance. "Mom, what do we do now? What if they come back?"

"I can put it in the box at the bank."

There was nowhere safer, only the two of them knew of the safe deposit box. Sam swore she didn't want the money but Brenda made her swear she would keep it "just in case". The question was never did she need it, it was whether she would ever touch it or let it rot on principle.

"Do you still have your key?" Sam asked without argument.

"Yep, I keep it in my purse." Wriggling out from under Sam who let her head rest against the back cushions, Brenda scooted her thick body forward and heaved herself up and onto her feet. " Pete's too good a cook," she joked.

Her reference to the extra twenty or so pounds she now carried since marrying Pete Tolliver five years ago drew a small snort from Sam. Personally, she thought it was great that her mother was happy. In all of Sam's childhood memories her mother was fretting and troubled. She'd been dangerously thin several times from stress. Sam watched her mother disappear around the corner into the front hall to grab the cylinder from the kitchen counter. Reentering the living room, Brenda held the troublesome tube in her palm, examining it. "Wish me luck." Brenda placed it in an interior fabric pouch at the top of her purse designed for sunglasses or a cell phone.

One final affectionate stroke of her daughter's cheek and Brenda let herself out. Sam watched her go and was getting up to lock her door when she was seized by a sudden panic. She couldn't let her mother carry that thing around. *What am I thinking?*

While she was lying there, wallowing in a self-indulgent pity party, her mother was taking a huge risk carrying that thing around. If those people came back they might go after someone leaving her apartment. They could hurt Brenda. Why had Sam involved her? It was stupid of her. She needed to get the tube back and send her mom away until it was safe. Or maybe it would be easier if *she* went away for a while. Frantic, she threw the deadbolt the other way and dashed out. She caught her at the elevators.

"Mom."

Brenda spun around, alarmed at the panic in Sam's voice. "What is it?" Her light brown eyes, the same as Sam's only minus the thin green band around the outside of her golden irises given to Sam by her father, had gone wide. She turned her head, scanning while clutching her purse to her chest protectively with both hands.

Sam held her hand out surprised it wasn't shaking. "Give it back, I can't let you take it. I'm going to hide it here."

Her unwillingness to go along with her daughter's change in plan was clear. "Sam," Brenda started.

Sam was just as stubborn, her mind made up. "No Mom, you're not going anywhere with that thing. Look what happened to the last person who got into this." A flash of her mother's face gone blue with dead eyes

42

temporarily superimposed itself over the plump, healthy face in front of her and Sam shuddered. "I can't have anything happen to you."

"How do you think *I* feel? What kind of mother would I be if I let you keep this thing?"

Goddamn tube, Sam thought trying not to grit her teeth. Appearing to fold, she let her shoulders droop and sighed before hugging her mother one more time. "All right Mom, thanks for doing this."

Satisfied she was being allowed to fulfill her motherly duty, Brenda smiled and kissed Sam's forehead. "Don't worry honey, we'll figure this thing out."

"I know." Sam smiled stiffly back and watched her mother get in the elevator, the doors closed, cutting them off from one another.

Sam's hand tightened around the cylinder she palmed during that last hug. She would be angry when she got to the bank but Sam could live with that. What she *couldn't* live with was letting her father hurt her mother again. From here out this was *her* burden and hers alone. The cylinder stayed with her.

Ch. 7

A pragmatic mind was a great thing in a time of crisis for several reasons. For one, it remained calm, for the most part, when emotion threatened to run amok. Second, it provided structure and order which set the stage for the third reason: planning. It was this last reason that controlled Sam's thoughts after her mother left.

Sam was assuming several things based on the evidence she saw around her apartment. She guessed, given the general disarray she'd seen initially, her home had been searched. A more thorough examination revealed that indeed it had. They might have thought they were putting things back but that was the funny thing about organizing someone else's belongings. You didn't know exactly how things were and if the homeowner was as meticulous as Sam, any "oddities" were easily noticed. Details such as pans having their handles turned the opposite way, sweaters being stacked off kilter, and most creepy of all, were her bras and underwear being twisted in their rows. However, it did make her feel more confident that with her apartment having already been searched it might be safe for a while before they came back inside to look again.

The fact that the entire unit had been searched so thoroughly while the cylinder remained untouched in the garbage gave Sam an idea. Careful not to drop it in case something inside might be fragile, never mind the fact that she'd whipped it into the garbage just yesterday, she pulled away the bag and slid the silver encased mystery tube down to the bottom between the white plastic container and bag. Same safe place, no nasty mush to dig through later.

With that handled and no more distractions, Sam

became painfully aware of the ghost of Paul lingering in her apartment. She desperately had to go to the bathroom only she couldn't bring herself to go in there. After a quick change from the work clothes she'd never changed out of into a green fitted tee and jeans, Sam made the decision to leave. It made sense that she would possibly be safer somewhere public anyway.

Pulling her black satchel purse over her shoulder she stepped out, locked the door behind her, and slid her keys into her pocket. Her favorite coffee shop was only a few blocks away and Sam made that her destination. A potty break and vanilla latte later, she was sitting at a small bistro table in the air-conditioned interior beside a large plate glass window, watching the passersby with unusually keen interest.

Any stranger could be the one responsible for Paul's death. Sam paid close attention to anyone who looked like he didn't belong. Sam hid her scrutiny behind a section of the local paper while painstakingly examining each man who walked past the window, taking special interest in any who looked her way. One attractive blonde man caught her eye and smiled, slowing by the doors. Feeling her heart rate triple, she watched him open the glass door and walk in. As the doors shut he looked right at her and one side of his lips tipped up. Embarrassed he clearly caught her staring, Sam straightened her face into a disinterested mask and dropped her eyes as he walked in and ordered, taking a seat somewhere behind her when he got his cup of plain black coffee and sandwich.

An employee of the shop came by long after she finished her drink asking if she needed anything more. Looking at the clock showed she'd been there over two hours. To avoid karmic penalty for bogarting a table, Sam asked for another latte and handed the girl a five.

What struck Sam, not usually a people watcher, was how tuned in to each other most people were as they moved amongst one another in such close quarters while still seemingly oblivious. Men watched almost all of the women and only those women who caught the men doing so too blatantly reacted as was expected of them, they acted uninterested except in the rarest of cases. Conversely, the women watched the men just as closely, although most had perfected their bored stares for when they were caught. It was both entertaining and educational and Sam found herself fascinated, smiling at the intricate dance more than a few times.

The vibrating phone in her pocket halfway through her second latte made her jump, she hadn't realized how on edge she was. *I'm going to have to switch to decaf* she teased herself.

"Hello?" She didn't readily recognize the number.

"Sam?" It was Pete and his voice was strange.

She put her finger against her other ear to block out the background noise, concentrating on her stepfather's voice. "What's going on Pete? Did you talk to Mom? She's out running an errand." Sam checked her watched. Come to think of it, where was her mother? She'd had enough time to get to the bank and back about ten times. Sam should have gotten an angry call by now. She had been so focused on her "surveillance" Sam had forgotten to worry about her mother. She couldn't be so single-minded if she was going to keep her mother and herself safe.

"Sam I just got a phone call from the Bloomington Police Department."

Now that she was listening Sam could hear the raw emotion in Pete's husky voice. She felt an

46

impending sense of dread pressing down on her so hard it was difficult to breathe.

"Sam, your mom's been in an accident. She's at Fairview Southdale. I'm going there now. Do you need me to pick you up?"

He was offering to be kind but Sam knew he wanted to get there without delay and she was twenty minutes out of the way for him. "No, I'll meet you there." She managed to squeak out around the lump in her throat.

Jumping up, she left her unfinished drink and dashed from the shop, oblivious to the two men who got up to follow. One had been watching her from the table at the café across the street, the other was the attractive blonde from two tables back in the coffee shop.

Ch. 8

The dark haired, balding and more senior of the two rose when she stepped out onto the street and waited for the younger blonde to jog across the street to join him. Watching her hurry blindly home to retrieve her car, the older man knew they had time to catch up with her nor did they have to worry about being stealthy. The girl wouldn't see anyone following her right now.

"Let's go." He spoke quietly to his partner, digging in his trouser pocket for his keys.

The younger of the two was in his early to late thirties, it was hard to tell with his boyish face and athletic build combining to give him a youthful appearance. Recently added to the team, his older partner didn't know much about his new junior partner, just that he was supposed to be a valuable addition. Now the younger man was in a huff. "I barely got to eat my sandwich."

"Are you sure she didn't have it on her?" the older man asked, ignoring his partner's complaint. "She gave it to her at the apartment. I heard it myself." He tapped the communication device in his ear linked up to the bugs they'd hastily planted earlier during their search when they discovered they would not be walking out with the lost cylinder after all.

This was turning from a simple recovery mission into a messy surveillance and cleanup operation. Things were bound to get worse if they delayed too long getting that cylinder. The lab was in a shambles after the scientist gone rogue had destroyed his research and stolen the formula. The deadlines for a completed product loomed and buyers were waiting. That damned doctor was in for it when they found him. They were authorized to use any means necessary to recover the formula or the scientist. Both men hunting Dr. James were good with any means necessary.

Nodding, the blonde answered while he checked the rearview mirror out of habit, even when he wasn't driving. They pulled out into traffic. "Yep, I'm sure. After I hit her I got out and was checking her out all 'concerned citizen' while I hollered for someone to call 911. It wasn't on her."

"What did you do with the car?" The older partner signaled his turn, carefully making his way back to the girl's apartment.

"Parked it back where I got it." He gave a snorting laugh. "Poor bastard won't know what hit him when the police come knocking."

The senior man grunted. His new partner wasn't impressing him thus far. The only thing he'd done correctly was to track the scientist to the courier service, although he hadn't been able to get the package before it was on a truck and gone. A little persuasion however, had at least yielded an address from the young clerk who had been at the register when Dr. James had come in. Unfortunately, he hadn't been able to get the young man alone until he was leaving after his shift and by the time they traced it, it was too late.

Things had only gone downhill from there. The girl was right that their search *had* been unexpectedly interrupted by the boyfriend who had to be disposed of after he'd proved not to know anything useful. His new partner's knowledge of the human body and how to inflict harm without leaving a mark was remarkable. However, they'd been left with evidence of their being there. If they'd had more time they would have taken him out of the building. It was cleaner that way, but that was impossible after he'd let on Sam was on her way home. The suicide ploy was a less than desirable solution reinforcing the older man's doubts about the wisdom of his new partner. The recklessness of his actions brought unnecessary risk. If the media got hold of the beating of the man from the courier service, the scientist would know they were getting close. And now, if he were watching his daughter, there would be no doubt.

"You're going to lose her." The blonde darted a frustrated scowl at the other one, sitting behind the wheel.

Sighing, he rolled his eyes. "You saw how she reacted to that call. We know what it was about and we know where she's going. Home for the car, then to the hospital. No need to hurry."

The younger man settled back in his seat still tense. "All right, but we'd better not lose her or you know they'll be pissed. We can't lose this thing."

The older man grunted again. Maybe his partner wasn't so dumb after all.

Ch. 9

Sam rushed through the hospital doors just shy of a run. Her mother was hurt and she knew it was no coincidence. That made two people hurt in the last twenty-four hours with the only thing in common being her, and the only thing that had changed in her world during that time had been the cylinder. It didn't take a genius to figure out that it was all related. Obviously they were watching her apartment and following anyone going out.

"Brenda Tolliver?" She asked the middle-aged nurse in blue scrubs awash with oddly colored cats monitoring the information desk.

Following her directions Sam sped into the elevator, taking it to the second floor. When she stepped off she trotted to where her stepfather was pacing outside the room a few doors down the hall. He stopped when he saw her, relief flooding his features.

"Sam!" He lowered his hands to her shoulders, pulling her into a tight hug and burying her nose against his chest. Usually awkward and shy, Sam knew Pete was upset if he was reaching out to her. He married her mother when she was grown negating the chances for a close "daddy-daughter" type relationship, especially considering her equal lack of affectionate overtures. "Thank God you're here."

Pulling back gently so as not to offend, Sam tried to get caught up. "Pete, what happened?"

Pete's narrow shoulders slumped as he leaned heavily against the wall. The out of place paunch that had recently begun to alter his long thin outline gave him the comical shape of a cartoon bear when he slouched that way.

"The police don't know exactly. Witnesses said she was walking across the street a few blocks from your house and this blue Subaru came screeching around the corner. Without so much as a honk to warn her, it hit her." Pete buried his face in his hands. "She's in a coma," he groaned through his fingers.

Her heart seized, tightening into a hard, painful ball in her chest. The words she forced out were barely a whisper, "A coma?"

This couldn't be happening. Brenda was the one constant in her world no matter what else happened in it. And her father's sudden *re*appearance had yielded the same result as his *dis*appearance; he hurt her mother yet again whether he meant to or not. Sam felt the last shred of longing she had to see the man dissolve.

Pete continued to hide his face behind his hands. "They've induced the coma while they wait for the swelling in her brain to come down. It's too soon to tell how much damage there is. They're in there now doing more tests."

A coma. Sam heard that word over and again in her head, tolling like a death knell for her mother. *No!* Her mind screamed, tipping her well into the danger zone for what she could handle. The extensive knowledge Sam had of head injuries due to her occupation inundated her conscious thoughts until she could think of nothing else. She shook off the negative prognosis she feared was coming. Her mother would wake up. She had to. Without her, Sam was alone. No family to speak of with the rest of them scattered and disconnected, few friends and no one special she could share herself with. Lonely took on a whole new meaning if her mother was taken from her.

52

The door to her mother's room opened and a doctor, followed closely by two nurses, strode out. The doctor approached Pete at an efficient clip. His report was clinical, sterile, giving nothing away. "Mr. Tolliver, your wife sustained a severe blow to her head. When she fell she struck it on the pavement." He cast a glance at Sam, deducing she was family by her proximity and attentiveness and included her in his report. "As you know we have induced a coma to allow her body and brain time to heal. The next few days will be critical." He patted Pete's arm and gave him a disingenuous smile. "I will keep you informed of any changes in her condition."

Another cursory glance her way before he turned on his heel and Sam decided she disliked the doctor. "Doctor," she called out behind him. He stopped. "Do you think my mother is going to wake up?" Her strength in business had always been her no nonsense approach. In times of upheaval she fell back on that; times like this, when her fear threatened to swallow her sanity without thinking twice.

He stared at her a long moment deciding whether she could handle an answer as direct as her question. Twitching his arms at his sides, he glanced down at the manila file he held, tapping it against his open palm before glancing back up to meet her level dark eyes. "I don't know."

"Thank you." She could hear his honesty this time and appreciated it even if it wasn't what she wanted to hear.

"Can I see her?"

"Yes. It might help to hear your voices."

The first nurse, a cute blonde nodded and added a

supportive touch to Sam's arm. "You can go in, sweetie."

Sam had heard or read that somewhere, that coma patients who woke up reported hearing people talking to them, that it helped them find their way back. Pete went straight in without speaking, Sam was right on his heels and stopped just inside the doorway to get the lay of the land. Brenda was lying in a big white hospital bed, face purple and swelling on one side, angry red scrapes on her face.

Automatically, Sam was reconstructing the accident from her pattern of injuries, deducing her mother had rolled after being struck and hitting her head, incurring the scratches after the fall. Tubes and wires stretched across her with monitors beeping and whirring all around the top of the bed. Sam took a shaky breath to steady herself, not wanting to shatter what was left of Pete's control.

He went straight to his wife's bed taking the seat scooted up against the taller bedside to be as close as possible. Reaching out he slid his hand into hers, holding on firmly as if this was exactly where he'd left off before the doctor's examination forced him out. As he mumbled his quiet words of encouragement for Brenda to come back to him, Sam could only hear her mother's voice as she swore to help her figure this thing out. "This thing" that had possibly cost her mother her life or precious brain function and cost Pete his wife. Sam's guilt and anger threatened to mire her in their depths.

Not one to show affection in front of others, Sam stepped forward and stroked the lump that was her mother's foot below the blankets. "I'll fix this Mom," she promised softly, "I'll make it right."

"What was that?" Pete sat up and twisted in his chair to face her.

She forced a half smile and patted her mother's foot farewell. "Nothing Pete. I said I have to go. I'm going to check in with the police to see about any leads they might have."

Pete had known Sam for long enough to know she was a "fix it" kind of person. She wouldn't be content to sit in a hospital room standing vigil when she felt there was something she could be doing. Kindly, he gave her his own "be brave" smile while he rubbed his wife's limp hand. "That's a good idea Sam."

"I'll let you know what I find out." She rested her hand on the door, poised to push. "Call me if anything changes?"

"I will."

Sam's mind was already spinning as she strode from the hospital and aimed her SUV toward the police station she'd been to on numerous occasions in the past. It wasn't far and she was already in full investigator mode when she reached their parking lot. Sam had been inside several police stations for business, requesting and picking up police reports for traffic accidents, and Bloomington's was like any of the others. It was more like an office than most people would think. The only thing especially "policey" about it was the fact that the people at the desks were all wearing dark blue uniforms and guns. The exception to that being the plain-clothes detectives housed in cubicles against the windows at the far end. Unlike television's version of a police station there were no prostitutes and drug dealers struggling in cuffs as they were led to a cell, Bloomington was too suburban for that. It was far more likely she would see a teenager waiting for his parents after getting caught with drugs on school grounds.

Sam went straight up to the front desk and asked

the middle-aged woman busily typing away on her out of date computer for assistance. "Excuse me, who could I speak with about a serial murder?"

As it had been intended, that got the attention of not only the receptionist but everyone else within earshot.

"Pardon me?" The woman's hands stopped typing and she repositioned her glasses over her small upturned nose. Her short, curly red hair that had been bouncing ever so slightly with her finger movements swayed abruptly to a halt. The only sounds to be heard came from the farthest reaches of the office where Sam's question hadn't been overheard and slowly those sounds too stopped as word spread.

Sam stood tall and made sure her professional "respect me" mask was firmly in place before continuing. All the attention had her wanting to turn tail and run until she girded herself with images of Paul's dead eyes and her mother's pale, battered face and held her ground. Their blood was on her hands, what was a little public humiliation? *I'd trade places with you in a heartbeat Mom and screw you Dad.* If there was a choice between loyalty to one of her parents there was no question. It was time to come clean to the police and get help.

"I would like to discuss a homicide that occurred at my apartment earlier today as well as an attempted homicide that happened a few hours ago."

Without missing a beat, the receptionist picked up her phone and made a call. Her voice remained low and even as she repeated Sam's message. Glancing up, she offered a small, stiff smile that didn't reach her eyes. "Come with me please?" She stood and walked around her desk, leading Sam to a nearby interview room; so said the metal plaque on the wall beside the opening. It was difficult but Sam ignored the curious stares. She didn't feel any better when she was ushered through the wooden door with a large glass window. The only sign this wasn't any other company orchestrating the sale of widgets was the metal mesh laced within the glass on the door. Sam felt the skin at the small of her back prickle with sweat.

The space was devoid of decoration, nearly equally empty of furniture. Only a plain gray table that could have been picked up at a second hand office supply store and equally abused upholstered chair on metal legs. The receptionist indicated Sam should sit, which she didn't, and backed to the door, fingers wrapped around the handle. "Someone will be right with you." And with that the door closed and the sounds of typing and phones ringing faded away leaving Sam alone with her thoughts.

Within minutes a short, heavyset man in a gray suit and blue tie opened the door, approaching Sam with his hand held out. "Detective Travis Cote, Homicide. I understand you have information regarding a homicide?" Sam faced him, struggling to remember to breathe and hoping he couldn't see the sweat she felt beading on her upper lip and forehead.

Detective Cote was a soft-spoken man whose physical bearing drew no more notice than did his voice. He wore his thin straight honey colored hair brushed neatly to the side, was clean shaven, and looked more like an accountant than homicide detective.

Sam cleared her throat. "Yes, um, Detective Cote. Uh, and an attempted homicide that just happened a few hours ago. I wanted to give you some information you don't have in your file." Sam wasn't willing to risk anyone else's safety while she waited for her father to come back from the dead and tell her what was going on. They could *all* be dead by then.

Holding up a hand, he stopped her. "Are you by chance Samantha James?" At Sam's shocked expression he smiled and held up his hands to point around them. "We don't have too many murders around here so I help out in other areas when I'm needed. The officers who handled a suicide earlier reported the girlfriend was pretty sure the death wasn't a suicide despite the evidence otherwise." Staring into his light eyes, she saw how wrong her first impression had been. His were not the eyes of an accountant. Sam saw nothing but cop in him as he stared her down.

Barely moving her head she nodded. "I didn't know if I should say anything before and then, a few hours ago my mother was involved in a hit and run." He failed to hide his initial shock before he hid it behind his blank expression. "Now that my mom has been targeted," she continued, "I wanted to come clean and see if there's anything you can do to stop these people and give my mom some protection until they're caught." Swallowing, she shifted her weight from one foot to the other. "My father sent me something yesterday. He always sends me something on my birthday, only this time he sent me this metal container. I don't know what's in it but he's a scientist, at least he was nineteen years ago when he disappeared." She licked her lips wondering where the moisture in her mouth had gone, wishing she had a drink to wash down the lump in her throat. "He sent me this thing and told me to keep it a secret because there were people after it. I didn't really think much about it only now two people are dead or hurt the day after I got it. I'm not keeping his secret anymore." The heat in her face threatened tears although Sam wouldn't give that up in front of a stranger. Taking a deep breath and letting it out slowly she forced herself to calm down so her voice didn't break. No one took an emotional woman seriously. "Can you protect my mom?"

The detective studied her, chewing the inside of his lower lip. That he didn't immediately dismiss her as a delusional conspiracy theorist Sam took as a good sign. However, his blank face was far from convincing that what Sam said made any sort of impact. "What kind of scientist is or was your father?"

"My mother said he was a geneticist. He was at Johns Hopkins before he disappeared. He was working on a research grant splicing DNA to isolate particular genes." Hearing the old pride she used to feel as a child that her father was a pioneer in his field, Sam swept it from her voice and continued coolly. "We moved here after he was gone. I couldn't tell you where he went." She stopped herself from gushing any more, she'd said enough. She watched closely for a reaction, seeing none.

"So your father was a genetic scientist nineteen years ago, left you, and now after all this time he sends you something and tells you to keep it for him without telling you what it is or why? And now your boyfriend has killed himself and your mother was hit by a car and you think it's more than unfortunate timing?"

She watched him blinking at her, feeling her heart clench yet she persevered in order to get her mother the protection she needed. "I know it sounds strange. I didn't really take his note seriously myself at first either, but how else to you explain someone breaking into my apartment and killing my boyfriend, and then trying to kill my mother..." Her breath hitched and she gulped air making an odd noise in her throat as she swallowed. "Nothing like this has ever happened to me before. It's got to be because of this thing with my father. There's no other explanation."

"Do you have this package?" He was still staring at her like she'd just read him her grocery list. "Do you know what's in it?"

"I don't have it on me, I didn't think it was safe to carry it around." She shrugged, feeling vulnerable and not liking it. "I tried but I can't figure out how to open it to see what's inside." Sam heard the facts stretching out before her and let her words die. It was starting to sound farfetched even to her.

The detective was clearly of the same mind. "Miss James, I understand after what's happened with your family that you might be under some strain." He slid his hands in his pants pockets and rocked back on his heels, his features softening for the first time. "The human mind has a need to explain things, to link events. Your friend killed himself today and your mother was involved in a simple, although unfortunate, accident. These things happen, at times in succession. It doesn't mean someone is out to get you," he paused, offering her a gentle smile and a pat on her forearm, "or your mother."

Sam struggled to keep her voice calm, hearing the beginnings of hysteria creeping in. "But what about the package? Why would my father ask me for help after so many years?"

He kept his expression carefully controlled, thanks no doubt to years of practice from dealing with loons and criminals. "You said it yourself, he sends you something every year on your birthday." His shrug was non-committal. "This time he's sent you a gift." He shook his head, trying to sound sympathetic. "I believe you have been the victim of misfortune and are trying to pull together some unrelated incidents. I also think you have a very active imagination and you would be well served to take a big step back and ask yourself if it's at least *possible* that I'm right. That maybe you've overreacted because you're upset."

She felt the wind go out of her and her mouth snapped shut with a pop; frustrated by his bland attempt to justify away her "misfortunes" instead of considering she might be telling the truth. This *was* happening, these things *were* related, and the only people she could think of who could help were laughing at her. If the authorities wouldn't listen and she couldn't risk involving anyone else, then from here out Sam was alone. Unfortunately, she had no clue what to do other than wait for her father to show up and that meant she had to stick to her patterns and risk injury to herself. At least if her mother was in the hospital that might keep her out of harms way, provided Sam stayed clear of her. Pain knifed through her chest.

Sam took a deep breath and counted to five. Without another word she stood up, turned on her heel and walked out of the building. She didn't see the Detective return to his desk shaking his head nor did she hear his call to Officers Davies and Nelson out on patrol across town.

"That lady stopped by the station, the girlfriend from your suicide from last night, Samantha James. I guess her mom was in an accident this morning and now she's having some trouble. You might want to have a social worker visit her. She was just here going on about a conspiracy with her dad and something he sent her. Now she says someone's after this thing he sent her only she doesn't know what it is." Exhaling, he rubbed his forehead. "It's your case but I think she could use a little intervention, you want me to send someone over?"

Officer Nelson's chuckle came over the radio. The older Officer Davies was more sympathetic when he answered. "She was pretty shook up. We'll have somebody by as soon as we can get them out there. You know how busy they are, it might be a few days. Maybe we can swing by in the meantime, I'll see if we can get time between calls later tonight." There was some grumbling from Nelson and Davies must have given him a look because it cut off abruptly.

"Thanks Davies."

"No problem, Detective." Davies hung up and, with an eye roll, replaced the radio.

"What do you want to do?" Nelson eyed his partner speculatively, not offended at being cut off for his dissention. It happened a lot when you were in a car together eight hours at a time.

They were parked on the street out in front of a greasy spoon Davies favored. "Eat. I'm hungry. We can see if we can find time to swing through tonight or tomorrow."

Not another word was said about the case they both had already closed. They had too many others that weren't.

Ch. 10

Jimmy Ramirez hung up his headphones and threw down his pen on top of the pile of notes he took daily. Monitoring communications chatter from several federal as well as local law enforcement channels was his daily routine, when he needed a break he fed it through a recording device and sifted through it simultaneously with the live streams. The others called him a savant, he flipped them off. It was easy for him. When they weren't listening for a few key names and tidbits, the likes of which he'd just heard, they stalked the frequencies for calls for men like them. Men with certain sets of skills who didn't mind hiring themselves out for a price. Those particular jobs, a few well-chosen per year, paid for all of their equipment so they could continue to search the airwaves for signs of the man they knew as "Doc".

After his interest was piqued, he jotted down a few key pieces of information for cross checking and additional information gathering on his laptop before calling his comrades in from outside. They were out in the field on the edge of the woods behind the farmstead they used as their base of operations. Judging from the sound of things they'd stopped with hand-to-hand practice and moved on to weapons practice.

When the shots paused long enough to signal the two men were reloading their magazines, Jimmy shouted out the second floor window where his listening station slash bedroom was located. He never liked being far from his babies. "Hey, Sarge, Marcus." They moved out from under the cover of the branches and looked up. Jimmy shook his notepad excitedly at them. "I got somethin'."

Justin Shaw, still "Sarge" to his men even if they

63

had been out almost ten years, holstered his 9 mm Glock on his black cargo clad thigh. Ruffling his unruly, sandy blonde hair with a sun darkened hand he lifted it off his sweaty forehead, shoving it away from his face. Having been working without a shirt in the sweltering summer heat, he crossed his arms across his bare chest while he waited, wishing he could cut down a few more trees to allow better air flow around the house. Unfortunately, less tree coverage meant greater visibility via satellite. Translation: they sweated.

Justin heard Evan Marcus slip his weapon into its shoulder holster as well, a .45 Heckler & Kosch he'd favored for as long as Justin had known him. The taller man's deep voice rumbled his annoyance as he sauntered up to stand next to Justin. "What do you mean we got *something*? What kind of something?"

Shaw held out a hand in Marcus's direction, cautioning. The two men were equally intense and disagreements were commonplace. Not that they ever amounted to much but they'd heard some things lately, nothing definitive, but hints that a chemical weapon was rumored to be hitting the market soon. Justin didn't have the patience to listen to his men do their dance. He was hot, he was bored, and he was ready to move as soon as they got some good Intel. The screen door slammed and their Communications Specialist took the steps two at a time. "What have you got, Jimmy?"

Jimmy glowed with pride as he raised his cell phone over his head. Five nine and shorter limbed than many of his peers, Jimmy had found a way to saunter at speed. He'd developed it in the Rangers, probably to keep pace while still maintaining his Mexican-American machismo. At present his strut was jerkier than usual, his legs moving fast. This brisk approach was the closest to breaking character Justin had ever seen in his companion. He was excited.

"I think I got a hit on the Doc through his kid."

Justin and Marcus's eyes bugged. "He's got a kid?" Marcus growled through clenched teeth. "How the hell does someone like that get to have a kid?"

Jimmy's grin disappeared and the intensity in the air ratcheted up a notch. Justin and Jimmy exchanged glances.

"Stay on target, Marcus," Justin's low warning served to keep the man from violence but only barely. "What'd you get, Jimmy?"

"I just picked up some chatter on a local police channel. A detective in Bloomington, Minnesota made a call to a squad that responded to a suicide yesterday. The boyfriend." He shifted his gaze from Marcus, still simmering just below boiling, back to Justin who continued to listen patiently, arms crossed and feet planted. "He says the girl ain't buyin' he did it himself. She says it ain't suicide, it's murder. But here's the kicker." His eyes danced in excitement. "She says it's all over this *package* her dad sent her." His black brows rose as did the corners of his mouth revealing two dimples, not that the guys cared though ladies generally reported wanting to kiss them, "her *scientist* dad. And she says whoever killed the boyfriend is after the mom now too. Sounds like the people the Doc works for don't it?" He was nodding eagerly, glancing between his compatriots, black eyes shining.

Shaw ducked his chin, toeing the trampled grass beneath his black booted foot. He bobbed his head slowly, not willing to get too excited over the possibility that they were finally getting close to a real trail that could lead them to the lab they'd once so desperately fled. The lab where they'd been held for almost six months enduring endless experiments, watching a parade of brave men die when those experiments failed. All conducted by the very country they'd pledged loyalty to.

The lab where they'd been held was dismantled after their escape but they knew the research continued and Justin's men had sought its replacement these last few years with little luck. It always seemed any leads dried up as they traced them back. It wasn't until nearly three years ago they'd started hearing underground reports of a hush-hush project in the Midwest and bought the old rundown farmhouse in eastern Wisconsin from an old woman's family just happy to unload it. They'd not even questioned it when Justin offered cash.

The area was rural, gunshots and hunting were common, and local law enforcement left them alone. Thus, without external interference, they were able to come and go on missions with their long absences unnoticed by their lack of neighbors and conduct their search for the mysterious "Doc" when they were home.

"A daughter?" Something dark and dangerous crossed behind Marcus's blue green eyes. Holding his glare fixed but sightless on Jimmy for a beat, he spun and ran his hands over his tightly-cropped, black curly hair. "Fuck!" he barked.

"Maybe I should try to sweet talk her a little. See what she knows, what daddy sent." Jimmy aimed for levity.

"Didn't you say the boyfriend *just* died?" Justin's subtle drawl became more pronounced with stress. That it was coming on now told his men he was equally affected by the first real lead they'd gotten in years. "That's not a prime candidate for your charms, Ramirez, and we don't want to make ourselves known too quickly. We have no idea what her father's told her or where her loyalties lie." Shaw pointed out. "For now we set up surveillance and wait to see what happens." Inwardly he groaned in unison with the two men who were sufficiently vocal about the suggestion they continue to wait. His men preferred action, not sitting around waiting and he agreed. "If time goes by and we don't see Doc, we pick her up and see what she knows."

"And if she doesn't want to talk?" Marcus asked him evenly, tension visible in the tightly bunched muscles in his arms as his hands gripped the back of his neck.

Shaw didn't flinch. "Then we *make* her. We're not losing him."

The others agreed with the plan, talking out the details. Marcus went out to "borrow" the necessary transportation and by nightfall they were parked outside her apartment. They waited until all the lights were off, almost midnight, before Marcus, outfitted in the urban commando camouflage of dark jeans and a tight long-sleeved black Henley, scaled the outside wall of her building. Starting at the bottom he climbed from deck to deck, making it to hers in just under a minute to place several tiny devices, each the size of a watch battery, on the top, outside corners of her living room and bedroom windows. Returning to their white cargo van with "Metro Water Solutions" emblazoned in red and blue letters on the side, he slid into the driver's seat and gave his team a small tip of his head. It was done.

Jimmy settled on his folding chair and got straight to work donning a pair of headphones and adjusting several knobs on his machine, mounted on a portable workstation bolted to the floor to keep it from sliding, before pressing record. He grinned. "She sleeps to music."

Marcus smiled grimly, his animosity toward the

girl not entirely forgotten. "What does she listen to?" He wanted to know how well they picked up through the glass, these were new devices for them.

Jimmy frowned, listening. "I'm not sure. Here, listen." With the flick of a switch the van was filled with the sound of strings laying out a melancholy tune.

Shaw's fingers paused only for a moment on his laptop where he was hunting the internet for all things Samantha James while simultaneously performing a thorough background check including her credit history. Spotless, all of it. She was squeaky clean. The music bouncing off the metal walls made it tinny but it was still recognizable. His memories brought him back to the humble Tennessee dirt farm just outside Nashville where he'd grown up, evenings spent listening to music on the porch with his parents. Sometimes his father and his friends played, sometimes they listened to recordings. His mother was partial to classical on warm summer nights. "It's Vivaldi's Four Seasons. Winter." He informed them absently. It had been his mother's favorite.

"Who says a hick can't be cultured?" Marcus usually downplayed that fact that he was not only the smartest of the three but was also from money. Apparently he was in the mood to dig at his "Sarge" tonight, probably out of boredom. He'd double majored in Physics and Chemistry at Pepperdine before being recruited.

"Mom liked classical," Justin lifted a shoulder in a non-committal shrug.

"Didn't know you had running water in that little shack, much less electricity." Marcus snorted.

Done with being teased, Justin eyed him with a

cool stare until Marcus found something that required his attention in the paperwork resting on the makeshift worktable beside Jimmy's equipment.

Soft female whimpering filled a gap in the music.

"Nightmare," Jimmy muttered, some of the joviality gone from his tone.

Justin's jaw worked. "Jimmy, turn that down. I can't think."

Ch. 11

Sam spent a restless night, waking often from her fitful sleep. When she rose the next morning she already had a message from Paul's mother, the service was going to be that day at ten. They wanted to be able to put things behind them, the sooner the better. Sam phoned her boss knowing she wouldn't be going to work for a few days.

"Mr. Silverstein, I'd like to use some of my vacation time." Citing her mother's accident as cause Sam left out anything about Paul, figuring she'd shared enough for the time being.

As could be expected Mr. Silverstein, old enough to be her father, and a doting one to his four children, was more than understanding. He told her to "take the rest of the week. We'll talk next week to see how things are going." He insisted she take care of her family and the office would send flowers to the hospital. *What would he say if he knew it was family who brought this on Brenda, and Paul?* She tried to imagine his kind, understanding brown eyes crinkling around fat cheeks when she told him how her father had orchestrated this mess, intentional or not. *Doubtful.* After a few more well wishes she hung up the phone to shuffle into her kitchen and brew a pot of some very strong coffee. The day sat uncertain before her and she had no idea what to do.

With a real fear of drawing any more unwanted attention to her mother by visiting, Sam was unable to even consider a secret visit leaving only Paul's service to attend. That would be enough. She had to force herself into the bathroom to shower, scrubbing her hair so hard in her anxious state her scalp was overly sensitive to the brush's bristles going through it afterward and she felt her eyes stinging from the sensation.

Donning a simple black sheath dress, Sam covered it with a black blazer appropriate for the occasion and walked out the door at nine thirty. When she pulled into the lot fifteen minutes later, she wondered if she should go in early and offer to help. *I wonder if I could get the hell out of here before anyone sees me?*

There weren't many cars out front and Sam was around for a year. She recognized each one. All close family. *Shit.* Being that it was an intimate gathering she assumed they knew what had happened, making her even more awkward having had it happen in her house. Surely they knew that too. *They know it's my fault. His family loved Paul.* Everybody *loved Paul.* She closed her eyes and let her chin sink to her chest feeling her lungs rise and fall with each breath. At times it helped her to relax to be aware of her body's movements. This time, all it did was make her think about how Paul would never take another breath and that concept left her feeling oddly empty. "I'm sorry Paul," she muttered impotently.

The service was awful. Not because anyone was mean or rude, in fact, nobody was *anything* to her. Sam walked in and aside from a distant, awkward hug from his mother and a nod from his father, no one acknowledged her presence. Not even to shoot her a dirty look. It was as if she didn't exist. Last Christmas, those few weekends last summer at the lake, shared family brunches, none of it. The nail that was her guilt stabbing her in the chest was hit on the head with the hammer of their disdain and Sam thought she would fly apart from her very center. Taking the hint that she no longer existed in their world, Sam sat in the back row where no one else would see her. After the eulogy had been read and his mother broke down into a wailing, pitiful wreck, Sam made a silent dash for the door. In that small of a group it was impossible to hide, everyone saw her. The accusation she saw in their eyes told her whom they blamed for Paul's death. She agreed. They were right.

She got home, slipped out of her dress and into a soft pink tank and her favorite cotton pajama pants, pink and black striped with images of Elvis dancing across them in his famous Jailhouse Rock tiptoe move. Clicker in hand, Bill on her lap, and a glass of water beside her, Sam didn't move until two whole movies passed her by.

The only movies she could find were about young women being stalked by their ex-husbands or hitmen hired by their ex-husbands to take out their women. Coincidentally, in both movies she watched, the police didn't listen until it was too late. More than a little freaked, she turned it off feeling much worse about her situation. The overwhelming cinematic consensus seemed to be for her to take matters into her own hands and shoot the responsible parties and, because she'd warned a few people along the way, she wouldn't even go to jail. For fear Hollywood might steer her wrong, Sam refrained from running to the nearest gun store.

It was nearly three-thirty. Checking the gym schedule posted on her fridge, Sam decided to hit an early kickboxing session that started in an hour. She had no interest in sitting around waiting for something bad to happen and for the foreseeable future she had no solid plans. Besides, now more than ever she needed to clear her head. Maybe something would come to her if she could just think, if she could see something other than glassy eyes and scraped skin.

The instructor was curious at her unusually early arrival yet quickly folded her into the class. Apparently it was larger than her normal evening class with a number of high school and college kids cramming in some last daytime sessions before school started next week. The class ended at half past five but the ring was open for another hour and Sam stayed after to "bounce around" with some other diehards. She finally took off her gloves when she was both exhausted and starving. By the time she showered and walked out into the fading heat it was a little after seven and the sun was beginning to cast long evening shadows across the parking lot. Her light blue tank top clung to her still damp skin, the top brushing the waist of her denim skirt to show off the pattern on her tan leather belt. No need to dress up, Sam was wearing a pair of flip flops with delicate butterflies stitched into the brown leather straps. They were her favorites and one of the things she missed most about summer in Minnesota when her feet were locked up in boots.

Returning to her apartment held no appeal and Sam fell back on the hope that public places were safe, deciding to wander into a sandwich shop kitty corner to the gym to grab a smoked turkey on sourdough. As much as she wanted to be out of the house, the constant coming and going of people on such a busy street had her stomach in ropes and her anxiety at an all time high. She put down the second half of her sandwich and headed back to her car by eight worried she'd puke before she got home.

Sam had just stepped off the curb and into the street across from the gym parking lot when a car's engine revved in the distance, catching her ear. Instantly watchful she glanced around to see nothing of consequence, only a work van across the street down the block as well as some other random cars. All were dark inside and unattended. She chastised herself for being paranoid and crossed the street concentrating on not running. Halfway across, the sound of an engine winding out caught her ear and she looked up to glimpse the very big grill of a very big car bearing down on her and already way too close.

Dropping her bag, Sam threw herself toward the

opposite curb and out of the car's path. It screeched around the corner and she shakily got to her feet. Tentative movements of her extremities confirmed she was not injured beyond scraped skin and promises of bruises to come. Sam glanced around, seeing no sign of the car or witnesses of any kind. Thinking she was in an episode of The Twilight Zone, waiting for some guy with a third arm to offer her a cigarette, she leaned stiffly down to grab her bag before making her way toward the gap in the fence several paces away. It was faster than going around the far side to get to the end of the chain link and she was in no mood to be exposed one second longer than was absolutely necessary. Her car was still a good distance across the parking lot from there and she doubled her speed to make it before anything else happened or she had an anxiety attack waiting for it to. In her haste she failed to notice the same big grilled car coming back around the block. It pulled up to the curb on the street perpendicular to the one it had nearly run her down on and stopped in the shadow of a large building. Sam also failed to see two men get out to jog across the lot until they were nearly upon her.

Catching them out of her peripheral vision when they were way too close for comfort, Sam tried to remain calm and outwardly oblivious as she took stock of her situation. Inside she was having trouble hearing over her hammering heart and blood roaring in her ears as adrenaline pumped through her system. She tried to keep calm by breaking down what she knew of the situation and looking at the facts. There were a few other cars in the lot and, not having seen where these two came from, she couldn't throw out the notion they were going to their car just like her. They were dressed in white dress shirts and dark ties, alleviating some of her apprehension. Then she mentally slapped herself, *what is appropriate attire for murder and hit and runs?* Sam measured the distance from her to the car deeming it too close to call on whether or not she could make it before they reached her if they *were* baddies. Her hand went to her phone, getting ready to dial 911.

When she sped up she heard the hard soles of their dress shoes slam down faster, echoing off the brick of the gym now beside her in the quiet of the area, mostly abandoned this time of night, she knew she was in trouble. They were moving faster and already close enough she swore any second a hand would clamp down on her collar or something sharp would poke into her back. Her bag was slipping; she hiked it on her shoulder at the same time she asked her body for more.

Sam had her key fob in hand and pressed the button to unlock her driver's side door. The lights flashed, the lock clicked, and she afforded herself a fleeting look to her side only to have her panic escalate at the sight of her would-be attackers nearly upon her. Her chest burned, not from exertion, but from sheer terror. Turning back, she wrapped her fingers around the handle and swung the door open only to have it kicked shut by a black loafer at the same time a hand clamp onto her shoulder. *Clearly there wasn't a dress code for killers. Who wore loafers to a street fight?* Gritting her teeth, Sam prepared to attack as she spun around and her back slammed into the side of the vehicle.

Her eyes went wide as she recognized the attractive blonde man from the coffee shop, only this time he didn't smile at her. This time he was glaring with cold eyes that said he wouldn't think twice about hurting her. She wondered if his was the last face Paul saw before he died and felt her hearth clench. His forearm smacked across her chest and throat, pinning her back tight against her car. The second man, reasonably attractive in a mature way if you liked a shaved head, was easily old enough to be her father even if there was nothing paternal about him. He regarded her coolly from behind the blonde. His eyes, less aggressive than the younger man's looked black in the shadows as they bored into hers.

"Give it to us and nobody dies today," the younger one threatened through bared teeth.

His voice snapped her out of her frozen state and Sam felt her fear turning to anger boiling inside her. Eyes narrowing, she snapped back at him surprising herself with her boldness. "You killed my boyfriend and my mom might die because of you." Nothing, no guilt, no fear, nothing human flickered behind his eyes. Sam's insides went cold. "I'm not telling you anything." She didn't sound very convincing. Probably because she wasn't sure she would die to protect her god damned father's secret tube of whatever.

Younger one shifted his arm, threatening to cut off Sam's air supply. She went up on her tiptoes to keep the tiny gap allowing her breath. The older one took a step forward, setting a hand on the other's shoulder. "That would be a mistake."

Sam shifted her attention to the older man. He seemed equally dangerous but maybe a hair more reasonable and she set her hopes on him. Those hopes were slim; she hadn't seen anything yet that would make her doubt that they both intended for her to die after they got what they were after. Not that she was going to give it to them. Anyone who would hire professional killers like these two couldn't be out to save the world with whatever was in that cylinder. Whatever it was, it wasn't good. *Steven what have you done?*

The older one leaned in, his lips pulling back to threaten her again when a ruckus on the far side of the lot snapped both men's heads around. Sam's too. Turning, she saw two men stepping out of the shadows and heading their way. They passed under a streetlight affording Sam and her two "friends" a clear view. The shorter of the two was darker, maybe Hispanic and staggered drunkenly. The other man walked more steadily but had a loose rolling gait, like he hadn't a care in the world. For a fleeting moment she envied him. Both were dressed casually, jeans and tshirts as far as she could tell. Sights set on the more steady of the two, she considered calling for help then he staggered as well, his long legs buckling at the knees. Her dreams of their coming to her aid were gone but, her mind still clicking through options, she figured they could prove to be a useful distraction. A surreptitious glance out of the corner of her eye and Sam saw her attackers were focused on the approaching men, deciding how best to handle them.

It might not be enough against trained killers, but two years of kickboxing and a smattering of martial arts when the coach decided to throw it in hadn't left Sam completely defenseless. When the blonde's arm relaxed ever so slightly she made her move. Dropping down below his arm, her fists shot out in a double punch to the solar plexus taking the wind from his lungs and doubling him over. She followed up with a leg sweep that took him down hard on the asphalt where he lay gasping for breath.

It wouldn't be long before he was up. Sam had to move fast. She craned her neck to locate the other man already lunging for her. Sam scurried backward, losing her balance in her haste and toppled sideways. He was on her in a heartbeat, twisting her arm behind her back and instantly immobilizing her, his weight crushing her to the asphalt. Loose gravel cut into her cheek and bare skin.

Suddenly his weight was gone and her arm fell free. Sam rolled to her hands and knees, eyes following the sound of the scuffle behind her. The drunks had arrived. *That was weirdly fast.* And the taller of the two was fighting the older would-be killer with a speed and skill that would have made her boxing coach weep with envy. She pushed up to her feet and scanned the ground for her keys, dropped when she'd been pinned.

Vice-like hands clamped around one of her ankles and Sam's leg was jerked back hard enough to knock her off her feet again. The top of her shoulders took the brunt of the fall, sparing her neck by mere inches. The pain between her shoulders was instant and brought with it a flash of light behind her eyes. Her vision danced, threatening to go dark.

Struggling against the hands that held her leg Sam jerked her trapped limb while aiming for his head with her other one. His hands loosened only enough to slide up her leg and clamp down again closer to her knee, pulling her painfully across the gravel simultaneously. His move brought his body closer and a painful grunt rewarded her efforts as she landed a heel on something solid. A flip flop went flying. Up on his knees now, one of his hands came off her leg as he knelt by her hip. The fingers no longer holding her bit hard into her side. Sam clenched her teeth to keep from screaming, her eyes watered from the excruciating pain he was inflicting.

"That's your kidney," he hissed. "They're important, you'd hate to lose one." He leaned in close enough Sam could smell the hazelnut from his coffee. "I can make this *very* painful for you if I want to. Now be a good girl and tell me, where's Daddy's package?"

Sam was powerless under his cruel hands. The searing pain in her side had her completely helpless, she could barely think. She gritted her teeth and growled back, "I don't have it."

The fingers dug deeper and Sam's vision shorted

out as her mind sought the reprieve offered by passing out. Sam saw a flash of movement behind the blonde and heard a crack as the smaller drunk brought his gun down, hard, against the side of her attacker's head. His eyes rolled back as he collapsed next to her. His fingers went away but the pain remained.

Panting, Sam rolled onto her side and curled around her stomach. Her hands clutched at her middle attempting to bring comfort. She barely noticed when the lot grew silent and the sounds of fighting disappeared. Someone's hand touched her arm. Instinctively she launched a fist that got no farther than her shoulder when his hand caught it. Moving sent her inside into spasm and her shoulders announced they weren't happy either.

"Hey *chica*, we're not here to hurt you. We're the cavalry." The soft Spanish accent gave away his identity. He wasn't slurring, he sounded perfectly alert.

She took a halting breath and rolled her eyes toward his voice. He was a good-looking guy, *hot* actually, if she was totally honest. Passing him on the street on a normal day she'd give him a second look, and a third. His toothy white smile was gentle, meant to put her at ease. Again, maybe on a normal day, which this wasn't. Her defenses relaxed only minutely.

Rocking back, Dark and Handsome stood and offered her a hand. "Can you stand?"

Her side was less painful but Sam was scared to move too much, worried she'd cracked something in her back when she fell. "I think so." Refusing the hand, she rolled onto her knees and brought first one leg then the other underneath her to stand. She took a few unsteady steps and was able to lean against the side of her car while she waited for the stars to clear. Fainting wasn't a good idea at the moment.

These guys had saved her from killers although that didn't necessarily mean they were good guys. From the way they fought and the odd timing of their arrival she could guess their appearance on the scene wasn't random. With any luck they wouldn't try to hurt her just yet. Sam was spent and couldn't put up a decent fight if it came to that.

The taller one walked over, also *hot*. Long and lean, his narrow hips drew her eyes down to take in strong legs that looked awesome in jeans and would probably be even better out. *What the hell?* Disgust with herself brought her eyes rocketing back up to his face. That was no better. Well, actually, it was pretty great too. Shaggy brown hair sun-streaked with caramel and maybe a hint of auburn curled around his collar and ears. He was about two weeks past needing a haircut but it worked for him. A superficial cut over one eye and some blood at the corner of his mouth drew her attention back to the fact that she was standing, or leaning, on her car in the parking lot of her gym with two bodies at her feet. Tall Sexy guy's injuries were indicators that the older killer hadn't gone down easily. She looked down at the loser of that face off. She stared at his prone body watching for signs of life and gulped. His chest wasn't moving. That was two dead bodies in as many days. She worked in insurance. Dead cars were her specialty, not people. Sam took another gulp of air struggling to keep control of her dinner.

"Hey you don't look so good. Are you okay?" Dark and Handsome asked her.

Unable to control her sarcasm, always amplified by nerves, she snapped at him. "Sure, I always wanted to join a fight club."

Bursting into laughter, he turned to his quiet companion. "Yeah, she's gonna be okay." Seeing the blood and rapidly darkening around one eye he frowned. "You okay Sarge?" Tall Sexy Scary didn't break eye contact with Sam. He stared evenly at her, intense green eyes boring into hers, his rough angular jaw tight. He scared the shit out of her.

Dropping her eyes for a beat before she forced them back up and her shoulders straight, Sam winced. Trying to hide it, she moved her hand to tuck a chunk of hair behind her ear. "Who are you guys?"

Blinking, Tall Sexy Scary didn't answer her. Instead, speaking without looking at Dark and Handsome. "Jimmy, bring her to the van. We need to get her out of here. There might be more coming."

"But Sarge, you said not to..."

A cold look silenced Dark and Handsome. *Yep, scary.*

Shrugging, Dark and Handsome aka Jimmy gave a brief nod and reached out to take hold of her upper arm.

Sam jerked away ignoring the pain that sent racing through her back and guts. Living past the next 24 hours was more important than discomfort. "I'm not going *anywhere* with *anyone*. Who the hell *are* you guys and who the hell are *they*?" Pointing at the corpse at his feet, she glared at Tall Sexy Scary aka Sarge. His order to have her dragged along with them only served to prove these weren't good guys either. Mentally she cursed her father calling him names that would have gotten her a mouthful of soap if her mother heard. *Well, maybe after today she'd curse him with me.* The image of her mother in the hospital brought on a fresh wave of fury and she clenched her fists at her sides. "As far as I can see you're killers just like *they* are." She pointed a shaking finger at the blonde first, swinging it over to include the now dead bald attacker.

"We don't have time for this." Shaw growled and turned to his friend. "Jimmy, bring her." He spun on his heel and strode off to the edge of the lot where the white work van she'd seen earlier waited, its engine running. She'd been too busy fighting for her life and checking out her rescuers turned captors to hear it pull up. *Way to be watchful.* She chastised herself for being preoccupied with ogling the hotties.

Jimmy shifted beside her and Sam felt his hand tighten around her arm. Jerking it instinctively she found herself unable to escape and, for the second time in ten minutes, being held against her will. Just as she was about to yell, Jimmy's other hand clamped down over her mouth.

"Sorry *chica*." He sounded genuinely apologetic as he moved her along, forcing her to walk or be dragged. "When the sarge says move, we move."

The side door of the van was open and Sam stared at a bank of equipment that had nothing to do with the water solutions the van professed to handle. Fortunately no hacksaws or nooses or other obvious devices of torture. *Who are these guys?*

Jimmy pushed her not unkindly into the van and hopped in, sliding the door shut behind them. Sam examined her situation pragmatically, forcing down the panic bubbling in her chest and body aches, which now included abraded skin on her cheek, upper arm, and leg. She'd been too busy to notice before but now that her adrenaline was draining away she was feeling every scrape and bruise. Sarge and Jimmy had blocked her in by sitting on either side and the driver in the front prevented her from going over the seats for a front door if she were so inclined.

Jimmy, apparently the social one, offered introductions. "I'm Jimmy, this is Sergeant First Class Shaw, and," he pointed to the tall black man driving, "that's Marcus." He smiled, flashing another toothy smile that could have landed him on a magazine. *Maybe he models when he's not abducting and killing people.* "And you're Samantha James. We know your dad."

Ch. 12

Sam felt dizzy. She must have hit her head harder than she thought. "You know Steven? I don't understand any of this." Making a cradle with her hands, elbows on knees, she rested her face against her palms, flinching when she touched the side of her face that had been ground across the gravel. Her back was tightening up fast, the beginnings of a headache bothered at the back of her eyes. It was getting harder to act strong in front of these guys but showing weakness could get her killed. *There are three of them and just one of them could kick your ass.*

Jimmy was still going for kindness. "We'll explain later. Right now we have to get you outta here." He eyed her face, squinting then let his eyes slowly sweep down her body. His assessment stalled at her chest on the way down and back up. "Yep, you got some nice road rash there." He rustled under the table holding the bank of electronics lining the side of the van opposite their two seats, his knee pressing against hers when he moved. Sarge, Shaw, Tall Scary Sexy, whatever his name was, rested on a toolbox pulled up on her other side. Not meant for three bodies, it was tight quarters.

Sam pulled away while Jimmy wrestled with a big black mass hard to see in the dim light. Spinning her chair she unintentionally banged her other knee against Shaw's. She decided since she wasn't in the Army and she didn't want to think of him being hot, Shaw was safest. Shaw stared at her, no sign he'd felt her touch him. She carefully brought her chair back to center seeking some distance from her abductors. All this moving around was killing her battered body. Staying centered and still was about her only option unless she wanted to be in traction. *If I live that long.*

"Here we go." Jimmy sat up, big black box in hand. Flipping open the lid he produced a packaged antibacterial wipe and waved it in the air.

Her hand flashed out to take the packet but Jimmy was faster, grabbing her hand before she saw him move. He had her hand pinned to her side, his chocolate eyes darkened for only a second before he loosened his grip and laughed, showing her his teeth again. He pointed to her cheek. "Here *chica,* let me see that." He shook the packet making it crackle.

"Quit messing around, Jimmy." Shaw's authoritative voice cut through the tiny space. "Marcus, let's go."

"Where to?" Marcus glanced up in the rearview mirror to watch the goings on. Sam caught a glimpse of blue eyes, tight curly black hair, and caramel skin in the glow of the streetlights. Mixed race, he'd gotten the best of both. Like his partners in crime Marcus was a pleasure to look at. They were like the male version of Charlie's Angels, multicultural edition. She turned back to Shaw, waiting for his answer too since it had a direct bearing on her future, however short that might be.

"The farm." He stared at Sam, blank expression unreadable, adding, "Stop at her place first so she can pack."

Jimmy's eyes got wide. Shaw's decision was clearly unexpected by his crew as well as his captive. Sam wasn't sure if that was good or bad. Either way, she knew she didn't want to be taken to a farm. *Don't they feed bodies to pigs to dispose of them?*

Sam bristled, fear coiling in the pit of her stomach. "You're kidnapping me?" She finally gave voice to her fear, frustrated at the nervous quake in her voice.

Jimmy inhaled to speak except Shaw beat him to it. His voice was even and controlled, Sam heard the hint of a soft southern drawl.

Tall Sexy Scary and *Southern, he has the quadruple hot factor.* One word worked to bring her wildly zinging thoughts and fear induced, she hoped that was all it was, hormones back under control. *Paul.* What if these guys were Paul's killers, not the other two? What if Shaw was the one who'd slipped the noose around his neck? Had Marcus or Jimmy wrestled him into the shower? Which one kept him from crying out and alerting the neighbors? Who ran her mother down in the street and left her unconscious and bleeding? She felt sick.

Shaw was watching her carefully. For a moment she thought she saw something strange happening behind his eyes before he walled himself off again. "We're here to help you. I would recommend you come along with us."

"Or what?" She couldn't help but push back.

His eyes hardened. "Or you'll die."

Sam sank back into her chair, staring at the blinking lights on the console in front of her, raw cheek forgotten as Marcus put the vehicle in drive. She didn't stir until she felt Jimmy move away and the door behind her slid open.

"I'll go with her, Sarge." Jimmy hopped out to make room for her to exit.

Shaw was already out, landing lightly on the balls of his feet on the opposite side of the door. He moved like a fighter. Sam had seen a few truly good ones at the gym and at least Shaw was better than any she'd seen before. She would be willing to bet the other two weren't slouches either. "No, I will." He waited for Sam to take the lead, surveying the streets for threats. "Hear anything, Jimmy?"

Sam watched Jimmy grab headphones off a hook below the narrow table serving as a desk in the cramped van. He listened for a minute and shook his head. "Nope. Can't hear anything but that don't mean it's clear."

They exchanged a look Sam didn't understand. She considered making a break for it and Shaw closed the distance between them, not touching but his message clear.

Shaw let her open the outer security door leading into the complex then followed her into the building, but put his hand over hers when she slid the key into her lock. She jumped at his warm touch, noting in passing his hands felt calloused but not overly rough. Her eyes went to where their hands were stacked on her door and wondered how many people his hands had broken. *How many women has he touched?* Mortified at herself, she dropped her hand and stepped aside to let him open the door. He eased past and held a hand out indicating she should stay behind him. Seeing the way the men worked together and had her covered, Sam pretty much figured it was pointless to stage an escape attempt in her building or try to cry out and involve someone else. She couldn't handle any more guilt, and apparently she was having some sort of breakdown brought on by stress. Thus, she was relatively subdued as she followed his silent command though she glared daggers at his well-developed back as he crept into her apartment.

They were a few feet down the hall when Sam heard something tap the bathroom door, making her jump. She spun to face it and before she could do anything else, Shaw had his arm wrapped around her waist pulling her tight up against him with one hand, a gun appearing in his other. It was so fast she barely had time to recognize what was happening. Just one minute she was facing the bathroom, the next she was staring at a blue tshirt stretched snug over broad shoulders smelling a combination of fabric softener and hot man. Heart beating wildly, Sam put her hands out to push against his back and peer around him. His muscles were hard under her hands as he turned his head, placing his profile a hand's breadth from hers. She could see the glints of gold and definitely auburn in the stubble on his jaw. He hadn't shaved in at least a day.

"Stay close." He commanded in a whisper, taking his hand from her waist and pushing her back with his body, giving him room to open the door while hugging the wall as tightly as possible. Frightened enough to listen Sam stayed close, feeling the cool wall behind her. The result was a Sam sandwich. She breathed short, shallow breaths and moved with him.

One hand reached out and twisted the knob, shoving it open in one fluid motion. Into the hall flashed a gray streak, low to the ground and yowling the whole time. Sam saw the gun tracking it and brought her hand down on his forearm, instantly re-aiming the gun's muzzle at the floor away from its target.

"Wait. It's Bill," she cried in a panic. The tension in his arm eased and she wriggled herself out from behind him to dash after her terrified cat.

"Easy baby. Settle down big man," she cooed, forcing herself to be calm and not clutch him against her body for her own comfort.

Bill yowled in reply, dancing circles around his food dish.

"Haven't you learned not to play with your toys behind a door?" She produced a heaping scoop of food for the hungry tom, sitting on the floor to stroke him while he crunched and purred loudly. Bill locked himself in a room about twice a month playing with his crinkle toys. Normally it was no big deal, then again, normally there wasn't a man with a gun on the other side of the door.

Feeling eyes burning into her Sam looked up to see Shaw staring, again that something strange in his face. The gun had disappeared. Color crept up her neck. She snuck fleeting glimpses at him while she petted her cat, reassessing the man after seeing him in action.

His selfless response to a perceived threat had been automatic. When he could have just as easily reversed them and used her as a shield he'd used himself to shield her. There was no doubt Sergeant Shaw's first instinct was to protect her. And if she was any judge of ability, he certainly could.

Tall and lean sure but as she'd felt while pressed up against him from tits to toes, every inch of him was hardened. And as she'd seen when he fought, that was through training not just a gym membership. Even without the title she could tell he was military, maybe Special Forces considering how effectively he used his body. Also, he wore his wavy mess of light brown hair like a bum. Special Forces did that to fit in, or maybe he was out and hiding. *From whom?* But there was no hiding what she saw in his eyes. Soft green when he wasn't glaring at her, they hinted at who he was when he wasn't busy being "Sarge". The tightness in his features as well as the way he held himself spoke of battles he'd been fighting for a long time. Sergeant Shaw and his men had been soldiers. Maybe still were. *What does Steven have to do with soldiers?* He might still be planning on killing her but he wasn't going to let anyone else. Exhausted both mentally and physically, Sam blinked up at him.

"What's going on Shaw? Why is all of this happening?" Her hands fell to her sides, palms down on the cool linoleum helping to ground her to reality. She felt her life whirling out of her control. Sam hated the insecurity she heard in her own voice while she pleaded for answers.

***

Shaw stared down at Samantha James. An only child, she and her mother left Maryland nineteen years ago and came to Minnesota to live. No sign of Doc after they left Maryland. Here Samantha had done well in school, completed a year of her college credits while still in high school and graduated at the top of her class from the University of Minnesota on an academic scholarship. She'd worked as an insurance adjuster since. Paid her bills on time, respectable retirement and savings accounts, good credit. Just turned twenty-eight years old. A hell of a thing for her father to do, drawing her into his fucked up shit on her birthday. A sliver of sympathy for her drove itself into his battle hardened psyche.

The girl was impressive he'd give her that. He'd seen with his own eyes she was an adept fighter. She could probably hold her own against a normal opponent despite being such a little thing. When he had her body pressed against him he'd felt hard muscle under that woman softness. The girl was no waif nor was she a coward. It took a lot of nerve to go up against those two the way she had especially since he was pretty sure she was close to her limit. He'd seen that same expression on the faces of men in war when they were done in, when they'd taken all that they could.

Her pleas and battle fatigue tugged at a place he'd tucked away a long time ago when his life had changed forever, forcing him to leave everything he fought for behind. All of them did. What Doc and his team did to them, took from them, it was unforgiveable. Shaw inhaled through his nose, not allowing his anger to surface. Not now, not on a mission. That was how men died and he wasn't losing any more men. Roughly he reminded himself of what the girl represented. That she was the one who would lead them to Doc and the lab they sought to destroy, the deaths *they* had to stop. Any warmth he showed her was to be feigned to ingratiate her to him. Nothing more. Turning his back to the wall Shaw slid down to sit next to her. When his shoulder touched hers she didn't pull away this time. He was right, she was fried.

"I don't know much about your dad just that he's a scientist who works for some very bad men specializing in chemical weapons." He gave her enough to hopefully shock her into questioning her father's culpability. If she doubted him enough she might willingly give them the package before her father came for it. Then no one had to get hurt. He ignored the relief that offered him.

Other than an elevated pulse he could see thumping in her throat and accelerated breathing, the girl maintained her composure. "He sent you something, a weapon they've been developing." Shaw watched her closely.

Samantha's forehead wrinkled and she sat up giving him a more dead on view of her features. Her eyes filled and Shaw felt that tug again as he waited for the tears sure to come. Her jaw stiffened and he watched her withdraw to lock herself safely away from her emotions. And him.

"Ms. James, what do you know about your

91

father?" He tried to draw her out, knowing Jimmy and Marcus were listening. No need to catch them up later.

"Steven's a geneticist. At least he was last time I saw him, before he walked out on us when I was nine." Her thin shoulders rose and fell, defeated. "He worked with gene splicing at Johns Hopkins until one day he just," her eyes flicked up not quite reaching his before going back down, "he just left." Her voice wavered and she ducked her head, running her hand down her cat's back, sliding it up his tail. He rammed his big gray head into her other hand and the side of her mouth lifted in a small smile. "Sam," she added belatedly.

"Hmm?" He'd been trying to read her body language to determine whether she sincerely disliked her father or was just hurt by his leaving. He'd noticed she intentionally used his name and hadn't referred to him in familiar terms but that didn't mean anything. Could be she was desperate enough for old daddy's affections she'd do anything to please him. Like hide something for him and lie about it.

"Call me Sam. He's the only one who's called me Samantha since I was a kid." Her flat tone was unreadable.

"Okay, Sam." A quick glance at his watch and Shaw cursed under his breath. Standing, he fought the ingrained compulsion to help her to her feet. She hadn't wanted Jimmy's help nor would she want his. Polite upbringing took a backseat. "You have to pack. We're borrowing trouble if we stay here much longer."

Pushing her back against the wall to get her feet under her, Sam stumbled then caught herself and a low groan escaped her lips. She saw him hold an arm out to catch her and she shot him a warning look. Sam Young wasn't weak and he would do well to remember that.

Hands going back to his sides, Shaw hid his amusement at her threat knowing that tough as she was he could take her down in a heartbeat. The thought of being on top of her, her lean limbs wrapped around him as she moved against him brought back a quick flash of how her body felt against his and he shrugged it off. He couldn't lose sight of their primary objective just because a girl who looked pretty when she tried not to cry came along. That hadn't been a problem before. Not for *him* anyway. It wouldn't be now. *Especially* this girl. Frustrated with himself he ordered her, his tone gruff. "Grab the package. If we have it with us we can keep them from getting their hands on it."

Her eyes met his unflinching. "It's safe. Don't worry about it."

Only due to years of practice was Shaw able to keep the fury from his expression. "Then go get what you need and hurry." He would have to coax it out of her and they didn't have the time now, they'd already been in the apartment too long. Surely there were eyes on it.

Sam moved. Slow and painful, yet under her own prideful power to her room. Shaw waited politely in the hall leaning against the wall with a watchful eye on the door and a clear view out the windows facing the back of the complex where it backed up to some woods. The cover they afforded in the height of summer was enough to make him start seeing guns in every leave flutter. He was antsy; they needed to move.

"How much am I packing?" Sam called from the bedroom. She didn't even try to hide her displeasure. "How long before I can come home?"

"Enough for a few days." Shaw's roving eyes happened to catch sight of a small black square sticking out a fraction of an inch from the tan air vent across the living room from where he stood. He stepped up on the back of the sofa to get a better look. The device was just inside the metal slats. Pulling up the leg of his jeans he withdrew a small Ka-Bar knife from inside his black boot. Using the tip he pried the small listening device from its adhesive grip, examined it, and replaced it. Then he slipped the knife back in its home and resumed his post against the wall. As he suspected *his* team hadn't been the only ears on Doc's daughter. Were they tracking the package unaware of who Sam was or had they known Sam was Doc's daughter? If not, their conversation put her in further danger. That was careless and stupid of him. An ungentlemanly oath slipped out. Probably the only thing keeping them from busting in here right now was Shaw's team and the hurt they'd put on two of their guys. Provided they had more, and he was sure they did, they'd be more careful before they sent them out so they came back in one piece. A cold grin twisted his lips.

"What?" Sam came out of her bedroom, rolling bag in hand. She looked more curious than offended at his use of language.

"Nothing," he lied. There was no point worrying her, soon they would be gone and it wouldn't matter. "Are you ready?"

"Almost." She moved toward the bathroom. Shaw saw her hesitate before entering and guessed at the cause of her reluctance.

"Is that where you found him?" he asked softly from the doorway. He knew it was, he wasn't sure why he asked. Maybe he wanted to see how she reacted. Had she loved him?

Her entire body was tense, her face pale as she

94

grabbed at her toiletries on the shelves. Her hairbrush fell from her arms in her haste to get out of the room. "Uh huh," she muttered quietly without turning her head. He barely heard her.

In a few steps he was behind her and put his hands on her arms to gently move her aside. "Put those in your bag and tell me what else you need."

Sam put up no resistance letting him push her out easily. He knew she was troubled if she was being so pliable. That didn't seem to be her usual MO. She seemed a little better with distance from the room, pointing at a little travel clutch below the sink and asking him to throw the bag to her. When he tossed it he heard pills rattle among other things. Shaw looked back to ask if she wanted anything from her shower and saw the hurt in her rapidly paling face. She was fading. Guilt snuck under his guard and into his conscience. The girl was mourning her dead lover and he was pretending to be her ally to get what he needed, even if that meant physical harm. *If I wasn't already going it's safe to say I'm headed straight to hell.*

A quick scan for anything obvious she might use daily and he started to retract his head from the shower, then stopped. He ran his hand over two cracked tiles where tub met wall. No further questions were necessary. He had enough experience with death and torture to know that this was exactly where the boyfriend died. Paul had been his name. He'd been choked to death, probably more before that though Shaw couldn't be sure without seeing the body. After what he'd seen the blonde do to Sam with his hands tonight, he would imagine Paul's death hadn't been an easy one. He was certain they interrogated the guy looking for the package.

Assuming the package was a sample of the

chemical they sought to destroy, Shaw was equally eager to get his hands on it. He would not lose his resolve to get it by "any means necessary." Even if she was the sweetest thing on the planet, he could save a thousand men from suffering by closing down the Doc's project. With so many lives on the line he refused to entertain any thoughts of leniency toward Doc's daughter. Their hunt for the Doc, the lab, the chemical they were trying to produce; it had gone on too long. He was tired and racked with doubts about whether he could succeed in capturing Doc and the package as well as keeping his remaining men safe now that they were out in the open. This operation had exposed them. When the other side figured out who he and the boys were they would become just as valuable as the chemical inside the package. It was their blood, after all, that led to its creation.

Shaw's watch clicked an alert and he touched the tiny piece in his ear. "Yeah?"

The tiny device chirped back. "Come on Sarge. Enough Oprah time, we gotta go. I got a feeling."

"Yep," he answered sharply. He'd been soft with her, he wasn't going to hear the end of this one any time soon. Shaw lowered his voice so no one other than those on the other end of the speaker would hear. "Heads up for unfriendlies. We've got ears in here. Not ours."

He heard two sets of curses but Jimmy's voice over the comm device. "Got it, Sarge."

"We're out of here Sam," he called into the bedroom, chancing a glimpse inside. She wasn't in there and for the briefest of moments he felt his heart leap. Had he let her sneak past him? No, the bag was sitting inside the room's entrance.

"Okay, we're ready." She came into view.

As she came around the corner to grab her bag, Shaw grimaced. "Are you kidding?" He eyeballed the cat she held in her arms.

Her back stiffened and, in spite of a wince, she held firm. "Bill goes with me."

Not wanting to linger any longer fearing the competition would get antsy and act out of boldness instead of intelligence and storm in here, Shaw threw up a hand. "Fine. Bring the cat. Anything else? Maybe you could call a friend, make it a sleepover." He fumed and, ripping the bag from around the doorway, he banged it on the wood as he slipped the strap over his shoulder. Bowing sarcastically, he opened the door and gestured for her to lead the way. Offended, Sam stormed out ahead of him making for the stairs so he had to carry her luggage farther. Petty yes, and deserved she reassured herself.

Ch. 13

They put her in between Marcus and Shaw in the front. Jimmy stayed in back with his equipment, listening. Sam held Bill on her lap and he settled after only a few minutes of squalling. She petted him absently as she watched the road and mile markers reflecting the glow of their headlights slide by the driver's side window.

"Where are we going?" she asked of no one in particular.

"East," Marcus answered without turning away from the road.

"If I'm not *really* being kidnapped, maybe you could fill me in on where I'm going to be held, I mean *staying*."

None of them answered and Sam scratched Bill's ears aggressively until he objected with a nip to her knuckle. She checked her watch and saw it was almost midnight, stifling a yawn with the back of her fist. Wherever they were taking her she hoped it had a bed. The miles rolled on and her lids got heavy.

Sam must have dozed off because the next thing she knew Jimmy's hand was gently shaking her awake and Bill was gone, leaving her hands clasped emptily in her lap.

"We're here." Jimmy prodded her again.

Sam looked around in alarm. "Where's Bill?"

"He made a new friend." He stuck a thumb at the windshield and Sam followed his finger to see her cat curled up in Marcus's arms while he stood outside, looking idly at the trees. The cat's head was twisted upside down so Marcus could better reach his chin. She was sure she could hear him purring.

"Traitor," she mumbled crossly.

She slid over and swung her legs over the side of the seat. Standing and stepping in one move, Sam's back spasmed again and she cried out involuntarily as she went to a knee on the running board, clutching at the door handle to keep from going all the way down.

Jimmy was at her side at once. "Hey, you okay?" His hands ran over her back and arms searching for injury. When he went over her upper back, he whistled. "Man that's tight. I can feel it twitching. You must a hit it in the parking lot, huh?"

He rubbed gently between her shoulder blades and Sam hissed through clenched teeth. "It's fine, my legs just got stiff. It was a long drive."

He pulled his hand off and held up both palms in surrender. "I didn't mean anything by it. But the best thing for a back spasm is to rub it out, trust me," he winked, "I know my way around a body."

Gaining her feet painfully, Sam glared at him. He was a flirt as she had surmised at the start and she didn't want him thinking this was going to be anything. A hot date was the last thing she needed. That familiar guilty pang knifed her ribs; sightless eyes stared at her from her memory. The weight of his death grew heavier with the addition of the guilt that she'd failed him even in mourning. When it came to love Sam was broken. *I should have let you go and I didn't because I didn't want to hurt you and now you're dead. I'm so sorry, Paul.* Stinging, she lashed out. "I'll handle it."

"Jimmy," Shaw called sharply. "Grab her bag and put her in the spare room."

Snapping his hand to his brow, Jimmy saluted smartly. "Yes Sir." He kept most of the sarcasm out of it but not entirely.

Shaw shot him a glare. "Now!" he snapped, his face dark.

Shooting him a curious look, Jimmy grabbed the bag and strutted off unhindered by its minimal weight.

Marcus went on ahead carrying the cat right past Sam and into the house. She cast them both an evil glance Marcus failed to acknowledge. Sam was left alone, holding herself up against the van's side, staring at Shaw's shadowy features in the glow from the house's front light.

His posture was tight, his tone hard. "Can you make it? There are some stairs. Your room's on the second story, end of the hall."

She heard his irritation loud and clear and refused to prove herself a burden. Sam forced her feet forward. "I'm fine," she repeated through gritted teeth.

Shaw nodded once and led the way, not looking back once.

It was nearly full dark outside. Inside was plagued by more shadows working to keep the interior a secret from her curious eyes. This was where she would be kept for the foreseeable future and now that she was here she still had no idea where "here" was. Shaw turned on the lights behind her as she ascended the stairs bathing the pale walls in light, revealing nothing. No decorations were hung, no hint at the personality of the house or its

100

occupants marred its surfaces.

"Yours is this one up here on the left after the bathroom."

The upstairs hall was long, spanning the entire length of the house and Sam had to walk past a closed door on her left side, the sounds of someone shuffling around and soft music playing marked it as occupied. By some miracle Sam made it to her room.

They came to her open door. The light had been turned on and her bag was already lying on the bed. Sam wanted to cry, she so badly wanted to be in that bed. Sliding a hand under her elbow Shaw shifted her over to get past her and heft the bag to the ground. Before he backed away, in a kind gesture, he pulled back the light blue blanket motioning that it was all hers.

Sam shuffled past him and eased herself onto the bed, drawing her knees up to get her feet in without much luck. Tightening her muscles sent her back into full-fledged revolt. She couldn't help feeling like an old woman, complaining about her pains yet here she was, a virtual invalid because of it and she wasn't even thirty. There was no way Shaw and his men weren't getting a chuckle out of this. Giving up with *most* of her body on the bed, her feet and bent knees hanging over, Sam threw her arm over her face to hide the tears she felt coming. Tired, in pain, and frustrated she was teetering on the edge of losing it and had no desire to have a witness to her meltdown.

"Can I be alone? Please?" Her voice cracked and she sniffled.

Without a word Shaw lifted her feet up and slid her shoes off. He raised the blanket to her waist and she saw the edges of the light disappear from around her arm as he flicked off the switch. The last thing she heard was the latch catch as he softly closed her door. Scared and alone, Sam cried herself quietly to sleep.

Ch. 14

It was before sunrise, the sky was jut beginning to glow with predawn light when something woke her and before she remembered what happened Sam sat up, screeching as her shoulders tied themselves together in a knot and her body convulsed in protest. She was only vaguely aware of the top layer of scabbing on her thigh deciding to remain on the sheets when the rest of her was not. Thinking about not wanting to bleed on the sheets gave her something to think about while she waited for the ability to breathe to return to her.

Loud footsteps sounded in the hall and someone knocked at the door. "Everything's okay." She managed to whimper through locked jaws.

The door opened anyway and Sam would have sighed sarcastically if drawing breath didn't hurt so badly. She screwed her eyes shut and tried to pretend she didn't exist. "Do I have *any* say around here?"

"Not when you're up here making enough noise to wake the dead. Thought we were under fire."

Sam's eyes snapped open to reveal Marcus standing beside her bed. Wearing only blue flannel pants with his arms crossed and a stern expression darkening his wrinkled brow he was plenty intimidating. And, yep, hot. She tried not to stare but he was ripped. The tattoo of a girl's name marred his left bicep, Marianna. There were also countless scars darkening his light brown flesh in deeper shades, bordering on purple. Yep again, he was as hard as the other two.

"Like what you see?" He raised an eyebrow mildly.

Heat rushed up Sam's neck and she felt her face go red.

Marcus rolled his eyes and grunted. "I'm kidding." He pointed and rolled his finger looking none too happy. "Come on, roll over. We're getting rid of this thing now. You're no good like this. We got to move and you're a problem unless we get you functional again."

Past arguing or being offended, Sam did as she was told. He sat down next to her and put one big fist between her shoulder blades and pressed down. When he pushed, Sam screamed into her pillow feeling tears burn her eyes.

"Don't be such a baby." He reprimanded, his other fist joining the first on her shoulders and rolling the opposite way. "It has to be worked out or it'll never get better."

Sam clenched her teeth and shoved her face deeper into the pillow, muffling her whimpers. When the door opened she didn't look up, already humiliated enough to know who else was audience to her pain and manhandling. Her face remained jammed hard into the pillows as she tried to pretend she wasn't there. Then his knuckles stopped pressing on her and she panted gratefully into the down, making an unintentional little whimper of relief. Sam hardly noticed when the mattress shifted and depressed on either side of her.

When his hands touched her again they were flat and rubbed instead of pushing on her poor, tortured muscles. This time, they started their path at the outside, wrapping around her sides, making their way to the center of the large knots in long, sweeping strokes. One hand ran down the neck opening in her shirt to reach her skin. Warmth began spreading at once through her skin everywhere his hands touched, easing the tension in her muscles and starting to untangle the knots holding her shoulder blades tied invisibly to the back of her head. A deep exhale was tainted with a low moan. After a few minutes Sam was able to turn her head and caught the scent of cinnamon. "Marcus what is that? Why is it so warm?"

It was Shaw's southern drawl that answered, not Marcus's impatient clip. "Tiger Balm. Best thing for muscle pain. Marcus was right, it has to be worked out but there *are* more humane ways than what he was doing to you. You'll have to excuse him, it's been a long time since he's done anything but soldiering."

Back stiffening again, Sam processed her change in masseuses on the fly.

Sam strove to match Shaw's cool demeanor despite her *very* compromising position. Her muscles demanded it, they begged for it. They were slowly letting go and the release was absolute heaven. She would have put up with anything to keep him right where he was. "Thank you, I can't tell you how good that feels." With her face sideways on the pillow she could watch what he was doing out of the corner of her eye as well as see what he was using on her when he reached past her face to dip his fingers in the small container on her nightstand.

"I'm going to pull up your shirt in back so I can reach better, is that okay?" he asked her, pausing in his ministrations.

Completely lost in focusing on the movements of his hands easing her pain, Sam readily accepted his offer. "Sure." She shifted her lower body to get her shirt out from under her hips, a simple task with him keeping all of his weight on his knees, and waited for the wonderful balm to continue it's magic on the rest of her aching back.

Shaw caught the edge of the shirt under his fingertips and raised it to expose Sam's long, shapely back, tucking the edge up over her shoulders to keep it out of the way. He tried to be a gentleman and ignore the curve of her breasts peeking out as they pressed against the mattress. She'd removed her bra in the night. Out of courtesy he stared at the side window trying to interest himself in the gently shifting trees or the rising sun or anything other than the warm body of a far too intriguing woman beneath him. It had been a while since he'd been this close to a woman and the experience was proving a bit heady. He continued rubbing. Another groan escaped Sam's lips. Shaw's hands immediately came off of her skin.

"Did I hurt you?"

"No," she giggled, uncharacteristically giddy with relief. "It just feels so good."

Gingerly he went back to untying her muscles, working quietly and giving his mind nothing to do but speculate. And because she was underneath him, his thoughts turned again to her. Out of nowhere he blurted, "I'm sorry about Paul." He felt the muscles go rigid almost at once and the resulting wince at her tender muscles' movement. Mentally he kicked himself for his blunder. *Fucking smooth asshole.* "Uh, did you want to talk about it?" He hadn't spoken to a woman, really spoken to one, for so long he was painfully awkward. Maybe that was good considering she was exactly the wrong woman he should be thinking *anything* about. She was their ticket to Doc. That was it. *Get that shit out of your head.* He blamed his sexual interest in her on the fact that he hadn't visited a woman in over a year. It was purely physical need getting in his way. Maybe he should get that taken care of before he fucked things up because he couldn't stop thinking with his dick.

***

Beyond the initial conversation with her mother, Sam hadn't talked about Paul's death. Quite honestly there hadn't been time and who did she really have to talk to anyway? She couldn't call Maria and burden her with this. Not one normally to bare her soul, Sam was shocked to hear the words come tumbling out. "I was going to break it off that night, I was going to like five times before that too but I didn't. I wasn't as into it as him and I knew it was wrong to keep leading him on but I couldn't admit it." She waited for him to pass some sort of judgment, shame her for speaking so frankly of the dead.

He said nothing. Shaw's smooth pressing and easing of her knots worked to loosen her tongue as well and she went on. "He was a really nice guy. Everybody loved Paul." Her voice quavered when she said his name. "I tried to feel more, I just couldn't." Sam waited for some sort of reaction, wanting him to say something, needing him to pass judgment. The hands never broke their rhythm. "You know what the worst part is? The part I wish I could take back?" She didn't wait, no need for a response. She was talking to herself now. "He died for me. Not like he did it on purpose, but I sent him there to wait for me and they got him." She felt a few tears leaking out across her nose sideways wetting the pillow beneath her face. "What if he thought he was protecting me? His worthless girlfriend who didn't even have the decency to love him. That was all he wanted from me and I couldn't give him that one thing." Sam brought her hand up to cover her face, ashamed to admit how cold she really was. *"A cold bitch"* to quote a past boyfriend who hadn't been so happy with her breakup speech outlining their insurmountable differences. Read, "Sam couldn't make herself love him either though he professed his love for her." She couldn't hide her tears nor her body's quaking when the real crying hit.

One long leg swung off and Sam was sure he was going to leave at last. Curiously, her relief at having him bail on her disgrace was tempered by disappointment at being left alone. She was surprised she would even consider wanting someone there to watch her fall apart. That wasn't her. But he didn't leave. He sat down on the bed beside her, his back curved against the hard wooden slats of the headboard. Curious, she turned her head enough to sneak a peek at him and was shocked at what she saw. He was observing her, not even a hint of disgust in his face.

"It wasn't your fault," he said, not commenting when her jaw dropped. "Your father didn't give you fair warning they were onto you." His gentle smile was encouraging. "I'm not sure I would have done anything differently." *But who's to say he would feel bad to have someone die for him.* She immediately chastised herself for that unfair assessment. Other than "kidnapping" her, Shaw and his men hadn't been unkind to her. Sure, they were probably using her to get to her father, but that didn't make them killers. When she'd decided these three weren't Paul's killers or her mother's attackers wasn't clear but there it was.

He lifted an arm from his side making a space for her, a wordless invitation for the human reassurance she needed so badly at the moment. Too mentally spent to pretend she was harder than she really was, Sam eased her upper body over to lay her head on his chest. Closing her eyes against the appalling lack of dignity she was showing, Sam waited for the usual uneasiness at the intimate gesture to drive her away from him. Yet even when his arm wrapped around her, his hand moving to stroke her shoulder, she felt only peace. "Thank you, Sergeant Shaw." Soon she began to drift.

"Justin." His hushed voice was loud in the morning stillness of the room.

"Hmm?" She was too near sleep to raise her head or open her eyes.

"Call me Justin."

"Okay Justin." She sighed as she drifted off.

She didn't see the smile curl his lips.

Ch. 15

Soft rapping at the door stayed Justin's hand against her head. After she'd fallen asleep he went to stroking her dark silky hair, toying with it and letting the longer strands cascade through his fingers. A tactile person, he'd forgotten the sensations that accompanied laying with a woman not purely for sexual gratification.

"Come in," he called softly, suddenly conscious of their intimate positioning. As she'd slept Sam had pulled herself up to lie snugly against his side.

Marcus stepped into the room, crossing his arms and frowning down at his Sergeant. "Think that's a good idea?" He nodded at the prone woman's form taking too long to assess, starting at her bare legs. Justin caught the flare as he hit her ass and went up. Reflexively he tugged at her shirt to work it down as far as it would go, not coming past her hip.

"Eyes front," Justin cautioned, a hint of warning in his tone.

Making no response beyond following the order, Marcus kept his voice low. "You two're getting cozy awful fast. That part of your plan in bringing her here?"

"She's been through a lot," he said quietly. "I'm getting her through it. She's no use to us if she's a mess." He turned a blind eye to what he felt awakening inside him. It would only confuse matters if they saw him distracted right now when the team was so close. He was already worried enough for all of them. "I've always said I'd do whatever it takes Marcus." Justin felt her shift and cut their session short. "I would assume you have a reason for coming in here?"

Back to business, Marcus jabbed a thumb over his shoulder toward the hall. "Somebody tripped an alarm on the northern edge of the perimeter. Jimmy thinks we might have been followed. He wants to go check it out. I'm going with him."

Shaking his head, Justin eased himself out from under Sam's sleeping form taking great care not to wake her. When he looked up again he saw Marcus' frown deepening. "There's no rule that says I have to be an asshole just because I need something from her. You know it might help move things along faster if she trusts us." His was mildly unsettled at the prospect of betraying the woman, she'd been betrayed enough. *She's one person. There are a lot more lives at stake than just hers.*

Shrugging, Marcus spun on his heel and exited the room. "We're heading out in ten. Jimmy's gearing up as we speak."

Justin glanced back one more time, pausing to throw the blanket up over her nearly naked form and closed the door.

Upon entering the kitchen Justin saw the small arsenal lying out on the table. Jimmy's strength as a sniper and preference for long range tracking aside, he also carried a bigger version of Justin's Ka-Bar knife at his hip. Not standard issue, it dated back to his days growing up in East LA when he carried a smaller version and it wasn't just for show. If his stories were to be believed, he'd been quite adept with it. Having seen him in action, Justin didn't doubt the tales.

Marcus, on the other hand, liked his guns. He carried his HK45 holstered under his arm with two smaller 9mm Glocks mounted on his thighs. A hunting rifle was slung across his back.

No one carried fully automatic weapons for secrecy sake. Here on the border where Minnesota met Wisconsin hunting and shooting were acceptable, the sound of sporadic gunfire easily explained. However a fully automatic, military grade weapon would call immediate attention to them. Because they didn't want to lose this base of operations, they kept those locked away and only took them out to clean and take on assignments when they were contracted for mercenary work. The men were taking this threat seriously if they'd brought them out.

Jimmy was sullen, his enormous ego bruised no doubt by Sam's rejection last night in the van and no doubt it hadn't escaped his notice Justin had been found in her room this morning. Jimmy fancied himself quite a ladies' man and, although Sam herself meant nothing of significance, the denial of a conquest would bother the proud man. At least for a little while.

"Hey Jimmy," Justin leaned against the doorway. "Be careful out there, huh?"

He stared at his commanding officer for a second before cracking a smile. "Sure thing, Sarge."

Turning to Marcus, he added. "Take them alive if you can." *We're gonna get them this time.* There was no feeling of satisfaction at the thought of impending vengeance, that passed a long time ago. It was the right thing to do but it would never give them back what they'd lost. *Who* they'd lost.

Marcus nodded his understanding. If these were the type of men the team suspected they were, they might have information. If they knew the location of the lab, Marcus could get it out of them. He was one of the few who had a gift for extracting information. Having seen it on more than a few occasions, Justin swallowed the acidic taste of bile and reminded himself the people these men worked for. If they got their hands on any one of his men, or Sam, they wouldn't hesitate to do the same things to them. He saw a Sam in his mind's eye, crying and vulnerable, and felt an overwhelming urge to scoop her up and run away from there. His chivalrous upbringing hadn't been completely eradicated by over a decade of soldiering.

After the two evaporated like smoke into the woods either one on a side to come in and flank the intruders, Justin took what remained on the table and armed himself should anyone reach the house. The alarm wires were run around the outer edges of the property, sixty-seven acres of farmland and woods. They had heavy forests in this part of the country and, while it provided convenient cover for them to keep their bodies and minds sharp through drills and military exercises, it also provided sufficient cover for an intruder to get within twenty yards of the house. Too close for his tastes.

Justin tucked his Glock into his waistband behind his back and slid a hunting rifle off the table, checking the scope before going upstairs to the attic. With windows at both ends and its height it was the closest thing to a watchtower they could get. He laid the rifle muzzle on the window ledge and settled in at the western facing window with the sun at his back to wait.

Ch. 16

Back up a few days

Dr. Steven James knew sending the last remaining sample of the chemical to his daughter was dangerous yet he had done it, confident in her level head and quick wit. She'd been that way even as a child, sitting back and studying something instead of reacting emotionally. "She gets that from me," he used to boast with pride. He was betting his career and both their lives on her still having it. However, he hadn't considered Management would move so quickly at the lab, scrambling two of their top thugs to track him as soon as his duplicity was discovered. They'd even untangled his false trail faster than anticipated. He'd seen the blip in the newspaper about a clerk at the courier's office being accosted and knew the men would be onto Samantha. Given their shared last name it would be easy for them to deduce she was his daughter thereby making her even more valuable. They wouldn't let her go once they got a hold of her; she was leverage to bring their top scientist to heel. *Shit.*

He wanted to warn her but by the time he arrived at her apartment there were police everywhere. Fearing the worst, he played the part of a curious onlooker. "What happened? Did somebody get robbed or something?" He approached an officer standing outside his squad car.

The blue clad paunchy gentleman hitched up his belt and rested a hand lazily on the gun. He failed to hide his pride when the spectator widened his eyes at the weapon, feigning admiration for the man.

"No, sir." He tipped his head toward the ambulance turning into the lot. "Suicide."

The doctor's stomach clenched and he ducked his head to hide his visceral reaction. He hoped he hadn't gotten her killed. Could they have found the sample?

"Poor guy. Hung himself in his girlfriend's shower." The officer was eager to appear important, sharing more than he should.

"Oh." He had to keep his face down to hide his relief. "That's a shame."

More people were approaching to hear the officer's words and Dr. James was able to melt back into the growing crowd with ease. From his rental car parked across the street he watched the police leave and Brenda arrive shortly afterward.

Seeing his ex-wife did nothing for the doctor. She'd been easier to leave than his child. Their problems were well established when he'd been forced to make his decision to go. Brenda didn't understand the importance of what he did, she never did. She might have *said* she supported him but when the hours got long she often complained, talking about family and commitments. To avoid the fights he worked longer hours.

Brenda left Sam's apartment not long after she arrived, clutching her purse tightly to her plump body. By the way she swiveled her head left to right, jumping at a distant car horn, James could assume his daughter told her mother about the package. He felt a twinge of disappointment in the girl. He'd told her not to speak a word. Perhaps Brenda's weakness bled over to his child supplanting his teachings of being strong and logical.

He remained on the street the rest of the day not leaving until he followed Samantha's easily tracked bright green Ford when she left that evening. Starving, he decided to grab a bite when she walked into the gym.

She would be there for a while judging from the shape she kept herself in.

He thought about approaching her there until he saw the same silver Chrysler do a pass twice in five minutes shortly after he parked. Dr. James couldn't contact her and recover his sample yet, not with her being watched so closely. It wouldn't do for both of them to be lost and he had to survive if he was to protect his legacy.

When the two sent by Management accosted her in the parking lot he'd been petrified, frozen with fear and unable to move from his vehicle. He had never been more of a failure as a father than at that moment as he watched his daughter fight for her life. Fear for his daughter and for himself had shocked him into a state of paralysis. Thankfully those men had come along and interrupted the attack. His gratitude was fleeting.

When the newcomers disarmed the two men leaving one dead, the other unconscious he realized too late that their intervention was not coincidence. Their maneuvers were too smooth, too practiced. They were professionals. Something about them was familiar. It was too far away and dark to make out more than the two forms. Several rather important members of the Armed Forces and government had been to visit the lab in recent months as they neared completion of the formula but those had been older men. He doubted any of those men could move with such efficiency. These were younger men. Soldiers maybe, but working for whom? Fearing they were hired by a third party and might take Sam *and* his sample, he jumped from his car to run after her only he was too slow, leaving him to watch helplessly as she was ushered forcefully into a work van. It was too dark make out anyone's features or the plates of the van. The doctor swore, kicking a glass bottle lying nearby. Before the sound of their van disappeared with it around the corner, he pulled his phone from his pocket and dialed.

"Nate Fowler."

"Nate I need to call in that favor."

Ch. 17

"I got one at the Northeast corner," Jimmy whispered excitedly into his comm device. "Big fella, bet he can fight."

"Don't be stupid Jimmy," Marcus cautioned. The man's hot blood caused him to make some bad decisions sometimes. They'd all paid for them more than once.

"Not to worry man, I got this."

Marcus cursed under his breath. His approach was slower, more methodical. His background in science was what made him attractive to the Army and with the promise of more money for college where he hoped to pursue a doctorate in chemistry. He'd enlisted right before the Second Iraq War in 2003. Ironically, when he finally got inside a lab it wasn't as a researcher but as a test subject.

There was a new arms race going on in the world, had been since the seventies when DNA splicing was first discovered. Some sick fuck somewhere hit on the possibility of "dirty bombs" and the rest took care of itself. Everyone wanted the option. But it wasn't until Saddam got caught testing them on people that the populace became aware of his now infamous weapons of mass destruction or WMD.

Iraq's weapons program had been no joke no matter what the political spin machine made of it. The thing was, they weren't weapons of mass destruction like people were *used* to thinking of them. These weapons were genetic. They messed with the victim's DNA. And not all of them were designed to kill. Some of the stuff Saddam was testing on his own people was rumored to make them indestructible; "Saddam's immortal army."

Rumors of a compound where the WMD were being kept were behind their last mission in Iraq for the US Army.

Corporal Evan Marcus had been teamed up with a small Ranger team led by Sergeant First Class Justin Shaw. Their communications officer, Specialist Jimmy Ramirez was tough as nails from growing up on the streets but their fourth, Corporal Henry Mills had been their philosopher. Mills was no slouch in combat he just didn't have the same balls out attitude the rest of them did back then. His strength was in reading people and understanding their angle, he was invaluable in negotiating and strategy. Shaw often sought his council and the rest of them respected him.

Mills could tell what a guy was going to do before even *he* knew he was going to do it. They should have listened when he told them they were in trouble. On that last mission north of Baghdad, outside Tikrit they were to go into the lab to recover the weapon Intell said was stashed there in one of Saddam's strongholds. It turned out to be a metal canister the size of a sausage. Kind of anticlimactic after all they'd done to get there. Iraq was in chaos, soldiers were everywhere and had Saddam's army on the run. Shaw's team slipped in right under their noses with minimal fuss. Relieved at the ease with which they'd gotten hold of it, they laughed off Mills's warning that something was amiss. There was a small guard on the facility, no match for a Ranger team and Shaw had put a hand on Mills's shoulder, smiling. "Relax, Mills. This one's in the bag." That was before the truck was hit and the canister in Shaw's pack was punctured by a piece of metal from the truck's underbelly, spraying all four of them with its contents.

They were evacuated immediately and sent to what they thought was a government facility to be debriefed and decontaminated only that wasn't how it went. The team turned captives were held for six torturous months. The cost to their team: six long months filled with experiments, the life of Lance Corporal Henry Mills, the loss of their loved ones when they'd been reported as casualties of war, and section of Shaw's right pinky finger. The toll was a heavy one, one they all wanted payback on. Especially Marcus. But the real kicker was the stream of test subjects they brought in for trials. Each one a man who swore loyalty to the very country that killed him when the tests failed.

Movement to his right caught Marcus's eye and he adjusted his rifle to use the scope. "Got one hugging the outer perimeter of the woods." He whistled low. "No joke, he's a big one."

Nearly a quarter mile away Justin shifted to the other window using his own rifle's scope to see into the woods. Something moved just outside the house and he tightened his finger on the trigger taking up the slack.

"Damn," he muttered, laying the rifle down. Sam was outside and heading for the woods.

Ch. 18

Sam woke up feeling better than she had in a while, not all of it due to the balm now elevated in her mind to miracle drug status. A tentative shoulder roll revealed only mild tenderness. Opening up about her guilt had been cathartic for her. And, shockingly, in Justin she'd found an unexpected ally. He knew about her father and wanted to find him, not necessarily to kill though the jury was still out on that one. Their talk had done a lot to help her accept that Paul's death, while horribly tragic and unnecessary, had been an accident brought on by her father's actions, not solely hers. What happened to her mother though, that was all Sam's and she knew it. She couldn't discuss that one, even with him. But she was willing to go with these three, for the time being, to take down the baddies, make her mother safe, and find her father to give him back his god damn present from hell. Chemical weapons? *Seriously Steven, what the fuck?* One thing was certain: Sam wasn't capable of making all of this happen by herself, she needed them. At least for now.

Sitting up carefully, Sam glanced around the silent room noticing the light curtains moving in the breeze. Walking to the window, she looked out at the property Justin called home. Justin. It suited him better than just Shaw or even Sarge. At least it suited the man he revealed to her this morning. That man was kind, honorable, and compassionate. She felt she could trust that man and her instincts rarely led her wrong. They also rarely steered her toward trusting a total stranger, but bizarre circumstances made for bizarre bedfellows.

She'd slept with him. *Shit, what was that all about?*

While she was staring at the tree line deep in

thought, her big gray tabby hopped off the front porch underneath the window and trotted toward the woods. Bill was a city cat who panicked the few times she'd tried to bring him out on the grass at home. It was outrageous to see him leave the house and Sam immediately went into protective mode.

"Bill!" she called. His furry gray ass picked up speed and jogged into the woods.

"Shit!"

Sam pulled her pants, hopping one legged around the room and toeing on the flip flops she'd grabbed last night at home. Throwing open the door she rushed out of the house, calling for her cat.

Cats are notoriously selfish and unstable creatures. As such, Sam didn't dare yell or point out how he shouldn't be in the woods trying to get himself killed. Instead she had to play the sweet card despite the fact she wanted to wring his fuzzy neck. "Bill," she called lightly. "Here Bill. Come on, baby." Sam was mortified one of the men might hear her calling her cat "baby" though she kept at it hoping to find him before he was eaten by a wolf or cougar or some other rabid creature. Fortunately they were far from the main road so a car wasn't of immediate concern. "I'm going to put a bell on you, you little monster," she muttered under her breath. "Here Bill."

Brush rustled off to her right, deeper in the woods. It was farther in than expected, although she'd seen Bill run before and it wasn't out of the realm of possibilities for him to cover that much ground if he was on a mission. She jogged through the thick brush, sweeping it aside as she passed. It was thicker than expected and the tangles caught her shoes and clothes, poking her mostly exposed feet. Cursing several times when branches caught her hair and legs of wild blackberry bushes scratched her arms, she made her way to where she thought she heard her errant cat.

"Bill?" she called out low and soothing. "Please be here, baby."

A twig snapped behind her and she whirled just in time to see the blonde man from the coffee shop/ gym parking lot rushing at her. As served her in the kickboxing ring, time slowed and Sam stepped to the side and jumped, bringing a leg up to kick him in the ribs, her hands pushing his back, holding him to feel the full impact.

Her kick caught him unawares and he took the full impact. Grabbing at his rib cage, he stumbled before recovering himself. "You little bitch, I've had it with you." His lips pulled back into a snarl. Nothing but pure black hatred filled his eyes. "I'm going to take my time with you. I'll enjoy making you tell me where it is." He reached behind his back, hand returning with an incredibly large knife that appeared quite capable of making good his threat.

Sam backed up, her hand out behind her feeling for bushes or trees she might hit her head on or trip over. "What's in that container anyway? Why don't you just make more and leave me alone?" She was terrified she was going to die, or worse given what she assumed he meant by "enjoying" making her tell. Still, she wanted to know what it was everyone was after. And hoping against the mounting evidence that her father wasn't working with bad men to make a chemical weapon.

He sneered at her. "No, we can't just *make more*," he mocked. "Your daddy took care of that when he trashed his records and bailed. All we have left is that one sample. Now, we need it back if you don't mind."

Her feet continued to move backward and, without the benefit of sight, her heel caught on some underbrush bringing her down on her backside. He was on her in a minute. Sam tried to bring her knees up too late.

Knife pressed firmly against her throat, he hissed in her face. "Where's the sample? Are you going to tell me or do I have to carve it out of you?" The blade's tip trailed down her throat and rested against the top of her breast. He raised the hilt as if he was going to shove it right down into her heart.

"If you do that you'll never find it," she reminded him, feeling sweat bead up on her lip. "Who'll be in trouble then?"

Hesitation flickered in his eyes and Sam felt a gush of elation. "You need to keep me alive because I've hidden it and you won't find it if you kill me and then you'll be in trouble with your boss."

The pressure on the knife's blade eased up and Sam could breathe again. He got off her and grabbed her arm, pulling her roughly to her feet. The knife hovered loosely by her side.

***

Justin watched from the cover of the dense brush, ignoring the sticks stabbing into his leg and back. He knew he couldn't reach Sam before the bastard could take his blade to her. Close enough to hear their conversation Justin was impressed when Sam talked sense into her attacker. She was composed in the face of death. That was something you couldn't teach, he'd known some good soldiers who hadn't done as well.

When the hired gun jerked her ahead of him and shoved her into the dense brush, knife hanging at the ready, Justin let them gain some distance before he whispered into his comm device. "The guy from last night's here. He's got Sam and they're heading northeast about forty meters from the wood's edge. I'm following."

Marcus finished tying off his man's arms to the tree he'd wrapped him around and stuffed a wad of the man's own shirt into his mouth to keep him from yelling. Patting his man's back, he smiled into his glaring face. "Hold tight. I'll be right back." He pushed the button on his comm. "On my way."

Jimmy was just wiping off his blade. "You shouldn't have fought me, man. I told you it would end this way." His feet were already moving when he pushed the button and responded simply, "Comin.'"

Ch. 19

Sam led the way, guided by repeated rough prodding at her back. He seemed to have a knack for hitting the spot he'd thrown her on last night.

"So do you know my father?" She forced herself to call him a title he didn't deserve.

"Sort of." He pushed again. "I've seen him around. We don't really mix, my type and the scientists. He's been there a long time though, I heard."

She didn't ask what she really wanted to know. How was this guy up and moving? She swore he'd have a concussion at the least, more like a cracked skull from the way he went down after Jimmy hit him with that gun. "He makes weapons? Don't you worry about the chemicals, being there every day?" She figured if she could keep him talking he might give something away. Something she could use to find her father. If she found him she could find out what he wanted with the cylinder of chemicals and then she could kick his ass for being a shithead.

The part of her that remembered her father's warm voice when he read her bedtime stories and put bandages on her knees when she fell off of her bike wanted to believe that he had some noble plan for what he'd clearly stolen. That was the part keeping her from getting rid of it once she knew what it was. That and the fact that she might inadvertently cause harm to a lot of people by disposing of it improperly. She couldn't just throw it away or flush it down the toilet. It was a chemical weapon for crying out loud. Who knew its full potential for destruction?

"Ingesting chemicals isn't the kind of harmful

work environment I worry about."

Sam stumbled over a fallen log partially hidden by low growing shrubbery. The man behind her grabbed her shirt and jerked her back up. When she gained her feet and looked forward, she stopped. Justin stood less than twenty feet away, calm and easy like they were old friends meeting on the trail.

Predictably, she was yanked backward and the knife again pressed to her throat. Her eyes locked onto Justin's. Gone was the soft green she'd seen this morning having been replaced by the cold, piercing glare she was more familiar with from last night.

"Do you know who I am?" he asked the man behind her, managing to stand loose, a skill she'd never been able to master in a fight. Tension served as a "tell" for when she was going to move, not so with Justin. He was cool and easy.

The man holding her laughed harshly. "No, should I? Far as I know you're a pain in my ass just like this one, only there's *nothing* stopping me from killing *you*." He moved the knife to gesture in a cutting motion at Justin.

Then Justin's face broke into a slow smile and he drawled, his accent more pronounced than she'd heard it before. Sam shivered. "Well, I know for a fact the people you work for would love to get their hands on me just as much as they want that little package you're after. So why don't we do a little trade?" He inclined his head at Sam. "Her for me."

Blondie was thinking about it, his silence told her that. Sam went cold, images of Justin's body covered in blood with a knife sticking out of his muscular chest raced through her mind inducing an irrational panic.

Blondie's sharp retort yanked her back to the horrific reality of the present. "No way. I have my orders and they want *her*. I don't know anything about you except you're dead." His knife hand continued to hold the blade in front of her neck while his body shifted behind her. She felt his free hand moving down toward his waist. She felt the gun just before it was in his hand aimed . directly at Justin's chest.

Sam's cry of warning was drowned out by the bark of the gun. She screamed as she watched the closest thing she had to a friend in this awful new reality go down. "Justin!"

The arm attached to the hand holding the knife blocked her from running to him. Her heart ached to see him give his life for nothing. Sam wanted to find her father and throttle him.

"Gotcha." Jimmy's voice came out of nowhere and she felt the arm against her fall away. A tan hand flashed out to grab the wrist and keep the knife from accidentally cutting her as it dropped. Spinning, she watched Blondie slide down to his knees.

As he tipped sideways, she saw the blade in his back. He blinked and Jimmy knelt down beside him. "Let's have a little chat shall we?" The look on his face sent chills down her spine.

The promise of more blood and pain made her stomach lurch. Eyes straight ahead, she followed her gaze with her feet straight to the body lying on the ground up ahead. She rushed, tripping and sliding, to his side and fell to her knees. An enormous spread of blood surrounded a black hole in the middle of his pale blue tshirt.

"Justin?" She called his name, her voice breaking

as she placed trembling fingers on his neck. No pulse. "Please don't die," she whispered. Clearing her throat and wiping the back of her hand across her cheek angrily brushing away tears, Sam continued to prattle on at him. She told him how it was going to be okay and Jimmy had the guy. They were safe for now. Sam waited with her ear to his mouth, praying for him to breathe. There was nothing.

Sam climbed on top of him to begin chest compressions the way she'd learned each year when she was certified for First Aid through work. She paused only to breathe precious air into his unresponsive lips. After her third set Marcus's voice reached her from where he stood over Justin's head.

"You can stop now." He wasn't upset. He actually seemed strangely detached. "That's not going to help."

Sam's face was drenched with sweat from a combination of stress, exertion and heat. "How far is the hospital? If I can keep oxygen going to his brain they might be able to restart his heart. Call 911." She shouted too loud in the peace of the forest.

Marcus saw she wasn't listening and took matters into his own hands. Without another word he walked up to her, circled behind her, and swept her up pinning her arms to her sides in the process.

She fought him as he pulled her off, kicking and yelling for him to let her go. Even level headed Sam could only see so much death without having a meltdown. "Please Marcus. Please. He can't die too. He can't." Body going limp she pleaded though not really with Marcus.

Marcus eased her back onto her feet when he felt the fight go out of her. "Hey, Marcus," Jimmy called from his position with the forgotten blonde killer. "Check this out."

Letting go of Sam, Marcus marched over to Jimmy and bent at the waist to hear what the dying man was saying. She heard the hum of male voices in the heavy silence of the trees though his words failed to register, her thoughts on the unmoving body of the virtual stranger who'd died. For her. Eyes wide, she let her tears course undaunted down her cheeks.

Sam numbly sunk down to her knees where Justin was lying in the brush. His arms bent awkwardly out to his sides, frozen where he landed. He hadn't tried to break his fall, he'd been dead before he hit the ground. She gently tucked them against his sides in a way that looked more comfortable and brushed his hair from his face.

Too worn from years of stress and worry, his face couldn't be considered beautiful like Jimmy's. Justin had been handsome in a different way, his features strong and defined; masculine without being heavy. Most compelling was the open honesty she could see in his unguarded face. In death Justin dropped the guises he'd assumed in life.

She wished she could look in his eyes one more time to apologize properly for drawing him into her father's mess. "I'm sorry Justin. I keep getting good men killed." She leaned down and kissed his cheek, letting her finger trail along the rough edge of his jaw. He had at least two days' stubble. She wondered if they would shave him for his funeral. She thought of Paul's funeral. Until Paul's Sam had been to two funerals in her life, now she would have two in a week. She wanted to check in on Brenda, she considered visiting her in a disguise of some sort. Sam's people were falling away from her faster than she could save them and she didn't have many to start with. Her grief warred with the burning rage building inside her demanding satisfaction.

Without warning there was a huge, wet, gasping sound next to her and Justin sat bolt upright.

Screaming, Sam scrambled back until she was jammed up hard against a tree. Justin's eyes were wild, scanning his surroundings.

Marcus sauntered up, casually checking his watch. "Down four minutes, Sarge," he remarked looking unperturbed by his comrade's resurrection.

"Still hurts like a bitch, don't it?" Jimmy was grinning as he joined them.

Justin nodded, hands going to his chest, feeling the hole in his shirt.

Marcus walked around his back. "No exit wound, Sarge."

***

"Damn." Justin frowned. His eyes ran across Sam and stopped. She was staring at him in a way that made him hate the men who'd done this to them more than ever. His chest burned like a bitch as he breathed in to speak. "You guys want to take care of this?" He inclined his head in the direction of the man who'd killed him. "I'll meet you back at the house."

Marcus eyed him warily. "We're at least five hundred meters over rough terrain. You sure you don't need some help?"

"I'll make it." His lips pressed together in a

grimace. It would be rough going but he wanted some time to explain things to Sam. For some reason, he believed she would take the explanation best from him. They'd gotten at least that far this morning.

Jimmy glanced from Sam to Justin seeing their eyes locked on one another. "Don't get started without me," Jimmy teased.

Justin gritted his teeth. "Call me crazy, but I think you like this part."

Jimmy went back to the blonde's body and removed his knife, still smiling. Grabbing the body by the belt, he dragged it off toward the deeper part of the woods. Marcus headed off in a different direction.

Eventually the sounds of their passing died away and Justin and Sam found themselves alone. He broke the silence. "Are you okay?"

"Am *I* okay? You were *dead*." She sounded rational with just a hint of hysteria creeping in. "Your heart stopped beating. You weren't breathing. I did CPR until Marcus pulled me off of you." Her brow furrowed, most likely going back there in her head. Justin got a strange thrill at the knowledge that his death had hurt her. Then he felt like an asshole for hurting her.

He rubbed his chest again. Compressions, that explained the bruising he felt starting in his ribs. Lucky for him he was dead at the time and blood wasn't flowing so the bruising would be minimal. Not that it mattered, he tended to be a fast healer. Eyes not leaving her face, he watched her expression closely. It shouldn't have surprised him that he needed her to understand. He didn't want her to see him as a thing to be feared, it went against his mission. "When we were in Iraq we were sent into one of Saddam's lab for a weapon. We'd heard

132

rumors but we didn't know how accurate they were." He tried to smile to lighten the mood. It got no response from the shell-shocked Sam. "You know how some of these guys are, 'I'm a god,' 'I figured out how to live forever.' We'd been hearing all sorts of bizarre claims through his rumor mill. All we knew for sure was that they were producing something and we were supposed to bring it back." That's how the Army works. They say, you do. No questions."

Sam blinked. No other movement or sound giving a hint as to where her head was at. Justin took a breath and dove into the rest, feeling his chest burn with the familiar sting of impotent rage.

"After we got it we destroyed the place. Those were our orders. We reached the pickup spot with no trouble and were being transported as a part of a supply caravan. We thought we were clear." He was back in the truck, remembering. "The attack came out of nowhere and our truck was hit by a mortar. The driver was killed and we were tossed around when it flipped. A piece of the truck blew and it went through my pack. The pack probably saved my life except the canister exploded when it was hit. It sprayed all four of us. After we got back they figured they could reverse engineer the chemical we'd lost using us. They figured out that when our heart stops beating, an electrical impulse restarts it and they put in an implant." He lowered his shirt's neckline to reveal a thin vertical scar. "It's like a pacemaker. Once the heart restarts, the chemical restructuring of our DNA lets the cells regenerate quickly. We heal and live to die another day. The people we're dealing with." He leaned forward, wanting to touch her yet afraid physical contact might break the tether keeping her there, listening. "They've been trying to replicate this for years. It took a lot of tries before they figured out how to kill us permanently." He held up his right hand showing Sam part of a missing digit she

133

hadn't noticed before. "We can't grow things back, we can only heal. They called it a breakthrough, figuring that out." His eyes narrowed, lips stretched tight. "The one we lost, Mills, they took his head off. They were ecstatic when it worked and he was dead." Justin straightened his shoulders, forcing himself back under control. "When we left they lost the chemical but they still had all their research. As far as we know they're still testing it on soldiers. Killing them when it doesn't work. If we're right, that's what's in that package your father sent you; they've finally succeeded. That's why they want it so badly. Think of what an army of soldiers who don't die could do."

***

Blinking again, Sam's eyes traveled down to the black hole in his shirt, still shining with fresh, wet blood. Her eyes widened in disbelief as blood started to pump out in a thin stream. It had really happened. He'd been shot and yet here he was, talking to her. This couldn't be. "Is Steven responsible for any of this?" She felt her stomach churn, an unbidden image of her father standing over Justin's body with a scalpel. "Did *he* hurt you?"

Justin shook his head and she exhaled a breath she hadn't realized she was holding. "He works for the men trying to reconfigure the chemical but no, he didn't take part in the tests. Actually, he's how we got out." A ghost of a smile twisted his lips at her shock. "When he was supposed to be helping transport us to another lab he let us go. He said he'd tell his people we escaped. When we went back to destroy it we found out they beat us to it. It was gone. They moved somewhere new and we've been trying to find the new lab ever since." His hand came up in the space between them and for a second Sam thought he was reaching for her but then it dropped. An odd sensation of loss tugged at her. "All we knew was the

134

Doc's face and he hasn't been easy to find. You've been our first real lead in a long time."

Sam watched his chest as it continued oozing blood. Pointing at it she remarked in a flat tone. "You should get that looked at." Her voice sounded funny even to her. Was she in shock? *Or going nuts.* She wasn't sure she could take much more, she was about at capacity at this point.

He gave it a cursory glance then looked in the direction his man had taken. "It'll hold until Jimmy digs the bullet out. Then it'll bleed like crazy."

Her eyes popped. "What? He's got to take it out?"

Brow furrowed, Justin nodded. "Yep. Otherwise it heals inside and then he's really got to dig."

"We should go." Her jaw clenched against the distinct taste of bile as it climbed up the back of her throat. Her mind couldn't completely comprehend what he was saying only that the immediate need for action was clear. Using the tree behind her for support she stood and held out a hand. "Let's go."

He hesitated for only a second before he took it and gained his feet, stumbling as he did so. The blood coursing out picked up speed.

Ch. 20

Thankfully the walk back to the house was short. Unfortunately, the dense underbrush proved to be a challenge for the wounded Justin as he weakened rapidly from the continuing loss of blood. A few yards in and the blood increased yet again, his steps turning to stumbles. Grudgingly he accepted her offer of support, wrapping an arm over her shoulders. Though his intent was merely to use her as a stabilizer soon he was leaning heavily on her.

"Damn bullet. It's shifting." Justin cursed, his fingers probing the injury site. Moving had brought it dangerously close to what was most likely his aorta or some other vitally important bit of his circulatory system considering the fact that he hadn't yet ceased spewing blood and was growing progressively weaker as a result.

"How can you be so calm?" Sam slowed her pace, forcing him to do the same. "You've got a bullet inside you and you're losing a ton of blood. It's getting worse." Her eyes were on the front of his shirt, dropping to take in the red path that continued down his pants, now completely red to his knees. He knew from experience his color had to be getting close to gray if it wasn't there already. Clearly she was having renewed doubts about his ability to live through this. Again.

Justin cast a tired gaze her direction. "I have died exactly fourteen times, fifteen counting this one. That doesn't include near misses and wounds that might have killed me in time if I hadn't healed quick enough. Trust me, I'll tell you if I'm in trouble." He caught the way her face paled and felt like an asshole. *What the hell am I doing? Bragging like some macho man jackass? Like this is supposed to be impressive, not totally crazy shit that'll send her running, screaming for the hills?*

"You're losing a lot of blood." She stared at his wet shirt, mouth gaping as she struggled to take it all in and not freak. Justin caught the way her body was beginning to shake under his arm and it wasn't from taking his weight though that had to be wearing on her by now.

Nodding toward the opening in the trees marking the edge of the lawn, Justin sighed in relief. "We're here." He would never tell her how every step burned his oxygen-deprived muscles or how the bullet had shifted again and was scraping his a rib with every breath. *Macho my ass,* he thought. Besides, those were things only his men could understand. No normal human being had taken the kind of damage they had and lived to tell about it. Those bits of the hell they'd endured as test subjects, continued to endure now for money, weren't for idle chitchat. Together they had suffered more than any man and would forever bear the scars, both inside and out.

Making it to the front porch without assistance, Justin grabbed the rail to pull himself up the three steps to the door feeling he'd just climbed a pyramid. Sam opened it before resuming her position under his arm, leaving him for only seconds. It was only a few more feet yet he accepted her help readily. Justin's legs were nearing failure.

***

Glancing around, Sam saw that they were alone and her shoulders sagged. The others were back in the woods, "cleaning up." She barely suppressed the shudder that ran through her body. No one had to tell her Justin was fading fast, she wasn't a fool. He was about to die again of blood loss if she didn't do something and, even if he acted like it was about as eventful as Sunday at Walmart, Sam didn't want to watch him do it again. *Why had it bothered her so much? She'd begged him not to leave her. What was that about?*

So naturally Sam looked for somewhere to get him off his feet before he collapsed. They'd mentioned having to take the bullet out. Sam's stomach twirled and her eyes strayed back to the blood staining Justin's shirtfront, plastering it to his chest. If it was water and not blood and nobody was talking about dying she would have taken the opportunity to admire his chest. It really was a crime not to. *And it was a crime to let Paul die just because he was a sweet guy.* Her knees wobbled and Sam's search for an "operating surface" grew more desperate. Her eyes lit upon the kitchen table, the only area large enough for a man Justin's size and hard enough to keep the blood from completely saturating it. She was fairly certain they didn't want him ruining the couch and there was no way he was going to make it up the stairs.

Taking a huge gulp of air to settle herself, Sam made her decision. "Lie down." She pointed at the table and closed the gap until they stood beside it.

Without argument Justin rested his backside against it, grunting in pain when he eased himself back and eased his shoulders down. Sam helped to support him, hustling to bring his legs up once his torso was on and he was lying flat.

"Thank you." He smiled tightly, forehead bathed in sweat.

Part of Sam's education had included Biology. Granted, it was all animals and animal parts, but she had significant experience with a scalpel and was growing steadily more concerned with each passing second that the bullet was causing far more problems than Justin would let on. Taking in his colorless lips, pale face, and glazing eyes Sam swallowed the squeamishness twisting her guts.

"Take off your shirt," she commanded.

He didn't argue although he struggled to comply. Standing at his head, Sam grabbed the lower hem of his shirt and pulled up. Justin could barely raise his arms to let the garment slide over his head. Putting a hand out she caught his head to keep it from thunking against the wooden table once it cleared the neck hole.

Chest bare, Justin lay panting shallowly, covered in sweat and blood. Sam could only gasp at the sight before her. His discipline carved body was awash in scars of various sizes and shapes. Some, round like this one with ragged edges, she guessed were bullets. There were at least five gashes of varying lengths that must have come from blades of some sort.

"What did they do to you?" she whispered, horrified, letting the fingers of her left hand touch the round, puckered scar on his left shoulder. Sam gazed upon his strong features now pinched in pain. Eyes closed beneath a furrowed brow.

"They wanted to know what made us live, so we lived. Then they wanted to know what made us die, so we died," he answered without opening his eyes.

Sam cast her eyes about for a tool that would be useful for the extraction already growing more complicated as the hole over his heart began closing itself before her eyes. Tearing herself from him she dug in the drawers and came out with chopsticks and a steak knife.

"What do you think you're doing?" He cracked an

eyelid at the sounds of her foraging.

"There's no sign of Jimmy or Marcus so I'm getting this thing out before it turns into a worse ordeal than it has to be." She stared at the hole gone back to leaking only a small stream of blood, dread settling in her guts telling her she couldn't do this. She pushed it away. "What do we do for the pain?"

"First Aid kit's in the van still. Locked. Jimmy's got the key." His hand was unsteady as he gestured toward the cabinets by the sink. "Whiskey. Use it to clean and some for me." Justin's voice was becoming steadily weaker. The image of his features frozen in death flashed before her eyes and she vowed she wouldn't see it again. Definitely not twice in a day if there was anything she could do about it. *You think it's going to be uncomfortable for* you? *she chided herself.* Unwilling to allow her thoughts to have much say in what was about to happen, she jogged to the sink and found the bottle. When she presented it, he drank eagerly. The amount he put down was impressive.

"Take it easy, you're going to get alcohol poisoning," she cautioned.

An unfocused green eye peered out from under his long brown lashes, striking against his deathly pale skin. "Have you ever had a bullet dug out of your chest?" He stared at her, sort of, considering his eyes were visibly struggling to focus. Blood loss was making the alcohol go right to his head. "All right then." Eyes closed again, exhaustion and pain combined with the whiskey to take him under.

With no experience at all with living subjects Sam was terrified she would cause more harm to the weakening man. A man who had a hole in his chest because of her. She placed her small hand over his chest

140

to feel his heartbeat while she waited until she was sure the alcohol had taken effect.

After what felt like an eternity his breathing deepened and she could tell he was at least partially unconscious. Sam doused the end of the knife with whiskey and stood with it poised over the hole, staring at it, wondering how to start. Her throat closed as it always did when she prepared to make the first incision. Reason number one why she wasn't a surgeon or vet.

"Get to it then." His voice was slow and thick. "It's just gonna get worse."

Sam jumped at the unexpected prompting. "I don't want to hurt you," she shot back, nerves fried.

His hand reached out and wrapped itself around hers on the knife's handle. Justin rolled his head sideways and opened his eyes, bright green and fierce. "You won't." With that, he guided the knife's tip to his chest and pushed.

Sam watched the blade disappear into his battle-scarred flesh and Justin flinched, groaning from the pain, his hand weakening. He continued to push until Sam felt the tip hit something. For a second she worried it was a rib but Justin managed a weak, "Bingo," before he passed out and she rapidly set about digging it out before he woke.

The smashed metal shell was not very deep inside his body. Luckily glancing off his ribs had slowed its progress. Her chopsticks were useless at first. Sam had to tap it with the end of the knife several times to better get behind it and push it into a position that would let her get a hold of it. Using the tip of the blade she was able to drag it close enough to the surface to grab it with her "forceps." Just as she reached in to pull the crushed shell out of the wound the front door opened and in walked the crew, Jimmy leading the way.

"What the hell?" He took in the scene and his eyes went wide. "What the hell're you doing? Get away from him." Jimmy rushed to intervene.

Free hand out, Sam waved him aside while trying not to lose her grip on the hard won metal. "I have it. Let me finish." She finally had the bullet and she was not letting it go. A line of sweat ran down her spine, stopping at the top of her jeans.

"She's doing all right." Marcus spoke quietly, stepping around Jimmy, eyes intent upon their teammate lying on the "operating table." "Let her finish, Jimmy."

Keeping his eyes glued to her hands, Jimmy grumbled and stepped back. Sam gave one last tug and out popped the bullet. She dropped it on the table and breathed, wiping her wet brow with the back of a suddenly shaky hand.

"Now what do we do?" She looked from one to the other.

"Nothing." Marcus shrugged. "It'll take care of itself." He nodded at the wound and Sam could already see the blood slowing as it began to close up from the inside first.

She couldn't stand around doing nothing but watching him heal the wound *she'd* reopened, so Sam grabbed a dishtowel, moved to the sink, and wetted it. Returning to Justin's unconscious body she set about cleaning his chest. It took some time and several rinses of the towel. There was so much blood. While she washed his body, Jimmy and Marcus stayed out of the way, never out of touching distance of their sergeant. It seemed even with assurances he would heal they would not trust him to her entirely. *They know my father.* That alone would make her suspect in their eyes and Justin was vulnerable. His team was protective. Sam envied them their close ties, more than shared service bound these men. They were bound by blood. *So much blood.* She went back to cleaning though it was no longer necessary.

Body washed and healing, Justin was ready for the recovery room. Marcus stepped in, scooped him up over his shoulder and carried him up the stairs to his room across the hall from Sam's, and plopping him down on the dark blue sheets.

"He needs to rest." He turned and stood, arms crossed. A roadblock for Sam, who had trotted after him upstairs and hovered in the doorway.

"I'd like to be here if he needs anything, if that's all right with you." She watched his mouth open to protest and risked a step closer. "He's here because of me." Unbidden, her eyes stung and her vision blurred with unshed tears. Her voice cracked and she frowned, not wanting to be weak in front of these men. Justin might be kind, but Marcus certainly was not and Jimmy was a wild card. Sam thought he was a player for sure and maybe a few fries short of a happy meal. Her eyes strayed past Marcus's imposing form to where Justin lay very still. Too still. Guilt made her brave. Squaring her shoulders, she forced her eyes up to his. "He died for me, Marcus."

After what seemed an interminably long time during which Sam decided Marcus was going to throw her bodily from the room, he bobbed his head once. "Good." His dark eyes softened the slightest bit. "We have work to do and he shouldn't be alone when he wakes up. It's always a little disorienting to die and he's come close to two in an hour. That's hard."

"How many times have you," Sam's curiosity made her bold, "you know, died." It felt weird saying that to someone standing in front of her, breathing.

Marcus growled through clenched teeth. "Enough."

Staring in bewilderment at Marcus, Sam figured she was now firmly in the Twilight Zone. "These men work for the men who hurt you, don't they?" Marcus responded with a barely there nod. "Why do you keep fighting? I mean, why not just disappear? You could leave the country, go some island somewhere and they'd never find you. You wouldn't have to…" Her eyes again found Justin's form, "die."

"Because you grew up with the Doc I don't expect you to understand this, but we took an oath to protect our country and our fellow soldiers." He leveled a cold glare at her and Sam wanted to back out the door. "A man doesn't run and hide from his trouble. Not if he wants to respect himself or his family to."

"Marianna?" She remembered the name he had tattooed on his arm. "Do you ever see her?"

His hand subconsciously touched the place Sam had seen her name inked onto his dark flesh and surprised her by answering. "My daughter. She was three when I left. I check in on her whenever I can, make sure she's doing okay but she doesn't see me."

It was impossible for Sam not to think of her own absent father and how often she'd wished for a call, a visit, anything personal. Not a pile of guilt money with nothing else in it, no clue where he was or how he was doing. "Don't you ever talk to her? Does she know you're still out there?"

His eyes clouded with pain and regret. "They told our families we were dead but they're still watching them." His thumb stroked his arm. "If we went home it would put our families in danger." He took a deep breath. "Sometimes to protect someone you have to walk away."

Sam absorbed that, considering the possibility that very thing had been behind her father's decision to leave them. Maybe he'd been trying to protect them from the same people who ruined the lives of these men, taking them from their families as well. Sam couldn't imagine how difficult it would be to walk away from her mother if this didn't end, yet she would to keep her safe. All of these men had left something behind. What had Justin left behind? Did he have a family too? For some odd reason that idea bothered her. *The last thing I need to be thinking about right now is a guy,* she thought bitterly. *No one else is getting hurt on my account.*

He nodded back toward the bed. "You do anything to freak him out or hurt him, you answer to me." The look he gave her telling her just how unpleasant she would find that experience.

She licked her lips and swallowed. "I won't hurt him."

Apparently he believed her sincerity because he gave her another unhappy eyeballing and grunted.

Sam moved out of the way and stood back to give Marcus sufficient clearance to get through the door but Marcus turned to the bed, not the door. For a moment Marcus fidgeted at Justin's bedside, his body blocking her view then stepped around to the foot of the bed. Without warning he grabbed both pant legs at the cuff and jerked, bringing the bloodied jeans off and revealing unsoiled black boxer briefs; the only thing that allowed Justin to be deemed *not* naked.

Marcus flipped the blanket over Justin covering him up to his chest, healed except for a new pink scar a few inches from his implant scar. "Sleep well, Sarge." He patted his shoulder tenderly and cast Sam a last cautionary glance on his way out.

Alone at last, thinking of her mother and the state she might be in, Sam pulled her phone from her pocket and dialed.

"Hello?" Pete answered on the fourth ring.

Sam kept her voice down to avoid disturbing the sleeping Justin. "Um, Pete. Hey, how's Mom? Have there been any changes?" Averting her eyes to concentrate, she stared out his window at the sun shining high overhead. All this and it was barely noon.

"Sam." His voice was hoarse and scratchy. He sounded like he'd been crying. *Oh God, Pete never cries.* He cleared his throat. "Where are you?"

Sam's lungs tightened. *What do I tell him? What's a good reason not to be sitting there holding my mother's hand while she's in a coma?* "Pete, I," she barely whispered, voice breaking with grief and shame. "I'll visit as soon as I can."

There was a long, heavy pause. Sam bit her lip, debating the possible costumes she could don to go to her mother's bedside. It was okay if Pete went on thinking she was a terrible daughter but what about her mother? She should be hearing Sam's voice, her pleas to come back. She could sing the songs Brenda sang to her as a child, remind her of the stories they shared and their

146

happiest memories. She snorted thinking of herself in full clown gear holding Brenda's hand. Would she be kicked out? That's it, *I'm cracking up.* How did Marcus do it? How did any of them do it? She wasn't a day from seeing her mother and already she was going nuts. Mercifully, Pete was called away by a doctor before he could push her. Good thing. She wasn't sure she could say no if he asked. Hanging up the phone, Sam slid it into her back pocket and closed her eyes. *Marcus wouldn't let me go anyway,* she reminded, herself though it did nothing to ease her conscience.

Justin moved in his sleep, throwing an arm over his head with a low moan. Sam jumped up to quiet him, thinking he shouldn't be moving around as he healed. Internal bleeding could still probably happen and that wasn't good for anybody, even genetically altered super soldiers. *Get a grip.* Sam ran a hand over his face, brushing back his hair and watching as his tense expression eased. Perching on the edge of the bed she thought for a long time about how she'd watched Pete sit vigil for her mother, wishing she could let someone get close enough to be that for her. It remained highly unlikely given her crippled heart. That was Sam, an unreachable island a college boyfriend had once called her. But it wasn't entirely true, was it? The image of Paul's dead eyes brought with them the sting of tears to the backs of her eyelids and she blinked. *He deserved someone who would have held his hand. Someone to mourn him.* And Sam knew, beyond the shadow of a doubt, that she was broken. At fault for the death of a good man and she was sitting here worrying about her mother and this unknown man. *Handsome man.* The knifepoint of guilt wedged itself firmly between her ribs and twisted. If she were a good person she would be so blind with love and loss that she wouldn't even *see* Justin. Not that she was lusting for him, but she still shouldn't even be looking at anyone even if he was better than most male models she'd seen hawking

147

underwear and cologne. There were no delicate cheekbones and carefully crafted hairstyles here. No, Justin was a man. A man who had a body sculpted by use and training. Hours in a gym with a personal trainer and dietitian were in no way responsible for what she'd had her hands on as she dug out a bullet to save his life. Well, sort of. *What the fuck is wrong with me?* she shook her head. *I'm going fucking crazy.* Not usually one to curse quite so badly, it seemed fitting as she slid over the edge of reality that her linguistic skills would also take the plunge with her. *He might also kill me when he wakes up.*

Sobered, at least temporarily, Sam recalled she was sitting in his room. Alone, she had ample time to look around and maybe learn something about the man himself. His likes, dislikes, hobbies, favorite color, loyalties. Did he have a poster that said, "Will kill the daughter of the man I hate yet helped me escape from a hellish lab?" Oddly, there was nothing personal on the walls, desk or even piled on the floor. The only thing in the room, aside from a bed, nightstand, and dresser was a full to overflowing bookshelf in the corner. So out of character for the sparseness of the rest of the room it could have been Photoshopped into the scene. Picking an interesting looking paperback that might move fast enough to hold her limited attention span given the myriad distractions she faced, Sam sat down on the bed next to him. There seemed to be a lack of a chair in the room and hardwood floors didn't look comfy long term. For modesty sake, she scooted well over to the foot of the bed on the far side.

Sam sat. And sat. The only time she left her post was to grab a bite when Jimmy poked his head in to invite her to dinner. Her eating was rushed, fearing Justin would wake alone. Having failed the last man who'd given his life for her she was determined to repay him even if it was only to ease his first few moments of awakening. From there, who knew? The likelihood of him or one of his teammates killing her at present was low, provided he remembered he needed her to find Steven's fabulous birthday gift. Sam barely tasted the arroz con pollo Jimmy made, much to his highly vocalized dismay. Complaining about having to cook during Justin's week, apparently they shared chores like any other ordinary, non-mercenary roommates, he excused her from the table after she'd startled at the tenth unknown sound as the house creaked and cracked, cooling as the sun sank lower on the horizon.

Released from the obligation of pleasantries she didn't object, jogging in her haste to return to his side where she studied him and found no changes, picked up her book and resumed her duty. Sam had just finished the book when the combined efforts of her dinner and the constant strain made her eyes grow heavy. Cautiously she laid her head on the pillow next to his thinking she would only close her eyes for a minute. She hadn't had more than a few stolen hours for what seemed an eternity. Had this whole thing started three days ago? It felt more like months to her fatigued body and mind. *How much longer could it go on?* Even the notion that she might face a life on the run sent Sam into panic mode and she willed her mind to quiet. Eventually, though she thought it would never happen, she finally found sleep.

Ch. 21

As always, he startled awake. At first he was surprised to find a body next to him, unmoving, he took a few moments to acclimate and assess any possible threats. Had he fallen in the field? No, no gunfire and he was laying in a bed. He was in a house. The farmhouse in Wisconsin, he recognized the pale blue walls. His tense muscles relaxed by a few degrees. The constant, all-over, bone-deep pain he wrestled daily returned with gusto; more than its usual dull ache. Justin had noticed it on the team's last two freelance jobs as well. Precious fractions of a second off his reaction time and his muscles weren't responding like they used to either. Justin wondered, not for the first time, if there were a finite number of regenerations to this interminable science experiment. Irritated, he pushed the possibility aside as inconvenient. There was no way he was dying for good before he shut down the Doc and the people behind the research. If he had to face the man on one leg he'd do it. He owed that to his men. All of them.

Blinking, his mind caught up to the present and the face beside his became familiar. Olive skin darkened by the summer sun, dark hair cut nearly boy short with long bangs. Awake she was intriguing, strong and confident though he'd seen a few chinks in her armor. Asleep, that armor gone, she looked small and vulnerable and had his Y chromosome charging to the front raising its sword, demanding he protect her from all those he knew would keep coming for her until he and his men took them out first. He watched Sam sleep, her face smooth and unburdened by the concerns that weighed on her so heavily, when someone tapped on the door. The cat who'd rejoined them some time in the night squawked his welcome.

"Come in." He beckoned low so as not to disturb

her, rolling over to face the newcomer.

Marcus stepped in first, Jimmy close behind. "Getting to be a habit. A bad one." The thin man commented.

Jimmy raised an eyebrow. "Good for you, Sarge."

Justin thought he was going to have to bring the mouthy playboy into line until Jimmy surprised him with touch of sentimentality.

"You work your angle right and you could come out of it with her too." He furrowed his brow. "This thing ain't gonna last forever and when it's over," he tipped his head toward the girl. "It'd be good to have something to go home to."

Marcus scowled at his mention of home. And despite Jimmy's positive thoughts, Justin considered the warm body behind him almost wistfully. "That would be something, but unlikely."

"Is it still there, the pain?" Marcus was back to business.

He and Jimmy started to feel it as well though not as bad, yet. They hadn't had to come back from the dead as often. That seemed to be the catalyst. No surprise that being resurrected through unnatural means would affect a body. *I just need a little more time.* Justin forced his mind back to the men eyeing him expectantly. Justin nodded grimly. "Worse."

Jimmy cursed quietly in Spanish. Marcus was thoughtful, pointing to the figure beside Justin. "We don't know how this is all going to go down. Let's not get too attached here before we know how we're going to end this thing." His brown eyes darkened. "Sacrifices need to be made."

His lips pulled tight as Justin gritted his teeth. "I'm aware of that possibility, Marcus." Then, taking a deep breath, he added, "But let's not forget what she means for us. We lose her and Doc's in the wind again."

"Maybe, maybe not. Who says we need her to find the Doc?"

"Are you fucking kidding me?" Justin couldn't believe his ears. "Have you completely lost it? We've been hunting these monsters for how long with nothing solid. Now we get our first solid lead, hell, we've got a direct line to the Doc with his fucking daughter and you're ready to throw that away because you're pissed off?" Justin pushed up, disregarding the agony the quick action sent firing through his abused body. On his feet he took a step and wobbled. Rage at his weakness pushed him over the edge and he shuffled another foot right into Marcus's space. Sam shifted, drawing all of their eyes, and he lowered his voice to a harsh growl. If he knew it wouldn't land him flat on his face he would push them out into the hall. Instead he gave Marcus his best hardass glare. "You're not the only one whose lost something, Marcus."

The muscle in Marcus's jaw twitched as he clenched his teeth, his nostrils flared. "You keep telling yourself you're the same as us, that you're some sort of victim, but we know on whose shoulders the blame falls. Don't you dare put yourself on the same level as me." Emotion fractured his voice. "Nobody's given up more than me."

Justin and Marcus faced off, fists clenched, when Jimmy broke in. "Marcus, you gonna tell him what you got from your man, buddy? Come on, this is huge." His brown eyes were shining as he bounced on the balls of

152

his feet.

"Right." Marcus blinked, withdrawing his challenge. For now. "I was able to interview *my* detainee," he flicked his chin over his shoulder, "whereas Jimmy here dispatched his catch before he could get anything other than 'ouch.'"

Jimmy glowered. "*He* picked the fight. Not me."

"We've got the lab." He spoke quietly, like it was nothing. No outward sign that this was what they'd been searching for since their escape. Jimmy was grinning from ear to ear. "It's outside Rochester, in Minnesota." Marcus let his eyes drift past Sam's sleeping form. "Apparently the Doc's gone AWOL but not before he destroyed his data and their supply. He left only one small sample." He was staring coolly at Sam. "Doc's going to be coming for that sample, guess he's got some plans of his own for it though he wasn't sure what those were." He lifted a shoulder and let it drop. "Doesn't matter. Point is, he's coming and so is his competition. These guys are under the gun. They've got a buyer coming in and they need to have something to sell. Without that sample the whole deal's over."

Not liking the cold calculation he saw in Marcus's eyes when he looked at her, Justin questioned the disturbing development. They knew it was inevitable once word got out that it wasn't just a rumor anymore. Still, knowing they'd reached that point sent a shiver down his spine that had nothing to do with the fact that Justin was standing there in his skivvies. "Buyer?"

Jimmy bobbed his head, all traces of his grin gone. "Yeah, they were working on selling this thing on the black market, man. It ain't just for enlisteds anymore." His eyes had gone dangerous. "These guys are thinking a little country or some warlord somewhere with big plans and an undersized army'll pay a lot for unlimited troops. They're thinkin' it'll offset some of their operating costs." He smiled darkly and Justin thought maybe Jimmy had officially tipped the scales of sanity. *How could he not? This much killing will loosen anybody's grip on reality.*

Justin could feel the familiar quickening of adrenaline an impending mission always sent pulsing through him. Add to that how personal this one was and he was nearly vibrating. It was sickening to think of the countless men and women who would be sent to rise and fall over and again. Shaking his head, he cleared the images of carnage the likes of which he'd seen in more countries than he cared to count from his mind's eye. "I have to think." He took a step to go around Marcus and stumbled, his hand shooting out to the dresser to steady himself. Over his head, the men shared a worried glance. Frustrated with his failing body, Justin grabbed clothes out of a drawer, yanking on a pair of cargo pants and pulling a black tee shirt over his head.

The two filed out in front of him. Justin was the last, taking care to close the door with a soft click. Downstairs, he left the others in the kitchen going out to be alone and think. Eight years and dozens of missions together, and the need to explain what he needed became superfluous. Jimmy poured himself a cup of coffee and sat down to wait for orders. Marcus opened a drawer and extracted a key. Jimmy raised an eyebrow.

"If this is it we need to be ready." He unlocked the door to the basement where the big guns were kept.

Ch. 22

"You know if I get caught it's my ass." Nate Fowler shuffled the phone to tuck it under his chin and the sound of rustling paper came across the line.

Dr. Steven James could picture the middle aged, heavyset man pushing his wire rimmed glasses up his snub nose, a tic he'd had back when they'd met at Johns Hopkins. Dr. James was working on the Genetics project and Fowler, already holding a Criminal Justice degree was finishing up his secondary degree in Farsi back then. Now, fifteen years later, Fowler was on staff at the NSA monitoring chatter.

Dr. James was not to be put off. His was an important mission, one that had countless lives riding on it.

"Nate, might I remind you what I put on the line when it was *your* kid?" He kept his tone even, counting on Fowler's fatherly guilt to do most of the work for him.

Nate grew quiet, no doubt recalling the chemical cocktail the doctor had given him when his daughter developed a rare blood disease. He'd saved her with experimental medicine that still hadn't been approved. If not for his aid, Fowler's little girl would be dead instead of graduating high school this year.

"All right." He caved. "Give me the number. It might take a while, I have to do it when no one's here."

Dr. James didn't comment on the time frame. He was by nature a patient man and a few days, after *years,* were acceptable. Reciting Samantha's social security number from memory, he heard Fowler's pen scratching them out followed by keystrokes as he plugged them into his computer. "Okay, I've got her cell number. Want it?" Dr. James grunted and Nate rattled off the ten digits Dr. James locked away in his more than adequate memory stores. "The last call she made was outside St. Croix, Wisconsin. That's not far from you, right?" Of course he would have already traced the line Dr. James was using. That didn't mean it didn't irritate the doctor. He made no comment. Nate cleared his throat. "Ah, I'll put a mark on her number and when she uses it again I'll have an exact location. Are you going out there now? So you're close?"

St. Croix was over an hour away and when the call came the doctor would want to be close. Assuming she was holed up with those men she would be stationary. Battle strategy wasn't his strong suit but he'd been working around military minds for some time and he'd picked up a few things. He ignored the paternal gut tightening that accompanied the thought of his daughter being held by three strange men. They wouldn't hurt her while she held the sample. He had to gamble on that. "Yes, I'll head out there now." He started to hang up then stopped, offering a sincere "Thank you, Nate."

Nate wasn't as happy as the doctor. "We're even now," he replied brusquely.

Dr. James hung up and leaned over to open the glove box and check, yet again, that the gun hadn't disappeared since the last time he looked. He'd purchased the handgun months ago as he planned his departure from the lab. Not generally a gun enthusiast, the doctor knew that his separation from his employer would not be easy and there was a possibility he would need to protect himself. As far as accuracy went, well, he would have to hope they got close since he'd yet to fire it more than the few times he'd snuck off to the range when making supply runs for the research team. A skeleton crew of researchers and assistants, they saw to their own needs. The speed and accuracy with which the two men now holding his daughter had taken down her attackers brought the reality of what he faced home. What he'd seen of them in action made him hope they were sleeping or that he could catch her alone. A fight wouldn't end well for the doctor. Either way it was time. He'd temporarily shaken those on his tail and was fast running out of money. He needed that sample.

Ch. 23

Sam woke to a dark room. Stretching luxuriously with her eyes still closed she rolled over and caught a whiff of Justin's mixture of smells from his pillow. The clean fresh scent of his shampoo and the mildly spicy tang of his cologne filled her nostrils. Her lips parted in a lazy smile. *What the hell is* that? Her heartbeat took off just before her throat slammed shut. Then she froze. *Holy shit! Where was Justin?* He'd woken and she was sleeping. The one thing she was supposed to do and she'd botched it. She could see Marcus's scowl in her mind's eye. Hoping Justin hadn't been disoriented or afraid when he'd come to, she leapt from the bed to go searching. Her quick escape was complicated when she managed to get her legs tangled in the blankets he'd tossed back when he rose. Cursing and wrestling with the sheets turned cling wrap, Sam finally won. Sort of. She fell off the bed, catching herself with her palms inches before her knees hit the floor.

Troubled she sat up and listened. It was *too* quiet. Had they left her? Sam was ready to go charging down the stairs when she glanced down and caught sight of her rumpled and *bloody* clothing. Ducking into her room she dug in her bag and quickly shucked off her soiled clothes and threw on a pair of tan cargo shorts and an orange tank top befitting the heat. She could feel the day's lingering humidity in the still night air barely flowing through the open windows.

Continuing down the hall at a somewhat calmer pace, Sam scanned and saw that the other two bedroom doors were closed. She cracked them enough to peek in both as well as the bathroom as she trotted past. No Justin. Hurrying downstairs she fought down her rising panic. If they were gone and more of those men came back. She slammed the door shut on that line of thinking as unproductive. Yet the feeling of being held against her will, of being helpless, pervaded her senses and her knees wobbled. For the first time in her life she feared being alone. Desperate for some amount of control over her deteriorating thoughts she ran through the possibilities, settling on a simple supply run. *They must have gone to the store or something.* Then, she quickly dispelled that assumption as ridiculous.

All three of them went to the store and left her, the keeper of the sample and key to their hunt for her father? Highly unlikely. And after what had happened just that morning she couldn't believe Justin would leave her alone. Not with more of those men out there. All sentimentality aside, their need to keep her safe and in custody wasn't a question. If the other side got to her and found the tube from her father that would leave Justin and his men high and dry and there was no way they were going to accept that. Sam was certain that need for that damned tube and whatever was in it was the only thing keeping Marcus from walking her off into the woods just like he had that man this morning.

She burst into the kitchen, already in the throes of a panic attack. Her pills were upstairs in the same toiletry bag as her birth control, the bag Justin had gotten for her when he'd helped her pack. She couldn't remember having taken either pill today, maybe even yesterday. That couldn't be helping. Her chest felt like someone was standing on it. The air in her lungs turned to sludge, her chest heaved as it worked to keep it moving. Her calm, cool façade, so contrived out of a need to protect herself was a joke but one only her mother and Maria had any clue about.

"Coffee?" Jimmy asked pleasantly from the corner by the sink.

Sam squeaked before slapping a hand over her

159

mouth, trying to cover the sounds of her panicked breathing. "Um, sure." She welcomed anything that might give her a chance to collect herself. Maybe it would even stop him from staring at her.

Setting down his cup on the counter beside his hip, Jimmy reached up and pulled one off a hook under the cabinet. "How do you like it?" He lifted the carafe and poured.

"Black is fine." She forced a smile, her chest still burning. She pulled out a chair and fell into it, dropping her forehead into her hands.

The cup clunked down on the table in front of her and Sam reached for it, her mouth parched. Jimmy's hand flashed out lightning quick and grabbed her wrist, his grasp light but solid. A small cry escaped her lips as her heart banged painfully against her ribs, black fog appeared at the periphery of her vision threatening a blackout.

"Just relax." He spoke gently, flashing his teeth in a grin. Wow, he was pretty close up.

Of their own will her eyes went to where his strong hand encircled her limb. Shaky, she couldn't form any words to point out the ludicrousness of his request. The most she could manage was a high-pitched, borderline hysterical laugh.

"Easy *chica*." His hand didn't loosen though his words were soft.

Trying to force her body to relax was impossible and Sam was rapidly losing the means by which she could struggle as her shallow breaths robbed her of precious oxygen. The blackness closed in, reinforcing the terror gripping her. When her arm went limp in

Jimmy's grasp, he slid his fingers around to the underside and applied pressure with his middle finger to the soft underpart of her wrist as well as pushing against the meaty base of her thumb with his index finger. The weight on her chest eased and she greedily gulped a huge lungful of air.

"You're a nervous one, huh *chica*?" He smiled and shrugged at her awed expression. "It figures." His other hand covered her trapped one and he gave it a gentle pat then rub. "The ones that seem like they can handle anything are usually wound too tight."

Sam stared at the startlingly astute man and drew a shaky breath. "And the ones who seem like they don't see anything are usually the keenest observers?" she shot back not unkindly.

He cocked his head and a sly grin spread slowly across his face. "I like you, *chica*." He pointed at her. "So are you goin' to tell me why you busted in here like somebody was chasin' you? Were you looking for something? Or maybe some*one*?" Jimmy raised his cup to his lips while his eyes stayed with hers.

Sam gaped at his insinuation. "Marcus told me to stay with Justin, er, I mean Sergeant Shaw and to be there when he woke up so he wasn't afraid and I fell asleep. I was looking for him, that's all."

"The Sarge can handle himself. He went out a bit ago lookin' just fine." He lowered his mug to his chest, still not averting his gaze. Sam felt a new kinship with a lab rat. "He's had to do this part alone before. Marcus just wanted you out of the way." He shrugged his shoulders and added mildly. "Besides, what man would want to wake up to Marcus's ugly mug when he could open his eyes and see your pretty face?"

His reassurance of Justin's wellbeing let her finally shake the last of her nerves. Then his insinuation hit and she felt a need to remind him of a detail he had forgotten. "Until three days ago I had a boyfriend. Remember?"

Jimmy's eyes crinkled over his cup, back up for another sip. He was getting a kick out of her being flustered. She could feel the flush in her cheeks. "Is that why we keep catching you two in bed together? One of you was in your underwear too." He wagged his eyebrows.

Offense borne of guilt sent Sam shooting out of her chair, her hands bracing on the table. "It's not like that! Justin has kept me safe during this nightmare; he died for me for God's sake. It's the least I can do to make sure he's okay."

Empty palm and coffee hands both out in supplication Jimmy chuckled, his expression anything but apologetic. "Hey don't get mad at me, I just call it like I see it." He eyed her speculatively, his features growing thoughtful. The steam from the mug curled and wafted around his face lending him the mien of a holy man extolling wisdom. "You know, I knew this guy once. His wife, she died in a car accident and he was real tore up. Not because he missed her but because he *didn't.*" He barely blinked. "See they'd been at each other non-stop for years and they were finally gonna get a divorce, only she died before he filed. When he met this other lady." Jimmy shook his head and rolled his eyes skyward. "Man, she was something. Totally hot for him too." He lifted his shoulders again. "He didn't go for it, said it wouldn't be right. Bad timing and all." Jimmy's dark head shook back and forth. "He never found nobody like her again." Setting down his cup with a resounding thunk on the counter, he headed up the stairs calling over his shoulder. "Sometimes you just gotta go

162

for it you know? You got no idea what's around the next corner." His footsteps faded and Sam sank down into her chair.

She was sitting at the table studying a bowl of grapes she'd been plucking pieces of stem from from for the past half hour, her head gone from tangled to borderline numb while she listened to the crickets through the open windows when the screen door opened and Justin's body filled the doorframe, backlit by the porch light.

"You're up," he said simply. No comment about having woken up in bed with her though what she expected, she wasn't sure. His lack of mention of being dead once, almost twice in the last twenty-four hours seemingly stranger than the fact that it'd happened at all.

"Jimmy made coffee." She pointed at the pot. "I could heat up a cup for you."

"That'd be good." He came in and walked straight to the sink next to her to wash up. Walking past the table he tossed the tshirt in his hand over the back of one of the chairs.

Sam turned to say something and caught an eyeful of his bare upper body. His attention was on something he was scrubbing at on one of his fingers giving her the opportunity to look at him. His scars were less visible in the low light and he looked like a regular guy. She had a flash of cooking beside him, having her parents over for dinner or Maria and her boyfriend Tim for a double date. She felt the image settle in and Sam froze, staring at him agog. *What the hell is happening to me?*

Sam, for the first time in her life, wanted someone. Not merely on a physical level. That had happened before, that was easier. She wanted him to *be with her.* She wanted to know him, wanted to feel him lying against her in bed at night, to come home to tell him about nothing at all. The revelation floored her leaving her able only to stare dumbly at him, this virtual stranger. And *now* of all times. Dead boyfriend, men coming after her, some potentially fatal biological weapon everyone and his psycho brother wanted to get his hands on hidden in her trash, and *now* she thought she found the one? *If* that one didn't decide to kill her first. *Only me.* Instantly she felt the familiar stab of guilt. *Poor you for being sad. Paul would probably like to still be breathing.*

Justin sensed her eyes on him and met her gaze, brows pulled together in confusion. "What?" His voice was abrupt, shockingly loud against the gentleness of the night sounds that had filled the room before his entry.

"I'm, uh, I'm glad you're okay," she choked out. "And I'm sorry I wasn't there when you woke up." She dropped her eyes, fearing he could somehow see her shameful thoughts. "Marcus said it would be easier if you weren't alone." She stared at her bare feet and freshly painted coral toenails. She'd painted them on her birthday. Oddly the memory of that day brought with it a few bars of her mother's voice singing and Sam felt the pricking of tears behind her eyelids.

"It's fine," Justin reassured her, his drawl creeping in to soften his words. "It comes with the territory."

"As long as you're okay." She winced when her voice cracked and she sniffed. Hand to her mouth, Sam wheeled and ran up the stairs.

"Sam," he called after her but she didn't stop until she was in her room with the door shut.

Flinging herself on the bed, Sam let grief overtake

her.

Sam stayed in her room through the night and into the next day. At one point there was a knock on her door an announcement of breakfast. She didn't answer. When Jimmy beckoned her to come out for lunch she grunted her answer of "not hungry." When her body demanded she relieve herself she crept to the door, listened to the silence, and hurried to relieve herself before rushing back to her room and the safety of her bed. At nightfall the gentle knock was followed by the click of the handle releasing and the door being pushed open. Choosing the coward's way, Sam closed her eyes and pulled up the blanket to cover her face.

A plate scraped on the nightstand just before he cleared his throat. "We've been watching your apartment."

Justin. She continued to feign sleep.

"They've been in and tossed the place but they must not have found it since there's still a car out front, watching."

Sam felt an odd sense of relief. They'd been through her apartment and hadn't found it. That meant she still had some value to Justin and his team. That meant she was safe here. For now. There was that thought again. *For now.* Everything felt temporary: her mother's safety, Sam's situation. It was like she was floating in some sort of limbo, waiting for her life to return to normal. *And how great was my normal?* A job she was good at but didn't get excited over, a boyfriend who was good to her but she didn't love, and friends who she went out with but never confided in. Except to some extent Maria, though even then that was limited. *I wasn't exactly setting the world on fire.* But she knew what to expect from day to day and no one was dying or getting put in a coma because of her.

"We can't afford to let them know it's us who's got you." Justin interrupted her thoughts, taking the no-nonsense tone of a leader commanding his troops. "And by now they know it's us." He paused, waiting for her to poke her head out but she didn't. "You'll stay here while we wait for a break before we can go in there and you get it for us."

There it was. She was worth something only as long as she provided them a tie to what they wanted most. Her father and that stupid lab. Granted, she couldn't fault them for wanting to shut it down. Having seen the reality of their brand of immortality she wouldn't wish it on anyone. And what if it was used on other soldiers? On anyone? No one deserved to go through that kind of pain and suffering over and over again. She saw his disoriented eyes when he woke in the woods and felt her heart clench. He only wanted her for what she could give him for his mission. *And this is the man I think I want? It has to be something to do with adrenaline and threats of death.*

When Sam finally found her voice and managed to ask, barely above a whisper, "What happens to me then?" he was gone. The metal latched and the door was closed. Pushing the blanket down her eyes fell on the light green fiesta ware on her nightstand. The sandwich and apple stared back. Sam sighed, rolling over and curling into herself for the night.

Ch. 24

Justin closed Sam's door and let his head fall forward. *The mission is the most important thing.* The soldier in him knew he was playing it smart. Sam was the only person who knew where her father's package was and that they had her meant they, in turn, had it. That didn't help him feel like less of an asshole when he watched her lay curled up, pretending to sleep while he pointed out to her she was a means to an end for his team. The poor woman was going through hell and they weren't doing anything to help that. Jimmy had expressed an interest in her, maybe he could let him spend a little time with her. *No!* The violence of his reaction to even the idea of another man with her sent a shock through him. He had to remind himself she was an asset, nothing more.

Footsteps came up the stairs and his head came up. "Marcus."

"Figured I'd find you here." Marcus's brown eyes were suspicious. "What were you doing?"

"Brought her dinner." He could see Marcus tighten and defended his actions. "She's no use to us if she's starved and too delirious to remember where she put it."

"Hunh." Marcus wasn't entirely convinced but had his own news to impart. "Jimmy's out checking the perimeter and his tripwires. I'm going to make a trip to town for ammo and a few things he needs, can you keep an eye on things?" He let his gaze slip to the door over Justin's shoulder. "If you can tear yourself away?"

Gritting his teeth, Justin gave a jerking nod. "Sure."

With a grunt Marcus turned and went back down the stairs. Justin went to Jimmy's room where the monitoring equipment was housed. Being a bit of a control freak himself and an insomniac Jimmy insisted on keeping it in his room. "It's my baby, I'll watch her," was his justification. It didn't matter enough to anyone else to argue with him.

It was just about midnight when Justin heard a door open and footsteps in the hall. All too familiar with the heavy footfalls of his teammates Justin knew immediately it was her. Her steps were halting as she first stepped out and the door to the bathroom shut. Water turned on and the metal rings slid on the shower rod. Images of her naked body; water running down her breasts, stomach, and lower caused his dick to twitch. He'd had a few passing fantasies of what that body looked like under her clothes after he'd felt it pressed against him back at her apartment. He *was* a man after all and it *had* been a while since he'd used that part of his anatomy for anything other than pissing. *She just buried her boyfriend, jackass.* Plus there was the fact that the last two times he'd been in the same room she'd run from him crying and refused to come out of her blankets. Sex was a fantasy, and one he didn't need clouding his thoughts. *We're close this time.* He couldn't mess it up. Marcus would accept nothing but success and, truth be told, so would Jimmy. And Justin owed them that.

They'd lost everything that made them who they were. Friends, family, all of their connections had to be severed when they'd been declared dead. And Mills. He'd been taken from them by enemies claiming allegiance to the same nation. The worst betrayal of all. He owed Mills vengeance. *Henry Mills wouldn't want vengeance. He wouldn't want any of this.* Roughly he cast it all aside and leaned forward, staring at the bank of monitors while he turned up the chatter in his headphones resting on one ear, leaving the other open to listen for danger in the house.

Sam woke to a loud clap of thunder. Hopping up, she rushed to shut the windows in her bedroom only to stare, blinking sleepily at the lawn and trees already glowing with the dawn's first rays. At first her sleep-addled brain couldn't make sense of why there was thunder and no clouds.

Crack! Crack! Crack!

The first pop made her drop and each after had her curling tighter and tighter into a fetal ball as she realized it wasn't a storm but gunfire she was hearing. Before she could crawl off to a dark closet and hide from the newest wave of assassins, Jimmy's voice floated in through the open window.

"Three shots, one hole." He was laughing. "Pay up, Marcus."

Climbing up on her knees Sam gripped the windowsill as her eyes searched the area below. There, at the edge of the trees, hidden mostly by overhanging branches in full foliage, a flash of movement. Watching a few moments more and she caught sight of Marcus stepping out, his hand messing in the back of his waistband. Apparently there was room in the back of his desert camo for a handgun. Something she would keep in mind from here out. The reminder that her captors were armed and comfortable with lethal force sent a spike of adrenaline through her.

A creak in the hall brought her heart to a near standstill just as knuckles rapped softly on the door.

"Come in." Well, that's what she meant to say.

What came out sounded more like a goose being strangled, "Gaaugh ahh."

The door swung open and Justin stood in the doorway dressed in olive green cargo pants over black boots, taking in her kneeling form as she overlooked the men below. A crease formed in his brow and Justin took a step inside, his arms crossing in a way that stressed his tan tshirt in the chest and sleeves. "Are you okay?"

Sam clamored to her feet and brushed off her knees. "Um, hey, yeah. What's up?"

To his credit, he kept his expression plain and gave no indication it might be a little weird for a grown woman in her pajamas to crouch at a window on a late summer morning, spying on people. "I thought you might want to know we haven't seen any movement from the guys on your apartment so we're here at least another day."

It was hard to hide her disappointment. She might not be especially eager to see what Justin and his men would do to get her to give up the hidden tube or what they might do once they had it, but she *knew* what the other side would do. The lesser of two evils, her nana would say.

"Can I shoot?" she blurted out.

He blinked. "You want to shoot?"

"Yeah, sure." She couldn't tell if he was displeased or just surprised at her odd request. She shrugged, trying to put him at ease. "If we're here all day I'd rather be doing something than sitting around wondering." Sam didn't want to give voice to what she figured would tie up her mind. What *had been* tying up her thoughts since she'd gotten there. *Has my mom woken up yet? Is she going to be okay?*

Seeming to read into her request, Justin softened and let his arms fall to his sides. "Sure. It's Jimmy's turn on the monitors, I was heading down there myself."

"Uh," Sam glanced down at her pink cami top and pink and white polka dot shorts and back up, crossing her arms over the nipples that chose that moment to wake up and come to the party. "I should get dressed."

A hint of something crossed his eyes too fast to quite get a handle on before it was gone, and he took a step back. "Meet me down there."

Before she could reply he was gone. In a scramble, Sam threw on a pair of short jean shorts and a light purple tshirt with pale pink swirls on one shoulder. It was from her favorite snowboard shop she and Maria stopped in at regularly to pick up funky clothes and earrings. Sam's job might be conservative but she had a few little flairs in which she still indulged. Cool, funky tshirts were one; kicky little tennies were another. Yeah, real wild. Maria often rolled her eyes at that one. A light purple and grey plaid pair of DCs worked with today's ensemble and Sam thought they were plenty cool.

A quick trip to the bathroom to run a brush through her hair and kill whatever died in her mouth overnight and she headed downstairs. Her step slowed when she hit the screen door and hesitantly pushed it open.

***

The door's hinges gave her away and Justin locked eyes with Marcus.

"What's she doing here?" Marcus' expression hardened.

Justin crossed his arms and settled his weight in his hips. He was ready should Marcus decide to take a swing. He kept his voice low and soothing, hoping to avoid a confrontation if possible. There was no reason for her to bear witness to their infighting and see possible weaknesses within their unit. "Tell me what it hurts to be friendly with her. She's scared, alone, and looking for a friendly face." He waited, watching his words fall on deaf ears.

Jimmy was uncharacteristically quiet. He merely leaned against the trunk of a tall tree a few feet away looking on in what appeared to be mild interest.

Marcus stared, unblinking for a long time before finally he exhaled, shaking his head. "You're not thinking clearly, Sarge. A night of her cuddling up with you telling you what a great big protector you are doesn't undo everything her dad's done."

"I'm not forgetting what *any* of them have done."

"Hi." Sam stopped a stone's throw from where the two men faced off. "I'm sorry. If it's a problem, I can go back in. I just didn't want to sit in there all day with nothing to do but think about," she took a deep breath, "about everything."

With a hard glare at Marcus, Justin broke off to give her a warmer reception. "Sure. Marcus was just heading in to take over the monitors." He offered her a small smile. "Jimmy, how about you go grab us another box of rounds for the Glock?"

"Can do, Sarge." Jimmy walked back with Marcus leaving the two of them alone.

Moving over to the double-stacked bales of straw covered with a simple blanket they used as a table, Justin watched her from his periphery. Pretending to focus on checking the weapons, he let his hands move over the weapons lying on and against their table as he watched her in his periphery. The woman was clearly nervous but good at putting up a brave front. He imagined she'd gotten used to that having grown up without her father to protect her from the slights of youth and even into adulthood. *Except her dad is the Doc. She was probably better off without that sort of influence in her life.*

That thought halted his hands as he thumbed all but two rounds from the magazine. Justin recognized the danger his feeling empathy for their hostage held and thrust it away with the mental image of Mills' dead body.

"Have you ever handled a gun before?" He asked over his shoulder, press checking the 9 mm in his hands.

"Yes, some."

Justin turned, gun in hand and caught the flicker of fear in her eyes before she jerked her gaze back to his face and hid it behind what he was coming to think of as her soldier face. It was certainly something he was familiar with; he'd seen it often in battle. Another full magazine went in his pocket.

"Come here," he waved her over, holding the gun muzzle up. Sam approached and he noted the ease with which she accepted the weapon. One hand remained beside the barrel, preventing her from swinging toward him should she get any ideas. "Finger is never on the trigger unless your sights are lined up and you don't point the muzzle at anything you don't intend to shoot. Got it?" He let his eyes wander from their hands on the gun back to her profile.

Her jaw was tight and her face pale. A whisper of a breeze ruffled her short hair and a section blew from behind her ear to brush against her cheek. When she turned to him, bringing their faces close, he heard her breath catch and saw a flash of pink as she ran her tongue over her lower lip. Willing to be called to action, his dick twitched. Sam's dark brown eyes widened and Justin noted flecks of gold he hadn't seen before.

Sam broke first. Twisting her neck, she nodded toward the human shaped targets mounted on more straw bales at the other end of their range. One was 6 yards, one at 25, and the third was at 40. "Which target do you want me to use?"

Curious her response, Justin shrugged. "Your choice."

Sam squared her shoulders to the targets, positioned her feet, and raised the gun in a two handed grip. Justin stepped behind her shoulder making it impossible for her to "accidentally" shoot him. She tipped her face toward him, a silent request.

"Whenever you're ready."

He watched her closely, sensitive to her steady breathing, her hands on the gun applying enough pressure to handle the kick but not white knuckling, and he caught the finger taking up the slack on the trigger as she aimed, took another breath and pulled.

Pop. Two seconds. *Pop. Click.* Empty.

"Your position's good. You just need to take a few more practice shots and you'll hit it."

"I did."

Squinting, he examined both the 6 and 25-yard targets and didn't see any new holes. Just the few dead on shots Jimmy put in this morning. "No, you didn't. Those Jimmy's shots."

"Look at the far one." She held the gun muzzle up by her shoulder and jutted her delicate chin toward the 40-yard target.

"Gawd damn," Justin drawled, forgetting himself temporarily. "Sorry," he flicked his eyes over in time to catch her smile. Then he blinked at the far target, now sporting two new holes where a man's stomach and shoulder would be. Not a sniper, but considering the distance they were respectable shots and would certainly do the job in real life. "How often do you go shooting?"

Pink colored her cheeks and Justin felt his dick again, reminding him it was there and willing to work. Stepping sideways he did the move and shift all guys mastered with their first boner.

"I used to date a guy who wanted to be a cop. We'd go to the range Friday nights."

Just as surprising as her time with a gun was his reaction to the revelation that another man had taught her. Probably stood behind her with his dick pressed to her ass, touching her arms as he adjusted her position. *What?*

"You must have gone a lot. That's some decent shooting."

175

Again her cheeks colored and he had to shift again, this time combined with a hand adjustment disguised as reaching for the magazine in his pocket. "Not really. We were only together a few months but he said I was a natural."

"Why'd you break up?" His question surprised them both. Her eyes went wide and her mouth parted before she shut it and her lips tightened.

"It just didn't work out." She held out a hand for the magazine he was holding. "Does that one have more than two rounds?"

Grinning at the attitude she was throwing at him, Justin handed it over.

Knock, knock

He heard blankets being thrown back and Justin felt a quiver of anticipation in his gut.

"Justin?" She opened the door, her hand rubbing at sleepy eyes. "What's up? Are we going?"

For a minute he forgot what he'd come to ask. Sam's lithe form was clearly visible through her tight grey tank and pink and white polka dotted girl boxers. Judging from what he could see through the thin material either she was cold or he'd surprised her. *Might have to start jumping out from behind corners.*

"Have you come to take me to my apartment?"

The dread he heard brought him out of his sex-starved depravity and he ran a hand through his too-long hair. He didn't like it so long and as disguises went it

176

wasn't much more than glasses on Clark Kent, but when you were on the run every second you could buy could be the one that mattered.

"No. Still no movement there." And standing there, her in her pajamas and him in his blue tshirt and grey sport shorts, Justin got bashful. *Bashful!* Like he was asking a girl on a date. Clearing his throat, he shifted his weight to the other foot and met her gaze evenly. "I wondered if you wanted to spar." Her brows shot up and her bow shaped lips fell open. "Jimmy's on monitors and Marcus ran to town." He shifted again. "And I know you kickbox so…"

"Uh, sure." Sam recovered herself and glanced down. "Give me a minute?"

He nodded. "I'll meet you in the kitchen."

Twenty minutes later, a piece of toast and glass of juice later, Sam faced Justin across a flat patch of grass in the yard. Her sparring outfit wasn't much different than her pajamas, he noted with a mixture of pleasure and nervous anticipation. The tank was fitted and pink and her girl version of sport shorts were black and significantly shorter than his. They revealed those shapely legs that although short were enough to do the trick for any healthy man with a pulse. It occurred to him this might not be the best idea. And then she moved.

Sam was fast. Justin felt her fist glance off his ear as he dodged almost too late. She spun with him and followed up with a round kick to his side.

"You're good."

She grinned and moved again.

Justin sparred with her, having to pull back a bit considering she was at least fifty pounds lighter than his usual opponents and he actually *could* hurt *her* if he went all out like he could with Marcus and Jimmy. Another advantage to their "condition" was quick healing. A concussion or deep bone bruise was gone in a few minutes for them. Sam would be feeling it for weeks. Close to an hour later they were back where they started, dripping wet with hands on knees and blowing hard when they heard Marcus pull up in the truck.

His vibe was unmistakable, fury spilled from the cab of the black four door pickup before he even stepped out around the front carrying his bags. "You teaching her how to dismantle the perimeter alarms too?" he growled.

"I haven't taught her anything she doesn't know." Justin straightened up.

Sam glanced back and forth between them and stood as well. "I'm gonna hit the shower." She hustled at a near jog back to the house.

"What the fuck, Shaw?" He spat, dropping any illusion of Justin's superior rank. Justin wasn't surprised; actually he was amazed it hadn't happened before now. "You're playing a dangerous game, man."

"What the hell else am I supposed to do with her while we're waiting? Stick her in a room and shove bread and water at her a couple times a day?" He put his hands on his hips and hissed back, keeping his voice low so it didn't carry through the open windows.

"It'd be better than playing best friends with her. Or is there something else you're after?"

Justin's voice dropped to a near whisper. "If we treat her like an animal, how are we any better than

178

them?"

Marcus's teeth ground together and his nostrils flared. Eyes narrowed it wouldn't have been a shock if steam started coming out of his ears. "Just remember the mission, *Sarge.*" Turning on his heel, he stalked back to the house.

Ch. 25

A week. That was how long it had been since Sam's last workout with Justin. Two since her world turned upside down. After their faceoff in the yard, which had been over before she could get to her room to spy on, Justin steered well clear of her. They all rattled around in the house ignoring the oppressive silence and each other for the most part. Flooring her, the day after he'd had a shout down with Justin, Marcus showed up at her door and wordlessly dropped a handful of paperbacks on her nightstand.

"Entertain yourself," he grunted and was gone.

She had. Good thing too since the rains started mid week stranding her in the house. Whenever she came across one of them she asked if she could call her mother and was always told the same thing. "No contact. Too risky." It was the implication that the risk was not just to her, but to her mom, that kept Sam from calling. That and the spotty reception. One of their Sat phones was her only option and they never left those lying around.

She suspected the men went running, or at least Justin and Marcus did, but she was never invited. She only saw soaking wet shoes by the door when she went in the kitchen to prepare her meals. Sam considered asking to go on a run to stretch her legs and breathe some fresh air but figured they wouldn't let her go alone nor would they want to go with her.

So now she sat on the edge of her bed staring at the watery sunset, more like watching someone slide a dimmer slowly down until the room went dark. Her hands rested idly on the open book on her lap and she felt her legs jerk for the thirtieth time in an hour. Hopping up, she threw the book aside and strode out of her room. Maybe if she caught Justin alone she could convince him to take her for a quick run before full dark, or a quick sparring session. Nothing huge, just *something.* She had to do something, anything physical or she was going to explode. She made it as far as the kitchen and came to a halt when she heard the door creak and Justin walked in.

Drenched, his sun-bleached hair was plastered to his forehead and his black tshirt neatly displayed every ripple on his chest and down his abdomen. To call it flat would be a disservice to those muscles he'd obviously carved into such painstaking perfection. Her hands twitched to touch them and she fisted them at her sides.

"Out for a run?" Her voice was breathy and she swallowed, looking past his intense scrutiny of her at the dark sky and hearing the maddening sound of rain for the fourth day in a row. She caught a glimpse of the half full coffee carafe on the counter and latched on to the excuse for being out of her room and opportunity to wrap her hands around something other than his neck and pulling him in to feel him against her body. *I've got some serious cabin fever.* "I came down for some coffee." She didn't bother to turn on the lights, the dim light coming through from outside was enough to see in the familiar space.

Pouring a cold cup for herself she put it in the microwave, pressed the buttons, and spun her body to lean her back against the stove, waiting for the timer.

"Yes."

"Huh?" His response didn't track with the direction her thoughts had taken.

"I was out for a run." He continued to stare at her. Though not as detached as the first time they'd met, he

181

remained untouchable. Apparently Justin's aloof Sergeant persona didn't leave him unless they were upstairs. Or maybe Marcus had succeeded in taking away her only "friend" here.

Ding

To stretch her legs, to push herself to exhaustion; she was starved for that mind numbing endorphin rush that only hard work could produce. Her shoulders drooped and a low moan rumbled in her throat. "I'd kill to work up a good sweat." As soon as the words left her lips, Sam felt her cheeks heat up. She watched his features harden and felt like an ass. She wondered if he would stop her if she ran outside, begging someone to shoot her right then.

He reached a hand up, past her head, and leaned in. Sam felt her breath hitch. *He thinks I was hitting on him. Oh my gosh! I should say something. What do I say, "I'm not turning you down, please don't kill me?"* What that said about her should she let him touch her so soon after Paul, or at all, she couldn't let solidify. The connotations alone without any actual words tied to them were enough to tear her to nothing.

When Justin leaned forward Sam stopped breathing. Watching him come closer she forgot to tell him she hadn't been hitting on him, she couldn't be. She wasn't the sort of woman who came onto strangers two weeks after she met them. No. Instead of being smart and strong, two things she prided herself on, she closed her eyes and waited. The sound of the microwave door jumping open with a spring loaded "pop" reached her ears, and her eyes cracked open. A quick peek upward offered only a glimpse of the underside of his jaw; no hint that he'd seen her misinterpretation of the "lean" and she reached both hands up to rub her heated face. Mortified, she felt a burning flush paint her cheeks.

182

"If you want." His voice was soft, her upstairs Justin. The puff of air on her cheek also told her if she opened her eyes he would be right there. Sam refused to open her eyes. "I'd work out with you."

There was something there, something she intuitively knew meant more than he was willing to spar with her or run. Justin was offering her what her conscience refused she ask for. Fingers brushed against the point of her jaw before slipping into her hair. Sam felt her head pulled forward and lips touched hers. Electricity jolted through her, her eyes popped open and she gasped. Justin's warm gaze caught fire and he opened his lips, crashing his mouth down on hers. Sam gave guilt a shove and let desire run free.

His hands cupped her face, holding Sam where he wanted her while he explored her mouth. The only parts of their bodies touching, it wasn't enough. Arching her back, Sam let her breasts fall into his hard chest and a low rumble erupted in his chest as water from his shirt wicked onto hers. Her hands, finally able to roam free on that body, did. Her fingers traced over his wet shirt, feeling the hard lines of his flat stomach, the angles of his wide shoulders. Roaming lower, she let her fingers slip under his waistband and trace from hip bone to the top of his backside.

Justin made a noise, purely masculine and one every woman recognizes. Sam's lips curled into a smile against his mouth and he pulled back enough for her to see he wasn't in the mood for jokes. Smile dying, Sam's lower muscles clenched and she molded her body against his. Her silent acceptance of his equally unspoken demand was met with another growl just before he dropped. One hand went around her shoulders, the other behind her knees and Sam gasped as she was lifted, pressed close enough to feel his muscles move against her. An eager shiver ran through her as Sam imagined feeling his muscles shift over her.

He took her to his room where he set her at the edge of the bed and gave her shoulder a gentle nudge. Taking it, Sam let her body fall back to sit on the mattress where she was granted a front row seat to Justin's own strip show. The shirt came off, hitting the ground with a slap, followed by sport shorts leaving him in dark blue boxer briefs while he finished toeing off his runners. Leaning one hand on the mattress beside her, he ran his tongue across her lips while he pulled off his socks. The silence, the lack of sweet talk, or any at all, had Sam hyperaware of her body and his. The tingling sensation as he stroked the underside of her breast, his thumb tracing her nipple before he gave it a soft pinch. She caught her breath and helped him when he reached the bottom of her shirt and together they yanked it over her head. Not a word as he pressed a calloused hand against her chest and gently pushed her back. Sam's shorts were tugged down and she lifted her hips to let him. Her fingers slipped into his boxers and he helped her take them off. Sam took a few seconds to admire the body about to cover her. Scars criss crossed it, marking him as a warrior, and Sam decided she'd never seen anything so beautiful. Eyes meeting his, she lay back and shivered when he covered her. Rain cooled flesh quickly heated as their bodies brushed and pressed together. Gasps as they explored each other were replaced by soft moans of pleasure and finally their panting as they caught their breath.

Sam held reality and the guilt for what her actions was sure to bring at bay while Justin's fingers ran through her hair, brushing it back. Eyes drifting closed, she didn't sleep as he head rested on his chest, but she let herself dream of what could be.

Ch. 26

"Getting something, Shaw?" Marcus' cutting words brought Justin's head up and Sam's entire body went rigid.

All too quickly, Sam squeaked and yanked the blanket around herself. "I'll let you two talk." Sam flew from the room and down the hall like she was on fire.

Justin said nothing as he watched her flee. He waited for his man, correction, his former man, to lay into him. And a part of him knew he deserved it. What had he done?

"Great plan, Shaw. Seduce it out of her," Marcus snapped heatedly as he stalked from one end of the room to the other. "It's a win-win for *you*."

Justin's face jerked around, glaring angrily at his accuser. "You're out of line, Marcus."

"Am I?" He was unfazed by the anger of his former sergeant. "We're this close to ending this thing and you pick now to start chasing a girl?" He pointed at the direction Sam had taken. "And not just any girl, *that* girl."

"Marcus, you know I'm not going to let anything interfere with getting Doc." Unable to have this conversation laying down and naked, Justin pointed and Marcus, frowning, tossed him his shorts before he stormed from the room. Justin yanked on his shorts and followed Marcus down the stairs. A quick glance and he saw that Sam had her door closed. He willed her to stay inside. Marcus was in a mood and he didn't want her to hear or possibly even get caught in the crossfire.

"What happens when she doesn't want to give up Daddy and keeps that package tucked away for leverage, hmm? Blood's thick, don't discount it." Stopping in the kitchen, his voice crept up again as his anger erupted. "Are you still willing to do whatever it takes to make her give it up? Are you willing to take her piece by piece while she screams and begs you to stop?" Marcus moved closer, the veins growing prominent on his forehead as he pushed. Justin stood his ground. "And what if we get the Doc right here in front of us?" he pointed vehemently at the floor, muscles cording in his neck and arms as his tension mounted. "If the Doc refuses to cooperate and won't give us the info on who he's working for, will you be able to use her to get him to listen?" Marcus stopped himself, chest heaving, nostrils flaring from the passion in his speech. He paused, working to sound more reasonable, appealing to Justin's sense of responsibility. "Have you forgotten the promise you made after those bastards killed Mills? After they took *our* lives away from us? Doc's weak stomach made him let us go, but it doesn't take away from the fact that he's in bed with these guys, that he's responsible for the whole program, and now he's got the only remaining sample. We wipe him and his bosses out and it's gone. This is it, Shaw. Is a little piece worth shitting all over that?"

Justin too struggled with his emotions. He knew what he was *supposed* to be saying. He was *supposed* to be agreeing with Marcus' single-minded focus; if that involved spilling Sam's blood and making her scream, cry, and plead for mercy then so be it. They'd done it on a few jobs before for information nowhere near this vital. It wasn't something he was proud of but sometimes found necessary when dealing with bad guys hiding information on more bad guys. But he couldn't. God help him, he couldn't. Not with this woman. He'd felt it even before what happened upstairs. Now that he had tasted her, he knew he would protect her no matter

186

the cost to him.

Marcus saw Justin's answer and roared, clutching his head with both hands. "I can't *believe* you! You're cool for how many missions? I've stuck with you when I *hated* you because no one's got a better head when it comes to strategy and here we are, the biggest mission of our lives and you pick *now* to screw it all up? God damn it Shaw. Forget this one. After we're done we can go anywhere you want and I'll get you *two* girls." He held up two fingers for emphasis. Spittle was forming in the corner of his mouth the more he shouted, the whites of his eyes flashing in the dim lighting.

If he didn't defend himself he was going to lose the loyalty of his men and Marcus was right about that much. They needed to be at their best right now. He spat back, telling Marcus what he needed to hear even if it turned his stomach. "I told you, this goes easier if she trusts me. If she thinks I'm with her she'll give up the package. We get word out and boom, we have Doc on a platter. If she doesn't cooperate I'll be the first in line to make sure she does. Is that enough for you?" Justin had his back to the stairs and hadn't seen where Sam stopped on the steps at Marcus' initial outburst.

***

Sam's feet froze at the top of the stairs when she heard Marcus' accusation and she lowered her seat to the step to listen since it was clear they were discussing her. Quickly pulling on shorts and a shirt, she'd planned to come down and at least be in the room while they discussed going forward. She'd find out their plan and maybe give them the sample once and for all. If they stood with Justin they couldn't be all bad. Surely they knew what to do with the stupid thing and their plan had to be better than hers, which pretty much consisted of

187

hiding it while she waited to see who tried to wheedle it out of her. But she'd arrived in time to catch most of their conversation. She heard every horrible, gut-wrenching thing Marcus said about her father. Her hand flew to her mouth, bile rising at his detailed torture scenario he described for her. And then, most crushing of all were the words that came from Justin's own mouth.

He would be able and *willing* to hurt her for that damned package. He would kill her with a clear conscience, if necessary. Her body sagged hard against the wall beside her, too heavy to move. It had all been a lie, his kindness an act. His mouth hadn't been all that fooled her. Her fingers touched where his hand had caressed her cheeks less than ten minutes ago. He was no different than those men who'd come to kill her. No, he was different. *He* lied to her. At least the other killers were up front about what they planned to do to her. She'd never felt more alone.

Rage bubbled up when she thought of that stupid cylinder and the needless pain it had caused. She wished she'd never seen it. If she could go back, she would chuck the whole thing in the dumpster without ever having opened it or maybe she should have given it to the two killers in the parking lot and been done with it. *Someone* had to get it eventually and clearly Justin and his lot were no better than the scientists and their hired thugs at this point. They were all killers.

It always came back to that rotten package and her father. That was where this whole thing started. Marcus said it would draw out her father but to go home would also bring the other side down on her. Hell, they were sitting at her apartment right now according to surveillance. She again considered the benefits of a disguise. That cylinder was all that stood between her and a painful death. She could use it as leverage. And even if the other side got to her first she'd be able to lead

Justin, no, *Sergeant Shaw* and his crew to them when they followed her. Let them kill each other and that might end this whole thing.

Marcus' words about her father stung. Sam hadn't wanted to consider the possibility that her father was a truly *bad* man. He'd been an absentee father and a less than ideal husband, yet a small part of her had remained faithful to him, thinking of him out there somewhere doing important work. That the real reason he left them was to do something great, even if he couldn't handle the burden a family offered.

That he had a hand in the experiments that caused harm and death to human beings, was working to devise a chemical that would allow men to be killed repeatedly in the name of war, drove another stake through her already dying heart. A tiny voice, that of a nine-year-old little girl who still loved her dad, told her she couldn't believe what these men were saying. Sam resolved to see her father one more time. She had to ask him about his part in all of this, hear the words from his lips. After that, she would figure out what to do with the god awful cylinder. At present she was thinking a very deep hole befitting the toxic waste it was.

Everything in her told her to go home. Sure, she wanted to curl into her bed and hide under the covers until the end of time but more importantly, and more useful, Steven would find her there. Somehow she knew that just as the killers and Justin's men were watching her place, so was her father. Justin would follow her, she was sure but if she was careful she might be able to buy a few minutes with her father before they found her. *I put him on the same level as Paul. I thought he'd died for me but that was nothing for him.* She cringed at the memory of his body falling, covered in blood. *It was no worse than taking a punch to get a better position in a fight.* It was a good strategy; she'd done it herself in the ring. Shutting down the ache in her heart the thought of Justin's duplicity sent through her, Sam brought the shades down on her emotional side and fell back on what she *knew* wouldn't lie. Logic and reason. The same practicality that served her professionally would let her keep her wits to see this through.

The ground outside was far too rough to try to leave in her present state, barefoot, and she needed her cell phone. She didn't have a charger and kept it turned off to guarantee a charge. Since she'd been willing to keep it off and not call her mother, they hadn't argued about her keeping it. She sneaked backward up another stair to her room, hoping she could make it out the back door while the two were distracted. Once she cleared the house she could make it to the road. During her time with them she'd paid attention to the roads, noting which ones were busiest. There was one that looped out away from the property that had the most traffic. Not much, but enough to provide a chance for a ride to a young woman with "car trouble". She would aim for that.

"You don't mean it." Marcus lowered his voice. "She got to you with that whole doe eyed, lost girl act. That woman is our key to Doc. We're running out of time and if you can't man up and do what needs to be done, then I will. This is over, now." He got as far as the first step and Sam held her breath; all he had to do was look up and he would see her.

"No." Justin put his hand on his shoulder. "Marcus listen, let me talk to her…"

That was all he got out before Marcus spun, bringing his fist with him. It connected with his jaw in a bone-jarring crack. Stumbling back a few feet, Justin recovered and came up swinging. Sam stared, mesmerized by the speed and skill of the men trading blows.

Concerned only with the man in front of him, Justin delivered a powerful sidekick thrusting Marcus out of sight. A crash announced the death of the kitchen table. Another series of thuds, the sound of fists hitting flesh, and Justin was thrown to the ground in the doorway.

Freed for the briefest moment, he twisted his neck and saw her. Green eyes blazed up at her, the ache in her chest making her see a brief flash of tenderness she knew wasn't really there. Shaking herself free from her cruel disillusionment, she closed herself down and backed hurriedly up the stairs to her room. Another thud and grunt marked their renewed violence.

Sam broke into a run at the top step, skidding into her room and jamming on her running shoes over her bare feet. The breeze had picked up outside and faint rumbling could be heard in the distance through the open window. She dashed over to it and pulled the posts holding the screen in place, catching it and bringing it inside before it skittered down the steep slant of the small roof overhanging the front porch.

Legs dangling, Sam lowered herself to sit and scoot down the roof so as not to alert anyone inside to her escape. At the edge of the roof she rolled onto her stomach again and lowered herself as much as possible, still leaving a good seven-foot drop to the ground.

A loud peal of thunder rang out and Sam jumped into a run heading west. It occurred to her she'd watched the sun set that direction last night thinking she might have found an ally with Justin, maybe even Jimmy. Now she felt like a fool for letting herself be duped. A sad, scared fool. Letting angst and frustration fuel her, she broke into a run.

Ch. 27

The rising moon was three quarters full and shed precious light to her path. A boon considering she'd finally made it through the darkest part of the woods and was jogging across a soybean field. The growing light gave her the means to identify between the lighter soil and its large, bushy crop. Afraid she was going to roll an ankle any minute in the loose soil between rows, she watched the ground and gave a silent thank you to the neighbors for not being corn farmers. Sam never quite got over Children of the Corn.

Far ahead, at the edge of the field, Sam could see a car's headlights heading for the same bit of road she was only the car had the advantage of an unobstructed path. Seeing her potential ride, Sam grew anxious. *Slow down,* she willed it. All she needed was a few more minutes and she would reach the end of the field to make the turn and head straight toward the road. She couldn't switch her path yet or this would turn into a hurdling race. He didn't slow and her heart sank as her rubber soles hit asphalt behind his fading taillights. Worried they'd discovered her absence and were following she glanced back in the direction of the house. No sign of movement, no headlights. Safe for the moment, she struck out at a brisk walk aiming the direction from which the car had come.

By the time it was full dark her breathing had returned to normal and the light sheen of sweat that covered her after her run through the field had dried; she wriggled in her shirt to itch between her shoulder blades. Curious to know how long it had been, she checked her cell. Less than half an hour and she had no service. Not surprising. She was in the middle of nowhere. That's probably how they wanted it. There were fewer people to hear her scream when they went to work on her. Sam shook off the doubt trying to creep into her thoughts. *He was being nice just to trick me into giving that stupid thing to him,* she reminded herself. Only Justin hadn't been angry when he'd caught her listening to his argument turned brawl with Marcus. That look, it had been regret she'd seen in his eyes. He was acting, that was all. She shook off the urge to let sentiment beat out facts. He was acting all right, for her, not Marcus. She heard his words again. He would be the first to hurt her if it came to that. Sam lurched into a jog, the sounds of crickets and the occasional owl her only company.

After what seemed forever she checked her phone and found that no there was still no signal and it had only been an hour since she'd left. Her absence at the house would have been noticed by now. She thought about going off the road except it was so dark and quiet, the thought of hoofing it through the woods made her cringe. No, she'd chance the roadside and hope that she would hear or see an oncoming vehicle before it saw her.

All at once Sam's phone came back from the dead, drowning out the crickets' mind-numbing songs. It buzzed, chirped, and buzzed again announcing myriad messages both text and voice. Sam's spirits lifted; she was once again connected to the real world.

The first voice message was from Maria asking if she'd spoken to Paul and was she going to consider moving in with him or just end it and let him move on. Sam's stomach tightened. It was as if she'd stepped through a time portal and was returning to a life she'd abandoned years ago. Another message was from her supervisor asking how she was doing and if she would be in tomorrow. *Shit! I've been AWOL for over a week.* The third message was Peter letting her know her mother had woken up and was going to be released what was now yesterday and she would like to see Sam. She was adamant that Sam was in danger and wouldn't accept

193

Peter's assurances otherwise. He wanted her to come to the hospital and show her mother, in person, that she was okay. Then another from Maria that she wanted to know what the *fuckall* was going on with her. Her voice sounded garbled; either she was furious or upset, or both.

Knowing Pete would have his phone off while he was at the hospital, Sam figured it was safe to leave a message for her mother there.

"Pete, it's Sam. Please tell Mom I'm okay and not to worry. I'm taking care of some things and I don't want to involve her. I'll come home as soon as I can." She took a deep breath. "Tell her I love her." Sam pressed end and felt her eyes overflow, wetting her cheeks. *I'm so sorry I got you into this Mom.* Her mother was lying in a hospital, fresh from waking from a coma and her first thoughts were for Sam. *I should just disappear before someone else gets hurt.*

By the time she'd recovered and wiped her cheeks dry it was after nine, too late to call Maria on a work night. However, Sam took advantage of her reception, texting Maria that she was okay and she'd call and explain everything when she could.

No sooner had she pressed send than her phone buzzed.

"Hey Maria." She stopped for fear she'd lose the call. "Now's not a good time, can I call you later?"

Maria was not easily put off, instead giving a rare display of her slow burning but very hot temper. "Sam, what the *hell* is going on? Tim told me about Paul. Jesus honey, why didn't you call?" Tim, Maria's boyfriend, worked at the shop Paul's dealership used for repairs. Word would have gotten out by now no matter how quiet his family tried to keep things. Maria wasn't done. "I saw in the paper your mom was in a *hit and run* and I haven't been able to reach you for over a week. I thought we were friends." Sam winced at the hurt she heard in her friend's voice. "I got your building manager to let me into your apartment thinking maybe you were hiding out, maybe you needed a shoulder to cry on, not that you cry." She harrumphed. "You weren't even there! Either was your damned *cat*. He, the building manager, not your cat, said your mailbox was full and he put a stack on your table already so I know you haven't even been home in days."

Sam's stomach dropped. "You went to my apartment? You can't!" Sam yelled sharply. "It isn't safe." Too late she realized she'd said too much.

Maria's tone was careful. "What do you mean *it's not safe?*" She spoke those words deliberately. "Are you in some sort of trouble?" Maria was a good friend. She didn't question Sam's warning, strange as it sounded.

"Look, I can't tell you much just that you can't go anywhere near my place or my mom's for now. I'm trying to figure things out but it's going to take some time."

"You're freaking me out, Sam. How did you get involved in whatever this is? Is it somebody you denied at work?" It wasn't unusual for people to get mad at the claims adjuster when their claim was denied. Sam often got cussed out.

"No, it's my father."

Maria was quiet for a while. "Your father? You found him? I didn't know you were looking for him."

"*He* found *me*." She sighed then gave her the

195

basics. If she didn't tell her, Maria was likely to stake out her apartment and get herself in more trouble than if Sam spilled. "He's involved with some bad people and they're trying to find something he sent to me to keep safe. I can't give it to any of them, it's too dangerous."

"Any of them?"

Sam cursed her friend's acute hearing. "That's where I've been for the last week. Uh, there were these guys outside kickboxing and then this other couple of guys came in and took me back to their place in Wisconsin. They said it was for safekeeping. I was there for a while but now I'm on my own again."

Maria took a deep breath before asking very quietly. "Sam, sweetie, they didn't hurt you did they? Did they do anything to you while they had you? Do you need me to come get you?"

"No. I'm fine." She said quickly, leaving out her suspicions that she was about five minutes from having something very bad happen before she bolted, though not in the way Maria surely suspected. "Really, he's been really kind of..." She trailed off, surprised how naturally defending Justin came to her.

"He? I thought you said there were a few. Did you make a new friend while chaos surrounded you?"

"How can you ask that?" Pinching her nose, Sam closed her eyes against the assault of pain that accompanied the reminder of her disloyalty to her dead boyfriend.

The phone was silent long enough Sam pulled it away from her face to check she hadn't lost the call. "Still there?"

196

"It wasn't your fault, Sam. You didn't kill Paul."

"He died because he was at my house, Maria." She glanced back up at the house, worried she'd heard something. No lights. "If I'd been honest with him he'd never have been there. He'd be alive right now."

"Maybe. Or maybe he'd have been there waiting for you to come home so he could beg for you to come back. Or he could have died in a car accident picking up a pack of smokes."

"He didn't smoke."

"Or an airplane could have dropped on the showroom. You couldn't have known being with you put him in any more danger than anyone faces any day. It happened sweetie and it sucks, but that's it. It's over." And then Maria dropped a wisdom bomb, something at which she was quite adept. "Dying can be just as random as meeting Mr. Right."

"He's not Mr. Right, Maria. Sorry to disappoint you."

"Then maybe he's Mr. Right Now." She giggled and Sam found herself smiling. "Point is life comes at you how it wants to. I know you hate that but it's true and there's nothing you can do to change it. You can accept it or fight it but it's gonna happen all the same."

"Thanks Maria." Twisting, she strained to hear. She was sure she heard something this time. Sam took a few steps off the road and ducked a little, preparing to race into the trees. "I should get going."

"Just, take care of yourself okay?" The quaver in her voice burned Sam.

I could punch you Steven. "I'll be back soon, don't

worry. I'll call you as soon as I can." She hung up before she could lose her nerve and ask Maria to come get her.

Leaves in the trees ahead of her lit up, her shadow grew tall and blocked out the forest in front of her. Without hesitation she dove into the dark underbrush at the side of the road, rolling several feet down the embankment where she gained her feet and took off running into the trees.

Once under cover of the closely packed trees the partial moonlight did nothing to illuminate her path; Sam was running blind. She slowed her pace to avoid falling over the downed trees and leaf litter making the ground uneven, alternately solid and squishy under her feet. Several times she cursed when a branch slapped her in the face or tore at her hair.

Winded, Sam realized she had to stop before she got too lost and searched for a good spot to hide. Up ahead was the trunk of a large tree that had fallen over recently and caught in the crotch of another. With the branches full of leaves it provided a perfect blind while allowing some amount of light to filter through the gap it left in the canopy. Praying it would be enough Sam scurried around the top, tucking herself inside the protection of its boughs and waited. Her labored breathing was deafening to her sensitive ears. Despite the pain it caused her lungs she forced her panting to slow. The darkness around the edges of her vision could have been from the lack of light or oxygen, Sam couldn't be sure.

She waited what felt like an eternity before she heard the crack of a twig, the only sound of a pursuer she'd heard thus far confirming that the car had indeed been driven by one of Shaw's men. Furious tears pricked at the backs of her eyes and her nose burned. She hoped it wasn't Justin who had followed her. Angry, and though she didn't want to admit it, scared as she was she didn't want to face him worried she wouldn't be strong enough to keep herself from forgiving him. Maria hadn't done much to shore up Sam's defenses when it came to him. He'd been such a good con artist her gut *still* told her to trust him. Fortunately her head argued that if she did, he would kill her. For once she told her gut to shut up.

Another shuffling sound to her left and Sam held her breath. Her chest burned and fought with her, demanding fresh oxygen in greater doses. Her vision was spotting like a disco ball spun above when she finally let out a controlled breath and took in a long slow gulp.

The loud rustle and crash toward the back of the tree told her that her pursuer was moving past her. She gave it a slow count of sixty before easing herself out from her hidden nook and took painfully slow steps away in hopes of making it back to the road and aim toward civilization. She had to be getting close by now.

Looping back toward the road, Sam was beginning to feel safer when she didn't hear anything following her. When the trees thinned and the moon again cast the terrain in light and shadow, she breathed a relieved sigh. The car, now sans driver, was parked alongside the road about a quarter mile back, no signs of life from within. She picked up a jog the second her feet hit the path.

The voice was ahead of her in the shadow of a thick stand of trees. It stopped her in her tracks.

"Hey *chica*," he called. "You shouldn't run off like that. You had us worried."

She gasped, heart pounding in terror. "Jimmy, please." Her voice was barely audible. "Please don't take me back there."

He stepped out of the shadows just feet from her, scaring her even more. His hand closed around her upper arm just as headlights lit the road from the other direction. Turning to face the oncoming car at the same time, Sam was able to get a good look at Jimmy's face. The look he sent from moving car to parked car was easily read. He was wondering if he could get her inside before the other driver was close enough to interfere.

Sam made her decision. Locking her knees and throwing her weight into her hips she let herself fall backward onto the tar thereby complicating Jimmy's extraction plans for her with only a minor amount of bruising and road rash to show for it.

"Come on, *chica*. This ain't a good idea." He bent down and tugged on her arm, some sort of binoculars gripped in one palm kept him from using both hands. That explained how he'd been able to see her trail, they were night vision goggles unless she missed her guess.

Exactly like a toddler in a mall, Sam let her body go limp. Jimmy had nothing but dead weight answering his jerks. He cursed.

"You got no idea what kinda risk you're taking being out here."

Yanking her arm from his grasp, angry with him, angry with herself, Sam snarled at him. "Yes I do. I'm saving myself from *you* people. Marcus and Justin don't have to fight over who gets the pleasure of tearing me apart anymore."

The headlights coming straight at them allowed Sam full view of Jimmy's shocked expression. "The Sarge ain't gonna hurt you. He took a bullet for you."

Sam shrugged off his defense of his teammate. "What's one bullet when you can't die? He would have done anything to convince me to give him what he wanted." It was hard to hear how ugly she sounded. How hateful.

The car's tires crunched on loose gravel at the opposite side of the road behind her as it skidded to a halt. Jimmy's face was washed out in the bright light. He held up a hand to shield his eyes.

Twisting his neck, he spoke softly over his shoulder. "Yeah, but I don't think it's the package he wants anymore."

The car door opened behind them; neither was looking. "I'm not sure I can get my father to come out of hiding."

He shook his head "Doc ain't the most important person in your family anymore for the Sarge. He's all turned around cause a you, you gotta come back."

Shoes crunched on gravel and the driver walked through the headlights, breaking their beam.

"Is everything all right?" the driver asked. He sounded awfully calm for finding a man hovering over a woman lying on the side of an otherwise deserted country road after dark.

Sam's mind swirled, heart and head locked in combat over Jimmy's insinuation that her trust in Justin had not been misplaced. Her head turned toward the man's voice although her eyes saw nothing in the glare of the beams.

"Samantha?"

After nearly two decades his voice hadn't changed. Slicing through the years in an instant, it was as familiar to her as if he had called her in to dinner only the night before.

She blinked owlishly in the light. "Dad?"

Jimmy recovered faster. "Doc, good to see you again. We've been lookin' for you." His eyes strayed back up the road. "Got company coming if you want to hang around for a few minutes."

Sam hadn't seen the gun in her father's hand and screamed when it barked twice. Jimmy's body fell in the gravel beside her, rolling through the grass and down the small hill.

The shadow that was her father leaned down and put a hand under her arm to help her to her feet. "Come on, we have to hurry before the others get here."

She followed him in a daze, her body automatically opening the door and buckling herself in. Her father turned the car around and the tires squealed on the asphalt, briefly illuminating Jimmy's body in the glow of the lights before leaving him behind on the roadside.

Sam stared at her father's dim profile letting her memory fill in the gaps the shadows left between the hawk nose and pointed chin. She knew how he would have his lower lip sucked against his teeth as he concentrated. He hadn't changed, apart from some creases in his forehead and a few unruly grays jutting out from his neatly slicked back deep brown hair. Dr. Steven James was tall, his head nearly touched the roof of the car, and yet there was so little bulk to him she barely noticed him beside her.

His face was pinched in frustration. "Damn." His hand slammed the top of the steering wheel and he turned to face her. "Do you know who that *was* with you?"

She shook her head wanting to hear his side of things. She could play dumb if need be.

"This is going to sound strange," he began, turning the car the rest of the way to head back the direction he'd come. "But that man is wanted by the US Government for war crimes."

She could see the white of his eye as he glanced at her out of its corner. Sam said nothing, waiting.

"He and his men stole something during the war and there are people who would stop at nothing to get it back. Do you have any idea the danger you were in just being with him?" He sounded concerned, a point in his favor. "Was he alone, did you see the others he mentioned?"

"I didn't see anyone with him." Bewildered as to "why," Sam found herself unable to give up the rest of the men. She wasn't the same as Justin; she wouldn't be responsible for anyone's death if it could be helped. The fact that Steven was starting out by lying to her wasn't helping his cause.

Her father wasn't easily fooled. "Do you mean for me to believe that you have been missing for days and haven't seen any of his unit with him? I saw them take you."

Sam's jaw dropped. "You were there? The night I was attacked you were there and you didn't do anything? Where were you?"

He sucked air through his teeth and stared out the window not saying a word.

Of course he didn't do anything. He wanted them and he wanted the freaking thing he sent. He doesn't give a shit if I get killed so long as he gets the weapon. Probably figured if I got killed he'd be able to search my place without anyone interfering. Sam chewed her lip and sniffed against the stinging in her nose and eyes. *He doesn't get tears.* Instead, when she answered she was calm and mild. "All I'm saying is that I don't know who he was." She didn't turn her head, she couldn't look at him or she feared she would explode. "What was in the cylinder by the way? Did you know a man died in my apartment because of that thing?"

Steven's brows flicked up but he said nothing.

"And Mom got hit by a car. She was in a coma." Exhaustion and frustration long pent up were given a much-needed outlet and she got up a full head of steam in a hurry. Turning her head, she unleashed the fury that had been building for most of her life on her father.

"What the hell kind of a man, no what kind of a *father* puts his daughter and wife in the path of killers? I mean, wasn't it enough that you left us when I was a kid? Do you have any idea what that did to Mom? How about what it did to *me*? Did you know I used to go to bed every night and listen for your garage door to go up? I *knew* you were coming back. I used to tell Mom when I'd hear her crying at night. How could you show up out of nowhere and think I'd protect that thing for *you*?" Her heart leapt at his anxious reaction to her suggestion she might not have the package. She pounced on it, wanting to cut him.

"That's right, I got rid of it as soon as I figured out how dangerous it was. You're not getting it back.

Nobody needs something people are getting killed over, least of all me." Let him think she was a selfish bitch, maybe he'd drop her off and leave her. Suddenly Sam had a strong urge to be far away from him.

Steven's mouth tightened and she heard his teeth grind together as he glared at the road winding toward them in the headlights. He switched to his high beams. "You 'got rid of it'?" He asked very slowly.

"Yes, I threw it away days ago."

He was quiet for a few minutes, thinking and tapping his fingers on the steering wheel. Sam had drifted off into her own head. Running over the past week, dissecting each little thing, what she'd heard in the house, and what Jimmy said by the side of the road, searching for that angle that would tell her what to believe, she was taken by surprise when the car suddenly accelerated, forcing her back against her seat.

"What are you doing?"

"You're lying to me." He darted a quick look at her. "So just like any other problem, when the outcome doesn't follow the data, you go back to the beginning. So we're going back to the beginning."

She stared at him.

"You wouldn't throw it away. It was from me." Just like that. Matter of fact. Her father knew she would hold onto the one thing he'd ever sent her because it was from him. And in that moment she hated him more than she had every night she tucked her mother in and picked up her used tissues.

But beyond the hatred there was something else. The hair on the back of her neck itched as it began to go up. "And where's the beginning, *Steven*?"

Her use of his first name barely induced a flinch. "Your apartment Samantha. We're going back to your apartment and if we can't find the package, we're going to wait and see who shows up. Eventually, someone will know something."

"Are you crazy? Justin will find us there for sure. They want to..."

The car slowed down and he gave her a long look. Sam realized he'd baited her on purpose.

"Samantha, did you want to try *again* to tell me how much you know?" He averted his eyes back to the road and began to pick up speed again. "And why you're protecting those criminals?"

"I don't know who to trust, Steven," she confessed honestly, slumping in defeat. "They helped me when I was in trouble, but I heard them talking." She shrugged one rounded shoulder.

"They?" he perked up. "Are there still three of them?"

"Yes." There was no point trying to hide that from him, she figured. Once Jimmy was "back" or "up", whatever they called it, they'd be on the trail. Sam hoped to have her father out of her apartment before they got there. Uncertain of anyone's motives at this point she figured her best bet was to keep them all separate, if that was possible.

The miles rolled on, several markers flashed past before he spoke up and interrupted her thoughts again.

"Do you feel any loyalty to them?" It was gentler,

more of the man she used to call dad. When she didn't answer right away, Steven looked over at her. Illuminated by the dashboard's blue lights, she stared off into the night. "Samantha."

Sam became aware her father was waiting for an answer. "No," she replied without making eye contact.

***

Samantha was a bad liar. She always had been. She was lying now. Her response took away all doubt and Steven knew, for a fact, he was in trouble. He had approximately forty-five minutes, if he drove slow, to win back his daughter's trust enough he could count on her when things fell apart as he was anticipating they would. Once they got to her apartment there wouldn't be much time before either Management's thugs or the contaminated soldiers he'd helped escape in a moment of weakness came for them both. If he had any chance of carrying out his plan he would have to be gone by then.

Damn. He had never been a good gambler. He liked to know all of the potential outcomes and be prepared for any eventuality. Only he wasn't sure what to do with the wild card sitting beside him.

Ch. 28

"Where the hell is Jimmy?" Justin came back downstairs to the kitchen. Marcus was coming in from the garage where Jimmy kept most of his equipment.

"How am I supposed to know? I was busy handing you your ass," Marcus gloated.

He was right. *Fucker.* The betrayal he saw in Sam's eyes when he caught her listening had been a distraction, but not enough to explain what happened. Marcus came back from that kick and made quick work of Justin. Usually when they sparred they were evenly matched. Marcus bested Justin as often as the other way round. This time Justin's muscles screamed at the demand he placed on them, trying and failing to match blows with Marcus. He'd tired easily. Something was definitely wrong; he was getting slower, his movements more labored. Marcus knocked him out cold minutes after the fight started. When he'd come to Marcus announced Sam was gone but her things and her damned cat were still in her room. Her shoes and phone were missing and the screen was sitting leaned up against the dresser, which answered the question of how. While they were out searching the woods around the house on foot one of their cars passed them on the road. They assumed Jimmy had returned from the store, saw their note, and went out to search in a wider radius.

Their search having turned up nothing, the smart thing to do now was to wait for Jimmy to show up. His burner phone was sitting on the counter.

It was another half an hour before the roar of an engine coming in hot brought Marcus and Justin to their feet. Part of Justin was relieved when Jimmy walked up the sidewalk alone and stopped outside on the steps.

That relief passed quickly when the light hit him, revealing Jimmy's tshirt, soaked with blood. The other two immediately joined him on the porch.

Menace simmered in Marcus' words. "Did she do that?"

"No man, it was the Doc."

For Justin, everything stopped. "She's with her *father*? How did he find her here?" She said she didn't speak to her father. She said they hadn't been in contact since she was nine. Was it possible she'd played him? It had certainly happened before; his mother used to tell him he was a sucker for a stray. That was a lifetime ago. He hadn't left himself open to anyone, even a stray, for a long time.

The Doc was back. He was close. That fact should have brought with it a sense of victory. Justin and his men were nearing the end and now the men they sought were circling ever closer. It was a matter of time before they connected and brought an end to what had stolen years and so much more from them. Instead he felt only a sense of failure. He'd lost Sam and she was now directly in harm's way. What was worse, if she gave her father the package she would no longer hold any value for the other side. They would have no reason to leave her alive. That shouldn't bother him, but it did.

Jimmy nodded, moving past Justin and Marcus both to get into the kitchen. Flanking him, Marcus put a hand out to catch the door, pausing when he was even with Justin.

"Looks like we get to move to phase two faster than expected." The corner of his mouth quirked up. "Lucky for your girl she got to miss out on the fact finding bit."

Fists clenching, Justin's retort was cut off by Jimmy's stream of obscenities coming from inside.

"Somebody gonna help dig this thing out? I'm workin' on borrowed time here. Where the hell's the table?"

Marcus kept his voice low and threatening. "I've got this. You figure out where we're going next." He poked a finger at Justin's chest. "Keep in mind you aren't helping anyone by letting her get away. You know as well as I do she's best off if we get to her first." He pushed past Justin, letting the screen door slam behind him. "*You* can make it quick for her, they won't be so kind."

Though bridling at Marcus' insinuation that he would do something disloyal to his men, Justin had to admit he'd considered doing exactly that. He would have thought hard about letting her go had Marcus been determined to hurt her. Again, *what the hell was that?*

The question of where Sam would go with her father was a matter of trust to his thinking. Would she trust him enough to give him the package? She'd told Justin it was safe, being very careful not to say where that might be. The only places she'd gone since they'd been watching had been the gym and her home. He doubted she'd left it at the gym. The package had to be in her apartment.

In fact, before he'd seen the bug in the house and feared interruption, he'd intended to search the place even if he had to restrain her. The recollection brought with it a guilty pang and another flash of her injured expression in the stairway. Not the horror at what Marcus wanted done to her, it was the injury *he'd* caused that went much deeper. *Fuck!*

A loud curse from Jimmy followed by a muffled response from Marcus pulled Justin inside to stand by the couch where the work was being done.

"As soon as you're ready we head out."

"Where you think they went, Sarge?" Jimmy panted, fists wringing the life out of a cushion on the soon to be ruined couch. Chalk it up to machismo, Jimmy didn't resort to pain killers except in extreme cases. And sad fact of their lives, two bullets just weren't that extreme.

"Sam's." He started for the door and stopped. "Jimmy, what have you been using to listen in at her place?"

"Just the little monitor. We can tap into a few of Big Brother's lines that'll boost it so we can listen on the way." He guessed accurately at Justin's plan.

"They've got a big head start and the van's slow. I'll move the monitor into the truck." Justin clapped his hand on the doorframe, his missing digit catching his eye and bringing with it an image of Sam being held at knifepoint. "Marcus, grab the big guns."

Jimmy let out another stream of curses in his native tongue as Marcus went after the other round and Justin jogged out to make the truck ready to travel. Jimmy would have to recuperate in on the way; the clock on Sam's life and their end goal was ticking. It would all be over soon if they were lucky. By Justin's way of thinking, he was due some luck.

Ch. 29

Sam unlocked the door and followed her father into her apartment, automatically looking down, fully expecting a big gray ball of fur to hit her shins at any moment. It was weird not having him there; she'd never come home without Bill to greet her. The silence made her hyperaware of each little door slam and creak in the building, sure the next one would mean they'd been found.

She watched her father make a slow lap around the small unit, not sure she liked him there in her space. When he finally opened his mouth to speak it wasn't to comment on how well she'd done for herself or to ask about any of the framed pictures outlining the important moments in her life. No, he had a one-track mind.

"Where is it?"

She shook her head in disbelief. "You know, you've been gone the majority of my life. Do you think that just for a moment you could at least *pretend* to be somewhat interested in what you've missed?"

He blinked, once then twice. "Samantha we are being pursued by members of our government whom are intent upon recovering this technology at all costs. So intent as a matter of fact that they will most likely kill us both to obtain it." He stared evenly down his long thin nose at her. The same dark eyes she saw every day in the mirror held no hint of a smile. "But if you would like to stand around playing catch up, then by all means why don't you just brew up a pot of coffee and we can stay here talking about what I've missed while we wait for them and their guns."

"You don't have to be a dick." She wheeled and

stalked into her kitchen to grab a yogurt. They could spare the two minutes it would take her to ram that down. Besides, she hadn't eaten since she couldn't remember when, and she'd been up all night. Her father would find it horribly inconvenient if she fainted from low blood sugar. "Do you want anything?" No answer. Shrugging, she grabbed a Greek yogurt and spoon then returned to the common area to stand back and observe.

Sam watched her father search the space, making no attempt to hide it. With his constantly darting eyes and his lanky limbs twitching and scanning frantically, he reminded her of a junkie in need of a fix. His pale skin and lean frame didn't do anything do negate the comparison.

"Dad, why did you leave?" she asked his back and slipped a spoonful of yogurt into her mouth, watching Steven's frame stiffen at the directness of her inquiry. A chunk of cherry exploded on her tongue and she rolled it around, savoring it.

"It was for your own good."

She was unable to stop the sarcastic guffaw that rolled out of her mouth, the back of her hand flying up to halt any sort of oral shrapnel that might fly and land on the carpet.

"You don't think that's possible? To leave someone for their own good?" He turned to face her, dark eyes narrowed. "I'm not the bad guy here, Samantha." His expression lightened. "Do you doubt that I might have wanted to keep my family away from all of this? I'd hoped to keep you and your mother out of this mess once I found out what the research I was doing was being used for."

"You've been killing people in the name of

213

science for this long and you've only *now* decided to take it and run? What changed? Why the sudden crisis of conscience?"

It was Steven's turn to gape at Sam. "How much did they tell you?"

"Enough to know you're feeding me a line. You're the definition of a bad guy, Steven."

Eyes narrowing, Steven took a step toward her. "What else did they tell you?"

She stood her ground. "Justin told me they got splashed by a chemical weapon when they were taking it from an Iraqi lab. That when they got back from the war their own guys locked them in a lab where they had to endure horrible experiments while scientists like you tried to figure out how to recreate it. People died there." Sam watched his reaction closely, hoping for a sign of humanity somewhere in there.

Steven's angular shoulders drooped and some of the fire went out of his eyes. He motioned toward the couch while he lowered himself into the matched chair opposite her. "Would you like to hear my side?"

Sam plopped down, passing another spoonful of yogurt through her lips and making a show of being quiet while she chewed.

"No one wants to use their nuclear missiles and everyone knows it. The threat has lost its teeth and countries have been working to develop something else that would strike fear into the hearts of their enemies. The answer is chemical warfare.

It's not so shocking anymore, word has been leaking out for years. But in 1990 when we went to war with Iraq the first time, it wasn't for oil or the liberation of the Kuwaiti people. It was for their advances in the field. Unlike us, Saddam Hussein wasn't limited in his experiments by any sort of governmental controls. As a result he was able to excel, his program was the best in the world. Apparently, our intelligence community heard about some of the chemicals he'd produced. One in particular caught their attention; it was said to give a man countless lives." Steven rested his hands on his knees, staring down at his shoes.

"They missed it the first time and we continued with our own program. Because I was in charge I was able to steer the research away from anything like that. It worked until the Joint Chiefs convinced the president that Saddam still had weapons of mass destruction and that they were going to use them in an assault on our soil. After 9/11 nobody was taking any chances." Steven waved a hand and sighed. "So we went in *again*. These men in particular, the ones you met, were a top recon team sent in for the sole purpose of fetching the chemical and destroying the program so the US would be top dog again." He shook his head. "Only instead of bringing it home, they were exposed and it made *them* the chemical. Our government couldn't be caught conducting the sorts of experiments necessary to construct something like that, so they were sent to a lab that doesn't technically exist. They were subjected to tests you wouldn't put your worst enemy through. When I read the reports I was under the impression the test subjects were animals. Like we used in my program." He rubbed a hand over his eyes. "When I was brought in and saw that they were men..." He shook his head. "I had to do something. I helped them escape."

Sam felt a tightening in her stomach at the sight of her father gone pale at the memory. The memory of Justin being tortured.

"You asked how I could have been involved in this, knowing what I do. You have to understand, in the beginning, when they came to me, I was flattered with the attention. They told me they admired my work in the field. They told me they had scientists on a special project, it was very hush hush. I couldn't even tell my family what I would be doing but I would be in charge of my own program. At first we worked with diseases. I thought we were working to develop a genetic immunity. I was thrilled. After I'd been there a while I started to pick up on the fact that there were an unusual number of visits from men in uniform. Top generals. I started asking questions and they told me I was helping my country, that I would have an opportunity to pioneer the field in a whole new line of defense." Rubbing his arm, he grimaced. "Then, in '05 I heard we had acquired some exposed subjects. Lots of excitement and things sped up. Six months later they sent me to pick them up. I was to learn more about the project in its entirety by observing for a few days. Then they would move me up. Give me my own team." He swallowed, inhaled through his nose, and swallowed again. "After observing for twenty minutes I had serious doubts that I could do my job. Then they told me I was supposed to take these men to my facility, keep them for 'samples' until I isolated the gene affected by the chemical compound and extrapolate a new compound based upon my findings. Our methods weren't as refined as they are now. We had to take *so much more* material back then." His eyes were empty as he lost himself to his demons. "And there were so many test runs. So many young men." He trailed off and his shuddering breath shook his thin shoulders.

Sam raised her hand to swipe at her wet cheeks, sniffing. *How can anyone justify that sort of thing? Is* anything *worth that? Cold blooded* murder?

Steven recovered himself. "I told them I couldn't cut up live men. My previous experiments had been on cadavers at the hospital." He gave a choked laugh. "One of the other scientists told me it was okay, they could heal anything I cut out as long as it wasn't bone. On the day I was to move them I took them like I was supposed to, and I let them go. It wasn't hard to explain that three well-trained soldiers had gotten away from the two guards assisting and myself. For my part in their escape they left me alive only tying me up and knocking me out. They had to kill the guards; they put up more of a fight. I thought Management wouldn't need me anymore, I thought the program would go back to my research and I could delay it. Keep them from reaching the human test subject phase again. I thought I could go home. I was wrong. They still had the *body* of the fourth man. I tried leaving and they threatened my family; they'd kept track of you the whole time." His hand twitched, rising as if he would reach for her then settled back in his lap. "I left you and your mother because I had to. It was the only way to keep the two of you safe. Then, when they threatened you again, I knew *none of us* would be safe as long as the program was close. That was when I started to plan for how to bring down the program. Shutting them down is the only way to end this."

Unable to process her father's culpability, Sam focused on the facts. "So you were able to recreate the chemical from Mills' body?"

Steven inclined his head. "Yes, that and the data from the experiments. It took well over three years to come up with a viable replica, another two to begin human trials again..."

"What? *You* experimented on human beings?" The beginnings of sympathy she'd felt for her father vaporized.

He leaned toward her, extending a hand to rest

lightly on her knee. Pleading with her to understand. "The chemical I used for the tests had a flaw, it was never going to work. The subjects didn't pass the tests. I'm sorry but it was a necessary evil. Please know that I used as few subjects as I could without drawing too much scrutiny. It wasn't until a few months ago Management figured out I'd been tampering with my own research. That's why I destroyed everything and stole the only sample of the real chemical, the one that does work."

She stood, unable to look at her father. Regardless of his guilt or moral qualms about what he'd done, the fact remained that he'd done it. That he was a murderer of innocents. Disgusted, she stood up and he did as well.

"Samantha please, you have to listen to me. I have given up everything I hold dear in this life for this project believing I had no other choice. I've missed out on your life. I gave up my wife and my home. I even gave up my career, there's nothing for me after this. But I believe I *do* have a choice now and I cannot allow this death and misery to be all that I'm remembered for. This one remaining sample is enough to cure so many genetic diseases." He brightened and leaned forward.

"It's a foundation for a whole new line of research. So much *good* could come from this." His eyes burned with a wild intensity. "Please, I need to undo some of the wrongs I've committed. When I got into this field it was to help people, to find cures. I could still do that with your help."

His speech was a good one and she wanted to believe him not just as her father, but also as a human being seeking redemption for his burdened soul. However, she'd watched him shoot Jimmy without flinching. That was not the move of a man bent upon making things right.

"I would like to help you, I really would." Sam shrugged. "I just don't have it." She made to move past him.

Her father's face darkened. His chilled tone was unrecognizable from the contrite one he'd taken seconds ago. "Samantha, you *will* give me that sample."

Sam kept her face pleasant, hiding the sick feeling growing in the pit of her stomach. "Excuse me, I need to go to the bathroom." She was already working through her options. The sun would be coming up soon and the early risers in her building would be awake. If she could get around him she might be able to get out the front door and yell for help or call the police, though they would be more likely to send a padded van than squad car when they heard *her* name. She swept past him, feeling her adrenaline surge as she rounded the corner into the hallway leading not just to the bathroom but the front door.

Quickening her pace she sidled up to the door, laying one hand on it to hold it from shifting within the frame and making noise. With her other she eased the deadbolt into the open position. Her eyes were on the opening door when her father's palm hit it over her head, slamming it closed. His other hand clutched her shoulder and spun her around throwing her backward into the wall.

His eyes were black, cheeks red, nostrils flaring as he stood over her using his full height to intimidate her. "Give me the sample, Samantha." He visibly worked to control his rage yet his voice quivered with it. "I told you, this is my *legacy*. You will *not* take that from me."

Tipping her chin up to look at him Sam felt her own temper rising, fueled by the growing certainty that she made a colossal mistake in leaving the farmhouse and not going back with Jimmy. Add to that nearly twenty years of loss and false hope churning just below the surface and she wasn't backing down. She wasn't going to be cowed by a bully even if he was her father. He gave up that title up a long time ago when he abandoned his daughter. "What about me? Aren't *I* your legacy? What about the life *I'm* supposed to live? You haven't even given that the slightest consideration, have you?"

His lip curled, a frightening light reached his eyes. This man was half crazy, Sam realized. Two decades in a lab choosing who would live and die hadn't done his sanity any favors. "You have no idea the amount of devastation this project has cost in human life alone and will cost the people of this entire planet if it's not stopped. Do you think one person's career in insurance, a potential marriage and maybe a couple of children makes up for that?" he mocked. "Neither you or I can offset that kind of toll."

Sam's mouth had opened to snarl back when the door flew back, throwing her father into the hall toward the living room. The edge caught her arm and elbow with a resounding crack of oak on bone, sending the lower half of her arm into numb oblivion and spinning her into the living room. She looked from her father lying on the carpet glaring past her to the face of the man entering her home and felt her insides curl in on themselves in terror.

The dark faces of the two men were different from the others she faced in the parking lot that night, but the dead look in their eyes was the exact same. The difference between that time and this was that she didn't have the protection of Justin and his team. It was only her crazy father and herself against two stone cold killers.

She barely opened her mouth to scream for help when the first man's latex covered hand swept over her mouth. His other thrust her further inside allowing the second man to enter and lock the door behind him.

"Hello, Doctor James. Management sends their regards." The front man smiled unpleasantly. "We appreciate your enthusiasm here but I must insist on our taking over. My partner is far more experienced at extracting information, and time *is* of the essence thanks to your carelessness."

Ch. 30

Justin sat in the driver's seat of the truck, metal engine parts clicking and ticking as they continued to lament their rough handling. The drive took them less than thirty minutes, a feat worthy of pride though the men inside showed no signs of joy.

They were only a few miles away when Sam and her father arrived at the apartment. They heard him tell his daughter how he'd used their brother in arms' body for experimentation. Marcus punched the dashboard hard enough to crack the molded plastic. No one spoke but the electric vibe in the truck was unmistakable. Jimmy lay quietly in the back seat. His body too was slower in recovering this time. Justin had merely pressed his foot down harder on the accelerator, willing the vehicle to move even faster.

Their arrival had coincided with Doc's altercation with Sam at the door. When Sam tried to make a break for it, Justin's hand was on his door. At the introduction of the new men's voices, he jumped out. Marcus caught him at the outer door of the complex.

"Shaw, we can't go charging in there." His hand clamped down on the frantic man's shoulder. "Think about it. If we go in we force their hand and the girl *and* Doc die. We get nothing."

Justin ground his teeth together, answering without turning. "And what do you think happens to them if we *don't* go in there?"

Marcus eased his hand. "We have to wait, treat it like any other op." He twitched his hand back in the direction of the parked car. "Come on, we can wait and listen in. If they get too rough we bust down the door. If we wait, we learn something about who's behind this thing or we find the formula. We have a chance to do a lot of good here. We could get the guys in charge of the whole chemical program, who knows what other projects they have going."

The soldier in him agreed with Marcus' strategy. The man in him was unwilling to allow Sam to be in the same room as the two assassins for a second longer. She was his now. He'd taken her to his bed. It was as ancient a method as birth and death and just as final in his mind. Sam was his and he needed to protect her. Jimmy's tired voice called over the comm, too weak to yell out of the vehicle.

"Hey guys, get in here. You look suspicious out there holdin' on to each other being all intense. You're gonna have to kiss or break it up." Understanding his former superior's motives, he added, "Come on, Sarge. We're thirty-seconds from her door if things go bad. Let's see if she can get something out of them. Your girl's smart."

Cursing and pounding his fist against the metal doorframe, Justin wheeled around and stepped back into the truck, slamming his door. His men were right. *Fuck.* Jimmy was right; they were close enough to be there in under a half of a minute. *A bullet's faster.* He forced the thought from his mind. Clear thoughts were the only way to complete the op. His gut churned.

Over the monitor they heard one of the men, the only one who had spoken so far, order Sam and the Doc to sit down. There was a general rustling and the recognizable sound of zip strips. It was easy to picture the scene.

After the rustling quieted, he spoke again. "So this is your daughter, Doctor James? You've entrusted the future of our entire program to *her*? Hmm."

"She doesn't have it." The Doc was talking again, his tone begging respect. No hint of fear.

Justin had him figured as a coward and a bully. *You better not sacrifice her for your worthless skin.*

"I figured you would say that. The problem is I don't believe you. You see, for a man who hasn't seen fit to so much as call his daughter in years to all of a sudden go to her house and follow her around..." There was a pause. "Yes Doctor, we do pay attention to the habits of our employees. Now you can't leave her alone, and by Management's description, the package you sent her had something that didn't belong to you. Management wants it back and he's given us orders we are to use any means necessary to recover it. You know how this works: we start with her then we move on to you. It's all about motivation."

A loud crack echoed through the silent truck followed by a masculine grunt. Justin's nerves wound tighter as the situation escalated. He held out, secretly approving of the pain the Doctor was suffering.

"So you know what we're talking about here," the calm voice continued, trying to draw the information from the doctor.

"It wasn't in there. I send her a gift every year for her birthday. I have since she was ten years old, just ask her." The doctor was trying hard to sound calm. It was too bad men who dealt in death, as did the men with him and the soldiers listening from the car could hear Doc's fear underneath that facade. "I can get it for you."

The talkative fellow chuckled. "I don't believe you. However, it is very helpful to see that you want to protect your daughter. I think we can work with that."

Something happened. Something quiet but the Doc's violent reaction had Justin's hand on the door. Jimmy sat up.

"No, *no*! Please. I'll tell you, just put that down. I sent it to her. Samantha, please! Tell them where it is. You have no idea what's in that needle. *No!*" His objection rose to a fevered pitch. "It's here somewhere I know it. Giving her that won't do you any good. Please, I'll go with you. Without me you have nothing and you know it. So does Management."

"What do you think he has?" Marcus pondered aloud. His chemistry background had his curiosity piqued.

Jimmy rocked his head back and forth. "Hell man, I don't know but I wouldn't mess with the shit they got floating around that lab, especially something that's got Doc spooked."

Giving them both a look to quiet them, Justin continued to listen intently for any signs they were too late and at the same time petrified that they already were. A lot could happen in the half a minute it would take to get to her and now he was afraid that by barging in he might force them to inject her with something he couldn't save her from. *Talk Sam. Tell them anything, just save yourself.* The violence of his reaction would have shocked him had he given it thought. Considering the circumstances he didn't have the capacity to dissect it right now. It was enough to run their options for rescue in his head while he willed himself not to rush in there and kill both of those assholes before they touched her.

"What do you say, Samantha? Is it here?"

"What do you think? Your friends searched the place the day after I got it and didn't find anything."

"Don't taunt them." Justin cautioned her uselessly from afar. The quake he heard in her voice had him silently promising to make those men hurt.

The line was silent, not a sound came through the monitoring device. Impatient, Marcus struck the top of the box.

"Hey be nice to her, man," Jimmy snapped.

"If you're struggling to remember where you put it my partner will help jog your memory."

"Please, don't hurt her. I'll help you look, I'm sure I can find it. I know my daughter," Doc begged. The way he was going on, the men on both sides of the microphones were beginning to believe that he really did genuinely want Sam spared.

"First you say it isn't here, now you say it is. Which is it, Doc? How am I supposed to believe you when your story keeps changing? I think it's time we try my friend's way."

A crack shot through the line followed by a feminine gasp and Justin went still. Something inside him went absolutely dead calm, it was that same calm that preceded battle when Justin accepted what might happen but knew he would go in anyway. Justin would die for her and in that moment he knew it. Marcus held up one hand. "A few bruises for people's lives, Shaw. Perspective."

"You can give me the package or you can give me the location of the men we're looking for. Yes, we know about them too. They are criminals, Miss James. You gain nothing by protecting them."

"I don't know anything," she said firm but quiet.

A second crack followed by a third and a soft whimper. Doc was repeating himself, begging them to stop. Two more impacts and Justin had the door open. Marcus caught his arm.

"Wait Shaw, don't blow this."

Glaring, Justin jerked his arm free. "What? What could be important enough to let an innocent woman be beaten to death? Have we become so much like them we don't see right from wrong anymore?"

"What if they kill Doc too? Then we've got nothing."

Justin shut his door and leaned in. "Then neither do *they*." He challenged them with a glare. "I say we go in there and handle the situation like we've been *trained to do* before *any*body gets killed." The sound of something soft being hit and a muffled scream came through the speaker and he was running. Two doors shut behind him followed by the sounds of boots on asphalt.

"This ain't gonna end well." Jimmy held his hand to his barely healed chest where the rib still ached from the bullet ricocheting off it.

Ch. 31

In reality it took closer to two minutes to reach Sam's apartment by the time Marcus picked the security door and they charged up the stairs as stealthily as was possible at a run. Another few seconds for the lock on her unit's door to be tripped and Justin led the way inside, gun out and in tight for close quarters as he rounded the corner into the living room.

The back of only one of the men was to him. It was the one who had been working on Sam. He'd paused for a second, possibly to keep her from passing out from what Justin could see. Rage burned its way through Justin and he fought to stay his trigger finger.

Doc flicked his head their way at their movement and gave a small cry of surprise.

The woman beater turned as well and Justin's eyes bulged. Marcus, coming around to Justin's other side, swore. The black man, the mouthpiece of the pair, hopped backward, hands empty of a weapon.

"You?" Marcus growled at the man still partially turned toward Sam. His eyes grew wide as Marcus rushed Sam's abuser, tackling him to the ground.

Jimmy called out from behind Justin. "Hands up, *pendejo*."

As much as he wanted his pound of flesh from the traitor, Justin let Marcus handle him. The sounds of men fists hitting flesh ensued. Justin went to Sam first. She was listing against the side of the couch, hands and feet bound and covered in a significant amount of blood. Most of it was from the cut above her right eye, already swelling; it would be shut soon. The blood from her nose dripped steadily on her shirt and hands, which were bound in front of her. Gritting his teeth he holstered his gun to take his Ka-bar from its ankle sheath and released her bound wrists.

"Sam, Sam it's me Justin. You're going to be okay. We've got you." Tenderly, he rubbed the circulation back into her hands and reached out to briefly touch her face. He wanted to fold her into his arms yet he was afraid of her rejection, remembering the hurt on her face at Marcus' accusations. Everything had changed in a matter of hours.

Her left eye stopped rolling and blinking as she focused on him. "Justin, you came." She ran her tongue over her lips to wet them, grimacing. "I should have known."

Before he could determine her meaning, Jimmy called out behind him.

"Sarge."

Justin turned to see the mouthpiece had turned the tables on Jimmy and had a gun trained on him. Jimmy's hands were up, his weapon tucked in the other man's waistband at his back. Justin cursed himself for being blind to Jimmy's weakened state in his rush to get to Sam. A quick glance and he could see how Marcus and his wrestling partner had been used as cover for the mouthpiece to get close enough to Jimmy to outmaneuver him. Coming back from the dead took time to recover from. Jimmy wouldn't have had a chance against him in his state. He'd been a fool to leave his man exposed like that.

"Sergeant Shaw, is it, and his band of merry men?" The mouthpiece asked with a smile. "We heard you had resurfaced." He nodded over to where Marcus

229

had his man down and was punching him repeatedly in the face. "Kindly call your man off Mr. Trainer, would you?"

Moving protectively in front of Sam, he called, "Marcus, get off *Mr. Trainer.*"

Reluctant, Marcus stopped hitting the smaller man currently lying prone on the floor behind him.

"This is a game changer." Unconcerned with the body of his fallen partner, the man grinned smugly at them. Justin wanted to tear the smile from his lips. Mostly hidden by his position, the man's arm moved and they didn't see until it was too late and the tip of a knife appeared in the center of Jimmy's chest. A look of agony appeared on his face.

Marcus lunged and Trainer, having regained his feet, grabbed his shirt and whipped him back so he could slam a fist into his throat, crushing his windpipe and dropping him to his knees. In minutes Marcus would be dead.

"What do you want?" He drew their attention back to himself. Both of his men's injuries were recoverable as things stood, he hoped to keep it that way.

A nod from the mouthpiece and the other one angled closer to Sam.

Justin took a step backward planting himself between her and those fists. "She was telling you the truth, she doesn't have it." He inclined his head toward Doc, currently observing the two fallen men in an oddly clinical way. "Doc was right, *she* didn't take it out of here."

Trainer made an unhappy noise and shifted closer

to Sam.

Justin backed up until he felt her knee on his calf. "But she wasn't the only one here. You've been listening, I'm telling the truth." He forced a knowing smile. "I took it days ago. It's gone."

The mouthpiece's mildly pleasant façade slipped as he pointed a finger at Justin's chest. "Search him."

The overly rough search of his person didn't reveal what they were looking for and Justin felt naked as his guns and knives were stripped from their hidden places. "I told you it's gone. I'm the only one who knows where it is." His eyes were glued to the lead man, watching for signs that this might go wrong at any second. He'd failed his men for the last time.

"Bring him with us." The mouthpiece didn't bother to plaster his false face back on. "Even if he's stupid enough to destroy the formula we have him and the doctor. He's got the original chemical in him, not one of Doctor James' fakes. We have everything we need to replicate the chemical, although we have to work fast. If we miss our deadline there will be severe penalties." His dark countenance was enough to subdue any grumblings from the doctor, beaten in more ways than one. The top of one cheek was purpling rapidly.

Justin felt his stomach drop at the thought of being back in the lab. He trained his features into a blank expression, mastered long ago in Basic. As his hands were bound tightly behind his back his mind flashed back to that awful place: hell on earth. A parade of innocent faces walked through his mind and he considered finding a way to die before they could reach the human trial stage again. His imprisonment didn't have to be a complete failure. If he couldn't take down the entire program, he could at least destroy a part. Doc was going first, that much was certain.

Waiting for Doc to be wrangled to his feet, Justin turned his head to take a last look at Sam. She was watching him through one eye, brow furrowed. He would die to keep her safe even if it were his last time. He gave her a quick parting grin before he was pushed hard from behind.

Falling into step behind the lead man, he walked single file with Doc behind him and the little woman beater now calling himself Trainer bringing up the rear. By his reckoning Marcus would be up in another few minutes and once the knife was removed from Jimmy's heart, he wouldn't be far behind. One hand slid over the other and his index finger pressed a button on his wrist, activating the device hidden in his watch.

Ch. 32

Marcus came back first, gasping as his rapidly expanding trachea finally allowed air to flow into his oxygen starved lungs. He crawled to Jimmy, lying on his side, and extracted the knife to wait.

Sam watched, her head oddly calm while her cheek rested on the arm of the couch, hands lying limp in her lap. The blood itched where it had crusted on her face and she rubbed it gently with her fingertips in hopes of alleviating the tickling. From the blood spatter already drying into the fabric she could tell the couch was shot anyway.

After Marcus and Jimmy were both sitting upright, backs to the wall waiting for their strength to return, Sam spoke up. Her words were hard to annunciate through her bruised mouth. *I wish I could heal as fast as they do.* "They took him."

Marcus glared at her, making no move to get up. "I guessed as much."

She raised her head, frowning. "We should be going after them. You know what they're going to do to him and that doesn't bother you?" Her vision was blurry so she stared at his nose, oddly easier to focus on than his cold, dark eyes. "You're a real bastard, you know that? Well why don't you make yourself at home, maybe see if there's anything in the fridge while *I* go after them and try to help before they hurt him again." Her outrage pushed her to her feet and she swayed, glaring down at him.

"So now you're one of the team?" Marcus countered, showing not a hint of emotion. "You didn't want any part of us, remember? You left. You're why we're all sitting here trying not to bleed. You wanted to do things on your own, so go." He flicked his fingers toward the door.

Indignant, Sam put a hand out to steady herself. "As I recall you two were fighting over who got to torture me for that damned sample. And no, I *didn't* want to stick around for that." Ignoring his dismissal she swayed into the kitchen. She wouldn't get far looking like she'd just stepped out of a boxing ring.

Marcus' voice was low and deep, halting her in her tracks at the mouth of the kitchen. She had to strain to hear him. "You're only half right. *I* was willing to kill you to get the sample as well as your father."

Fighting down the flutter of hope she felt in her chest, she turned to face him. "I guess that's no longer an issue. At least where my father's concerned they beat you to it."

"Both really." He shrugged. "They have Shaw instead of the formula and they have Doc. It'll take them a lot longer to recreate it depending how much the Doc gives them since he destroyed everything except what's in his head." He tapped his forehead. "Smart guy, the Doc."

Sam was sick picturing Justin suffering in the name of personal gain. She grabbed a dishtowel and wet the corner to begin wiping the blood from her face. "Aren't we going to even try to find him?"

Jimmy raised his head, back among the living. Instead of answering he staggered to his feet and crossed the room to the air vent. Sam watched in fascination as he pulled a small black device from the grate and smashed it on the coffee table with his heel. Marcus, now also up and prowling the room, ran his fingers around the window and doorframes. Minutes later he dropped them on the coffee table and brought his boot down.

Now sure they didn't have an audience, Jimmy sank down on the couch and let his head fall back. Lines of exhaustion marred his handsome features. "Course we're goin' after the Sarge, we never leave a man behind." Clearing his throat, he tapped his watch at her. "Sarge activated his signal. We can track him within a fifty-mile radius. We're just giving him a head start so they don't see us coming."

Sam put a hand to her mouth to touch the tender lip she felt crack when she smiled. Blinking, she fought back the tears that pricked at her eyes. Let them think those were because of the cuts on her face, not the relief she felt that Justin wouldn't have to endure captivity again. That he knew help was on the way. Dabbing at her bloodied face with her wet towel she hid her moist eyes.

How she felt about her father was more complicated. She couldn't tell if there was anything left of the man she once called "Dad" or if his research had taken too great a toll on his morality and sanity to ever recover.

Ever the wet blanket, Marcus made sure she didn't get her hopes up. "We're up against nearly impossible odds, Sam. The only things we have going for us are surprise and Shaw's ability to die a few times before we can get to him. That buys us time but it doesn't make it any easier." There was something else bothering him but he drew his lips tight and was clearly finished talking.

Sam glanced at Jimmy who gave her a deliberate smile. Something was bothering him too. Something they weren't telling her about Justin that had them worried. Her heart clenched. *We'll get him back,* she promised. *He'd do it for me.* Regardless of her doubts about his motives she knew that much to be true.

Her fingers carefully probed the swelling already altering her features. Never quite dainty enough to make her beautiful, they weren't doing her any favors at present. Guilt slammed into her with a quick one two combination that had her leaning against the wall, panting. Paul, her mother, now Justin. She couldn't make things right for Paul and the only way she could help her mom was to steer clear of her until this was over. That left Justin. She *knew* she could do something for him. Confident she was making the right choice, she walked around Marcus and pulled her garbage can out from where it sat at the end of the cabinets.

Out of the corner of her eye she caught Jimmy and Marcus both watching her, puzzled when she pulled the bag away from the side and slid her hand down to the bottom. "We have one more thing going for us. We have exactly what they want." She opened her hand and showed them the silver cylinder.

"It was in the trash?" Marcus gaped.

"I threw it in there after I got it and when they left the trash alone," she shrugged, "I figured it was the safest place for it."

Shaking his head in disbelief, Jimmy laughed twice before putting his hand to his chest and grunting in pain.

Marcus held out his hand. "We'll take it from here."

Sam slid the cylinder into her pocket. "I'm going with you."

"No way *chica*," Jimmy interjected, "this is going to get ugly." He pointed at her pocket. "We're using that thing to get in but we ain't leavin' that place until there's nothing left but smoke."

"Then all the more reason you need me, I'm a nobody." She smiled at the looks they gave her. "I mean I'm not some super soldier. I'm just a girl they've already proven isn't a threat. They won't suspect anything from me. You can wire me up and I can get in and give you a lay of the land from the inside or something." Giving them no chance to refuse, she made her way through the living room calling over her shoulder, "I'm going to change my shirt before we go."

Five minutes later she emerged from her room in a clean shirt and jeans, socks and running shoes strapped on tight. It was the best outfit she could think of for sneaking into a lab and rescuing people. Patting her pocket and the precious cylinder inside, she grinned as best she could at them. "Shall we?"

They had no choice shy of wrestling their prize from her. Considering they would win, Sam considered it a sign of acceptance that, for the time being, the men kept their hands to themselves. *Or maybe they're just tired. They* were *both dead a half hour ago.*

Ch. 33

Justin and Doc rode in the backseat of the white SUV, Trainer drove, and the mouthpiece rode shotgun. He could see the black man's lips moving as he spoke into his cell phone, unfortunately the combination of talk radio and air blowing from the vents prevented him from hearing anything in any great detail.

What he *could* make out was the triumphant look plastered on his face when he twisted to take a peek at his prisoners, harmless with their hands bound behind their backs and ankles tied tight. "That's right, Ma'am, we've got Shaw *and* Doctor James," he boasted with a big toothy grin before going back to mumbling and facing the front.

"Thank you," Doc muttered under his breath.

Justin was drawn back from trying to listen in on the phone call. It was futile anyway. "Hmm?"

"I said thank you, for stepping in. Thank you for sparing Samantha."

He considered the doctor out of the corner of his eye. The lanky man's beady eyes were focused straight ahead, watching the road between the two front seats. He gave no indication that he was speaking.

"It's fine, Doc. That's what we were trained to do. We weren't always lab rats."

They rode in silence for some time. About twenty miles south the Doc's voice interrupted Justin's thoughts again.

"What do you think of Samantha, Sergeant

Shaw?"

"I'm sorry?" Justin turned and questioned the man unkindly.

Doc had turned and was studying him. It gave Justin the creeps. "I understand she was in your company for some time. I'm merely curious what you think of her presence of mind." Not the direction Justin was expecting. Doc jutted his chin toward the men in front of them. "During all of this she's been quite remarkable, don't you think?"

Justin detected a hint of fatherly pride in the man's words. Playing down his personal feelings for her, he bobbed his head. "I was impressed with her grace under fire, Doc. She's a steady-minded woman."

"Yes, she is isn't she?" Doc was thoughtful. "Her mother was always the flighty one. Whenever Samantha would fall or hurt herself I would dust her off and put her back on her feet. Brenda would get so upset, running for ice and bandages. She was never good with that sort of thing."

Justin snorted. From what he'd seen of the doctor both before their escape and since his return he would have to give the credit for Sam's cool to the parent he hadn't met yet. The mother he knew tried to redirect the attentions of killers from her daughter onto herself. He'd seen the same selfless cool time and again with Sam. This last time, when she was quietly taking blows he'd seen hard men fold under, she gave up nothing. She hadn't given them the package nor had she given up his men. That last part brought with it a painful reminder of the betrayal she'd thought him guilty of at the time, and still she'd refused to hand them over. He wished there had been time to explain at the farmhouse before she ran off. What a difference that would have made. She wouldn't have run. They wouldn't be here. If he had his way they would be in his bed right now, maybe still making love in the dusky hours before the dawn. Justin's dick twitched as he thought what he should be doing right now. His lips tightened wryly at the thought. *No, I'm sitting here with her father, tied up, waiting to die. Again. Fuck.*

Fearing he wouldn't get another chance to see her face to face and wanting to make things right, he spoke frankly. "Can you tell her something for me?"

Doc turned back to him, curious. "Of course. Anything."

Justin shifted uncomfortably. His arms were going numb and his body was no longer regenerating like it should. He was growing more certain he wouldn't walk out of the lab alive this time even if his team followed his signal. There was no telling how many more times he could make it back, but he was sure there weren't many. He swallowed against the swelling he felt in his throat. "Tell Sam I never would have let anything happen to her, no matter what I said."

"Did you threaten her, Sergeant Shaw?"

"Not in so many words, Doc." Justin looked out his window hiding his shamed face. "Just tell her, okay?"

He took long enough to answer, when he spoke Justin jumped. "I will, Sergeant."

***

Doctor James studied the brave Sergeant's profile. Samantha had been with the sergeant and his men for over a week. He'd seen the impression that time made on his daughter when she heard his name. The sergeant was right to think she was angry with him, although there was something else there underneath the anger. And now he understood what it was. It appeared Samantha wasn't the only one who had grown attached during their seclusion.

The doctor felt a quiver in his bowels. His daughter's words resonated with him. His legacy not need merely be professional. Maybe he could redeem himself with her as well. The doctor dared hope.

Ch. 34

Being in the best condition of the three, Marcus drove. Sam rode up front leaving the back for Jimmy to lie down. He was in rough shape. How much help he would be in a fight was uncertain. They were hopeful the drive would be long and afford him time to heal.

"Go south on 35W." Jimmy called through the seats.

Marcus did so without comment. Sam had her head ducked, relying on her hair to cover her face. She hadn't thought of hiding until someone's honking drew her attention. They'd pointed at her then Marcus then mouthed, "was she was safe". She attempted a smile and waved them off then went to riding with her face hidden, wishing it was still night and she could ride normally. She was getting a kink in her neck. Though honestly that could have been whiplash from the whole being punched thing.

When they drew away from the city and the lane beside her was clear, Sam risked an exploratory look in the rearview mirror and winced. She didn't know how much help *she* would be in a fight at this point. Her right eye was swollen almost entirely shut and, by the look of the puffy upper lid, there was no hope of it coming down any time soon. The right side of her upper lip looked like a botox treatment gone awry, lopsided as it was.

"Is there any chance we could stop for some ice?" She asked, poking at it tenderly. Her nose was swollen too though she doubted it was broken. The rest of the quiet man's blows had been to her stomach and although delivering serious pain, he hadn't caused her any severe damage. She didn't think.

Marcus grunted. "Next exit. I need a drink anyway."

They got off, swinging through a gas station where Marcus parked out back. "Stay here. The last thing we need is some good Samaritan calling the cops about our domestic problems."

"Did you make a joke?" Sam's mouth dropped and she winced. Marcus gave her a grumpy look as his eyes slid past her and into the back.

Jimmy asked for two energy bars and several sport drinks. "Dying takes a lot out of you," he told her when she gave him a brow raise. Marcus went in alone, coming out a minute later with two bags full of goodies. Once in the car he handed them out like gas station Santa. Jimmy got a handful of energy bars and three bottled drinks. Marcus handed Sam a bar and drink as well as a cup of ice and a packet of ibuprofen.

When she thanked him he replied coolly. "It's been a long day for everyone and we don't know when we're going to get another chance to eat." He pointed at her face. "You need to get that swelling down or you'll be useless."

"Thank you." She said again with a whole new meaning. More like *screw you.* Sam rested her elbow on the top of the car door, cold cup of ice pressed against her head and nearly cried for joy. The cold cup provided instant relief from the pain as well as hiding her face enough she could straighten her neck again.

They filled the tank and drove on for anther hour before Jimmy told Marcus to head east on I-90 toward Rochester.

"Rochester? He's been this close all along?"

"If he was really worried about keeping you off their radar it wouldn't matter if he was next door. He couldn't contact you."

Sam looked over at Marcus, remembering the name inked into his skin. "Marianna, who is she?"

He hid his reaction except for a minor twitch at the corner of his eye. "My daughter."

Softly, so that she didn't disrupt the fragile truce or whatever it was between them that had him temporarily not openly despising her, she asked, "Does *she* live far away?"

"She lives in Los Angeles."

"Isn't it hard? Don't you want to talk to her?" Her question was intrusive and transparent.

His lips tightened and his eye ticked twice. "Of course it's hard." He said before turning his head to look her in the eye. "But it is a lot easier than going to her funeral." He turned back to the road and Sam didn't say anything else until they hit the city limit sign for Rochester.

Ch. 35

The SUV was stopped in front of a good-sized auto repair shop that appeared to be abandoned. The name had long since faded from the chipping paint and the sign that rose above the rooftop had been denuded of its plastic facades. No hints of movement came from inside. Justin was only absently aware of the river bluffs rising dramatically beyond. It was beautiful there but his eyes were trained on the building and his companions. The plain tan painted cinderblock building was long and low with five white overhead garage doors along the front of it. The backside was partially protected by a mound of earth from an ancient septic system, stretching out beyond the edge of the shop. He wondered how long it had been since a legit business had been there; it looked like it hadn't been touched since the '40's, except for the shiny metal keypad hidden by the tan access panel. The driver got out, punched in a stream of numbers and got back in to wait. In a few seconds the overhead door farthest to the left rolled open allowing them to drive in.

It had been a long time since cars were the primary focus here. Inside, the building had been converted from a shop to a sterile lab. The bay where they pulled in was walled off from the rest of the building. Another smaller vehicle had been pulled up in front of theirs and the shop was deep enough for another small car to come behind them. The wall to their right was a solid corrugated steel wall with a single door, its high tech coded entry serving as a secondary guard against unwanted guests. Justin and Doc had their feet free to get out of the SUV and were ushered through the steel door. Justin didn't fail to notice the keypad on the inside of the door as well. Escape would be complicated. Once inside their hands were freed.

"Strip," the mouthpiece commanded.

Justin, rubbing his wrists and rolling his shoulders in an effort to regain circulation in his nearly numb limbs, took in his surroundings. What had obviously once been the service bays had been redone in lab chic. Stainless surfaces, white walls, easily mopped light tile. Just beyond where they stood was another steel door and keypad. During his eyes' swing he caught the mouthpiece's hand resting on the butt of his gun in a low shoulder holster. Trainer had his weapon out already, held low by his side and eagerly waiting for one of them to object.

Before he could make a smartass comment about his impending nudity an electric tone, a click and the far door opened to a man in light blue scrubs. The newcomer stepped through the door, motioning for them to follow.

"Welcome back Doctor James, Sergeant Shaw. The decontamination showers are this way." He cocked his head and addressed the mouthpiece. "She's waiting downstairs Mr. Smith."

Justin followed the mouthpiece and Doc fell into step behind him looking shaky and uncertain with the little gun toting woman beater, *Mister* Trainer bringing up the rear. Doc wasn't used to being handled this way and Justin almost felt bad for the man so clearly outside of his norm. An image of Mills' face frozen in death brought a quick close to his thoughts of sympathy.

Through the door in what was once a customer lounge, stood a large alcove on the outer wall with a bank of three large showerheads over the top and two jets on either size. Some might call it a spa shower. Its purpose was more clinical than pleasure. Justin was willing to bet the velocity of the streams would be nothing those at a spa. Two wall-mounted soap dispensers were lined up on the back wall.

When it turned on Justin washed first, the hard barrage of water sending sprays up his nose and into his eyes and ears as well as other more tender places, assaulting his senses with their concentrated and powerful spray patterns. Ranger training had involved being disoriented so Justin was much better able to function than the doctor. Using his hands to feel for the soap he followed orders, finally taking a waterfree breath again when he was allowed to step out from the white block-walled shower bay. The doctor clattered around for a few extra minutes while Justin dripped dry. When they both were declared officially clean they were handed light blue scrubs and slippers to don. Someone had already taken their street clothes and Justin's watch, discarding his last link to his men. Being back in scrubs slammed the reality home for him. There was no doubting where he was and what lay in store. His gut pitched and acid flowed up his throat, over his tongue.

Public nudity didn't bother Justin. Years of communal showers and living in the military pretty much killed any sense of modesty. Doc, however, was clearly uncomfortable being naked with an audience. He let his hands hang in front of him, covering his privates, as he reached for the scrubs presented by the man who led them here. For Doc, this treatment was humiliating. Justin was surprised when he bristled at their treatment of the doctor.

Their scrub-adorned guide had gray hair and a neatly trimmed mustache. He was holding Justin's clothes while staring unabashedly at his body as he tied the string waistband on the loose pants to keep them over his narrow hips. Justin glanced down, seeing the scars, most prominently his newest bullet hole and glared back at him. "Admiring your handiwork?"

247

"Mr. Trainer." Mr. Smith's voice prevented any sort of an answer.

Stepping in, Mr. Trainer, now wearing sterile gloves, put a new set of zip strips around their wrists binding their hands in front of them before shoving Doc forward to take the lead.

"You know where we're going." Trainer barked at Doc's slumped shoulders. "Lead the way." He gave a shove just to be an asshole.

Unprepared, the doctor was sent sprawling. Justin leaned down and clamped his hands over his bicep, tugging him to his feet. Doc nodded, mumbling a "thank you" and used his bound hands to smooth the front of his shirt.

Walking beside the doctor Justin took in their surroundings, mentally taking stock of the lack of exits and windows. As was the case with the previous lab it was a completely controlled environment and would be a bitch to break out of. Several computers lined the wall monitored by lab assistants made androgynous by their asexual medical garb. Clearly curious, they each twisted their heads in turn to watch the prisoners or "test subjects" parade by. Their glares, oddly, were directed toward Doc.

Justin's neck itched in anticipation of a blade against it. He needed to distract himself. "Is this where you've been since we escaped?" Justin kept up the charade of a real escape versus the truth that Doc had at least a shred of conscience back then.

"Yes, Sergeant Shaw, this is where I sold my soul bit by bit." Regret and resentment oozed from each word. His loathing for the part he played in this heinous program was too strong to be false. "I destroyed everything when I left here. I launched a virus. I ran the formula down the sink. Tissue samples left out and left to rot at my station. I thought I was so smart." Eyes wide and shining, Doc surprised Justin with the risks he'd taken. His demolition would have taken days during which he could easily have been found out. "Then they drag me back here and I find out they've gone and brought in new computers and the staff is already rebuilding." He must have understood what he saw on the monitors they walked past. "Plus now they have you again. My efforts were for nothing."

Justin wrestled with this side of the doctor. He and his men believed the worst of him, assuming his letting them go was merely one moment of pity for an otherwise dark soul. How else could he justify the part he played in this? What they heard over the monitors in the truck when Doc was spilling his guts to his daughter came back. *I couldn't cut up live men. I tried to leave.*

He gave up his life without much choice in the matter. Doc left the family and successful career as a research scientist on a promise, only to lose everything when it turned out he'd been misled.

A poke in his back got Justin's attention. Mr. Smith waved toward a gigantic open-faced elevator like one would find in a hospital with an open grate floor awaiting them at the edge of the clean room. That had to be how they got the equipment down to the lab. An unbidden shiver ran down Justin's spine. *They've got me. They'll leave the others alone now.* He consoled himself with thoughts of his teammates finally living in peace and Sam being able to go back to her life.

Justin nodded at Mr. Smith's street clothes. "No need for *you* to shower? Or do you just figure no amount of scrubbing will do?"

Chuckling, Smith answered mildly. "I'm not staying, and I've promised not to contaminate the sample."

Justin fumed. *A little longer, only a little longer,* he told himself to try to keep his anger in check. *I'll do what I need to do to destroy this thing for good then I'll end it.*

"Welcome back Sergeant Shaw. You're late but we've held a spot for you."

He hadn't heard that voice since he'd shipped out to Iraq. Her soft, husky tone hid the venom he knew lay beneath. "Colonel Meredith Lange." He felt his lip rise in a snarl. *His* former commanding officer had been behind all of this? He thought he was going to be sick, clamping his teeth shut against his stomach and exchanging the useless feeling with a more useful one: anger. "This is *your* operation?"

She bowed her elegant neck toward him as her hand touched her epaulet. "It's General now, and in a manner of speaking, yes. I have command of the operation." Her pride was sickening. "After our top generals discovered leaders in third world countries and dictatorships the world over were able to develop weapons we couldn't due to social 'limitations,'" she rolled her eyes, "I was brought in to oversee a small but necessary project guaranteeing our country's defensibility." She let her voice grow husky, intimate. "You should be thanking me, Sergeant. I had to call in a lot of favors and make quite a few promises to bring you here after what happened. They wanted to kill you." Frowning, General Lange actually managed to look offended. "And then you went AWOL on us. Do you know what I had to *do* to keep my position?"

Mouth falling open, Justin was too shocked to

even be pissed. *She's off her fucking nut.* Justin took a long look at her, searching for outward signs of her complete lunacy. Meredith had always been a relatively plain woman with ash blonde hair, although her big blue eyes and generous lips made her popular amongst the enlisted men. Nature hadn't given her exceptional looks but she knew how to use them. Combined with a position of power she'd been the ultimate forbidden fruit and reveled in it.

He too had fallen under her spell for a short time and she encouraged the interest of the young, promising sergeant. Theirs was a brief tryst ending when his request to depart Camp Pendleton for Iraq was granted. She wasn't pleased with his decision to leave. She was used to being the one who made the decisions, only this one was beyond her. The war was being run out of Washington and she had no pull there, not yet. When he announced that his orders had come through she was livid, swearing she would make him regret it. Her career aspirations had always been lofty but Justin would never have imagined her capable of sanctioning torture and murder. And even though their breakup couldn't have been the cause for her involvement he couldn't help feeling responsible.

Not much time had passed since he'd seen Meredith last yet the change was dramatic. Where her eyes had been open and bright, now they were heavy lidded and her cheeks red from a conscience filled with regret and nights most likely involving too much wine. Lastly, the biggest change he could see was the bitter twist to her lips. Her smile was no longer her most pleasant feature. Now it spoke of a tendency toward cruelty instead of her former ready laughter.

"You'll forgive me, *General*." Justin uttered the title with contempt. "I wasn't aware you were the one waiting for me." He stared her down. "If I'd known, I would have come willingly. With a grenade." His hand itched for a weapon. If he blew the place now he could take out the program and all its key players. He didn't give a shit if he died in the process, he was kind of thinking that was how this was going to end anyway.

Trainer drove the butt of his gun into Justin's kidneys, dropping him to his knees.

"Better late than never I say." The General's lips tightened, her eyes narrowing at his boldness. "Just think of all the catching up we have to do."

Ch. 36

Sam bit back her objection on their second drive by while her feet tapped out an impatient staccato on the floor mat.

"Do you mind?" Marcus snapped. "I can't think with all of your noise."

Her feet stopped their rhythm but the urge to move was unbearable. "What more do you need to see? You could drive by the place ten more times and not get anything new. They have all the doors closed and nobody's so much as peeked out a window when we've gone past. The only thing that's going to change is how much they hurt him. Them," she corrected herself.

I'm being practical, that's all. Her father was safe in there. He was *more* than safe now that he destroyed all of their research. Being the lead scientist on the project they would need him more than ever. Justin, on the other hand, was lead lab rat. They would be only too eager to get their scalpels on him again. Her foot began tapping its rhythm again. Marcus grumbled.

They drove another half mile down the gravel road, the repetitive pinging of stones against the wheel wells adding to Sam's insistent tapping. Stopping in the shadow of some overhanging trees off the side of the road, Marcus put the car in park and rested both hands on the wheel. Sam stared out her window; the leaves of one particular low hanging branch camouflaged her view of what lay beyond.

They were at the edge of where forest met field, an important divider in this community rooted in farming and moving quickly toward a future in medicine. With the world-renowned Mayo Clinic based here and its spider web network of supporting clinics and laboratories, Rochester's citizens now made their livings serving the needs of the world in an entirely new way. The skeleton of a partially erected office a few miles on the other side of the field stood in stark contrast.

"Why are we standing here doing nothing?" Marcus' plan was taking too long to unfold for her. Sam needed action now. Her imagination had Justin already bleeding. "We should be talking about how to get in there."

"We're waiting for Jimmy." Marcus replied flatly without affording her even a cursory glance. He flicked his eyes up at the rearview mirror. "Hey Jimmy. Rise and shine, Martinez, time for you to work your magic. Sarge's comm is gone, we're blind and deaf out here."

Jimmy was slow, and by the sound of the rustling as he moved around. He was still suffering from his wounds, both had been severe and his recovery brief and less than ideal. It was no surprise it was taking a while for him to bounce back. "What do you want, man?" Encouraging, his voice was strong despite his convalescent status. "You want eyes? I don't know what I can do with that block. It's hard to get a signal through that."

"Get what you can. I'll get your stuff out of the back." Marcus got out and unlocked the steel truckbox mounted against the back of the cab for a minute before swinging himself back into his seat and tossing Jimmy's black nylon bag to him.

Grunting upon impact he gave a sarcastic "thanks" before Sam heard the zipper and turned in her seat to watch. Jimmy was unpacking several mysterious pieces of technology before clicking them together and taking out headphones. The last piece Sam recognized. It was an extendable antenna and Jimmy held it out to Sam. Taking it, she opened her door and used the suction cup on the bottom to mount it on the roof before stepping back in and shutting the door, closing out the sound of the cicadas better enabling Jimmy's eavesdropping.

Once assembled, Jimmy's device consisted of a small box roughly the size of a hotel Bible with a handle on top and several dials along the front and an attached monitor with a screen the size of a phone. Putting the headphones in place and grabbing the black "megaphone" attached by a cord and sitting in his lap, he opened his door and tapped the back of Marcus' headrest. "Be right back." He slid out smoothly enough, considering.

Sam opened her door and jogged after him, falling in step beside him just past the tailgate. "I'm going with you," she declared firmly. Twisting around to look through the back window, she saw Marcus watching her in the rearview mirror making no move to stop her.

"Suit yourself but if you get dead, no complaining." He didn't slow down.

To reach the backside of the building without being seen they were forced to loop wide and come back along the road, crouching in the ditch for the final quarter mile before they reached the mound. The last dying heat of summer cooked the air around them, the lack of rain giving them only limited reprieve from the humidity normally causing endless misery this time of year. By the time they could hunker behind the shelter the mound provided Jimmy's shirt was damp and his face wet with sweat.

"I'm fine." He waved off Sam's concerned expression when she started to speak. "I gotta be," he joked with a stiff smile, "nobody else can make this stuff sing like I can." He held up the mini megaphone and aimed it at the only window; a glass block square about fifteen feet in from the outer edge.

Frowning, he concentrated as he juggled the handheld device and attachment in his damp hands. Sam reached out and slid her fingers around the handle of the megaphone. Jimmy flashed her a grateful smile and went back to turning his dials carefully and methodically. He would turn one half a click and wait several seconds, turn one half a click and wait several seconds. He continued that way for several minutes.

Sam's limited patience was maxed out keeping herself from fidgeting and messing up their "ears." She wanted desperately to jump up and knock on the nearest door, waving the cylinder she knew would gain her immediate entrance. The only thing holding her back was the fact that it could get her in, but she hadn't figured out yet what could get them out.

The idea of her father being free brought with it a whole new internal conflict for Sam. *What if he was free from all this?* she wondered. Would he *choose* to be a part of her life? Would he disappear again, never to be heard from except for the annual unwanted gift? She didn't want to admit it, but she was afraid of losing him again. The fact that she wanted a chance to know him knocked her on her ass.

"Hey, I got something," Jimmy whispered excitedly beside her.

Startled, Sam jumped and earned a sharp glance. She craned her neck to watch the monitor.

His finger traced a small red blur at the bottom of the screen. "The concrete block's distorting the sound."

He turned down the knobs and killed the warbling static coming over the small headphones he pulled down to hang around his neck. "See that? That's a heat signature. That's a person." He pointed to three others in the same general vicinity. "All people." He wrapped his hand over the back of hers and waved the attachment all the way around the opening then back, staring at the screen the whole time. Sam hopped up and followed when he ran, crouching, to the other side and repeated the swinging sweep from the other angle.

"What do you see?" The monitor was too small and her angle too severe to make out more than a few shadows. The colors of the blurs were a lost detail the further toward the edge the monitor they appeared. Everything looked a variation of gray from her position. She debated leaning in to see better and risk being yelled at or hit on.

His forehead wrinkled as he continued to stare at his monitor. Finally he shook his head. "There are two or three over here, this one is either two people standing next to each other or one fat one but the block is so thick I can't see more than this area." He lowered his device and frowned at the building. "I'd guess there's a basement in there. They need more space than this for what they do." Jimmy's dark head swung deliberately back and forth. He was too exhausted to be his usual animated self. "They picked the right place to put this thing. It's gonna take goin' in there to get a good look."

"I'm guessing you have some sort of wire or tiny camera or something?" Sam's gaze was fixed in front of her, decision already made.

"I can't let you go in there. You're a civilian." He didn't sound happy.

"They're not going to let *you* in." Blinking, she

turned her head and patted her pocket. "I have insurance as long as we have this."

Expression dark, he pointed at her face. The swelling had gone down from all the ice she'd been throwing at it. She'd even been able to open her eye when they'd reached town and considered it a major victory. Her speech was still slightly affected by the cut inside her lip, but overall Sam considered herself relatively okay. "Think you're ready for another round?"

"Don't worry about that, it's a few bruises that's all." Her fear was easier to swallow when she pictured Justin being picked apart; they would show him no kindness. Steeling herself for an argument, she set her jaw and crossed her arms. "I can get in there and get you the information you need. I'm the only one of us three they aren't going to want to do experiments on." Holding up a finger, Sam headed off Jimmy's objection. "They have everything they need to make the formula except time. Remember what their guy said? They have a deadline for results. A completed product is going to make them money now where a failed deal is going to cost them more than just money. Word will get around that they don't have the real thing and they'll be sunk." Sam looked meaningfully at Jimmy, "They need this sample bad. It will keep all of us safe if we do this right. I trust you guys to do the cavalry bit once I find Justin and my father." She gave him what she hoped was a reassuring smile. Her cheeks felt stiff and a spot of blood from her lip leaked into her mouth.

She saw him beginning to agree before he shook his head. "I'm not gettin' blamed if somethin' goes wrong. Sarge would have my ass if I got you killed. We're runnin' this one past Marcus before we make any sorta decision."

"Fine." Sam gritted her teeth and followed him

back to the car. She was going in there whether they agreed with her or not and each tick of the clock brought Justin closer to his last death.

Ch. 37

General Lange had very definite plans for Justin. Their brief ride down to the lower level brought them to an open space exactly the same size as the upstairs "shop" only without any of the dividers.

Smith and Trainer left Doc at a lab table complete with a white top and accordion power cords hanging down from the ceiling; one attached to a microscope, one to a laptop. Several racks of what looked like ice cube trays hovered nearby, stocked with test tubes. A half-size fridge whirred a few paces away. The laptop sat open, a happy face screen saver bounced from edge to edge. A sleek metal bar with clear glass containers in various sizes lined the far wall. The containers sat empty, waiting to be filled. A short metal rack filled with shallow trays hovered at the end of the bar burdened with metal clamps, gauze, and other various surgical supplies. Clean, tidy, spit polished. It was sparse but without a doubt a research laboratory, waiting for two crucial things: scientist and test subject. Justin stood straighter, squaring his shoulders.

"As you can see we've cleaned up your mess so get yourself set up, Dr. James." Smith's tone held a dangerous warning. "We've done our best on short notice to get you the basics. The rest of your team has been dispatched. By destroying the project and your notes you've made this a one-man show, Doctor. I would suggest you not delay any further or you will be dispatched as well."

Doc remained at his table, unable to meet his gaze as they led Justin forward to a white padded chair complete with movable panels for arms and legs to be strapped onto. The fact that the chair was mounted on top of an elevated bank of pale tiles with gutters along the outer edges didn't escape his notice. All's the better to keep the bodily fluids from pooling and causing the butchers to slip he thought contemptuously. Glancing around, he saw one huge difference between this lab and the previous one he and his men called home for six months. No cells. No living quarters for the test subjects. The message was clear. As soon as they had what they needed from him he was done. It didn't matter that he planned to die in here, facing it so blatantly laid out was chilling. He broke into a sweat.

Smith stood by being smug. "You remember the drill, don't you? You lay there and we take pieces off until we've got what we need." He tsk'd and wagged his head. "The doctor tossed all the tissue samples. Looks like you've got a big job ahead of you too."

"Go on, Sergeant Shaw." Trainer pushed him forward. "Climb up there."

"Why's he here?" Justin indicated Trainer with his chin, still refusing to say his name. "Can't wait to get his turn?" Justin had been horrified at learning that this soldier wasn't the usual unwilling participant. At least not once he learned the purpose of the tests. The bastard actually *wanted* to be one of them. They'd trained at Pendleton together and Justin always thought the guy was a little off. Too intense to be "right". When he jumped ship to the dark side he ceased to exist to Justin.

"Good question, Sergeant. I'll tell you." Smith smiled his bland smile. "Because as it turns out Dr. James has been fooling us for years with only partially complete formulas." He pointed at Trainer, currently turning a curious shade of purple and looking like he was going to have a seizure if he couldn't choke someone soon. "Mr. Trainer here is the last remaining subject from the last set of human trials and he's on borrowed time. The chemical he was given allowed him to regenerate like you boys only he's become more unstable each time he's come back. That isn't the kind of product we want to promote here. No one wants an army of deranged, hard to control killing machines. Although we've certainly found a use for his violent tendencies."

Justin glanced back to see Trainer grinning broadly at him. Smith was doing nothing to control the psychopath. Justin's hand clenched into a fist and for a second he saw it connecting with Smith's mocking lips and smashing Trainer's heavy Slavic nose.

"Go ahead." Trainer easily read the directions of Justin's thoughts. "You can have your moment's satisfaction." A dark shadow crossed behind his eyes. "Just remember, I get to make this hurt as much or as little as I want. *She* wants you left alive but with *you*," he grinned again, "that leaves me a lot of room for interpretation."

He could have fought although it would only put off the inevitable and he had no idea how many more of these he had left in him. He had to stay functional long enough to see this thing through to the end. Then he could let go. A pair of dark brown eyes hovered in his memory and Justin regretted there wasn't much of a chance of him making it out of here. If he had any life left when this was over he wanted to see Sam again. He wanted to see where things might lead without the threat of someone chasing her, of him living the life of a mercenary and hiding from Lange's hunters. Could they have a future together?

Feeling the pain of losing something before he ever had it, he stepped up to the chair and scooted into place, allowing Smith to buckle his arms and legs into the leather straps without a struggle.

Without waiting for any sort of surgical prep

Trainer closed the distance between them, a blade appearing in his hand. Resigned to his immediate fate, Justin watched him approach. His mind went back to the last time he and Trainer were in a lab together. The lab was about this size only there were more stations and white coats at each one. All four members of his unit were strapped in their hospital beds, hooked up to monitors that regulated and recorded their vitals and the changes when the "experiments" were conducted.

Trainer was in charge of sample collection where the scientists preferred to keep their hands clean. He also frequently got called upon to test the efficacy of the chemical, meaning "what types of expiration could they endure?" Blood loss, strangulation, drowning, internal hemorrhaging, the list goes on. Trainer seemed to take great joy in his work, cutting with both the precision of a surgeon and the gleeful abandon of an ax murderer. The only time he ever smiled was when one of Justin's men was screaming in agony.

That last time Trainer had come, before Doc was to take them to their new "home", he'd been tasked to obtain a few final samples from each of the men before they were transferred. Henry Mills was still healing from a particularly brutal extraction of liver tissue only two days prior. Seeing Trainer coming for him he seemed to give up, lolling his head to the side, his body gone limp. When the little man leaned in to carve out a section of skin from the inside of his mouth he hadn't hidden his pleasure. Justin saw him flash his nicotine stained smile. Believing Mills to have passed out, Trainer leaned in and put a hand on the side of his face, turning it to better see the flesh exposed. His tool was held loosely in his other hand.

Justin, watching his friend, was waiting for the screaming to start. It was a second form of torment for him not to be able to stop his men's suffering. He witnessed the strange glint in Mills' half closed eye as Trainer came for him sending a thrill through his devastated body, emaciated from the demands placed on it as well as from being led from cell to chair for six months with no real muscle use. Justin was staring, his mind mostly numb when the screaming started. Except when he heard it the sound wasn't coming from Mills. His eyes came back into focus, the other two caught on to what was happening as well.

"Rip 'em off man. Rip off his *cojones* and see if he can grow *those* back." Jimmy hooted, excitement bordering on hysteria.

Trainer's high-pitched screams filled the air as Mills twisted his hand, clenched tightly around his testicles. Mills was laughing hysterically. His tenuous hold on sanity seemed to have given way at last.

The area where they were held was in a far corner of the lab, the sounds well contained behind thick glass walls and solid steel doors. No one came to assist young Trainer as his sensitive parts were crushed in Mills' hand. However the little man was strong. He brought a fist up and delivered a well-aimed blow to Mills' temple. The relief was immediate as Mills' body went limp. Trainer wasn't done. The metal extraction tool in his hand clattered to the floor, his hand going to the hilt of the blade on his belt. The look in his eye sent a chill to Justin's core.

"Don't." That one word, spoken as a weak plea, was all he could think to say.

Trainer looked at him, all reason gone from his blue eyes rolling wildly in his pain flushed face. The knife came up and swept down in a vicious swipe across Mills' throat with such violence it cut through the flesh and into the bone.

Jimmy was cursing a steady stream in Spanish while Marcus remained dead silent, glaring his promise of vengeance. Justin watched, knowing this wasn't over. Trainer's arm drew back again and he brought it down several more times in rapid succession. The last time, the blade lodged in the bed and Mills' head hit the floor with a wet cracking noise as the bones crushed against the hard floor. And the scientists left the body for three days, waiting to see if by some bizarre happenstance it would grow back. By the end of the last day Justin was certain Jimmy was mad, Marcus was plotting killing each and every person in there, and Justin wanted to close his eyes and never wake up.

Back in this lab, seeing the knife in Trainer's hand as he approached, Justin was tempted to taunt him or hurt him like Mills and bring about his own lasting death. He could finally put an end to the nightmare of endless pain, a life as an undying soldier fighting other people's wars. Even if he could get free he couldn't best the man in a fight. Exposed to the reconfigured chemical, he was earlier in the process and was stronger. Then he saw Doc move into his field of vision and his thoughts turned to the doctor's daughter. *What if I made it out?* He pictured Sam's face when she thought he was going to kiss her. That image morphed into her body under him, cheeks flushed and eyes half-mast. *Fuck* but he wanted that. He couldn't give in now in a moment of weakness. It was almost over, he could last a while longer until it was finished. And maybe, just maybe he'd crawl out of here and get a chance to see if a good woman maybe wanted to try it too.

So it was with a tightly clenched jaw that Justin watched death approach and lower the knife to his throat. He worked to keep the dread from his eyes to cheat the little sociopath of his sick thrill as he felt the blade slice through his windpipe and artery. He felt the life pump out of him as he choked on his own blood, praying this would not be the last time for him.

Smith stepped up. Standing a few feet from Trainer's elbow, as a section of skin and muscle was removed. Justin felt him tugging, twisting to expose the desired flesh to be cut out.

"I said a sample damn it, you weren't supposed to kill him."

Shrugging, Trainer stared dull eyed at his superior. "Oops." He motioned to the blood pouring out. "You said the doctor was starting from scratch." He waved his knife at the source of the blood. "You can get plenty from that."

"Just go," Smith growled, watching the life fade from Justin's eyes.

Closing his eyes, Justin freed his mind from this place, picturing his boyhood home in the hills of Tennessee. The happiest of his memories got him through this before; he trusted them once again to keep from going mad. His visions of the hillside behind his house where he went shooting with his grandfather had been replaced though. In his mind's eye he saw a woman with dark eyes lying on a blanket under the familiar oak tree. Another haunt of his as a boy, this was a private place for him. It was where he went to think and find peace. He'd gone there after his grandfather's death.

In his vision he sat beside her, propped on an elbow. He reached out to smooth a few strands come loose in the breeze from her cheek. His face lowered and he imagined the feel of her full lips against his. Instead of providing him distraction, thoughts of Sam made the pain he felt all the more real. Because his home was memories of what was; Sam was what *could be* and damnit he wanted it. He heard a wet gurgle and knew it was him.

Smith's voice tied him back to the present. "What sucks for you is that this time *you're* our only materials source and we have people waiting for a demonstration of the new weapon they bought. You had better hope my partner here doesn't contaminate the samples by being sloppy or we have to start all over." His voice faded as death came to Justin, releasing him from the pain.

***

"How could you sell it? I... I took it before you could complete the final tests," Doc stammered. After all he'd done to prevent this, his whole plan had been for naught. He endangered his own daughter for nothing. His failure was devastating.

"We made the deals based on promise. Now it's up to you to help us deliver. We need a saleable quantity to keep our deadline. Our first delivery is scheduled for next week and we need to be punctual. We have a reputation to uphold." His footsteps faded and glass clattered as Doc fumbled his slide, dropping it on the table.

Ch. 38

"Absolutely not." Marcus leaned against the car shaking his head. "Sure, they'll let you in easily enough if you show them that." He pointed at the lump in her pocket. "Unfortunately it isn't that easy. We need to be able to get you both out, maybe the Doc too." He offered it, though Sam wasn't convinced he meant it. "Shaw is in who knows what kind of condition and you being fragile limits our rescue choices. Never mind the lack of leverage we have if *that* goes in."

Sam, pushed to take an unprecedented leap of faith by emotions she didn't dare explore quite yet, pulled the shiny cylinder from her pocket and held it out. "I'm going in. You decide if it's with or without that."

Wordless, Marcus held out a hand and she dropped it into his palm. He examined the metal tube closely before his grudging admission. Marcus flicked his eyes up to hers. "He's not going to *want* you in there."

Sam didn't care. They could fight about it when they were all out, safe and sound. As for their "permission" to go ahead with her plan, getting back out would be easier with their assistance though their cooperation wasn't necessary. "I've got the best chance."

Marcus' objection formed on his lips and he took a breath to give it voice.

"I haven't died yet today." She reminded them the cost their healing had taken on their bodies. "They're going to kill him for real when they don't need him anymore. Do you want that on your conscience?" Sam stuck out her chin and lied. "I know you'll get me out. I trust you."

"He's dead already." Marcus replied quietly, staring over her head in the direction of the building where his former leader was enduring God knew what.

"What? Like *really dead*?" She managed to keep most of the quaver out of her voice.

His gaze returned to her, nothing readable behind his eyes. "Did you ever wonder why they would keep us alive? Replicating every type of injury a human being can receive, each time taking a sample of our flesh or internal organs when they could simply pull the DNA out of a sample piece of any one of us and be done with the whole thing?"

Her father's chilling statement that he'd had a corpse to cut sections off after helping the other three escape came back to her. She stared at Marcus, waiting, unable to breathe.

"When they first got us back they weren't sure if what we'd been exposed to was the chemical we were sent after. Even then, having us already tainted gave them a chance to experiment on live subjects to see how accurate the reports had been. One of the techs took blood after they'd killed Jimmy the third or fourth time."

"Fourth." Jimmy clarified from where he at on the open tailgate. "Right after that one they gave us the implants."

Marcus frowned at the interruption. "That was when they noticed that the levels were all wrong. His white blood cell count had spiked. That sent them down a whole new road of 'what ifs'. It turns out when we die it triggers the enhanced cells to work overtime to heal the wounded area. The addition of the implant jumpstarts the organs like a super charged pacemaker. Each time it happens, it leaves more white blood cells in our systems.

It used to be we would die and be down for barely any time, getting right back up as strong as before. Now, even with the implants it takes longer each time. The restart causes less strain on the heart so it doesn't wear out as fast as they feared, but they were trying to figure out what the long term impact of the constant strain on the system and the addition of the residual white blood cells would be." He held out his hands. "So, they're going to be keeping him until they figure this out is my guess." His lips twisted bitterly. "They aren't going to want to ruin their newest specimen either. They'll keep Trainer intact as an example for buyers or top brass unless I miss my guess. He's fresh and he'll show better."

Sam shuddered to think that anyone, even a sadist like Trainer, would let himself be killed on purpose. "Well, whether you approve or not, *I'm* going. *You* get to decide whether you'll help me get him out or let us both die." Drawing herself up, Sam gave him her best disdainful look and fired a final shot meant to stir him to action. "He would go in there for you and you know it."

Her reminder of Justin's commitment to his men served its purpose. Marcus was angry, slamming a fist into the side of the vehicle. Sam couldn't help herself figuring the value of the damage. He stormed away, the sun glinting off the cylinder clenched tightly in his fist. She watched it go, thinking how much suffering could be avoided if she chucked it off of the highest cliff into the deepest pit on the planet. Then she snorted. No, sample or not these people would come for Justin, his men, her father, anyone who had any chance of helping them to recreate their precious formula as long as they were around. *That* was what had to disappear, not the cylinder. Sam considered what that meant.

Marcus came to a halt at the edge of the trees, staring at the tube in his hands and tapped it with a

270

finger. "Jimmy, rig her up. I want it invisible."

Sam turned to Jimmy, her victory tempered by the fact that it was possible she wasn't going to walk back out. She felt an odd sense of peace. Because with the same certainty with which she knew she was going in, she also knew she wouldn't come out without him.

At his direction Sam stripped off her shirt and leaned against the truck's black grill while Jimmy dug in the bag at his feet. Watching his hands helped alleviate some of the awkwardness of being half naked in front of the shameless flirt.

That he didn't use the opportunity to make jokes or cop a feel, Sam's stomach plummeted into her shoes. "You don't think this is going to work, do you?" She watched his hands slip into the lacy edge of her bra to secure a wireless microphone the size of a watch battery.

Jimmy's lips were tight, his brow creased in concentration. When he removed his hands, there was no hint of a bump. "Would it matter? You're gonna do it anyway." He went back to the tailgate. "You're gonna get in there fine. It's the gettin' out that's the problem."

Sam followed him, leaning with her hip against the sun-hot metal. "What would you do if you were me? Would you just stand around doing nothing? Would you wait for it all to be over so you could collect the bodies?"

Years of defenses layered on until she was untouchable had been punched full of holes in the last week. Witnessing the bravery of these men and watching them put themselves on the line for a much greater selfless cause over and again, she let go of the anger over Marcus' willingness to harm her for the sake of the greater good. She understood his motivation. They alone

271

bore the full weight of protecting the world from the fallout if this chemical got out. That was a heavy burden and one they didn't shirk. Her hand went out, reaching to touch Jimmy's forearm. "I have to do *something*." The raw emotion worked its way out of the depths of her heart. Intense to the point of a physical blow it hit her square in the chest, taking her breath with it. Her eyes stung and her voice cracked. "I can't leave him. I just can't." Sam physically felt the draw to the man inside. She couldn't leave this place without him if someone carried her.

Jimmy put a hand over hers and gave her a real smile, not bothering with his usual cocky show. "Me either *chica*." He gave her another pat and went back to his bag. "If we're gonna do this, let's do it right."

Ch. 39

"Sergeant Shaw, can I get you anything?" Lange's voice beckoned inches from his ear. Her multifaceted offer was transparent as well as nauseating. Justin's aversion to the woman was visceral.

Justin woke hungry among other things. He couldn't remember the last time he'd eaten other than grabbing something on the road. Healing was a huge calorie burn and he was giddy from fatigue. Every muscle burned and he had a raging headache from dehydration and blood loss, yet coming to consciousness he heaved a grateful sigh. *I came back.* Ignoring the piercing glare of the lights above, Justin opened his eyes. "Meredith," he began, making his revulsion obvious. "There is *nothing* you have that I want."

She sucked air noisily between her teeth, standing stiffly and smoothed a hand over her black sheath dress and blazer. "That's really too bad Justin. If you want to be a stubborn ass I can make your stay even more unpleasant. I see you're not interested in comfort."

The woman's need for control was ridiculous. When he was with her, brief as their affair was, he'd picked up on it. It had to be her choice where and when to eat, what they did and whom they did it with. When he spoke of breaking things off she alternated between shouting and tears, manipulating his sense of chivalry. He saw his deployment to Iraq as his escape. Now that very escape had brought him full circle, back into her hands. "Not only is there nothing that you can offer me Meredith, I won't let you take anything else from my men. Not anymore."

Justin avoided moving his head around to follow her as she paced behind the chair and out of sight. He could feel the skin, still torn and finding its way back together gradually, and painfully. It never failed to amaze him how his body could heal itself in a matter of minutes, now hours.

"I'm not interested in your men right now, Justin. There's a visitor at our door right now Mr. Smith says is a friend of yours *and* the key to finding our lost sample. Your cooperation could make all the difference in how we handle her." Her disembodied whisper was right in his ear. "I don't believe you destroyed it, *Justin*." She whispered his name like a caress. "I think you're too smart for that. You know what it's worth and you tried keeping it for yourself. Let's see if your friend is more willing to share."

Her? The air was squeezed from his lungs. Sam was here? *What the fuck is she thinking?* He could throttle her for putting herself in danger like this. Was she here for him? He checked himself for assuming too much. She'd come for her father, not him. Still, hope tickled in his chest.

Regardless of why she was here the fact remained that she *was*. What were Marcus and Jimmy thinking? They had to know what she was up against. He was too weak to protect her and Trainer and Smith both were armed. *He* might not survive a retrieval attempt and Sam definitely wouldn't if things got bad.

Fighting to keep his mounting apprehension from showing, he shrugged. "She's Doc's daughter she must have followed him here. I told you, I destroyed the sample. It's gone."

The general walked around his head and back into view. He eyed her warily, praying she would accept his explanation as truth. "She doesn't like Doc's work and wants to stop him working on this project. She's just

274

going to get in the way. If you're smart you'll get rid of her, you can't afford to lose the time if he's distracted."

"Hmm." She put her hand to her chin, index finger tapping absently in thought. "You know Sergeant, you bring up a valid point. Dr. James could benefit from some additional motivation; having his long lost daughter so close might prove to be just what he needs."

Justin's hands clenched at his sides and he willed them to open again. He rushed to shut her down. "He left her when she was a kid and hasn't had any contact with her since." She didn't need to know about the annual gifts. "The only reason she's even involved is because he used her to hide the formula and it pissed her off. She's probably here to give him a piece of her mind. He's not going to worry about her safety now. If he did care he wouldn't have involved her." Justin honestly believed at least some of what he said. The Doc was a shitty father and the best thing he could do for his daughter at this point was to send her packing before she got sucked in any farther.

Her eyes narrowed. "Has anyone ever told you that charming little accent of yours is more pronounced when you're nervous?" A slow, frightening smile thinned her lips. "I'm not so sure we should write off the value of our guest just yet."

Justin felt every aching inch of his body sink into the chair and let his heavy eyelids droop. His mission had been nearly complete. He was here. He found the hive and was fairly certain he was within spitting distance of the queen bee. All he had to do was get his hands on a few explosives and this program would no longer exist. The doctor going down with him gave him no qualms, he honestly had too much information in his head for Justin to be willing to let him loose on the world even if they did manage to survive this. That flicker of hope that he might complete his mission and manage to make it out *and* have some sort of a future with Sam burned down to nothing. Now he had to find a way to get a very killable Sam out without coming to harm on top of everything else. That was going to prove to be a hell of a challenge. Plus if she were in here she would see things she wasn't meant to. And he would face having to explain to her why he had to kill her father.

Ch. 40

Sam held her breath, fighting the urge to check her shirt for visible lines as she waited for someone to answer the white overhead shop door staring her in the face. The only human sized door was boarded up and there was no doorbell to be found so when she stood facing the large door she did the only reasonable thing she could think of. She banged on it and waited. She prayed her instincts were right and she was helping matters by going in. It was so difficult to sit out there and wait, wondering if he was alive. Although her father stood to face some consequences for trashing the program, he'd guaranteed his safety with that same move. At least in the short term.

Marcus, finally accepting that her going in was a decent idea, told her to get a read on Justin under the guise of seeing her father. He even smiled when he explained she was well equipped to play the bullheaded, well-intentioned daughter who wouldn't take no for an answer.

"Careful, your face might crack," she tried to act like she wasn't a ball of nerves. In her mind's eye she saw Justin broken and bleeding, unable to walk out. Would they be able to drag him out if he was hurt? Could she if it came to it? "Are we just going to hand it over if it comes to it?" *I knew they'd pull together if push came to shove. There's no way they could go through what they have and just leave him to suffer.* The hand clutching her stomach eased up a tiny bit.

"If it goes in, it's not making it out of there," Marcus replied without emotion.

Sam swallowed and set her jaw. What would her father do if he knew they were going to destroy everything, even his precious sample? Would he refuse to leave? Morally deficient or not, she couldn't just walk away and leave her father to die. "I won't need it." She reassured them, confident that once she found him, Justin and she would be able to handle anything, even persuade her father to walk away from the project that had stolen his life. "We'll get out." The men's estimation of her had grown; they didn't argue. Or, she considered with a sinking feeling, they already knew what she faced in there.

So Sam approached the lab/ garage half-sick and knocked on the giant door. She didn't wait long. After only a few seconds the door went up and Sam entered. There was the white SUV and a little blue Toyota in front of it. Regarding the wall of steel standing between her and her people, Sam felt the familiar prickling of the little hairs as they rose on the back of her neck. She worried she was putting it all on the line for someone who might not be all that appreciative. Two someones.

When the white door clanged shut behind her with a resounding rattle and her courage threatened to fail, Sam thought of the sacrifices both her father and Justin had made, each in his own way to stop this unnatural kind of zombie warfare becoming a reality. They both put themselves on the line for a higher purpose; so could she.

She drew her lip tight against her teeth, still painful and puffy despite the continued icing she'd given it while Jimmy wired her bra and the backup device hidden deep in her ear canal. The earpiece tickled and made it hard to hear, though he assured her if anything happened to the one in the lingerie she had the other as a backup. She didn't want to consider what might happen to the one that would require a backup. Straightening her back, Sam managed to offer a friendly greeting as a pale, mustached man in blue hospital scrubs opened the steel door to her right and stepped out. The sound of the metallic "clack" of the lock dared her to get by it. Stubborn, she straightened her shoulders.

"My name is Samantha James. I want to see my father, Dr. Steven James. I need to know that he's all right." The hands on her watch ticked audibly in the heavy silence as she waited for him to respond. He pulled a phone out of his breast pocket and dialed. After a minute he muttered her request to someone with more authority than him. Sam counted the ticks of her watch's second hand as she waited for approval.

Forty-three seconds after he dialed the phone, he clicked it shut and the twitchy little man re-deposited it in his pocket. "Come with me," he said simply and punched in a code on the silver pad beside the door. With a sigh the seal on the door released, opening wide and her escort stepped in waving her to follow.

She watched the quiet man, his face twitching nervously, and the mustache twisting sideways with each miniature convulsion. He was like a mouse on meth. Sam had to force her eyes to the ground as he led her deeper into the building, the door whispering shut behind them.

They passed another person, similarly garbed in blue, keying at a large desk computer. She counted only two people here and saw no signs of a lab. This was more library than lab. Several times as a kid she'd visited her dad at work and it looked nothing like this. The university where he worked before was bursting with scientists, students assisting, and technicians. Clusters of people hovered even in the outer rooms of the laboratories. Sam had never been allowed inside the sterile confines of the lab to see what it was like, though she'd sometimes watched through the big windows in the halls. That was back when she thought her father was a god. Before maturity and his own deeds took that away from her.

"Follow me." The twitchy little man hitched up his shoulder and sniffed. He'd caught her dawdling and picked up his pace, forcing her to take a quick step after him. Then, as they walked past the computer on the end, Sam slowed down to study the screen over the seated man's shoulder. She stopped and stared, her heart temporarily gone tender.

She recognized Justin's name and the picture from when he enlisted. Slow feet halting of their own accord, she stared. He looked like a kid. It hadn't been but eight years yet his eyes reflected each day he'd lived and died, each battle he fought for country and for money. The toll that took on him suddenly became clear. Now that she saw him staring back at her, twenty-six by the birth date on the screen: stern expression, a little cocky, yet somehow still hinting at the naiveté of youth, she thought of how he had looked the last time she'd seen him. When he'd come to save her at the apartment; when he'd traded himself for her. It was hard not to be moved to tears. He had lived a thousand lifetimes in those few years. Each one of those days leaving its mark on him. And yet she felt a surge of happiness. The youthful light in his eye captured on screen was the same one she saw at the farmhouse in those unguarded moments they'd shared before Marcus pointed out what lay between them and Justin pulled away. But she knew it was in there.

Somewhere in Sergeant Shaw's fatigued mind and body remained a hint of the man who was still willing to try. Whether it was an adventure or saving the world, Justin was willing to bring what he had to the fight. Sam wished she could inspire that passion, that spark in him on her own and not just for her father's gift. She could forgive what had come before if he were willing to start fresh; if Jimmy was right and he truly felt something for her.

The man in the mustache caught her eye and hurried back to tug her arm. "Come on. They're waiting." He frowned unapologetically when she jumped at his cool touch.

Sam was confused at first that they were waiting. Then her eyes scanned what she knew had to be there. *There they are.* The cameras over the entrance were probably only a few of many in the area. No one's coming or going would go unnoticed.

Curiosity overruled anger and Sam was able to keep her voice calm. "So, you know that these people are dealing with life and death. They're conducting human experiments right here and it doesn't bother you?" She pointed at her damaged face. "Your coworkers do this to people and you're okay with it?"

He stopped, rubbing his thigh absently with his palm. The beady eyes darted around under his bushy gray eyebrows then stopped on her for a long focused instant. "I believe in doing everything possible to defend my country." He twitched once. "To keep the rest of us safe some of us must get our hands dirty." His mustache bristled as he stared down at her.

Uncertain how to respond to his odd justification that seemed to validate the torture of American citizens, Sam followed him silently while he stalked ahead. The first inkling of what she might have gotten herself into itched at her. *There's no reasoning with zealots.* They walked through several apportioned areas lined by more computers and people monitoring them before turning a corner and staring directly into an industrial shower on the far wall. *You've got to be kidding me.*

"Strip." He pointed at her then swung his head toward the shower. Apparently that was an entire instruction manual for the icky creeper.

"Excuse me?" Sam blinked at him. "I'm not getting *naked* in front of you. I just changed before I got here, I'm clean."

In no way affected by her objection, he rocked back on his heels. "I can see the dust in your hair from here and that face is full of bacteria. Keeping this facility clean is my job and if you want to go any further you have to be clean. We're already behind schedule and we can't have you contaminating things should you touch either of the subjects." He waited, quietly smug in his little corner.

Sam feared losing not her bra but rather what was in it. Or worse, getting caught with it. She simultaneously tried to figure out how to get the bug out of her clothing *and* keep the one in her ear dry while doing as the hairy little ferret commanded. Two men of surprising importance to her were relying on it. Sam pictured only the one face to help motivate her to disrobe in front of a stranger. "What do I wear after I'm *bacteria free*? Are you expecting me to parade around in my birthday suit and give you all a little thrill?"

The mustache twitched. He knew he had her beat. "I'll bring you fresh clothing."

Putting both hands on her hips, she glared at him. "What about these clothes? I want them back."

"Put your clothes on the floor. We'll bag them for you and return them when you leave."

Sam had a hard time believing they would actually hold them for her. More than likely they didn't plan on her leaving here and those favorite jeans of hers were destined for a garbage can. That was a shame, good jeans were hard to find. She wanted to argue, to keep her clothes and her dignity, but it was time to take one for the team. "Okay." She put her hands on her hem to pull up her shirt.

He hesitated too long and Sam dropped her hands. "This isn't a show."

He flashed his teeth in a nervous smile at being caught and scurried out to grab her clothing.

In a rush, Sam tore the tiny microphone from her bra leaving a hole in the lace in her haste and let it fall to the floor kicking it down the drain. "Sorry guys, we're down to one." With a combination of head tipping and putting a finger in her ear Sam kept the ear bud, her last link to the men outside, dry and intact while she washed herself.

A polite cough behind her and Sam darted her eyes sideways to see a towel being offered. She took it, eager to be covered. She dabbed at the lip, shocked by the sight of her blood on the white fabric. She rolled it inward to hide it lest they find that reason enough to keep her from the "sterile area" where Justin and her father waited.

"Here, take these." His hand gripped blue scrubs like his.

"Can you at least turn around?" she growled.

He was watching her, making no effort to hide his eyes. "I'm a scientist." He told her flatly, like that gave him carte blanche to stare at absolutely anyone's nakedness.

"Well *I'm* not a specimen and *I* don't like to be stared at." She softened her tone hoping for some amount of courtesy. "*Please* give me a little privacy?"

Placing the stack of clothing on one hand he turned his body and eyes the opposite direction.

Sam dressed facing toward the inside of the three-walled shower. When she emerged, finger combing her wet hair, the microphone was still riding safely inside her ear.

Her escort gave her a cursory once over and nodded. "Follow me."

Sam was scared. She considered herself reasonably brave under most circumstances, but she'd never faced a situation like this. This wasn't just talking to someone in a bad neighborhood about minor injuries or a wrecked car. This was offering herself up to people who weren't afraid to kill. A million possibilities for this to go wrong pummeled her sensibilities. Swallowing hard, she cleared her throat. "Okay."

Seeing her following, he moved on another ten paces to a huge elevator. With no front doors and a grate for a floor it left them exposed as they rode down one floor. *Why would they need an open floor?* Images of bloody bodies filled her head and she gagged. Taking a few steadying breaths through her nose, Sam nervously smoothed the shirt of her boxy scrubs. Once she had herself under control again they'd reached the floor divider and she could see the lower level. Immediately her eyes studied everything in sight, keeping her part of the mission in mind. Having a job to focus on allowed her to settle her nerves from *holy shit* to *oh crap*. "This is a big elevator. You could move just about anything on it, huh?"

The little man gave her a queer look.

Sam offered him a lame smile. Subtlety wasn't her strong suit. She would have made a crap spy. When the platform touched the ground with a hollow metallic clang, Sam sucked in her lip trying to keep her reaction private. The tiles covering the large, open area went from the floors up the walls even rolling across the ceiling. The effect was immensely cold and suffocating all at the same time. Her knees trembled.

Her background with her father's previous lab should have had her taking in the details, determining whether they'd rebuilt the program enough to restart their experiments but her glance over the furnishings was cursory. Her eyes slid over her father, hunched over a computer at the table between her and the chair on the far side. As soon as she saw him, Sam forgot the ugly words at the farmhouse, her cover of being there for her father. Her feet were already moving before she had a conscious thought.

"Don't contaminate him." Mustache cautioned from behind her.

His objection barely registered as Sam jogged the short distance, her heart in her throat. Reaching Justin, Sam could see a thin red line across his throat. Marcus was right; they'd started already. *Bastards.* Glancing down she took in his bare chest. His shirt had been removed and the floor had been mopped but some blood remained, wet on the front of his pants. Sam bit her lip, sniffing sharply when her teeth bumped her temporarily forgotten injury.

***

Justin's eyes fluttered open and he moved to stroke her battered face, forgetting he was strapped down. He growled his frustration when he realized he could only move his shoulder. Horrified as he was to hear she was coming, in that moment, he was grateful to look once again upon her face. It was a pleasure he worried he wouldn't have again. Then he took in her wet hair and clothing. They'd made her shower. They made her strip in front of them. She caught him looking and a shadow passed behind her eyes before she hid it behind a brave face. His eyes cut to her escort and rage had him straining against his bonds. *I'm gonna fucking kill that motherfucker.* After he sent her way the hell away from here.

"Sam, you have to leave." He risked twisting his freshly healed neck trying to see where the general and her people had gone. They were down here a few minutes before when he drifted off. No one but Sam used the elevator; the thing was so loud it was impossible to sleep through even when he was half dead. Still there was no one in sight. Justin felt a guilty twinge as the lie rolled out. "I'll help Doc shake loose as soon I can but you can't be here."

Unable to look him in the eye, Sam reached a finger out to wipe away a tiny speck of blood on his cheek someone had missed. "He's not why I'm here." She admitted finally, her eyes flicked to his only briefly. Her brave front faltered, being so exposed left her shy.

Shocked as he was by her admission that she'd come for him, Justin couldn't deny the fullness in his chest. The skin where she touched him tingled. His fists clenched helplessly on the chair and he wished he could wrap his arms around her. The marks on her face and the troubled look in her eyes doubled his urge to protect her.

286

Yet here she was putting herself squarely in harm's way for him. *Fuck.* Speaking softly, he called her in close. "Sam, listen to me."

She leaned in close enough he could smell the same antiseptic soap from the shower neutralizing the soft, sweet smell he'd come to associate with her. For some strange reason he felt cheated. The unmarked side of her face rested inches from his as she waited dutifully for him to speak. Call it temporary insanity but without considering who might be watching, intent only upon doing that which he'd dreamt of since parting, he lifted his head to brush his lips whisper light across her cheek. If he didn't get the chance to touch her again he had to at least know her taste.

Startled, Sam turned her wide brown eyes to scan his features. Justin watched her, anxious as a teenager with his first crush, for a painful few seconds before her expression softened and she lowered her lips to his.

Very gently, he kissed her bruised mouth tasting traces of blood from her lip. Cursing the bands holding his arms and the tenderness of her bruises he was unable to give in to the need to crush her against him, to feel her body on his. It was one more thing they'd managed to take from him, he thought before remorsefully casting his desires aside.

Wrestling himself back under control, Justin pulled back catching a glimpse of regret in her eyes. "Sam you have to go. I've told them I destroyed the sample. You're safe. Doc and I will get out of here when we can." He saw her wanting to object. "We can spread this out for a day or so, that gives you and the guys plenty of time to get clear." He willed her to keep quiet and listen to him. Now was not the time for her to argue. Meredith had to be here somewhere.

Sam tapped her ear and turned her head giving Justin a glimpse of clear silicone shoved deep in the canal. She had ears to the outside. If it weren't for the fact that they were out there and she was in here he would have been ecstatic. As things stood she was still going to have to get past Meredith and her goons before he could breathe again.

On cue, a pressure seal released at the far end of the room and both heads turned toward the sound. A panel of tiles that had been bare wall moments ago was opening outward toward them. High heels clacked and men's shoes padded against the tile beneath them as General Lange, Smith, and Trainer approached.

Lange's venomous stare was fixed upon Sam, a viper stalking her prey. Mr. Smith grinned broadly and Trainer moved silently and without expression a few steps behind.

"This is fantastic." Smith chuckled, his voice boomed off the bare walls. "Not surprising I must say. I had a feeling after you got all 'knight in shining armor' at her apartment." Coming closer, he scrutinized Sam's face. "Yes, that was a bit much maybe for a first effort. You could try dialing it back next time Trainer." He winked at Sam. "My associate is not known for his finesse. Not like Mr. Young was, now *he* was gifted. You can thank your Sir Galahad for the personnel replacement."

Sam stared at him like he was speaking Chinese.

Smith enjoyed his game. "Forgive me, you might be more familiar with him by his work. I believe you saw what he did to the young man in your apartment?" Cracking a smile at the color draining from her face, he let his eyes linger on Justin's face then back to Sam's. "You certainly do get around don't you, young *lady*?"

288

His intimation had Justin's teeth clenched so tight he was likely to be molar free and choking on dust if the jackass didn't quit.

"Mr. Smith, let's not get off subject." General Lange cut him off. She was back to being the picture of cool and composed, her hand smoothed an imagined stray back into the flawless chignon holding her hair.

The woman in the black dress smiled graciously at Sam. She felt her hair rising on the nape of her neck. Her hand slid down and gripped Justin's, she felt him squeeze back. The woman's calm demeanor stuttered when she caught it, though she recovered so quickly Sam couldn't be sure what she saw.

"I think that we have been presented with a perfect time saving solution for our dilemma." Her head inclined toward their clasped hands. "We have something that Sergeant Shaw *obviously* cares about." Her tone grew icy. "So I say we use it to our advantage and find that elusive sample."

"No, please. Let her go." Doctor James called and started forward. Mustache caught and held him by the arm.

The distinct sound of metal sliding from a nylon sheath ripped at Justin's very soul. He glanced at Sam's face, the ghost of the blood he'd tasted in her kiss flitted across his tongue. In his head he saw her bravely taking Trainer's punishments. Down here, with no neighbors to hear her cries, he would do things she could have no way of imagining a human capable of doing to another human being. She could die here and there was nothing he could do. Tightening reflexively, he again cursed his bonds.

"Damn it, I *destroyed* it. I told you that before.

Don't bother with her, she doesn't know anything."
Justin kept his apprehension from his voice with
considerable effort. "General, I told you, you don't need
her." Sam looked at him and he gave her a look usually
reserved for those under his command. She couldn't
sense his physical weakness right now, not when it could
get both of them killed. "You have me, you don't need
anything else."

"And I told you, you're a bad liar." The general
eyed him, disbelief plain on her face. "Now is your
chance to save yourself and your girlfriend a *lot* of pain."
Lange motioned to Trainer who took another step toward
them.

Sam's hand tightened on his. Justin kept his eyes
on the advancing threat, not chancing a look at her for
fear what he saw there would distract him.
Concentrating was hard enough right now with his blood
thick as sludge, pushing its way too slow through his
veins, trying to delivery oxygen to his brain.

"Doctor James tells me he will need at least two
days to reconfigure a sample and that's just not fast
enough. The first buyer is coming tomorrow."

The first *buyer?*

"Sergeant Shaw, *you* are going to walk out of
here." Trainer sheathed his knife, working to free
Justin's legs before moving on to his wrists. "Miss James
is going to keep us company until you return with our
sample. That's pretty straight forward, isn't it?"

Justin rubbed his wrists and rolled his ankles to
get the blood flowing again. He was weak but he
imagined he could stand. Fighting was out of the
question, and foolhardy, he reminded himself. He'd gone
through Basic with Trainer. He'd seen the man's abilities

back then. He was legendary for his prowess, and tenuous hold on sanity. Who knew how good he was now, or sick. Justin knew the answer to that last question.

He shook his head at the general, seeing it was no use to continue the charade. It was helping no one at this point. "You're right. I didn't destroy it, but this has nothing to do with Sam. I know where it is. Send one of your grunts with me and I'll give it to them. You can have it as soon as I know Sam's safe."

"You insult my intelligence, Sergeant." Lange raised her brows at him. "I didn't get this far by being a fool. You've done nothing but lie to me today." She gave him an ugly grin. "I've finally got something that might motivate you to make the right choice. I'm not giving that up."

When Justin offered to retrieve the sample knowing he had no idea where it was, he did so with full knowledge that he was probably going to die for good when they figured out he did *not* have it. What he hadn't considered was that he would drag the woman he loved down with him.

The realization that he loved her barely caused a ripple in his consciousness. He'd known it since that first night when she lay against him. She'd needed his strength as much as he needed hers. Something in her called to him and that kiss had given his tired heart a glimpse of what a future with her would have been like. The loss of that future was a kick in the nuts and he called himself all kinds of a fool for what he'd unwittingly done to her by showing his heart where they could see. Why hadn't he seen that they would keep her as collateral? Damn it, his head was so murky. He tried to collect his thoughts but they moved too slowly to be any use to him.

"You don't look very good, Sergeant. Are you sure you're up to a little reconnaissance? It should be an easy one if you really have it. Easier for everyone." Justin let his eyes slide over to Sam.

Swinging his legs over the edge of the chair, he put out a hand to keep from swaying. Sam instinctively stepped in to give him her body to lean against. She wrapped an arm around his waist to look like she was cuddling up to him, hiding his swoon. Justin realized he'd underestimated her again. She knew what kind of shape he was in and automatically knew what to do. All too willingly, he let his arm roll across her back. His desperate grip on her had little to do with anemia.

Impatient, Smith stepped forward and took charge of him with one hand clamped on his shoulder and dragged him toward the elevator. Trainer took his place at Sam's side.

"Come on, soldier. Time's a wasting."

Justin hated the man's gloating but let it pass unanswered as he stared back over his shoulder at Sam and Trainer, holding her arms firmly at her sides. The sight of him touching her incensed him almost as much as her not struggling. She trusted him to save her.

"Don't hurt her," he ordered impotently. "I'll be back with what you want soon but the deal's off if I see any signs that you've laid a hand on her."

"I know, I know. Not a hair on her pretty little head. Got it." Lange raised her voice to be heard over the clanging of the elevator as it groaned into life. "My superiors are coming in the morning expecting a demonstration before our buyer arrives. I get what *I* want by nine a.m. or I let Trainer do what *he* wants."

The side of Trainer's thin lips twitched at the general's promise.

Doc was slouched against his lab table no further need to restrain him past his one pathetic objection. Years of subservience and a brief reminder of his powerlessness shackled him better than any physical chains.

Sam's white face next to Trainer's disappeared from his view as the elevator took him up and Smith ushered him past the gawking lab minions and through the steel door. At the touch of a button the white door rolled up and sunlight flooded in, blinding Justin in its sudden glare.

Smith pushed him forward and Justin fell weakly to his knees. "You heard the general, Sergeant. I hope you're a gentleman." He winked. "Because we both know Mr. Trainer is not."

Ch. 41

The door rolled back down and Justin was left alone in the heat and the dirt. His body ached and his legs threatened to revolt if he asked them to cooperate. Physically he could have stayed down, lain there until someone found him or the end finally came. He was so tired of their never-ending mission.

But Justin saw a beautiful pair of soft brown eyes in his mind's eye. There had been a break in their luck and in the same brief moment, a glimmer of joy in his life. He found someone who made him hope for a normal life. Sam had given him a picture of what his life could be when they were past this. For once he actually thought past this. For so long it has only been about the mission. With her, he found himself imagining being with her back home in Tennessee. He wanted to take her to see the farm where he'd been raised. Show her who he was before all this.

Before the service he had an honest job working with an uncle in his metal shop. Justin took to it immediately. With an artist's eye he created a few pieces they'd sold for good money in boutiques out in Nashville. He thought he could do that again. Giving up mercenary work would be a pleasure.

But here as soon as he considered his future with thoughts toward sharing it, she *and* his hope were snatched away. How was he supposed to save her when the one thing they wanted was the one thing he couldn't give them? His body was nearing its end, he could feel it. It was questionable whether he had the strength to do this one last mission. It didn't give him a whole lot of confidence for what would be left of him if he *did* manage to pull it off.

Climbing to his feet, Justin staggered as a wave of dizziness and nausea combined threatening to dump him in the dirt. Stubbornly he held on until his head cleared and began a steady march back toward town. Somewhere along the way he knew he would run into his unit. Before he'd gone half a mile and was hidden from sight behind a line of trees, crunching gravel and a purring motor crept up beside him. An automatic window whined and Marcus' voice called out.

"Going somewhere, Shaw?"

Stopping, Justin tipped his face up to squint at the sun just reaching its zenith. "I am. I'm just not sure where yet." He crossed over to the passenger side, climbing into the front seat.

Marcus grinned his grim smile. Jimmy clapped his shoulder wordlessly from the backseat. They'd been through hell together. These kinds of reunions needed no words. They'd happened too many times before. He knew they were glad to have him back, they knew he was grateful to have them at his side.

"Let's get some calories in that sorry ass of yours." Marcus picked up speed heading into town.

"Sorry about Sam," Jimmy offered. "She insisted on going in after you."

Justin shook his head slowly, his thoughts still too jumbled to think clearly. "We have to go back to her apartment," he said slowly. "It *has* to be there. I know she lied about getting rid of it. She wouldn't. We never had a chance to go back and search for it ourselves. Lange's crew must have missed it. They had to." He sounded desperate and hated it.

The car pulled in alongside the curb on the main

drag of town. Marcus pointed across Justin at a large plate glass window framed by a green awning. On the other side of the glass sat an older couple eating what appeared to be coleslaw and a sandwich on marbled rye. Frustrated to have them both so unconcerned for Sam's safety, and only for feeding his sorry ass, Justin glared at Marcus. "I told you we have to go back to her place. We're not stopping for a *sandwich* like it's a fucking Sunday after church. We only have until nine a.m. and I'm not sure that's going to be enough since I have no idea what I'm even looking for."

Jimmy opened his door and stepped out. He knocked on the trunk lid and Marcus hit a button. When Jimmy sauntered over to Shaw's window and tapped on it he had a shirt for him. Frustrated and quickly losing his patience, Justin lowered the window several inches and ripped it from his hands to jam it over his head, attacking the helpless gray cotton garment.

"Come get something to eat, Sarge. You'll come back faster and we need you at a hundred percent when we go get her." Seeing no movement from within the vehicle, he sighed. "There's no need to go looking. We got plenty of time for food."

His head whipped around and Justin was staring at Jimmy. The usual hint of a joke on the tip of his tongue was suspiciously absent. Jimmy looked troubled. Dread filled Justin's heart. He was afraid to ask.

Cutting short his opportunity, Jimmy stared down the street, squinting at the bright mid day sun. "Come on, man."

Justin let himself out and ambled his way to the door, Marcus opened it for him. A wooden sign on a post told them to seat themselves and they did so at a booth in the back. The orange vinyl seats squelched under them as they slid in and a twenty something brunette with short permed hair styled far too old for her face and a well-kept body set down three plastic coated menus.

"Would you like to hear the specials?" she asked cheerily.

"No thank you, Michelle." Marcus glanced at her nametag. "Could we have three large glasses and a pitcher of water?"

At her strange look he gave her a pleasant smile. "We've been outside all day."

"Oh." She smiled back. "It's really hot out there." Glancing around curiously at them again, probably noting the lack of dirt or evidence of hard labor on them, she spun on her heel. "I'll be right back with your waters."

Left alone for a few minutes Justin surveyed the restaurant for potential threats, a habit he was only vaguely aware of anymore. Safe from detection for the moment he leaned in, eyeing Jimmy and Marcus across the table. Both faces were grim and he made another quick scan of the restaurant in case there were armed gunmen storming in after them. Battled hardened, he usually didn't spook easily but Justin jumped when someone clattered plates in the kitchen. His head was starting to pound.

Bracing himself, he sat up straight and laid both hands flat on the table. Staring between them at a painting of a white barn with a grain silo and the yellow fields of fall corn going to silage in the background, Justin pushed aside all thoughts of his own farm and prepared himself for the worst. "Tell me."

Jimmy deferred to Marcus. He was Justin's

Second. Always had been. Except Marcus sat beside him, lips pressed tightly together. Jimmy could understand Marcus' reluctance to speak, they were still absorbing it themselves. Smith and General Lange dropped a hell of a bomb after the Sarge had been escorted out. He was not going to like what he was about to hear. Especially not now after what they'd heard pass between them. Shaw was really serious about the girl, no joke. He glanced over at Marcus again hoping he'd step up, rolling his eyes when he didn't, and finally broke the tense silence. "We got it."

At first Shaw just kept staring at the wall behind them. He didn't even blink.

Jimmy worried he'd been under too long this time. It had been getting worse for all of them, the sergeant especially since he'd gone down more than either of them. Maybe there'd been brain damage this time. "Did you hear me, Sarge? I said we got it. She gave it to us when we were at her place this morning. Just a little silver container no bigger than my thumb." He went on about how she'd hidden it in the garbage and then again how she'd insisted on being sent in as ears for them. "Pretty brave, that lady. You picked a good one, Sarge." Jimmy snapped his mouth shut. It probably wasn't a good idea to remind the sergeant how he felt about Sam right before they told him the bad news.

Michelle returned to a silent table while she poured the three waters and pulled out her pencil and notepad. "What can I get you?"

"What's your favorite?" Happy for the distraction, Jimmy turned on his charm. It took no special effort. He gave her a leisurely smile, hand coming up on the table to lean back on and watch her. Under his interested gaze she touched her hair, smiling nervously back.

"Um, well, I guess I like the club. You can get it with fries or a salad." She let her eyes run over his fit body and blushed.

"Give us three of those with salads." Jimmy gave her a wink and Michelle nearly floated back to the kitchen to put in their orders. The second she was out of sight his countenance was again severe.

Marcus pushed his water at him. "Drink. You'll think clearer."

Justin did as he was told. He had three glasses down before Michelle brought out their sandwiches, barely registering the exchange between the waitress and Jimmy as her hand lingered on his plate.

"You tell me if you need anything else?"

"Sure thing Michelle." Jimmy fanned her hopes.

"You shouldn't do that," Marcus warned him.

Shrugging, Jimmy took a cucumber off his plate and put it in his mouth. "When you look like this, you can't let it go to waste." He grinned as he crunched.

Glowering, Marcus unrolled the paper napkin holding his fork and, gripping it in his fist, he stabbed his lettuce clanking the metal on the porcelain of the plate. "They aren't there for your amusement, Ramirez."

Jimmy took a drink of his water, unaffected by Marcus' reprimand. "You brood, I flirt, the Sarge thinks. We all got our things."

Automatically and without speaking Justin ate until his plate was empty. He ignored the petty argument between the men. This wasn't the first time they'd had this conversation nor would it be the last. This time sounded a little strained, desperate. There was something going on here they weren't telling him. Something he wasn't going to like. He was putting off hearing it. The pounding in his head had grown so loud he could barely think.

***

Marcus poured Shaw another water and watched him swallow half the glass before placing it back on the harvest gold laminate tabletop. He too was worried about the sergeant. It could have been something triggered by being returned to custody or something those bastards did to him while they had him, although he doubted it. No, Shaw looked heartsick. He was waiting for the other shoe to drop. They weren't doing any favors by keeping what they'd heard from him.

He recognized Shaw's mood because that was how he felt the moment he realized what had happened to him and the four of them had walked out of the flipped transport truck, bleeding but alive. They were the only ones and even that was a miracle. A chunk of shrapnel lodged itself in Jimmy's leg, severing the femoral artery. Yet he'd removed the metal and, after a few gushes, the wound healed itself enough to walk in minutes, completely in hours. They'd healed so fast back then there had been barely any after effects. Now things were different. It was slower, more painful. When Marcus woke in the morning he felt like he was eighty years old and had just been in a fight.

When they were brought home and told they were to be debriefed, Marcus tried to use the phone to call his wife and daughter to tell them he was safe and would see them soon. The airmen shooed him off the phone before the call went through. That had been the first indication

300

that something was wrong. They'd been kept away from the general population between plane changes. Making their flights alone on cargo planes with changes in Germany and New York, eventually being brought back to base in Southern California where they'd all shipped out of initially.

Once their nightmare began it became apparent the reality of their walking out of that hellhole was nonexistent. He asked the officer in charge if he could have news of his death sent to his family. They would be upset but it was better than thinking of him lost out there, waiting for news that wouldn't come. This way they could mourn and move on. In the end, the others had all done the same for their families.

The look on Sergeant Justin Shaw's worn face mirrored Marcus' the day he had to give up his family. Shaw was in love and wasn't going to let it go easily. He was willing to give up his life for hers. Marcus ducked his head to hide his resentment. He couldn't allow anything to get in the way of their ultimate goal. Success was the only way to justify the incalculable toll it had taken on all of them, what it had cost Mills.

"We have to leave her in there until that meeting." He was frowning at his plate, his words bitter on his tongue. "You heard Lange, her superiors are coming in. We can get them all if we wait."

Justin's fork hovered forgotten halfway to his mouth, romaine dangling precariously from its tines. "They don't intend to keep her alive, you know that."

Marcus met Justin's gaze without flinching. His skin was pasty from blood loss yet it was the dead look in his eyes that bothered him. Marcus wondered if Justin was processing any of this in his state.

Jimmy listened, mouth hanging open expectantly. He knew Marcus was about to drop the hammer, although neither one envied the sergeant the pain it was going to bring.

"Yes they do. They're planning to bring her to the meeting. She's the demonstration."

Justin's fork clattered to his plate, his hands went down on the table gripping the edge. Jimmy's eyes bugged out, clearly anticipating Shaw flipping the table over. His eyes had gone all wild, there was no telling what he was going to do if he lost his shit.

"Are you kidding? Are you actually considering leaving her in there for that? How can we do that to her?"

Shrugging, Marcus continued staring at Justin. "For now she's okay. They aren't going to search her again so we have ears in there. And you heard Lange they've given you until morning to come up with it. They won't risk damaging her now that they're going to use her. We can use that time to listen and find out the scope of the entire project. We don't want to move too soon and blow this place just to find out there's another one in Boise or in some desert in New Mexico. Once we get what we need we pull her out and *then* blow the place and everyone in it. "He went back to eating, his piece had been said.

***

Jimmy glanced from one to the other, not sure why something felt wrong, like there was something else going on. It was a feeling he used to get even on the streets as a kid. He trusted it. Justin blinked at Marcus a few times, watching him eat before reclaiming his fork

302

and resuming his meal. His movements were deliberate and a slight tremor shook his fork. The sergeant was definitely not firing on all cylinders just yet.

After a silent end to their meal, Jimmy signaled for the check and Michelle brought it. He chuckled when he glanced at it and scanned the restaurant for their server. She gave him a little wave from behind the salad buffet and he lifted his chin at her with a wink and a grin. "She gave me her number. What do you think? We gonna be in town long? It's been a while, you know?" Baiting them, he hoped to break the tension. Neither bit while he fished in the back pocket of his jeans for his wallet.

***

Without a word Justin stood and left the table. He walked out of the restaurant and was heading back the way they'd come, already a block away before he felt the familiar bodies of Jimmy and Marcus as they each took up a flanking position.

"What are you doing Shaw?"

Justin didn't answer. He was too busy feeling the energy flowing back into his body, gauging his strength. Now nourished, his cells were rapidly replacing the blood he'd lost. The fatigue accompanying his anemia was falling away taking most of his headache with it and leaving him somewhat rejuvenated. The process ran slower and rougher each time. What he felt return came well appreciated this time.

"Shaw you have to give this a chance. This is what we've been working for, don't lose sight of that now." Marcus laid a hand on his shoulder, attempting to pull him back.

Shrugging him off Justin continued to walk. "I will not 'give this a chance', Marcus. She's there because we put her there. I had this thing handled until you let her go in there." He shook his head, willing his mind to clear faster so he could think. "So what if we have until morning? We still need to get in and get her out without giving ourselves away, and then we have to blow the place up. Do you have a plan? Something I don't know about? Some reason why you're not the slightest bit concerned?" Justin could hear his drawl grow stronger as the pressure built. Lange was right, he did have a tell when he was stressed. Funny he hadn't noticed that before.

They reached the stoplight and had to wait for an old rusted pickup turning left before crossing. While he waited, his thoughts finally caught up to him and his blood ran cold. Justin whirled on Marcus, alarm bells clattering in his head. "Why Marcus?" He stared the man down, moving into his space and backing him up against the brick of the corner building.

Marcus stared evenly back at him, unflinching.

Justin took a step forward and jabbed a finger into the black man's hard chest. "*Why* are you so cool about leaving her in there? Why aren't you worried about the extraction?" Apprehension gripped his throat tight, he couldn't breathe properly. Justin's headache came roaring back.

"Ease up, Shaw." Marcus blinked at him. "I'm trusting the girl to keep her head down and give us time. Don't *you* have any faith in her?" He lifted his shoulders. "If this goes right we take out the whole crew. If this goes wrong, Lange is forced to give it more time and still has her as bait. She won't get rid of her as long as

304

you're out here with the sample. I don't see it as a problem."

Angered by Marcus' unemotional assessment, honestly the same one he would have if it was anyone else they were talking about, Justin reluctantly agreed she wasn't in any immediate danger. That gave him some time to get his wits about him and put a plan together. "We only have a few hours. Jimmy, you stay glued to her audio feed. Let me know if anything, and I mean *anything* happens. Marcus, I want you to quietly go buy enough fertilizer and heating oil to blow up a small country. Don't do it all in one county and be quick about it. We'll meet at that Mom and Pop motel we passed on the way into town."

"Yes Sir." Marcus' frown eased only barely.

Taking a step and then stopping again, Justin turned to Jimmy. "While you were listening did you hear anything about their plans for Doc?"

The dark man's cocky smile wavered. "Uh, no man."

"You're lying, Jimmy." Justin's eyes narrowed and he shot an accusatory look Marcus' way. "What else is going on? Is it something with her father?" He held out his hands palm up. "How can I put a plan together if I don't have all the facts? You know this shit." He gave Jimmy his best hardass glare; he would be the first to give way.

Predictably, Jimmy broke first. "He and the general were talking right after they took you up. Lange was askin' him about some other project." He paused, shooting a look at Marcus who was fuming silently.

"Spill."

His shoulders sagged and he did. "Well, you know how Doc was talkin' about a legacy when he was with Sam? It sounds like he's been workin' on that about as long as he's been workin' on this formula for the general. There's another side effect to the agent we got sprayed with." The look that passed between the three was enough, they all knew there were side effects. They'd been progressing for a while. The clock ticked for all of them. "So, Doc's been working on findin' ways to get the good and take out the bad and he's got it, sort of." Jimmy ran a hand over his intentionally messy black hair. "'Cept he's only tried it on himself so only his DNA works with it."

Justin thought he was going to puke. "And Sam's."

"She's their new prototype." Marcus confirmed for him. "They're going to expose her and run a few tests after you come back with their sample or Doc gives them something. From there they plan on taking samples directly from their new incubator to make a version 2.0."

"I have to go back." Justin stepped off the curb, Marcus and Jimmy following close behind. "If I'm with her maybe I can convince Lange to synch it with *my* DNA. I'm farther gone and they'd see the results faster. Maybe I can convince them they'd lose too much time bringing her this far." Bile rose in his throat at the thought of what they would have to do to her in order to induce the kind of slow recovery he and his crew were suffering. What was left of his cool slipped, and Marcus' eyes narrowed.

They were nearly to the opposite curb when his hand caught Justin's shoulder and he spun him around. Eyes dark, he pointed a long finger at his former sergeant's chest. "You're not going in there again. We need you out here to put this thing together." Admitting

306

they needed Justin had a cost, Marcus' grim expression said as much. "Like Jimmy said, we each have our roles and yours is strategy. *She* demanded she go in after you and we let her. She *knew* the risks if we couldn't get her out. If you didn't want her to come after you, you shouldn't have been working that angle so hard."

"Hey man, let's take this off the street." Jimmy sounded agitated.

Neither man budged. "Don't push this off on her. She couldn't know what she was in for, not like you or I do." He shoved Marcus with both hands, pinning him to the streetlight's heavy base. Craving an outlet for his impotent rage, Justin was shaking with the effort of not pummeling the taller man and leaving him there for someone else to scrape off the sidewalk. "She put herself on the line for us, all of us, and you're willing to sacrifice her just like that? You're not even thinking of extraction, what you're thinking is more like murder. That's not how this team operates."

Marcus brought his hands up on the inside, breaking Justin's grip with an outward sweep and followed up with a fist in his side. Justin backpedaled into the wooden side of the corner store, narrowly missing a plate glass window.

"Come on guys, not here." Jimmy was more forceful. "*Really* not a good time."

Nostrils flaring, Marcus followed Justin as he stumbled putting both hands on his shoulders, thumping him back into the wood and holding him firm. "Don't you *dare* call her part of this team, *Sergeant*." Voice rising, he lowered his face to come nose to nose with Justin. "To hear *you* talk about sacrifice makes me sick. I gave up my whole world for this hunt. I left my baby girl to be raised by another man. Every night, my wife sleeps next to the man who used to be my best friend, instead of me." Blue eyes burned with a mixture of fury and anguish. "What did *you* give up? Your parents are dead. You have no woman or child. You never cared enough about anyone to know the agony of true sacrifice. You sat there and let Mills die when you were right there. Tell me how that isn't how this team operates."

Both fists flew in rapid succession, the first hitting Marcus' stomach hard enough to break his hold and the second catching him full in the mouth. His teeth cut the knuckles on Justin's left hand. "What did you expect me to do? *I* couldn't fight any more than *you* could."

Marcus condemned him, disgust twisting his features. "You could have talked Mills down. He bought every goddamn line you ever sold him about duty and the job. But when it mattered," he sneered, "you didn't say a word. You just let him get himself killed. This one's all yours, Sergeant." Spittle gathered unnoticed in the corners of his mouth. "*This* is your sacrifice. Learn to live with it. *We* did. We're blowing that building up in the morning when Lange's superiors get there. When everyone's there, waiting to see something amazing, we're going to give it to them."

Justin's shoulders slumped under the weight of Marcus' accusation. It was the same one he'd aimed at himself a thousand times. Worse, it was true. He *could* have talked Mills out of getting himself killed. Although honestly, watching Trainer pull the knife, seeing his comrade fighting back, he wanted his friend to attack, to go out fighting. It was better than being sliced and diced until there was nothing left. And ever since that failing he'd been angry: angry with himself for not doing more, angry with Mills for dying. And envious. Envious that Mills found a way out and he was still here, fighting. God help him, Justin wished it had been him. He had wished it had been *his* head to hit the floor, his blood to stain the walls. Not just because he should have protected his man back then. It was because at least the torment of being a part of this endless impossible mission would have had an end. Mills found peace, none of the others had. They were still living in hell; fearing the worst, never allowed anything better.

Sirens blasted behind them seconds before the sound of an officer's gun chambering a round.

"Freeze."

Justin and Marcus were both breathing hard as they raised their hands, lacing their fingers behind their heads. Jimmy was gone.

Ch. 42

Sam sat on the floor, back to the wall reflecting on how everything had changed in minutes. *What the hell happened?* She'd heard the group discussing the demonstration and her role in it. Her father was escorted by the mustache to a door hidden in the wall at the back of the room after Justin left. For what purpose she couldn't guess. She was musing on how synchronizing his DNA with the chemical he'd developed fit in with his desire for a lasting legacy. *Dad, what have you done*, she asked of the ether, rubbing her hands over her tired eyes.

With a troubled heart she watched Justin disappear up the elevator, her skin crawling where Trainer's hands had touched her. Justin's ashen pallor making her thankful for the proximity of his team and the experience they had in helping each other when they came back. They would get him right again.

As far as their commitment to her she couldn't ask for more, although she was more certain of one than the other. Jimmy for all that swagger and good-time guy front, had a good heart. Despite his cockiness, she felt she could trust him. And she had, with her life.

Marcus was another story. His certainty that she was expendable for the cause that night couldn't be discounted. That her life was forfeit to him for the right reason was something not easily reversed in a day. Suspicion reigned supreme when it came to him, aided by the fact that he had not only let her, he *encouraged* her to walk in here assuring her they would find a way to get her and Justin out alive. Except now there was no Justin. It was only Sam and her father in a building filled with people they were sworn to destroy. Sam had a hard time believing anyone other than Justin would be willing to risk a rescue attempt. He would come for her, wouldn't he?

Her fingertips traced her lips delicately before she stopped herself. She was reading a lot into a kiss. He hadn't said anything that would lead her to believe that kiss was more than a momentary impulse. He was probably just glad to be alive and to see a friendly face. A lot of things had to happen before there was a chance of finding out if there was anything more to Justin's and her. For one, she had to get out of here and that was something she intended to do for herself, regardless of whether they were coming for her. She wasn't one to play damsel in distress very well.

Coming back to the present, Sam could feel Lange's eyes on her. She was watching her from where she stood beside the tiled door, Trainer flanking her. It was easy even for a novice like Sam to figure out that her best bet for survival lay in not provoking the general. She wouldn't think twice about killing someone who meant as little as Sam in the grand scheme of things.

"Miss James you are free to roam about down here." She spoke quietly and the sound carried across the hard surfaces. "Your father will be out shortly." Without changing her matter of fact tone or her bland expression, her words were all the more menacing. "I feel I should warn you, if you set one foot on the lift I will see to it you never walk again." The general gave her a quick smile.

It seemed Sam had already failed in her endeavor to remain inoffensive. "Um, yes Ma'am."

Lange studied her a moment, her thin lips pinched together in a grimace, accentuating the few lines around her mouth and adding years to her appearance. "Good."

The general made her way to the elevator, her

mute blonde guard dog in tow and waited for it to return after Smith's ride up top with Justin. While she stood waiting, she told Trainer loud enough for Sam to hear.

"Keep her in line, nothing permanent and nothing obvious. She has enough damage for the demonstration to impress them. Afterward though, you'll have ample opportunity." She cast a glance in Sam's direction.

Trainer gave a half bow and stepped back when she entered the elevator. After she disappeared he took up a loose-limbed guard position next to the square of steel marking Sam's only real exit. His face expressionless and eyes focused straight ahead, Trainer made for a perfect bouncer.

Too bad they don't have drinks here. The strain was wearing on her and she was worried she was cracking up. Sam watched her guard out of her periphery, not entirely trusting him to follow orders and keep his hands off. He made no move toward her though, and after a while she relaxed in increments, exhaling loudly and leaning back on the chair where Justin had been kept. Her fingers traced the leather straps and she felt an odd sense of pride. Because of her he was out there walking around. No matter what happened in here today, the lab and the minds who were behind its atrocities wouldn't live past tomorrow. For the people she'd failed she hoped that meant something. It might not redeem her or make up for what had happened, but she at least felt she could hang her hat on that small victory.

Her hand went to her face, feeling the swelling pressing painfully on the eye and the lumpy lip and she heard a throat clear. Sam jumped and checked he hadn't moved. Trainer remained perfectly motionless, no evidence that he was even aware of her presence. Yet she knew better no matter how bored he tried to look.

The sound of the pressure seal on the tiled door caused a hitch in her breath. Not excited to be spending a second in the same room as General Lange. Her girlie senses were tingling about *why* the woman was being such a bitch to her. *Did she have a thing with Justin at one time or is it a one-sided thing? Unrequited love? What do they do in that room anyway? It can't be that big.* She pictured the three of them jammed shoulder to shoulder in a closet whispering their evil plans and had to stifle a laugh. Feeling eyes on her, she glanced at Trainer and caught him just as he spun back to watch the unholy trinity exit their secret room.

Her father approached and as he got closer she could see the strain in the lines around his eyes and downturned mouth. Sam glanced over again to catch Trainer watching her openly this time. Just as she was about to snap on him about being a creeper, her father called out in relief.

"Samantha, I'm so sorry." He stopped short of putting his arms around her, settling for resting an awkward long fingered hand on her shoulder.

Putting her hand on his to give it a comforting squeeze, Sam offered him a tense smile. She had no idea how she felt about him or what he'd done but the fact remained. He was her dad and they were both here against their will. That made them allies.

"Don't forget our deal." Trainer's voice was loud and rough in the quiet room. "You better not screw me or you're dead."

Bewildered, Sam turned to her father. "What's he talking about?"

"*You're* not the one who's getting the upgraded version." Obviously Trainer was listening in when Lange and company were discussing who was going to be the guinea pig for the bigger, better, faster, more version of the stupid chemical. "Doc promised to fix me so I don't end up like those other sad sacks." Trainer cocked his head, his eyes a little too wide for her to trust in his sanity. "He's going to make me the perfect soldier. Better than even your precious Sergeant Shaw."

"When are you going to tell Lange the change in plans?" Sam looked from one man to the other.

Trainer shrugged and her father's hand tightened on her shoulder, urging her to be careful. "I thought it would be a nice surprise to let them do a 'head to head' test tomorrow. You know, 'this is what happens with and this is what happens without the super soldier juice'." Yellow teeth flashed wickedly, he was awed by his own wit.

***

Several miles away from inside a motel room decorated in enough flowers to make an old woman proud, Jimmy leaned back against the back of his stiff backed white and blue flowered chair and cursed. "Aw shit."

Ch. 43

Justin sat in the backseat of the squad car, hands cuffed behind him. Miserable, he leaned forward to ease the discomfort in his shoulders. The physical discomfort was nothing to the emotional toll the last fifteen minutes, hell, the last five years, had taken. The burning stiffness in his shoulders was a small but welcome penance for his failure to his men. He'd promised to get them home from Iraq and he had. Until that last mission. Since Mills' death he let nothing save his duty to his men and country drive him, determined not to lose another man whether in his unit or fellow soldier, needlessly. And he had been relentless, putting his men's lives and interests before his own more than once.

Justin never spared his pocketbook when he could provide them some physical comfort nor denied a request to go and look in on one's family in whatever way they saw fit. Both "checked in" often, unbeknownst to their relatives. Yet, in doing so he lost sight of another kind of loss. The loss of one's soul that comes from killing men for someone else's cause; being a killer for hire. Knowing he brought death to so many while the other side couldn't reciprocate so easily left a black mark, a hollow place inside him. Inside all of them. The lines between black and white, right and wrong were blurred for all of them while their invincibility went to their heads. And the fallout should have been predictable.

He should have seen it coming. Really it was inevitable that things would come to this for at least one of them. Jimmy came from a close-knit family he'd given up. And Marcus walked away from a wife and young daughter. The loss damaged them both irreparably, but it hit Marcus especially hard.

If he was honest with himself, he could track the fracture between them to that first visit Marcus made to look in on his daughter after a particularly ugly job. His wife had been out, the sitter was playing with the little girl in the front yard. As he was leaving he watched the car pull up and his wife get out with another man, Marcus' former best friend Russell Williams. When he returned from his visit, Marcus was changed. Never a big talker, he closed himself off for weeks with hardly a word spoken beyond a grunt here and there. Eventually he returned to speech though he was never the same. He became sullen and introverted and there was something else. It was nothing Justin was able to put a finger on. Not that there was much time for that sort of introspection or therapizing, even if they *were* inclined toward that sort of thing. Which they most definitely weren't. "Pussy shit," Jimmy called it when Justin tried to talk about anything. Marcus usually left the room. *That's fucked up if I'm the one being all touchy feely,* Justin thought.

Since going out on their own, hiring out their services, they always had one ear glued to the radiowaves. Chatter was constant. There was always a report coming in on a small skirmish here or another weapons lab turning up there. Wherever there were reports of activity involving weapons or chemical agents, Justin and his men followed. Often ending up in the thick of things getting hired on by whichever side got them closest to the action so they could investigate.

There was nothing connecting the three to the real world anymore. They just drifted through the world from war to war, always searching, always killing with no end in sight. It was a wonder no one had gone off the deep end before now. But never in all that time had Justin stopped to consider that either Jimmy or Marcus held him in such utter contempt. It was a devastating blow. Sitting next to the man was like being pressed against a furnace, the heat of the rage rolling off of him was palatable.

"Got a problem with each other, you keep it off the street." The young redheaded officer in the passenger seat was shaking his head in disapproval. "You guys are old enough to know better." The wizened old cop routine didn't suit him even if he was right. The older Latino officer's cheek twitched, probably fighting a smile.

Justin and Marcus remained silent. It wasn't a good thing to be in police custody. If they hadn't been on Main Street with so many potential witnesses, things wouldn't have gotten *this* far. Now they would end up being detained and lose precious time in addition to the risk brought by having their prints run. Imagining Sam with Lange and Trainer after their deadline made Justin frantic. Yet as much as he hated her being in there the soldier in him recognized the strategic advantage. She was their window. He itched to get in front of Jimmy's monitors to hear how she was doing in there. He prayed they were keeping their word and no harm had come to her.

***

Rochester's police station was only a few blocks off the main drag and the drive a short one. Minutes after being collected the officers were maneuvering Justin and Marcus out, guarding their heads from striking the roof as they extracted them from the vehicle. Escape would be complicated if they had to do it from inside the station. It had to end here.

Marcus glared at Justin when they faced each other over the top of the car, then abruptly turned away. Failing to catch Marcus' eye, Justin had to gamble that he would work with him. He couldn't afford being captured any more than Justin. Taking a breath and hoping for the best Justin stumbled intentionally, going down on one knee and his arresting officer stopped.

"Are you okay buddy?" The redhead's grip loosened.

The other officer was bringing Marcus around the nose of the car. "Hey, what's going on?"

His head was hanging down in front, hiding his face. Taking a deep breath, bracing himself, Justin stuck out his tongue and brought his teeth down hard. Blood instantly pooled in his mouth. He opened his lips, letting it run down his shirt. The light gray fabric aided in the dramatic visual he was hoping for. Going ramrod stiff he threw himself down on his side, twitching and convulsing in his best mock seizure. Predictably, his hands were released as he flopped around on the hard pavement, rocks grinding into his arm. The officer's hands shook when they came back with the key to unlock him. Good thing his mouth hurt like hell or he'd have smiled when his hands fell free of the cuffs. Getting into it, he let one arm flail and clipped the cop upside the head.

"Holy shit! I think he bit off his tongue. Look at all the blood!" No one touched Justin. The fear of blood borne disease was so great no officer was allowed to touch anyone without protective gear. "Call for an ambulance, I'm going to get some gloves out of the kit."

Marcus' voice chimed in right on cue. "I was a medic in the service. Let me loose and I'll hold him down so he don't hurt himself."

The sound of metal sliding out of metal was the next thing he heard as Justin lay twitching in the parking lot. The asphalt had ground his ear bloody while he kept his back to them. Rolling his eyes back for too long gave him a headache, this was easier. All he had to do was twitch at this point. Big hands pushed his body straight, rolling him over and jamming his spine into the loose pieces of rock and asphalt lying on the ground. Cutting a warning glance at Marcus, Justin could see he was enjoying his role a little too much.

"I got this. Y'all make the call and I'll keep him still." Watching them over his shoulder Marcus made a show of rolling his eyes dramatically and sighing. "We ain't gonna fight with him twitching like this now are we? It was a disagreement, that's all. I ain't gonna hurt 'im while he's all fucked up." His urban, uneducated mien was a fallback whenever he needed to make himself non-threatening. Marcus pointed out once that if the people thought you were dumb they didn't see you as a threat, not unless you were armed. Then they shot you.

Marcus was right again. Both officers hustled into the station house, one declaring he was calling an ambulance, the other looking for gloves to assist. As soon as they were gone Justin popped up and ran as fast as he could, pulling his phone and dialing as he ran. Marcus was close on his heels as they turned down the alley behind the station. Tongue nearly healed but not quite, Justin's words were too thick for Jimmy to make out. Puffing and annoyed, he tossed the phone to Marcus already running abreast of him. He was always faster once he got going even if Justin could beat him off the line every time.

"Yeah, I know. We're on the move, three blocks off Main heading west out of town. There's a warehouse up ahead." He was repeating something Jimmy was feeding him. A genius on his equipment, he was already dialed into their position and helping with tactical. "Yeah, I can see it. We'll find somewhere to hole up till you get there. The cops will be on us any minute." Justin

319

clenched his jaw against his screaming muscles while they pounded down the block, Marcus opened a growing gap between them.

Sirens wailed from not far off. Glancing behind them, Justin panted. "They're at least a street over, they can't see us yet."

Nodding, Marcus saved his breath. In three more strides they were able to cut over another street and did, legging back west another block up and into the large faded parking lot behind the decaying gray metal warehouse. It was a good place to hide; long since abandoned judging from the height and bloom of the weeds coming through the cracks in the asphalt and the number of broken windows. The two didn't break stride until they were around the side of the building, temporarily dimming the sound of pursuit and telling them they had a brief reprieve in which to find a hiding spot. A large pile of discarded pallets was stacked cattywhompus creating holes large enough for the panting men to crawl in to wait. Marcus glanced over at Justin, again pale as death from exerting himself too much too soon and called Jimmy back to update him as to their exact whereabouts.

"He's about seven to ten minutes out unless we want him to come in hot and draw attention. I asked him not to." His speech was short and clipped. Still pissed. He reached out a big hand and shifted the front pallet to hide Justin then do the same for himself.

"Sounds good."

An uncomfortable silence filled the hot air, pungent in the small space, too small for two grown men. Way too small when they were dripping sweat in the late summer sun with no breeze. The sound of an engine growling up, tires crunching on the pavement as a truck slowly trolled the lot had them both holding their breath. The tires stopped when they were even with the pallets.

Lying down on his stomach to peer out under a gap in the stack, Justin heaved a grateful sigh and stood, waving Marcus up from behind him. Another cautious glance around and they made the short jog to the truck. Jimmy got out and gave Marcus the driver's seat. He was always the driver. But Justin signaled Jimmy over the roof that *he* would sit in back this time. No arguments, just a raised eyebrow, and Jimmy trotted around the back and took shotgun.

Just as he raised his leg to step into the car Marcus twisted his head not far enough to look directly at Justin, but enough that his displeasure could be seen by his profile. "This," he wagged a finger between he and Shaw, "doesn't mean we're okay. We live through this I walk."

"You're right, it doesn't." Justin inhaled deeply. "We make it through this we can *all* walk. I promise." *You'll be free of all this. I'll make sure of it.*

Ch. 44

"Samantha, I never thought it would come to this." Dr. James began, moving not toward her but toward his worktable.

"It doesn't matter, we can't change what's already done. The point is we're here now and we have *another* problem." She glanced over his shoulder at Trainer, still guarding the elevator like it was Buckingham Palace. The image of him in a furry hat brought a giggle up her throat.

Her father's features clouded, perhaps thinking she was cracking up. Her finger went up, freezing him in place. Before she spent another minute with him, Sam had to set something straight with her estranged father. "First things first. I want to make sure something is perfectly clear and *then* we can move on." Her gaze didn't waver. She drew upon an inner strength that served her many a night when she had to comfort her grieving mother. Another casualty in this madness. If this was it for her, Dr. Steven James needed to know where he stood. "You are my father and a certain amount of respect goes with the office but you *left*. You didn't raise me and you didn't earn the right to ever speak to me like you did back there. Okay?" Sam held back most of the venom the years had amassed but there was no keeping it all out of her words.

"I'll play along with the general's crazy plan but just so you know I'm not staying. As soon as I can swing it, I'm out of here." She didn't say out loud who she hoped would be helping with that venture. It would do more than embarrass her if he left her there and she would hold onto that. *Not the time to try to make sense of how I feel about him or what that kiss meant.* "You should come too." The relief that washed over his face at that made her throat swell shut. Blinking away the dampness in her eyes that went with the throat lump she sniffed sharply. "You tried to make things right here so you can't be all bad, but don't believe for a minute that means we walk out of here and all's forgiven." She had to establish distance from him. Everything was getting so confused with him, with Justin, the guilt over Paul and her mother was still there at her periphery, waiting for her to let down her guard so it could sucker punch her. Used to keeping her feelings at a safe distance Sam was finding herself rapidly reaching her breaking point and she'd be damned if she broke down here in front of the general and her two trained dogs.

***

Dr. James soberly dipped his chin in agreement. He wanted to smile not out of amusement but satisfaction. His daughter was strong, not like her mother. Brenda was always the first to defer to him in an argument and give ground. She was a peacemaker, not a fighter. Their daughter had inherited none of her mother's weaknesses. Thus far, she had only displayed a fortitude that made his chest swell with paternal pride. She was an intriguing young woman, surprising him at every turn. This crisis he drew her into on a gamble had proven that she was not only strong in spirit but also in body and intelligence.

That she'd endured some amount of bodily harm was an understandable, if unfortunate happenstance. He shrugged it off. She came out of that okay and soon he would have the altered formula ready and this would be over.

Her sergeant would come back for her, that he would bet on even if she doubted it. She did though, he saw it and the sadness that accompanied it behind her eyes. Despite *her* reservations about him, her father knew Sergeant Shaw wouldn't abandon her to this place. Even if he didn't care for her, which he clearly did, the honor that drove him wouldn't let him. And when he came the doctor would be ready. He was nearly there already. And the soldiers would destroy the lab as well as the people in it. They had to, their intentions were well known to the man who helped them escape once years ago in a weak moment. Free of the general, armed with the altered chemical, he could cure countless diseases. Dr. James could feel it, his legacy and exoneration were within his grasp.

Calling the doctor's attention away from his glorious, much anticipated return to the medical community, Sam cleared her throat. He glanced up to see her tip her head sideways indicating the man at the elevator. "How are you going to come up with the formula in time? You don't have the sample to go off of."

Not answering, he looked over his daughter's shoulder, making eye contact with the intense man he'd used as a test subject all those years ago. Volunteering, he endured the tests willingly only to be crushed by the realization that the process took a toll. He would deteriorate over time. Of course hearing that the doctor found a way to counter it, he was first in line, again eager to prove himself to his superiors. Raising his hand to wave the man forward, Dr. James beckoned. "Step over here Mr. Trainer and we can begin."

Seeing neither man was interested in her being there and having no desire herself, Sam crawled back up into the chair, pulling her feet up and curled on her side. She closed her eyes in hopes she could pretend they were far away and she was somewhere else with him, maybe an island somewhere with the sun on them as they made love on the beach. She imagined she could catch the residual smell of him on the cold vinyl.

"Steven?" She sat up and fixed her gaze on him, ignoring Trainer's glare.

"Mmm?" He was drawing blood, too busy to debate titles. Trainer was holding a cotton ball against the crook of his elbow, a kit containing vials and cotton swabs lay on a sterile tray between them.

She watched him empty the vial of blood into a test tube and click it into a centrifuge. While it began to spin he took a dropper and prepared a slide. Several other vials sat in metal racking to the left side of her father's table, far too much to have just been drawn from a normal needle such as this. It would have taken time or a significant injury. "Is that his, from what they did?" Her eyes ran over Trainer's face. There wasn't a flicker of emotion from the man. He seriously creeped her out, there was something so not right with him.

The doctor snapped the slide into the microscope's tray and turned on the light before looking up. "Yes." He studied her reaction.

Her nose stung. She tried to assure herself it was the same compassion she would have for *anyone* who had to endure torture. "Is there really a difference from one regeneration to another?"

His eyebrows shot up and Trainer's entire body stiffened. "How did you know that?"

"Marcus told me." She assumed it wouldn't be giving anything away that the men themselves had figured that much out. "He said they would have," she pointed at the chair, "you know, done it to Justin again to see the changes since he's been gone." Her brow furrowed. "Isn't it bad to have that many white blood cells in a body for that long unless you're sick?"

The doctor nodded. "The goal was to take enough of their DNA to run whatever tests they'd like and destroy the evidence." He snorted and gave a wry little smile. "The problem with that was no one knew how to destroy them. We tried the usual means: lethal injection, shooting, strangulation, slitting their throats, drowning, poison…" He trailed off when he saw her tip in her chair. "Anyway, at first the change was barely perceptible." Lowering his eyes to the slide he took a quick glimpse through the lens and frowned, rubbing his nose before peeking around the eyepiece at her. "You can see it quite plainly now. Come, take a look."

Sam popped off the chair and scooted around the table to see. Her father took a step back, grinning excitedly. Ignoring his discomfiting ability to let science supersede humanity, Sam settled her face against the binocular eyepiece, letting her eyes adjust and waited for what she was seeing to make sense.

The red streaks of blood outlined the small white orbs. Although she could guess at the fact that the orbs were white blood cells from her high school and college Biology classes, anything more was beyond her ken. Rearing back, she shook her head. "I don't know what I'm looking at."

Puffing up, the doctor found himself in his element and prepared to lecture his audience. Sam foresaw it being far longer and more complicated than she needed and headed him off in a rush. She held up a hand. "In layman's terms. Please."

Only mildly put off, Dr. James cleared his throat. "The initial change in cell structure is simple. The chemical bonds itself to the blood cells and encourages regeneration at the site of injury. If it's only a few regenerations they die without making any significant impact on the body and their systems eventually return to normal. But after as many regenerations as these men have had, their bodies are teeming with extra cells. They can't get rid of them quickly enough and their bodies look for something to do with them. They begin to form masses."

That word was universally understood. Gasping, her hand flew to her mouth and her eyes instantly wetted. "Masses? They have cancer?"

"Yes." Despite his initial excitement, his confirmation was less than enthusiastic.

"Do they know that, Justin and his men?"

"No, they were gone before we figured it out." He held out a hand Sam deftly avoided. "I'm sorry Samantha, by what I'm seeing here it's progressed significantly since they've been gone. They don't have much longer."

Returning to her seat she curled up on the chair with her back to the men as her father recommenced collecting data using Trainer's blood and felt the tears roll down her cheeks.

Ch. 45

Jimmy watched the faces of the other two as they listened to the recorded conversation between Doc and Sam. Marcus paled slightly before recovering his usual stoicism. Justin on the other hand, wasn't surprised. It was as though he knew it somehow already and this evidence was merely the final bell tolling for him. The only sounds in their motel room were Sam's muffled sniffles at the end of the tape.

"Turn that off." Justin got up and walked out of their room opening straight to the parking lot. They were at the end and abutted a natural area. Walking down the footpath, he stopped at the railing overlooking the small creek and series of miniature waterfalls. Only instead of soothing, its soft tinkling served to further annoy, grating on his nerves and adding to the tension making his nerves hum. He needed to think but all he could hear was Doc's prognosis. It would have been funny if it didn't piss him off so much. Justin had always believed his death would be a violent one, most likely alone and in some godforsaken jungle.

As hard as he tried to concentrate on their plan of attack and all the variables: whether he could get Sam out, what to do about Doc and how to explain that to Sam, how Trainer was best dealt with; he only succeeded in becoming more mired in self-pity and despair. For once in his career Justin was drawing a blank. Every way he worked it no version ended with Sam walking free and the general and her superiors not. That meant giving up the first person he'd cared about in a very long time. It was hard to distinguish between all the curses flying through his head.

Hadn't he given up enough already? No contact with his family for years, no one in his life that meant anything to him, never staying in one place for long enough to make any sort of home. Justin hadn't been close to anyone since his parents' deaths the year before his enlistment. And here he was with their mission nearly accomplished and he was going to have nothing left on the other side to look forward to than a lonely, painful end. *That's what I get after all this?* It was hard not to feel cheated. Not that any of them expected a reward or even a thank you when they were done, but to only have the promise of more loss? It was too much.

"The hits just keep coming, don't they?"

Justin didn't turn around. Marcus leaned on the railing next to him. Both watched the water, listening to its happy burbling. Nature had the luxury of endless time, going on about its cycles blissfully unaware of the petty dramas in the lives of those mortals around it.

Justin glanced sideways at Marcus' grim features, noting the way his knuckles whitened and filled as he gripped and released the rail. "You wanted me to suffer, to feel what it's like to have to leave someone behind." He laughed bitterly. "You got your wish."

He said nothing, only squinting into the glow of the setting sun over the tree line. Pinks and oranges were beginning to tint the wispy cirrus clouds blowing in for the evening.

"I get it." Frowning, Justin stared at the white foam floating on top of the water, churning merrily along. "I get why you leave every few weeks. I get why you live cheap and all of your money goes to her under the guise of a survivor benefit from the Army." Justin considered the stockpile of money he had set aside over the years and where it would go when he was gone. "You were right, you know. When you said I'd never given anything up before. My parents' dying wasn't something I had to choose. After they died I enlisted and then we changed, and that was that. There wasn't time for anything else. It was always the mission. I always did the best I could for you guys. There was nothing I could do to make things right, to make things normal again. God knows I wanted to except I didn't have that kind of power. Nobody did." He confessed his burden, the burden of leadership one keeps to himself because that's the responsibility that goes with the position. It no longer mattered since they were coming to the end of their too long run. "I have regretted letting Mills go every day." Justin was thinking not of the past but of his future that would never be. Rubbing one hand over the back of the other, he saw her in his mind's eye when she told him she'd come for *him* and not her father.

"I have enough stuff to level that place. It would take me about two hours to get it ready." Marcus spoke in a monotone, gazing off unblinking and disengaged. His thoughts were far away on a young woman he had most likely seen for the last time. "I say at nine a.m. tomorrow morning we give them a demonstration of our own. I don't know how high this goes and I don't know if we have the time or strength to get them all, but I'm taking as many of these bastards with me as I can and tomorrow may be our only shot to deal them a blow they can't recover from."

"All I ask is for you not to blow it until I get in there and see if I can save her." Justin raised a hand to stay Marcus' obvious objection. "I won't put the mission in jeopardy. My time is up at nine. Give me that long." He kept his eyes on Marcus until the man turned to face him. "You don't need me anymore and I need to try. Let me get her back to her mother." He let that sink in. "Just like Marianna and Tammy," he spoke the names of Marcus' family out loud for the first time in five years. "She doesn't have to be alone."

330

Eyes growing wide at their mention, Marcus' nostrils flared in anger for only a brief moment. Eventually, he gave a curt nod. "Maybe you're right. They didn't ask for this. We can try to make things right for them for when we're gone."

The relief he'd expected at Marcus' forgiveness of Sam's lineage was empty. Instead of being pleased, Justin pushed away from the rail and walked back to Jimmy's room, his heart heavy. The man had been glued to his monitors for the better part of a day. Justin could spell him for a while and let him get some sleep. He knew he wasn't going to get any himself.

Ch. 46

Sam woke when the elevator growled to life. Looking around, she saw her father hard at work taking turns hunkering over his microscope and keying in the computer. The soon to be genetically repaired Trainer was smoothing his tshirt. Lounging against the bare metal elevator supports, he came back on alert at their arrival. No bandage on his arm hinted at his secret agreement with her father. While she slept the doctor had taped a cotton ball inside her elbow should anyone check that things were coming along. Sam stood up and stretched. Her father's shoulders pinched at the sound of the gears although he did not stop working.

When the elevator stopped it was just the general. She was alone and had a briefcase in her hand. General Lange made a beeline for Dr. James. "Doctor, we have only a day for you to develop a match for the formula should the sergeant fail to return and we're relying upon your memory of years of research." She cast her eyes Sam's direction giving her a disapproving once over. "You'll forgive me for not trusting entirely in your memory but I'm not filled with a ton of confidence in your ability."

Straightening, her father couldn't help but bristle at her taunt. "I have an incredible memory and yes I *can* have a match before your deadline. The question is *will* I."

"You will do *exactly* that or you serve no further purpose for me. You should know that I will personally throw you in a cell in some hellhole and let you rot." The general's emotionless response was far more effective than yelling. Sam and, it appeared, her father, had no doubts about her willingness to carry out her threat.

Paler and ego temporarily in check, the doctor smiled weakly. "I will do my best, General."

Sam saw the cruelty in the woman's eyes and also a pettiness that she had come to associate with those who weren't at the top of the food chain. General Lange was someone else's whipping boy. Stepping forward, she cocked her head and brought the bug in her ear closer. She hoped the men were still listening. "Don't worry about it, Sergeant Shaw will come and you'll have what you need." She guessed at the root of General Lange's instant dislike of her and poked her. "He'll come for *me*."

The general's puffy eyes narrowed into slits. Sam fought the childish urge to squeal at her. "How sure you are of yourself. How long have you and the sergeant known each other? A few weeks, a month maybe?" Lang's doubt was clear in her snide tone.

She pushed away the queasy feeling that accompanied her fear no one was coming and she wouldn't find her own way out. She didn't want to die in here but if she did, at least she could feed as much to Justin's team as possible. Sam kept her voice calm and even. "We've known each other just over a week."

Lange grinned, proud to one up her. "I have known him for years," she preened. "We used to be *very* close."

"I hope it doesn't bother you then that he's moved on. I'm sure *you* have as well." Sam opened her eyes wide, acting every bit the innocent. "This can't be *all* you have. Your boss has to give you time to go out in the world. There's a 'Mister' General out there, right? Something waiting for you after you're done wreaking havoc all day?" Not usually catty, Sam was getting a bit of a kick out of needling the bitch.

Pig eyes full of loathing and mouth tight, Lange spit back. "I have been running this program since you were a child you self-important brat. My superiors have no idea what I've put into this but when they see what I've done for them, what progress we've made, I will be writing my own ticket." Finger pointing angrily at the doctor she spat, "Get back to work or I'll have Mr. Trainer motivate you by breaking every bone in *her* precious little body." She gestured at Sam. "Starting with her jaw."

It wasn't until the elevator's noise filled the chamber that Sam finally exhaled the breath she hadn't realized she'd been holding. "I hope you're there," she mumbled. "I hate to think I'm poking the bear with a stick for nothing."

When it was just she and her two very different roommates again, Sam checked in on her father's progress. "How's it going?" She leaned on the counter, fidgeting with an empty slide. "Will you have it ready?"

He sighed. "It'll be ready."

"Great." Her hollow words fell flat in the empty space.

Sam watched the glass rectangle catch the light from above as she turned it end over end between her fingers. "I never asked, is there a cure? For Justin," she didn't try to hide it anymore. Her father was smart. He had to know she had feelings for the "soldier" as he called him. "Is there some way to reverse the process or are they too far gone?" Sam bit her lip, willing him to answer correctly.

He regarded her carefully for some time before answering. "I've been testing some theories although there is nothing tested, nothing proven."

Hope flickered in Sam's breast. "What theories? How close are they to being the real deal?"

Dr. James' brows knitted. Letting his eyes wander over to their constant voyeur, he took a step toward her and lowered his voice. "In theory, if we were to expose someone who is already affected *again* only this time with the altered compound, it would effectively 'reset' him. And yes, I would be confident enough in the process to test it on a human subject."

"Normal, like *normal* normal? Can't come back from the dead normal?" Sam had to forcibly contain her enthusiasm and keep her voice down. "Are you sure?"

"As sure as anyone can be." He managed a smile.

"Would you consider running a test on someone?"

Pushing himself away from the table, her father crossed his arms and gave his daughter a long knowing look. "You're speaking of your soldier friend I'm guessing?"

Her jaw set tight against the argument she could hear coming, Sam nodded.

"I thought you might feel that way about him although I don't entirely understand why. Do you really know him?" He studied her closely, trying to understand his daughter's reasoning. "Do you know what he's done, what kind of man he is?"

"There was a time when I wasn't so sure. This has all happened so fast." Lowering her voice she confided her thoughts, not caring that they were being broadcast. "When I first met Justin he wasn't concerned with being my friend or playing the nice guy to ingratiate himself with me. He was cold and kind of scary. I thought that was who he was. And then, when we were at my apartment and he thought I was in danger his first instinct was to put himself between the threat and me. There was no way he could have faked that. There were other things that happened, things that made me think it was all for the sample or to get to you." She took a breath to steady herself. "Then I remembered that moment in my apartment." Sam shook her head. "I won't doubt him again."

Dr. James wasn't visibly affected by her speech, he only continued to stare at her, thinking.

"You want something great to be remembered for. Why not the cure for cancer? Isn't that what we're dealing with here? There's no greater plague for us worldwide right now. You would be among the greats: Pasteur, Physick, Schweitzer. You'd be a shoe in for the Nobel." Her heart raced, waiting for him to respond.

Pensive, he rubbed his jaw, rolling his eyes up. Soon his lips began to move, index finger punctuating points to himself as he began to pace up and down the room, growing lost in his thoughts. Now and again he would come back to his computer and type something in. "We're linked to the original files stored remotely." He told her without looking up. "They're very basic and hold little of the formulaic composition but I have some of the subjects' basic information. It could save us some time in the sequencing but everything else is gone with my notes. I destroyed it all when I left." Fingers tapped the keys and the doctor was off.

Sam settled back on the chair to watch him pace and think. From her post she could see Trainer watching her father suspiciously. After a few minutes, he stalked over.

"What's happened? Are you done with my

changes? It's nearly nightfall, there isn't much time left." He frowned from one to the other.

"Don't worry Mr. Trainer, I'm nearly finished with all I need to synchronize the formula to your DNA. It will take a few minor tweaks when we combine the two and voila, you'll be all you can be." His lips curved into a smile.

Watching Trainer fade back to his post, Sam saw her father immediately return to work and she wandered over to sit on the foot of the chair and watch, feeling utterly alone. "I wish I could just talk to you Justin, *you'd* know what to do." Sighing, Sam felt some of her nerves settling. Even if he wasn't listening she felt better thinking he might be on the other end of the microphone. Part of her was embarrassed he might have heard what she'd told her father. Part of her hoped he had. It might serve as an apology for her having run off and gotten Jimmy shot, and ending up with her father, and, well, there was a lot to be sorry for. "I hope you're doing okay out there. I'm trying to figure things out as best I can." She cast a glance over at Trainer. "I'm not sure I'm doing any of it right."

Seeing Trainer eyeing her in return, Sam stopped talking. Sitting quietly for a while, she lost track of time. No windows, watch or clocks had that effect. Her father's computer might have a clock but she, not wanting to interrupt him, left him alone. They would let her know when she was "on".

Ch. 47

A steady knocking at the door woke Justin from the troubled sleep he'd fallen into just before dawn. Rising with the instant alertness a life of paranoia brings with it, he whipped open his door.

"Morning." A somber faced Marcus handed him a styrofoam cup with a plastic lid. "Get up, we need to move."

"What's happened? What are we looking at?" He asked his Second for the important points.

Without hesitation Marcus launched into his report no different than he would have the day before. No more emotional, no less. Unsurprised by the soldier's professionalism, Justin kept his own emotions in check. They had work to do.

"Jimmy's got some action from what sounds like NSA. Our General Lange has been to meet with a Colonel Daleque who came in from DC. No entourage, no official orders just your run of the mill secret meeting at a coffee shop. They were in there for a while and now Daleque is coming back with Lange to take a look at the program and meet the scientist behind it all." Taking a gulp of his own coffee, Marcus' grim face broke into a nasty smile. "Sounds to me like Lange might be feeling some heat."

Justin tested his coffee with a small sip. Finding it reasonably cool, he took a larger swallow. "Looks like you're going to get your wish Marcus. We'll blow up lots of people today." He joked coldly.

"It's been quiet in there. Jimmy hasn't heard anything since you handed it off after midnight.

338

Trainer's been quiet too. We've heard enough mumbling and equipment rattling to know Doc's been working all night, which has to be good. He might have us all cured by dinner," Marcus reported. "She did good, Shaw. She's been helpful to have in there," he admitted, watching his bootlaces and lowering his voice. "We'd better get moving if we're going to beat the deadline and mount our rescue op."

"We?"

"I've been listening to Jimmy's tapes and I've heard enough to know you were right," he admitted painfully. "They aren't the ones we're after. They don't deserve to die."

"Give me two minutes, I'll meet you at Jimmy's room." Justin closed the door and threw on a clean shirt and jeans, slipping on his usual pair of black boots. A quick visit to the bathroom and he had himself put together enough he could set out from Jimmy's without being mistaken for a transient. No matter what their operation, they always fell back on the basic strategy of blending in. The average person paid no attention to others like themselves. A few minutes of basic hygiene and no one bothered them.

Less than five minutes later he was knocking on Jimmy's door. Marcus opened it and retreated into the interior to sit behind Jimmy on the edge of the peach and teal floral bedcovering. Jimmy sat in the chair lording over his equipment with earphones on his head, a notepad in his lap filled with illegible shorthand notes and a pencil in his hand.

His listening station was cobbled together, a somewhat comical mish mash of high tech and MacGuyver like urban engineering. He'd taken the speakers out of the car, a series of small black boxes he kept in the trunk, and ran them to his laptop on the desk against the far wall.

"What's been happening, Jimmy?" Justin took up a post beside them, watching the man's hand write furiously in a shorthand only he could understand. Part of Justin believed he did that on purpose. Pausing only for a fraction of a second to hold up a finger to stay any interruptions, Jimmy continued writing for a few minutes more.

Finally he slid the earphone back off one ear and twisted his neck to look Justin in the eye. "I think we got something big happenin'." He tapped the end of his pencil against his notes for emphasis. "I been doin' some diggin' and this Daleque who's meeting with Lange is a heavy hitter with the NSA." Jimmy's hacking skills were criminal. "Fifteen years ago he was an officer in the Army with a bright future. He was sent over to Afghanistan for two tours. Guessin' he did stuff off book. Hard to find any real details on it." He patted the top of the laptop's monitor like a trusty Collie. "About ten years ago he disappeared. I got a pattern I'm seein' every time his name comes up in a file." One brow cocked. "He goes in and whatever it was they didn't like just gets wiped off the map, never a mention of it again. He's a 'Cleaner'." Jimmy turned his shoulders to better face Justin. "He's on his way back with Lange now. He ain't here for no demonstration, Sarge, he's comin' to shut this thing down."

Can we not catch a fucking break? "How long?"

"They met outside St. Paul, left twenty minutes ago." He grinned. "Lange must be buying Doc time, she took the long way. I'd say we got an hour and a half."

"Does Lange have any idea?"

Jimmy was thoughtful. "I didn't hear while they were inside, just the street and her call in to let them know she was coming back with a plus one. Sounds nervous though. She knows she doesn't have anything without you and it don't sound like she trusts you to come through. Doc's a hail Mary at this point. She doesn't think he'll deliver in time." Jimmy watched his commanding officer, complete faith in Justin's decision. "What do you think? You want to go in now before she gets back?"

"What do we have? Two, maybe three people on computers depending on the shift, the guy with the mustache, I don't see them as more than a nuisance. Do we have tranqs?"

"Yep," Marcus answered.

Justin roughed his neck, frowning. "What about Smith. Do you know if he's still there or did he go with Lange?"

"I ain't heard him in a long time, Sarge. Trainer either. Didn't you say Sam was talking about him before she nodded off? We know he's gonna be there pretty quick if he ain't already for his big graduation to Super Soldier."

When she started talking Jimmy handed it over to him saying he was going to catch some sleep. It brought a smile to his face to hear her say his name with such absolute faith believing he could help her, that thinking of him brought her comfort. It resonated on a basic, testosterone filled level. He was a protector by nature and she was a woman who wanted him to do that for her. Justin would have taken on the Taliban singlehanded. But what they were doing wasn't just for them, it was for their loved ones. Those they'd given up and who'd buried them and moved on not knowing their fallen continued to live and toil alone.

"Right, that gives us three plus Trainer and Smith who might be there but upstairs where we can't hear." Turning away, Justin walked to the window to look out on the parking lot. The day was gloomy and windy. Leaves were beginning to fade on their farthest tips as their host trees began the slow steady march toward dormancy for the long winter ahead. Too soon they would have one last burst of brilliance before death. How appropriate, thought Justin with a bitter snort. "I say we go now. Our best bet is to move before we have more firepower to face. Then we level the place when the General and her guest get back. Agreed?" He heard the two "ayes" behind him and grunted once to himself, already setting the plan in motion in his head. "Let's do this."

Together Marcus and Justin filed out, Jimmy remained plugged in to keep them apprised of any changes. Pushing the button opening communications through the device in his wristwatch, Justin gave a test call to Jimmy and heard it back in the tiny earpiece he popped in. They were live. Marcus popped the trunk and Justin pulled several guns, checking the chambers on all three before stowing them on his person. Two nine millimeters and one tranquilizer gun with a full load of seven darts went on first. Two extra clips of real ammo and a knife for his ankle and Justin felt reasonably prepared.

"Let's go." Closing the trunk, Justin had a clear view of the street and the patrol car pulling into the narrow lot. "Damn." There was no point running so Justin didn't.

Following the direction of his eyes to the source of displeasure, Marcus startled when his eyes landed on the black and white rolling up on them. "Standby to evac

342

Jimmy. Cops in front." He pretended to scratch his temple to hide his muttered warning in his comm.

"Rochester Police, freeze!" The passenger jumped out of the car, his red hair instantly recognizable. The gun in his hands was steady. He wouldn't be fooled twice.

Marcus and Justin exchanged glances. Justin lifted his arms over his head, sliding sideways to within arms reach of his companion.

"I said freeze!" the young officer shouted again.

By now his older partner was out, his gun raised as well. "Get your arms up, both of you."

"On three," Marcus murmured, his arms started to spread out like wings and coming up in a wide arc toward his head.

"One, two," and while the officers were approaching them, guns trained, Marcus' hand flew forward, fingers curling around the butt of the tranquilizer gun. On "three" Marcus pulled it free of Justin's waistband and Justin dove behind the car.

The older partner saw what was happening first, his gun shifted to Marcus. Justin watched his eyes go wide as he yelled a warning. "Gun!"

Years of combat on top of extensive training gave Marcus a marked advantage. As easily as pointing a finger, Marcus shot the older officer first before swinging his sidearm to the youth.

But even an inexperienced rookie has ample time to take a shot when he's the second target. This one was no exception. The standard issue nine millimeter barked just as the first officer's knees buckled. The shot went wide hitting Marcus in the left thigh and blood exploded from the wound. Marcus staggered forward, his gun never wobbled as he put the youngster down before the report of his weapon had finished echoing off the pavement.

"Jimmy we're clear out here. Marcus is hit," Justin reported in.

"Man, I tore my wires all to shit just now. I'm gonna have to cut 'em all down to get 'em to talk nice again," Jimmy grumbled.

Sergeant Shaw didn't bother to comment, going to the side of the older officer first to make sure he was properly under before checking the redhead. They were both out.

"Holy shit, Sarge. Seriously?" Jimmy opened the door to his room assessing the scene. "How we gonna explain this?"

There weren't many guests in the low budget motel, part of its appeal for Justin and his men. Although squad cars and gun fights were probably not the norm here and tended to draw attention. Sure enough, the manager was already stepping out of the office, a cordless phone visible in his hand.

"We're not. Grab what you can, we have less than two minutes before backup arrives."

Scuffling and crashing from within the room was the only response to the command.

He pointed at the leg, the blood seeping through the blue material of his jeans already slowing of its own accord. "How is it?"

"Went through. It's fine." Marcus gave a half of a headshake. "Doesn't matter how many bullets you take, they still burn like a son of a bitch."

Justin rubbed his chest. "Don't I know it."

Marcus slid into the driver's seat with only the slightest hint of a limp and the engine roared to life. Justin dragged the officers to lean them up against their car to protect them from the other cars sure to arrive shortly. Justin was busily making adjustments for this new complication. The truck would need to be ditched now that they could be tied to it through the motel logs.

"One more stop and we're out of here." Checking his watch, he saw that they were drawing close to one hour from their deadline. It was going to be tight to get Sam before the general and her guest returned. Sam couldn't be there when Daleque got there. There was no way of knowing when he would begin his "cleanup" and Justin couldn't have her caught in the crossfire.

More sirens wailed in the distance.

"Jimmy!"

"Right here, Sarge." The man's arms were loaded with his tech gear, bag on his back barely zipped enough to keep the computer from flying out, notepad flapping wildly as he ran out. "Little help." He stood at the back door, arms too full to open it for himself.

Justin hurried to let him in, slamming the door shut behind him and jogged around the front of the car to take a seat. Marcus threw the car into drive and shot out of the parking lot, fishtailing as the car hit the street still accelerating.

"Hold on Sam," Justin muttered. Marcus looked at

him out of the corner of his eye.

Ch. 48

General Lange drove slowly in hopes that when they arrived back at the shop turned laboratory the pain in the ass Dr. James would have by some miracle recreated the chemical. She needed it to be right so she could show Colonel Daleque and those he represented she was capable of producing results. She didn't really believe Shaw would show with the sample. No one walked into certain death for a pretty face and perky tits. Not in real life.

A lot of eyes were on her for this. And after the doctor's attempt to jump ship she needed a miracle to avoid a shut down. This project being closed would mean pretty much the same thing for her career. This was all she'd done for nearly a decade. Without it she'd probably end up in some outpost on the edge of civilization where she could quietly rot out the rest of her days until Malaria or a polar bear took her. That prissy bitch of the doctor's was right, this *was* all she had.

Barely turning her head, she glanced over at the colonel. The second she shook his hand she'd wanted to wash it. She wasn't sure what it was, there was something about him that made her feel unclean. Maybe it was the way he looked at her, or rather *through* her with his watery blue eyes so light they nearly blended with the surrounding whites. Or maybe it was the smoothness of his hands, like a woman's. Her father told her, "You can't trust someone without a few calluses on their hands. They don't know the value of an honest day's work."

Daleque was average height, thin as a whip, and fair skinned. The shock of black hair sticking out at odd angles left him looking sickly and mentally unbalanced.

But appearances could be deceiving. Lange was willing to wager that the man seated next to her wasn't sick and could actually put up one hell of a fight if need be. His mental state was definitely a crapshoot though. It was the eyes. They were chilling in their dullness. Anyone with that kind of flat expression is either trying too hard to appear uninterested or truly isn't, and that scared her more.

The bored looking Colonel was supposed to be getting an update from her on the project that once was a top priority for their government, yet he was barely listening as she made her points. It was as if he'd already made up his mind about it. That wasn't good. She began to stutter when it came to their budget. By the time they crossed the border she was almost pleading to keep her doors open. As soon as she realized it was over, she stopped.

Wordless, he sat next to her barely blinking. Her limbs were heavy with exhaustion. Exhaustion from working eighteen-hour days under constant pressure from above to produce after years of extensions and budget increases. And when she finally had something, their lead scientist sabotaged the entire project. Now that she had him back there would be no more excuses. She would tear his smart-mouthed daughter apart before his very eyes if that was what it took to get results. Lange wasn't one to go out without a fight.

The girl bothered her from the start when she saw the way he looked at her. Justin hadn't looked at *her* that way when they'd been together. He hadn't been hers from the beginning but she figured she'd win him over. She always did. But he wasn't to be won, instead he left. He humiliated her. It would only be fair to make him watch Trainer work on the girl as payback. The horrible little psychopath was all too eager to kill when it came to those soldiers. If only he had been in the van with them instead of those two amateurs they never would have escaped.

Even driving slowly, the road eventually ended and Lange and Daleque arrived at their destination ahead of schedule. Daleque got out first, taking in the old decrepit looking shop with the same bored expression. Lange felt a cold sense of foreboding curl itself around her middle. Stepping past him to lead the way into the shop, she plastered on a pleasant face.

"This way please, Colonel."

The hard soles of his hyper polished black dress shoes slapped softly on the crushed rock drive. Knowing they saw her on camera, she waited only a few seconds before she heard the gears catch and raise the white overhead door to allow them entry.

She led him in, explaining each computer station's purpose. The operators, lab techs, not enlisted, knew enough to keep their eyes on their screens. "This particular unit," she waved a hand to indicate the second computer in the row, "is tied into our satellite system. We've devoted this station to monitoring communications networks all over the world. We are of course looking for several different things: competing chemical programs, prospective buyers for materials such as ours…"

"I'm here for a demonstration of your project, not a lesson in telecommunications." Daleque cut her off sharply.

Lange gave him a polite smile, one he returned equally disingenuously. "As I've explained, we have our lead scientist working on the project as we speak. There was a slight delay and some data was lost. In my report I explained that we would be more than ready by early next week." With as much respect as she could muster, she endeavored to remind him she'd been granted more time by Washington. She had a strong suspicion he was here to shut them down. If she impressed him, she hoped to be assigned to a new project instead of being put out to pasture. Her career was all she had.

"I would like to see that." He clasped his hands behind his back and raised his brows at her.

"Of course." She slammed her heels against the impact absorbing flooring imagining it was his face she was punching holes in with her patent leather black heels. They walked into the open lift and her finger jabbed the button to bring them down to the lower level. Fuming on the inside, she was the picture of professionalism on the outside.

Ch. 49

Doctor James summoned her quietly. "Samantha could you come over here please?"

Sitting up and rubbing her eyes, Sam pulled her shoes back on and shuffled sleepily to lean against her father's worktable. Though her thoughts were swirling too fast for real sleep, Sam closed her eyes and feigned sleep well enough to give herself much needed quiet time. Her father continued his frenetic pacing and muttering all night and the few stolen glances she'd aimed at Trainer revealed he allowed himself to rest his back against the wall, knees pulled up with his eyes open. Always open.

"What is it?" She matched her father's soft tone.

He was pulling on a fresh pair of latex gloves. "I need an extra set of hands for a minute."

Shrugging, Sam stepped around the table and donned a pair of gloves from the box in the drawer on the side of his table. "What do you need me to do?"

He pointed to the fridge standing on the outer wall across from his table and held up his gloves, keeping them clear of any surfaces. "Could you remove the materials from the cooler?"

She slid the tray onto the table and watched her father take what bore a striking resemblance to a metal cuticle tool and dip it into one tube to tap out a small portion on a slide.

After he finished preparing his slide he handed the tool to Sam. "Take a sterile wipe from that box and give this a thorough cleaning." He pointed to another box sitting on the edge of the table.

Sam wiped it and laid it back down with the edge propped up off of the table with the folded wipe.

The doctor was on his third slide when he caught her attention. He was whispering.

"What?"

Eyes still fixed on the microscope's eyepieces, Dr. James repeated himself so quietly she had to lean in to hear him. "I said I've got it ready, I've got the cure for your soldier and his friends."

Her heart leaped in her chest. "How?"

He gave her a cautionary glare before going back to his eyepiece.

"Okay, but how can you be sure it's right?" She watched his fingers dexterously maneuver three tubes into a separate wire rack. "How do you know it won't do the opposite and make them more sick?" Sam stared at the vials trying to keep her hopes realistic. *Are they hearing this?* Butterflies exploded in her stomach.

"Think about it. The chemical itself allows a body to heal from virtually anything. The only thing it *can't* do is regrow parts that are removed entirely. Limiting it to one small dose will reset the body back to its initial status, healing them one last time only this one," he tapped the slide, "*doesn't* attach itself to the DNA so once it's done its job it disappears." He pointed to the three special vials. "I've pulled as much information as possible from their medical records. It should be enough to make it compatible with their blood types and biological makeup. All we need is the sample." He eyed her and gave a tiny wink. He knew Justin was coming.

Sam beamed at her father before he she tucked her lips between her teeth and clamped down. "What about him?" She gestured toward Trainer.

Dr. James cracked a smile. It was the smile she remembered, before things got complicated. She grinned back. Instead of answering he returned to his work. That he was cooking something special up for Trainer was obvious. Sam could only imagine what that might be. She hoped it hurt.

She watched his thin shoulders hunch over his microscope and frowned. He was already being sucked back into his research. His work was his life. As an adult she could see that clearly. Yet the realization didn't hurt now that she was old enough to understand. The world needed people like him just like it needed people who were family people. That he would give up everything in his life for the pursuit of his true passion, science, made her father a good man in his own right and Sam was surprised at the pride she felt.

"Thank you, Dad."

"You're welcome, Samantha."

Ch. 50

Marcus sped out of town making it to the shop ten minutes after they left the motel parking lot except it was too late. The dark blue sedan in the driveway told them the general beat them there.

"Holy shit guys, ho-ly shit!" Jimmy called out. He slid the headphones back on the one side. "He figured it out. Doc's got our cure."

Justin and Marcus exchanged glances. "Now we *really* need you out of there before we blow the place. Shouldn't be a problem, right Shaw?" Marcus joked but his concern was clear.

Equally worried he'd prove too weak, but not willing to trust either of the other men to retrieve his woman, Justin shot Marcus a look. *My woman? Get your head on, dumbass.* "Do we have locations on our threats?"

"No man, I got Sam and Doc having a little moment here and that's it. Everything else is quiet."

"Okay, then I think we take them down before they go below." Justin began to run through their roles out loud.

"Sarge, wait." Everybody stopped. "I hear the elevator I think." Jimmy pressed his headphones tightly against his head. "Yep, they're goin' below right now." He met Justin's gaze, his face falling. "We're too late."

Justin felt his stomach twist. "The fuck we are." He pulled his guns from his waistband and did a quick press check making sure a round was in the chamber before replacing them out of sight. "Nothing changes.

354

Jimmy, keep ears on. Tell me if things go south or if Smith turns up." He turned to Marcus and gave him a tight smile. "Marcus you do what you need to do up here to wipe the place off the map. If this goes to hell, I want you to know it's been a pleasure serving with you both."

"Sarge, think about this," Jimmy argued. "Once Marcus sets those charges, we're committed to this. We don't know how long you're gonna be in there with all these unknowns. What if they evac? Marcus' gotta blow it even if you're in there. It ain't smart."

"I know." He refused to make eye contact with his men. Justin was putting them in a terrible position and he knew it. Marcus would hold off as long as possible, that was as much as he could ask. Cure or no they had to end this and they might not get an opportunity like this again. Personal sacrifice was a soldier's duty and they all accepted that without question.

"We all have our jobs, Jimmy." Marcus opened his door and stepped out.

Following suit, Justin did too and watched Marcus over the truck bed. "Sergeant Shaw knows his." Though the words were cold, the crisp salute he gave lightened the burden on Justin's mind. If things went badly, Marcus wouldn't relish his duty nor would he shirk it. Justin was counting on it.

"All right then. I have thirty minutes before the show." Everyone took a moment to sync their watches. "If we're not out, blow the building." Justin cracked a hand on the metal and set off for the white door.

Ch. 51

"Colonel Daleque, let me introduce you to our Chief Scientist on Project Phoenix, Dr. Steven James."

"Doctor."

The visiting colonel turned his translucent eyes on Sam and she had the same gut reaction as Lange had. Her breath caught in her chest and the hairs on the back of her neck stood straight up.

"And who might this be?" He stared at her, his lack of emotion oddly inhuman. That and his angular jaw and chin had Sam thinking lizard.

Lange grudgingly introduced him to the thorn in her side. "That is Dr. James' daughter, Samantha. She is here to *assist* the doctor with his demonstration today."

His black brows peaked at her inflection. His constantly roving eyes caught sight of Trainer, initially hidden by Lange when they stepped off the elevator. Trainer stood, arms apart from his body in a ready stance. The men were staring each other down, two hunters recognizing each other for what they were.

Taking both superiors by surprise, Trainer spoke first. "Actually, the doctor decided *I'm* better suited for the demonstration today."

General Lange didn't like the impromptu personnel change. "I don't think that will be necessary Mr. Trainer. We will proceed as planned with the girl acting the part of the test subject."

Ignoring Lange, Daleque squared himself to Trainer and cocked his head, studying him. "Do I know you?"

"Mr. Trainer came to us at the beginning of the project." A tremor had crept into Lange's voice. "He was a recruit who served under me at Camp Pendleton. I doubt he ran in your circles, Colonel."

But Trainer and Daleque were oblivious to General Lange's explanations or anyone else in the room frankly.

Alarm bells clanged in Sam's head. She moved closer to her father who was blinking at the happenings, seeming lost. He inched toward her. They could both feel the tension mounting rapidly between the two men. *Something* was going to happen, she just didn't know what. Her throat tightened. She doubted she could find somewhere for her and her father to take cover if it came to gunfire. Scanning the sparse room once again, the best options were the chair and the lab table. Both of which were in the middle of the room and neither presented the best shield if bullets started flying.

"Things are about to go very, very bad."

"What was that?" Dr. James frowned down at her.

She forced herself to sound calmer than she was. "I don't think this is going to go well." Suddenly, Sam was seized by inspiration. Tipping her face up she whispered, "Dad, think of a reason for us to get into that back room." The room hidden by the tiled wall was at least twenty feet away and they couldn't make it over there without being noticed. They had to have a reason to go in there.

His eyes flitted from Daleque to Trainer and back to Sam, realization finally dawning. "Oh no." She watched fear freeze his features. Sam's initial assumption was right; her father wasn't a fighter. "What should we do?"

"Dad." She reached out and squeezed his arm, bringing him back to her. "Dad, you've been in that room down there. Tell me what's in it and how do we make them buy that we need to get in?"

Dr. James pursed his lips in thought. He grunted to himself a few times before his finger stilled. "Just some monitoring devices for the facility, there's no reason for us to use those."

"Why were you back there before?" She could feel the nerves building.

Her father actually blushed. "You being here and so much pressure with your life on the line, I wasn't feeling well." He paid particular attention to his gloves. "I was using the bathroom."

Daleque spoke again, commanding control of the room even if his words were for just the one. "I know I know you." He cocked his head the other way. "It was Tel Aviv back in '04. You were a Ranger then." He cocked his head the other way. "From what I saw you do to those Palestinians I wouldn't have thought you'd settle for some sort of guard duty. You got them to sing when no one else could get them to talk. Why are you really here?"

There was no twitch or external hint that he was at all surprised by Daleque's recollection. The only thing that moved on Trainer was his mouth. "And you were on the wet team cleaning up my mess." That same unpleasant grin he wore when beating up girls spread across his face. "How did you go from janitor to boss?"

General Lange, forgotten entirely to this point by

both men, spun with her mouth wide to watch Daleque's reaction. She didn't exist for them.

Daleque snorted at the question. "My title changed, not my duty. I'm sure you've already guessed that's why I'm here, am I right?" He lifted his chin. "What do *you* really want here?"

"What everyone wants, I want to be unstoppable. It appears our causes are at odds." His conversational tone gave Sam chills.

It wouldn't have surprised her to hear one offer the other a drink. They were professional killers, complete emotional detachment from the battle that was coming.

Trainer shrugged. "The doctor has prepared a version of his chemical compound specifically engineered for my DNA to make me the ultimate soldier. That's all I want," he pointed at the wire rack on the edge of the table, "and you can do what you need to do here without my interference."

Turning to see Daleque's's reaction, Sam watched his hand slide up and into his coat. She squeaked. In that moment she made a decision. She brought her hands up to her face, cupping her sound back toward herself to carry it to her ear. "This is going bad right now. Steer clear." Getting out of here was up to her. She couldn't ask them to walk into a firefight for her and this was shaping up to be exactly that in a hurry.

"Dad we need to move, now." She elbowed him in the ribs. They both began to shuffle forward, Sam willing the others not to see.

"A bold request," Daleque chuckled. "And one I can't grant."

Sam's footsteps sped up.

Trainer harrumphed. "Typical. You charge in here ready to start shooting, but you should know that if you delete this place you're leaving three very important parts of the puzzle out there."

"What?" The head tipped. "You mean the last three subjects?" Daleque was well informed about the players.

"One of whom is coming back here right now with the last bit of the chemical compound. The good doctor's pretty smart, he kept some for himself to sell."

The two spun to face her father. Trainer was glaring at the doctor. Sam's disappointment in losing their bid for safety evaporated at Trainer's accusation.

"Dad, what is he talking about?" She was rooted to the spot, horror planting her feet. "*You* weren't going to sell this, w*ere you*?"

Dr. James stood blinking, staring at his accuser. His prominent Adams apple bobbed up and down as he gulped to wet his mouth and find his voice. His answer was directed past Sam, at Trainer. "You're wrong. I had no intention of selling it. I was going to use it to heal people." Turning to Sam, he tried to explain himself in a rush. "Samantha, please listen to me. I intended it to help people. It's my legacy."

She stared, numb.

"I've been working on it for years. It's been my goal to take the formula to the public and use it to cure diseases. While we've been here I've come to understand it so much better. I have a cure for so many different diseases, not just for your soldiers but for

360

genetic diseases, blood diseases, the possibilities are endless. In small doses, this compound can cure nearly anything." His glazed, frantic eyes were frightening.

Sam backed away from him.

Dr. James turned and leaned in, both hands palms up as he pleaded with the general, Daleque, and Trainer. "Don't you see? With this formula so many lives can be saved. It doesn't have to be a means of destruction. It can be our salvation."

Looking to Daleque, Trainer went on unaffected by the doctor's impassioned pleas. "With the doctor's alterations think of the possbilities." He glanced at the vials on the worktable. "It'll make *me* invincible, think what he could do for *you*."

The elevator groaned and Sam felt her insides turn to stone. "Ohpleaseno." The legs that came into view as it made its descent should have lifted her heart, they only made her want to scream.

Colonel Daleque twisted his body to watch the body coming into view. "Sergeant Shaw, I presume." Smiling for the first time he aimed his curious expression toward the occupant of the noisy box. His hand flashed from under his coat.

Sam saw the light reflect on metal and screamed a warning just as the gun barked.

Ch. 52

When the elevator stopped at the bottom, Justin's body lay face down on the white floor. Already in motion, Sam didn't stop until she had Justin's hand in hers, willing him to come back fast. She doubted her ability to defend him and herself when all hell broke loose.

Laughing, Daleque turned to Trainer now coming around Lange staring stricken at the fallen soldier. "Now there are only two."

Except the sadistic soldier was shaking his head. He waved a hand toward the would-be corpse. "Do you not understand *anything* about this project? Didn't she tell you?" He inclined his head toward the mystified general who, until approximately seven minutes ago, thought she was in charge. "You haven't killed him, not permanently. When he comes back he'll be closer to death, but you can be sure he *will* come back to life."

"I know the identities of the three subjects and I've been briefed on the entire project. I know the important details. My goal was to stop him, not kill. The one piece of evidence she overlooked telling me is how to kill them. *You* know obviously?" Daleque became the student.

Exasperated at his ignorant pupil, Trainer advanced to where Sam hovered protectively over Justin's body. "Of course, I killed the last one." He raised his voice unnecessarily to be heard. "They regenerate life, not limbs or bones. You have to decapitate him unless you'd like to feed him a grenade."

Their casual talk of killing Justin was too terrible and, clutching at his hand with one of hers, Sam patted the pockets of his jeans, praying he'd brought it as a bargaining chip. That's what she would have done. Finding it quickly, she extracted the cylinder from Justin's pants pocket, too frightened for him to be relieved to have it here.

"No, please stop!" She held up the cylinder in her hand, waving it for them to see. "Don't hurt him. I'll give you this if you'll let us go."

"Samantha, you can't give that to them," her father chastised her, aghast.

General Lange became functional again, striding forward. "Give me that."

Trainer got to her first and snatched it roughly from her hand. "He brought it." Turning his body, he held it up to examine it in the light, incredulous. "Doctor, I believe you have what you need to finish your tweaking."

Daleque watched the cylinder in Trainer's hand with marked interest. Sam got the impression he might be under orders to wipe out the hierarchy but that cylinder wasn't on the list of things to be destroyed.

"If you want to see the future of warfare, Daleque hold off for a few minutes." Trainer gloated, taking his prize to the worktable.

With everyone focused on the cylinder, Sam tried to catch her father's eye. He was under its spell as well but cut a glimpse at his daughter, giving her the briefest tightening of his eye; not quite a wink. He was planning something.

Mumbling fast, voice shaking, she gave the men an update not knowing if they were listening or preparing to charge in or destroy the building any second. Her shoulders pinched tight, waiting for the sound of bombs or gunfire. "Hold off, I think I can get your vials if you give me a little time." She had no way of knowing that was the one thing she didn't have.

Dr. James was already busy using a strange clawlike device to open the metal cylinder and reveal a tiny bottle inside. Careful so as not to spill a drop, he uncorked it and took a syringe out to withdraw a small amount through the rubber cap. By the amount extracted, Sam figured that tiny sample had enough in it to expose at least ten men. The quantity was plenty sufficient to restart a whole new research lab in addition to selling a portion for profit.

"How were you going to pay for your new lab where you were planning on doing all of this great socially redeeming work, *Dr. James*? Sam felt like someone kicked her in the stomach as it dawned on her.

"Don't judge me, Samantha." Her father directed a dark look at his daughter and slid his syringe into one of the tubes in the rack apart from her three. A slight tremor shook his otherwise steady hands as he combined the two ingredients to complete Trainer's "upgrade."

Eager, Trainer held out an arm. "Okay Doctor, I'm ready."

Glancing around, Sam saw Daleque between her and Trainer intent upon what was happening at the white table and Lange merely standing off to the side looking ill. It was almost enough for Sam to feel bad for the woman. Both she and her entire life's work were about to be terminated and it wasn't even important enough for her executioner to afford her a second glance. He was already treating her like a ghost.

A celebratory whoop from Trainer made Sam jump. He held a gauze pad to the inside of his elbow, grinning ear to ear. It was the first human emotion she'd seen from the little man and it made her want to punch him.

"How long before it takes effect?" Daleque wanted to know.

Both men looked to the doctor who shrugged. "We should see the results momentarily." One long finger tapped the tabletop.

It was her father's nervous habit. She had a momentary fear that he'd been lying about the cure. He didn't really have one and this was all a bluff. The hand in hers twitched and Sam looked down at Justin's face, rapidly regaining color. Blood began to flow out of the hole in his side. She hoped the bullet had made it through; there was nothing she could do about it now if it hadn't.

Everything stopped when a hoarse scream rent the air. All eyes went to where Trainer stood. The gleeful expression had turned to abject horror. He was rubbing at his injection site.

"What did you do to me? Is it supposed to burn?"

The doctor made no move to help. He was stepping backward to put the table between them. Daleque blinked but showed no other sign of life. He seemed content to let the events play out, maybe figuring it would save him some trouble if he let the players do his work for him. "It will be over in a minute, Mr. Trainer. The agent is combining with your DNA now."

Another scream ripped through the otherwise silent room. Trainer went down to his knees. The skin around his eyes was turning black, the eyes themselves were rolled all the way up and the man's body gone rigid. A small trail of blood dripped from his nose and ears just before he collapsed dead.

"Is that my formula? What have you done to it?" Lange reminded everyone she was still there. Of course she would be worried about the chemical.

Without breaking his stare from the twisted body still tortured even in death, Dr. James spoke in a monotone. "I altered the formula to unravel his cell structure instead of repairing it, destruction is far simpler than creation." His shoulders slumped. "There's your weapon, General. I've done my part, now let my daughter go."

For a few seconds no one moved. Then, everything happened at once. General Lange jogged to the table attempting to snatch the vial from where it lay by the doctor's defeated form. Daleque sprang to life and Sam saw a blur of movement from his direction. His gun roared twice and Lange hit the table, bounced off, and slid to the ground where she got up on her hands and tried to belly crawl away.

Seeing the man temporarily distracted as he went to finish the job, Sam managed a glance at her father. He stood frozen, staring at the man he'd knowingly murdered, and Sam seized her chance to act. It took no time for her to reach her father's side and whisper, "Dad, come on." When there was no response she put a hand on his arm and tugged, attempting to draw him back to the elevator. "Dad, this is it. We have to go now."

The eyes that turned to her were not her father's. They were dead. Gone was the flicker of life and animation that marked him a brilliantly curious soul. The hands lying against his sides didn't move, even his fingers were still. "I did exactly what I swore I would never do. And now they have it. Anyone in the world, any single person or family can be killed now with one flake of skin or piece of hair, anything with DNA, and it's because of me. That's my legacy, Samantha, a killer of men. Presidents, dictators, entire bloodlines will die because of my vanity."

Temporarily, the man who was her father, flaws and myth she'd once layered him in, fell away and Sam saw him as a man who had a gift and wanted to leave a mark on the world. Only now that he had, he could only wish to take it all back. Uncertain what to say, she squeezed his arm.

Daleque's's gun reported one last time and he finished his business with Lange. Sam glanced over as her killer squatted down to confirm she was gone.

"Doctor, before I finish my business here I must ask if that is all that you have." He pointed to the tube.

"Yes, that's all that I've made."

"Thank you doctor."

Seeing the gun come up, Sam guessed the target. "Dad, watch out!" Tugging on his arm and using her weight to bring him to the ground was easy, he offered no resistance. A second later a deafening barrage of bullets filled the room. When nothing hit her she backed off to let her father get up.

"Dad, we have to get out of here."

He was shaking his head. "No, this won't be what I leave behind." Pain-filled eyes met hers. "You were right, Samantha, this isn't all there is." He touched the table. "It isn't too late."

Recognizing the debilitating effects of shock dulling her father's mind, panic seized her. She had no idea how she was going to get two barely functional men out of here. Twisting and leaning out around the table she saw that Justin was trying to move his leg. "Now's not the time, Dad." She turned back to try to reason with her father, only he was gone. Sam crawled around the other side of the table to see her father up and picking the three undisturbed vials from their rack and the vial that started it all off the white surface.

For a second she thought everything was going to be all right. She took a breath only to have it sucked from her lungs a second later. The gunshot knocked her father forward into the table. The brief hope that it wasn't fatal deflated when she saw that he'd gone white, the look on his face instantly obvious to her. Recently she'd come to know death well enough to recognize when it was coming.

Sam's father stretched a long arm across the table, four small vials holding three lives within them wrapped in one long fingered hand. Tears filled her eyes as she listened. "I knew he would come for you. Take these and go." His lips twitched at her, in some failed effort to reassure her. His expression grew stern. "Two ccs of the agent goes into each man's vial to heal them. It should counter any effects of their initial exposure. Any more and you cure the cancer but start it all over again." Her outstretched hand wrapped around the vials and her father curled her fingers tightly under his. "Destroy all of it when you're done. Leave nothing for anyone to find."

Before Sam could say anything her father pushed himself away from the table and turned to plant his body between her and the gunman. "Run." He ordered over his shoulder as he took a step out to block her path to the elevator. The gun went off again as Sam cried out even as she did as she was told. Sliding into the elevator she hit the button with an outstretched hand before she lay on the floor, counting the seconds before it began to crawl its way back up to the upper level and escape. The last glimpse she had of her father was his body folding to the ground, his blood pouring out on the light tile beneath him just as the lift reached the upper floor sealing her off from him and his murderer.

Several bullets hit the metal grate at her feet, shocking Sam into action. She could wrestle with her guilt and grief over her father's death later. Right now she was facing her own and Justin's and he still wasn't up yet.

Shoving the vials into the pockets of his jeans to free her hands, Sam grasped both his hands in hers. She spun him around and dragged him off of the platform while searching hurriedly for something she could use to jam the elevator or smash the box. The gears began to grind again. The elevator was going down.

Miraculously, Sam's frantic eyes fell on the only thing portable nearby that fit the bill. She picked up the little metal garbage can from where it sat on the other side of the elevator's frame. Without hesitation, Sam hefted it with both hands and spun, swinging it out in front of her to get maximum force. The can's lid flew open, scattering coffee cups, napkins, and food debris all over, while the bottom struck its target with deadly accuracy. Sparks flew, the black plastic buttons shattered and skittered along the floor and walls. The gears stopped. The elevator was stuck a few feet from the ceiling, buying her time before the killer found a way to reach it and pull himself up.

Jerking the mini mike from her ear and bringing it to her mouth, Sam shouted into it. "Marcus, Jimmy, if you can hear me hurry! Justin's down and we've got someone shooting at us. He's going to be here any minute. Please!" Her voice broke. She was close to losing control.

A series of tones crackled from Justin's wristwatch. Sam stared at it. A light was flashing on it. Twisting his wrist, she read the message:

Run. Bombs.

"Justin you have to wake up." She rubbed his arm rapidly, hoping to elicit a response. All she got for her efforts was a moan and useless twitch of his leg.

Seeing no other option but to get him out on her own, Sam reexamined the materials available to her. The nearby computer station gave her what she needed. Now she just hoped years of an athletic lifestyle would give her strength.

Ch. 53

Jimmy was watching his clock, feet tapping in a nervous frenzy as the clock approached twenty-six minutes. In four more minutes the entire place was going to blow. He had advised Marcus of Sam's predicament and, although neither man wanted to see their sergeant and friend as well as the girl working so hard to save him die, this was their chance to take out the project for good. Even if there were more people up the line they would never be able to replicate the program without the Doc and his notes. The charges would go at thirty minutes exactly. With them on a timer the men couldn't change their minds.

One minute later the white door went up and Jimmy stared in disbelief as he radioed Marcus coming back from setting the last of the charges on the far side of the building. "They're out."

"How many?"

"Sarge and Sam."

Jimmy didn't listen for Marcus' response as he stepped out of the truck, watching Sam's makeshift gurney jerk to a stop when the wheels hit the crushed rock driveway. Rushing out, he grabbed Justin's prone body from the office chair Sam had propped him in, threw him over his shoulder in a fireman's carry and ran side by side with Sam back to the truck. Marcus was running all out, reaching them just as they slid into their seats.

"Sam, you drive. Get us the hell out of here *now*." Marcus commanded. He knelt over Justin's body lying across the back seats. His knees were pulled up to close the door. Jimmy took shotgun.

No questions asked, Sam threw the already running vehicle in reverse and flew backward into the street before cranking the wheel and slamming her foot down on the accelerator. A few snatched glances in the rearview mirror and the sun's reflection off a blade and Sam knew Marcus was busy carving the bullet out of Justin's side. She worried at his slow recovery. His cancer was draining his reserves. She feared she was losing him. An unexpected sob erupted before she could stop it.

Jimmy was staring transfixed through a pair of binoculars at the building steadily growing smaller behind them. "Get it out yet?" He asked from behind his field glasses, one hand rested gently on her shoulder for just a moment. *Be strong. Now's not the time to fall apart.* She sniffed and swallowed her emotions.

"No, it's closed. Too much tissue in the way."

"We can stop, Sam." Jimmy told her quietly. "The blast won't reach us here."

Obedient, she did as she was told and put the car in park but left it running just in case. Just in case what, she didn't know. It seemed like a good idea and no one said otherwise.

"Got a kit up there?" Marcus called from the back.

"Yeah, what do you need? Tweezers?"

"Yep."

Silently Jimmy flipped open the glove box and fished inside to grab a small blue kit. Opening it, he extracted a pair of metal tweezers, much larger than the kind Sam had at home, and passed them back. That was where she lost sight of them. She couldn't bring herself

372

to watch Marcus digging around in Justin's beautiful body. He made a few painful sounds letting her know Marcus wasn't done yet. The binoculars trained back on the rear view immediately.

After what seemed like an incredibly long and anticlimactic minute, a series of distant pops sounded. Followed closely by rumbling not too different from the sound of rolling thunder. Sam watched the explosions in the mirror, fascinated by the implosion of the brick and cement building collapsing in on itself, billowing a mixture of intermingled plumes of black and light brown smoke filling her view. Turning around to see it firsthand she watched the explosions settle into a huge blaze sure to take out all evidence of the doings of the general and her people.

"Is everyone in there dead?" She couldn't remember exactly how many she counted yesterday upon arriving. It seemed forever ago.

"No. He tranqed and dragged the two desk jockeys clear. That little one with the mustache was crazy, he pulled a gun and Shaw had no choice." Marcus' voice was strained as he continued to struggle with the lodged bullet. "Jimmy? Anyone else?"

Lowering the binoculars, Jimmy's lips fixed in a straight line. "No movement over there. Nobody got out."

They exchanged a look and although neither looked pleased at what they'd done, Sam could feel their relief fill the car. If they could manage to not lose Justin, their mission would be a success. Her stomach tightened at the thought of losing him. Morbidly curious as to what was making the bullet's extraction so difficult, Sam pushed off the floorboards and craned her neck to see what Marcus was doing. The skin was growing, rapidly forming a lump on either side of the tweezers.

"What is that? Is that his body healing itself?" It was not at all like the previous time she'd seen Justin heal and come back from the dead. That had been just like the skin came back together and he was woke up a while later. This was awful and gross. His flesh was growing at an incredible rate. In that heart stopping moment Sam recognized what she was watching. "It's the cancer isn't it? Those are tumors. His body isn't putting itself back together right, it's too sick."

Marcus barely afforded her a grunt he was so feverishly trying to remove not only the bullet, but the tweezers now being hemmed in by the sick flesh as fast as he cut through it. He brought his knife, gripped in his other hand, down again and again, sawing a hole for him to remove the tweezers. Carving an extra amount of space that left a hole nearly big enough to put his fist through, Marcus bought himself a few seconds to pry loose the bullet.

"Got it." He held it up proudly, admiring it as he held it in front of his nose.

Sam watched in anguish as the new onslaught of tumors altered the man she'd come to care about so deeply. "The cancer is spreading so fast. Is it too late for the stuff my father gave me to work?" She studied Justin's face, one cheekbone now higher than the other.

Neither answered. They were busy having one of those unnerving silent discussions. While she waited for them to sort out the next step, Sam tore her gaze from the drama inside the car and watched her father's funeral pyre continue to burn in the distance. Far away, coming from the direction of town rose the inevitable wail of sirens.

"Sam, do you know where the hospital is from here?" Marcus' voice called her back from her mind's wanderings.

She'd been to Rochester only twice. Once for a medical records review and once for a visit with her mother when she was fifteen. It was a well-marked town built around the clinic. She could find it. "Yeah."

"Then get us there." Marcus told her. "We need a few things."

Ch. 54

Driving in a daze Sam kept her emotions in check as best she could, save for the errant tear that wetted her cheeks unattended every few minutes. She wanted to cry for poor Paul who died because she was too much of a coward to admit she didn't love him. She wanted to weep for her father who came back into her life for such a short period to redeem himself in his final moments, and for Justin who had awakened her heart only to tear it apart.

They had to swing wide and go back to the freeway in order to come back the other direction and avoid the police. Their recognizable truck was a liability and the town too small to hide in larger numbers. Their time was too limited to risk being taken in again. They would have to pray for luck, something they hadn't had much of. It took nearly ten minutes for them to reach the hospital during which time untold havoc was being wreaked upon Justin's body. The cancer was growing rapidly inside it as his body replaced healthy tissue with tainted.

"Park over there in the visitor's lot. It's busy and we'll blend." Jimmy directed her.

"Do you know what you need?" Marcus' voice was rough.

"Yeah, be right back." He was out the door, the slam nearly cutting off the last of his words.

Marcus and Sam waited silently in the car. She was guessing at what Jimmy was in there digging up and hoped that by some miracle they weren't too late. At least she brought up what the others needed and *they* would be spared Justin's fate. Closing her eyes, she made a silent wish that he wasn't in pain. People said cancer hurt and she hoped he was too far under to feel it.

The passenger door whipped open and shut. Sam jumped.

"Got it." He handed a syringe to Marcus, several extras clutched in his other hand.

Marcus laid it down on the seat and held out a hand to Sam. "I assume you remember what he told you to do?"

Holding her breath, Sam nodded. Her father's whispers must have come over the radio for all of them to hear. "Two ccs of this one into," she spun the larger vial looking for the one labeled with Justin Shaw's name, "into this one and it will clear up the cancer. More than that and it will make him, you know, so he can keep coming back again." Staring at Justin's uneven side she asked, "If he's too far gone we can give him more. We can save him."

No sign of doubt, Marcus locked eyes with her and took the vials. "We give him the two ccs and pray. He wouldn't want more. He'd rather die a normal human being than live like this again."

Her mouth opened and closed and she considered arguing in favor of Justin's life at all costs. A look at Marcus' set features and she knew he was right. She asked anyway, part of her unwilling to lose the man who'd unlocked her heart. "Are you sure?"

Marcus flicked his eyes at her. "I'm sure." Using the syringe he mixed the two liquids and turned it, tapping any air bubbles to the top and depressing the plunger to push them out.

Fascinated, Sam watched as Marcus inserted the needle tip into Justin's arm and sent its contents into his bloodstream. A hush filled the interior of the vehicle as Marcus hunched over Justin, his shoulders pressed up against the roof of the car and an empty syringe in his hand. "Please work." He closed his eyes and his lips moved. Marcus was praying.

Jimmy crossed himself and kissed his fingers.

Sam held her breath and clenched her fists.

Ch. 55

After a few minutes it became obvious nothing was going to happen right away. Marcus shifted Justin's legs toward the floor, gently easing him into a seated position and buckled him in. "Let's get back to the farm," he said quietly. "The longer we stay in town the more likely we are to be sleeping in a cell tonight."

No one said any different so Sam resumed her role as driver. She drove carefully, using back roads whenever possible and following the posted speed limits to the letter. It made the trip take nearly twice as long as it should. They were just pulling in as the sun began its descent behind the trees. Clouds were rolling in promising an evening shower.

Sam got out, hands on the small of her back and pushing to stretch against the stiffness that came from holding every muscle tight for way too long. She shivered in the cool air, tasting fall in its dry crispness. In the next few weeks there would be a short but dazzling display of reds, oranges, and golds she looked forward to every year. She hoped this year to be watching them with Justin by her side.

A grunt behind her spun Sam around in time to see the back of Justin's head as Marcus slung him over his shoulder and Jimmy followed them to the steps into the house. Sam trotted after them.

"What should *I* do?" She asked from Justin's doorway after Marcus laid him down and Jimmy pulled the covers over him. No sound came from the bed where she could see faint movement in his chest.

Backing away, Marcus rolled his shoulders and massaged the back of one. "I don't know. I guess you could make dinner while we put our gear away."

Sam had taken a breath to say, "Okay" only to groan it out when Marcus stepped aside and she caught sight of the face on the pillow. The growth had continued to distort his cheekbone until his skin looked waxy and stretched to the point of breaking on his right side. Her father's formula hadn't worked. Justin's cancer was spreading unchecked. She clapped a hand over her mouth to block the strangled cry that came out.

"Why don't you go down and make somethin'?" Jimmy placed a guiding hand on her back and moved her away. "Trust me, better to be busy right now than just sittin' and watitin'."

She let herself be expelled from the room hearing them mumble in low voices behind her.

Reaching the kitchen, Sam set about relocating several wooden crates formerly being used as end tables in the living room to replace the shattered kitchen table. That done, a sheet over the top serving as a table cloth and she began exploring cupboards determined to make something incredibly complicated and requiring the utmost concentration. A thorough search revealed a refrigerator of mostly condiments and a pantry of canned and dry goods.

She ended up settling on pasta primavera with frozen veggies instead of fresh. She would have preferred the tedium of chopping vegetables to staring at the water in the pot waiting for the tiny bubbles lining its edges to explode into a rolling boil. It was just coming off the stove when the kitchen door shut behind Jimmy after he brought in the last load.

"Smells good, Sam. Like my mama would have made," he chuckled, "if she was Italian."

380

Marcus washed up first and grabbed three beers out of the fridge while she plated dinner. When they sat down Marcus lifted his beer and took a long pull. Sam and Jimmy did the same and set about eating a quiet dinner punctuated only by a few brief questions and answers. They wanted to clarify what they hadn't been able to make out over the radio before she made her escape. They raised their bottles in a somber toast to the man who had brought them all together. In the end Doc had tried to do right.

Jimmy offered to clean up. "Why don't you go chill or somethin'? All we got now is waitin' time. You might as well get some sleep."

A shower and a fresh change of clothes sounded good and Sam let Jimmy take the stack of plates from her hands at the sink. "Thanks Jimmy." She gave him a grateful smile.

She did shower and change. Except when Sam lay down in her room she tossed and turned, unable to clear her mind. Bill was nowhere to be seen, he most likely abandoned her for Marcus again. With nothing to distract her all she could see was Justin's painfully deformed face and she worried he was hurting or scared. If it was the end for him, he shouldn't be alone.

The house was dark and settled for the night. She heard the other two doors shut nearly an hour before. Only one set of footsteps had gone to Justin's room across from hers and she heard them retreat shortly thereafter. Taking care to be quiet, Sam padded across the hall and gently eased his door open then closed it carefully behind her. A dim light offered a faint glow from the farthest corner of the room.

Justin's face was cast in shadow when she went in and the dimness of the room let her picture him as she preferred, in the condition her father had tried to return him to with his final sacrifice. It would have worked had it been one bullet sooner. To her thinking that was a good enough legacy for any man. To be given an opportunity to right the wrongs he'd done. To give the soldiers back their lives and save the daughter he'd abandoned was a lot for one man to accomplish in one night. Because of his last actions Marcus and Jimmy could live out their lives as they deserved. In peace.

Sam couldn't imagine how her mother would react to all of this. She tried to think of some way to let them honor the sacrifices of Dr. Steven James and let his sins be forgiven as he wished. The empty feeling in Sam's chest where she once carried the hope her father would someday return to her demanded comfort and she had no way of finding it. The only solace she'd been able to find apart from her mother had been when she'd lain with this man. The one who had shaken her carefully monitored, safely closed off little world.

Sam pulled back the covers and tucked herself in beside him, taking care not to bump him. She lay her head on the pillow next to his, her hand gently covering his arm, bare now that Marcus or Jimmy had stripped his bloodied clothing and dressed him in cotton drawstring pants. It was in that position that Sam felt a little bit of that aching empty hole in her chest ease, finally letting her sleep just before dawn.

Ch. 56

The sunlight streamed in as Sam woke from a
dead sleep. She tried to dig down and figure out what the
sound had been that woke her. Remembering the night
before, she slid her hand over to touch the cold sheets.
What? Worried something had happened to Justin in the
night, that one of the men had taken him for a burial
without telling her, she hopped up and raced down the
stairs.

When she reached the bottom she flew wild-eyed
into the kitchen and took a second to realize the sound
that woke her had been the voices of the *three* men
sitting at the short, makeshift breakfast table drinking
coffee.

Not surprisingly, Sam sought only one. He was
facing her head on, cup paused halfway to his mouth as
they all sat frozen for a heartbeat more. Slowly he
lowered his cup and Sam's hand flew to her mouth to
capture the relieved sob that caught in her throat. Her
eyes prickled and filled until they overflowed.
Thankyouthankyouthankyou. Her hand clutched at the
doorframe keeping her from keeling over and from
running to him. *What if he doesn't feel the same way?* A
heavy weight settled in her belly.

"Hey, I gotta do a thing. Be back in a bit, Sarge."
Jimmy got up first.

Rising a half second after, Marcus put a hand on
Justin's shoulder and clapped it.

"Thanks guys." His voice was weak but as the
door closed and left them alone, he smiled at her.

Sam's gaze was locked on the soft green eyes she

had feared were lost to her, she didn't want to blink. "You're okay?" she whispered hoarsely. "Did it work? Is it gone?"

His eyes never left hers as he dipped his smooth, non-lumpy chin in assent. "We think so. They're going to take some blood and get the numbers run. For the right price Marcus knows a guy. If it looks good, Marcus and Jimmy will do theirs. Then we get to start worrying about dying just like the rest of the world." He joked but his smile quickly faded. "I'm sorry about your father."

"He took those bullets for us." Her guilt would take time to fade, for so many things. His mention of death brought with it a pang she kept close, accepting it as a part of her now. "So, what does that mean for you in the long run? I mean you aren't able to heal yourself anymore but can the cancer come back?" *Will I lose you in a few years when this wears off?*

Justin rose and went to the cupboard to take out another cup, filling it for her and setting it on the table in front of her before retaking his seat. "No, we think the whole process has been cancelled out like Doc said it would. I even look a little older." He pointed at the corner of his eye and a few crow's feet that hadn't been there yesterday.

Sam pushed off from the doorway and took the seat where he'd put her cup, all the while giving him a thorough visual appraisal. She noticed a hint of gray at his temples and frown line at the top of his nose between his brows. He looked like any other man who had just come back from an illness, one who would take time to heal and get stronger. One who would always carry a reminder of the toll it had taken on his body.

"It isn't all going away?"

He shook his head. "No, this is different. It's been a long time since I've had to get better on my own, but I think this is normal. I guess it's over." He shrugged. "We need to figure out what to do with ourselves now." Justin frowned into his coffee, hiding his face. "What about you? Do you have a job to get back to?"

Suddenly unsure of herself, Sam took a sip of her coffee. "Well, I don't know what I would do here."

Justin's frown lines deepened and Sam waited for something from him, an invitation. Instead he set down his cup with a thump and stood up quickly, his knees upsetting the precarious table in the process and nearly capsizing both of their cups.

"I guess there's no point delaying then. We'd better get you home." He glanced at his watch. "Come on."

Sam watched his back as he strode stiffly to the door. "Wait a minute. After everything that's happened, that's it? You're dismissing me just like that?" She crossed her arms.

Wheeling, Justin fixed his gaze on hers. His expression was unreadable. "You said it yourself, there's nothing for you here."

Exasperated, Sam threw up her arms. "I said I didn't know what I would *do* here, not that there was *nothing here* for me." Angry with herself for saying too much when he was so unaffected by the prospect of her leaving, Sam turned and stormed to the stairs. "I'll get my things." Feeling foolish, she wiped at her cheeks with the back of her hand.

"Wait."

His one word stopped her and his hand on her shoulder turned her around.

"What?" Her control over herself was shaky. Sam felt a fool for having misread Justin's attentions and their one kiss. When it was only the two of them he'd been kind. Maybe that was all it was for him, a kindness while they were all tucked away from the greater world. Now that he had his life back and he no longer had to hide he didn't need her. She bit her lip to keep her face from doing that ugly crinkling thing it did when she cried.

"What's here for you?" he asked her softly.

Sam couldn't break away, his eyes creating a gravity that pulled her toward him regardless of how mortified she might be at mistaking his feelings. Hers had been true and she let the words come unchecked. What did it matter? He would be out of her life soon anyway. For the first time since her father left that little girl broken, Sam put her heart out there.

"When my father left I watched my mother fall apart and I helped her pick up the pieces. I swore that would never be me. No one would ever break me like that." She took a breath to steady her shaking voice. "Since I met you I haven't been able to think straight. You test my nerves and my sanity, two things I've never had trouble with before you came along." Sam gained strength, liking the way his eyes widened at her boldness. Shock was better than laughter. "You might have seen this as some sort of friendly face while we were all on hold, but I didn't. I've never felt this way about anyone in my life and I'm just sorry I had to go and fall in love with someone as unappreciative as you."

Sam waited several painful heartbeats. Nothing. Seeing the frozen expression on his face as her answer, Sam felt hers flushing. She was about to spin and run up the stairs, wondering how expensive a cab would be so she didn't have to endure an uncomfortable ride home when he stepped into her space. She parted her lips to ask him to move when the green of his eyes darkened and his lips met hers.

No warning, no words, Justin planted his soft lips on hers and the world stopped spinning. His demanding kiss proved something although what that might be had Sam at a loss. This kind of emotional back and forth had her out of her depth. She had just given him the ability to hurt her completely unbidden and now he was kissing her. She wasn't sure what that meant. Hating to do it, she tore herself away from him, suddenly feeling cold where his hands had been touching her back. *When did he put his arms around me?*

"Why are you kissing me?" Frustrated, she glared at him.

"I'm being appreciative." He grinned at her. One hand came up to tuck a chunk of hair behind her ear just like she would do right now if he wasn't so close.

"Don't mock me." Humiliation twisted her insides and she felt ill. "Just take me home."

"I thought you said you loved me." He teased lightly, his hand trailed lightly down her shoulder and making Sam acutely aware she was still wearing the tank top and shorts she slept in.

Growing steadily more frustrated the longer he went without giving her a straight answer, Sam reached up to knock his hand away and his hand shot out, catching her by the wrist. He lowered it to hold it between them. The intimacy of looking him in the eye from only inches away was too much.

Left with no other escape, Sam closed her eyes. "I didn't tell you those things so that you could make fun of me for it."

"Who says I'm making fun?" He was so close she felt his breath on her mouth.

Sam's eyes flew open.

"I love you too Sam. I love you and I don't care what you do *anywhere* as long as it's with me. We can stay here or I have a little place back home in Tennessee I was hoping to show you." It was his turn to be unsure, his accent growing more pronounced. "I always intended to go back when this was over. I was thinking you might want to go with me."

Sam blinked as confusion turned to joy, a smile slowly spreading across her face. "Well, I don't know what I'd do *there* either but I could think of something." Leaning in, she gave him back the kiss he'd given her, softer this time and with a promise of many more to come.

End

www.ingramcontent.com/pod-product-compliance
Lightning Source LLC
Chambersburg PA
CBHW051520250626
47156CB00001B/163